D0099442

Praise for *Uwem Akpan's*

Say You're One of Them

"Awe is the only appropriate response to Uwem Akpan's stunning debut, a collection of five stories so ravishing and sad that I regret ever wasting superlatives on fiction that was merely very good. . . . Akpan's characters are ordinary, flawed, sometimes funny kids who happen to be caught in a nightmare. . . . The book should be depressing, but the blazing humanity of the characters and the brilliance of Akpan's artistry make this one of the year's most exhilarating reads."   —Jennifer Reese, *Entertainment Weekly*

"All the promise and heartbreak of Africa today are brilliantly illuminated in this debut collection."

—John Marshall, *Seattle Post-Intelligencer*

"It is not merely the subject that makes Akpan's writing so astonishing, translucent, and horrifying all at once; it is his talent with metaphor and imagery, his immersion into character and place. . . . Uwem Akpan has given these children their voices, and for the compassion and art in his stories I am grateful and changed."   — Susan Straight, *Washington Post Book World*

"From the bowels of the most impoverished, war-ravaged continent comes this strong, brave offering from Uwem Akpan, a Jesuit priest. What better lens to view this landscape than through the eyes of children — siblings about to be sold into slavery by their uncle, a Muslim boy trying to pass as a Christian on a bus traversing a religious war. No news report or documentary evokes the desperate straits of the African people so keenly. Like Isaac Babel's *Red Calvary* stories and Michael Herr's *Dispatches, Say You're One of Them* has invented a new language — both for horror and for the relentless persistence of light in war-torn countries. I can't shake this book, and shouldn't."
          — Mary Karr, author of *The Liars' Club*

"Uwem Akpan writes with a political fierceness and a humanity so full of compassion it might just change the world. His is a burning talent."
          —Chris Abani, author of *GraceLand* and *The Virgin of Flames*

"Amazing and moving, and imbued with a powerful moral courage. . . . Akpan wants you to see and feel Africa, its glory and its pain. And you do, which makes this an extraordinary book."
          —Vince Passaro, *O: The Oprah* Magazine

"Amazing. . . . A book so overwhelming that when you put it down — if you can — it takes a minute to adjust to the world around you. . . . It takes a great writer to face the extremes of human depravity without either sensationalizing them or trivializing them with easy judgments. Akpan doesn't blink, yet these stories have none of the moral queasiness of voyeurism. And somehow the author manages to love his characters — even the killers. . . . Akpan has the largeness of soul to make his vision of the terrible transcendent. Beside these stories, other fiction seems to dry up and blow away like dust." —Craig Seligman, *Bloomberg News*

"Although they often deal with horrific material, these stories retain an astringent clarity. . . . This time the ballyhoo is real: Akpan is an important writer." —David Grylls, *Sunday Times*

"*Say You're One of Them* is a tour de force that takes readers into the lives glimpsed in passing on the evening news. . . . These are stories that could have been mired in sentimentality. But the spare, straightforward language — there are few overtly expressed emotions, few adjectives — keeps the narratives moving, unencumbered, and the pages turning to the end."
—Juliana Barbassa, Associated Press

"Akpan combines the strengths of both fiction and journalism — the dramatic potential of the one and the urgency of the other — to create a work of immense power. . . . He is a gifted storyteller capable of bringing to life myriad characters and points of view. . . . The result is admirable, artistically as well as morally."
—Adelle Waldman, *Christian Science Monitor*

"Stories that are as shocking as they are delicate."

— Cynthia Crossen, *Wall Street Journal*

"Uwem Akpan, a Nigerian Jesuit priest, has said he was inspired to write by the 'humor and endurance of the poor,' and his debut story collection about the gritty lives of African children speaks to the fearsome, illuminating truth of that impulse."

— Lisa Shea, *Elle*

"A beautiful, bitter, compelling read. The savagely strange juxtapositions in these stories are grounded by the loving relationships between brothers and sisters forced to survive in a world of dreamlike horror. Open the book at any page, as in divination, and a stunning sentence will leap out. Newspaper facts are molded by Akpan's sure touch into fictional works of great power."

— Louise Erdrich, author of *Love Medicine* and
The Plague of Doves

"A startling debut collection. . . . Akpan is not striving for surreal effects. He is summoning miseries that are real. . . . He fuses a knowledge of African poverty and strife with a conspicuously literary approach to storytelling, filtering tales of horror through the wide eyes of the young."

— Janet Maslin, *New York Times*

"In the corrupt, war-ravaged Africa of this starkly beautiful debut collection, identity is shifting, never to be trusted. . . . Akpan's people, and the dreamlike horror of the worlds they reveal, are impossible to forget."   — Kim Hubbard, *People*

"Akpan transports the reader into gritty scenes of chaos and fear in his rich debut collection. . . . His prose is beautiful and his stories are insightful and revealing, made even more harrowing because all the horror — and there is much — is seen through the eyes of children." — *Publishers Weekly* (starred review)

"Here is a truly unforgettable book. *Say You're One of Them* is an important, well-crafted, and ultimately devastating collection, and Akpan is a writer of rare gifts and deeply humane vision. I can't recommend these stories more highly."

— Peter Orner, author of *The Second Coming of Mavala Shikongo*

"An important literary debut. . . . Juxtaposed against the clarity and revelation in Akpan's prose — as translucent a style as I've read in a long while — we find subjects that nearly render the mind helpless and throw the heart into a hopeless erratic rhythm out of fear, out of pity, out of the shame of being only a few degrees of separation removed from these monstrous modern circumstances. . . . The reader discovers that no hiding place is good enough with these stories battering at your mind and heart."

— Alan Cheuse, *Chicago Tribune*

"A stunning short story collection. . . . *Say You're One of Them* offers a richer, more nuanced view of Africa than the one we often see on the news. . . . Akpan never lets us forget that the resilient youngsters caught up in these extraordinary circumstances are filled with their own hopes and dreams, even as he assuredly illuminates the harsh realities." — Patrik Henry Bass, *Essence*

"Uwem Akpan depicts the plight of African children with the kind of restraint only possible when an author fully inhabits his characters—he manages to be empathetic without being condescending." —Tatyana Gershkovich, *Village Voice*

"*Say You're One of Them* is one of those collections that drops the reader into the midst of wonderfully rendered worlds, and compellingly so. I hope it finds the wide readership it merits."
—Oscar Hijuelos, author of *The Mambo Kings Play Songs of Love*

"This fierce story collection from a Nigerian-born Jesuit priest brings home Africa's most haunting tragedies. . . . Akpan seems inspired by the biblical prophecy 'A little child will lead them.'"
—Margo Hammond and Ellen Heltzel, *Minneapolis Star Tribune*

"This astonishing first collection of short stories marks the arrival of a major writer. . . . It is a long time since I have been so moved and so disturbed. Any notion that the short-story form is languishing irrelevantly is disavowed by this terrific, and sometimes terrifying, collection." —Alastair Niven, *Independent*

"Searing. . . . In the end, the most enduring image of these disturbing, beautiful, and hopeful stories is that of slipping away. Children disappear into the anonymous blur of the big city or into the darkness of the all-encompassing bush. One can only hope that they survive to live another day and tell another tale."
—June Sawyers, *San Francisco Chronicle*

"Like Flannery O'Connor's best work, these stories absorb any light you project upon them; Akpan's characters are wrapped in the hard-edged, inscrutable armor of people in situations so desperate that superhuman instincts take over. . . . Akpan is such a clever, instinctual writer that even when his characters are providing testimony, it can feel like art. . . . These stories are complex, full of respect for the characters facing depravity, free of sensationalizing or glib judgments. They are dispatches from a journey, Akpan makes clear, which has only begun. It is to their credit that, grim as they are, you cannot but hope these tales have a sequel." —John Freeman, *Cleveland Plain Dealer*

"*Say You're One of Them* is astonishing, triumphantly unique. . . . Uwem Akpan has moral greatness—you can never again put out of your mind what he has taken you firmly by the hand to get a close look at. The startling newness of his language gives us no choice but to listen."
—Franz Wright, winner of the 2004 Pulitzer Prize for Poetry

"Brilliant. . . . *Say You're One of Them* proves that great fiction often can reveal more truth than a whole shelf of memoirs and histories." —Deirdre Donahue, *USA Today*

"With this heart-stopping collection Uwem Akpan relentlessly personalizes the unstable social conditions of sub-Saharan Africa. . . . The stories are lifted above consciousness-raising shockers by Akpan's sure characterizations, understated details, and culturally specific dialect."
—Jennifer Mattson, *Booklist* (starred review)

"*Say You're One of Them* gives voice to Africa's children in beautifully crafted prose and stunning detail. Uwem Akpan is a major new literary talent."

— Peter Godwin, author of *When a Crocodile Eats the Sun*

"Akpan has a real gift for bringing the day-to-day living of the downtrodden of Africa to life. . . . If he can sensitize a few of us toward keeping our humanitarian promises to Africa, this book will have achieved its purpose."

— Vikram Johri, *Milwaukee Journal Sentinel*

"There is an energy in Akpan's characterization that makes his book compelling rather than downbeat. . . . In the midst of his continent's crises, he has given vital voice to its children, naming them with true compassion in an unflinching collection."

— Isobel Dixon, *Financial Times*

"*Say You're One of Them* is not only good advice for surviving ethnic conflict; it's also, in Uwem Akpan's hands, an exercise in empathetic speculation — an exercise that, in this collection's case, seems nearly sacramental in the sobriety and miraculousness of its reach. Repeatedly these stories quietly enable us to imagine the unimaginable, and offer up to our view the unspeakable rendered with clarity and grace."

— Jim Shepard, author of *Like You'd Understand, Anyway*, 2007 National Book Award finalist

"*Say You're One of Them* is a book that belongs on every shelf."

— Sherryl Connelly, *New York Daily News*

Say You're One of Them

Uwem Akpan

BACK BAY BOOKS
LITTLE, BROWN AND COMPANY
New York Boston London

Back Bay Books / Little, Brown and Company
Hachette Book Group
237 Park Avenue, New York, NY 10017
Visit our website at www.HachetteBookGroup.com

Originally published in hardcover by Little, Brown and Company, June 2008
First Back Bay paperback edition, July 2009

Back Bay Books is an imprint of Little, Brown and Company. The Back Bay Books name and logo are trademarks of Hachette Book Group, Inc.

The characters and events in this book are fictitious. Any similarity to real persons, living or dead, is coincidental and not intended by the author.

Map designed by John Barnett

Acknowledgment is made to *The New Yorker,* where "An Ex-mas Feast" and "My Parents' Bedroom" first appeared, in slightly different form. "An Ex-mas Feast" also appeared, in different form, in *Kwani?* and the *Guardian* (Nigeria).

The interview with Uwem Akpan in the reading group guide at the back of this book originally appeared at www.newyorker.com. Copyright © 2005 Condé Nast Publications, Inc. Reprinted with permission.

Library of Congress Cataloging-in-Publication Data

Akpan, Uwem.
    Say you're one of them / Uwem Akpan. — 1st ed.
        p. cm.
    ISBN 978-0-316-08636-3 (hc) / 978-0-316-08637-0 (pb)
    1. Children — Africa — Fiction. I. Title.
    PR9387.9.A3935S29 2008
    823'.92 — dc22   2007041350

10 9 8 7 6 5 4 3 2 1

RRD-VA

Printed in the United States of America

FOR MY PARENTS,
LINUS AND MARGARET,
WHOSE LOVE IS A WORLD OF
STORIES BETWEEN THEM

AND FOR UNCLE GEORGE,
WHO WAS THERE

If our God, the one we serve, is able to save us from the burning fiery furnace and from your power, O king, he will save us; and even if he does not, then you must know, O king, that we will not serve your god or worship the statue you have erected.

DANIEL 3:17–18

What is good has been explained to you . . . to act justly, to love tenderly, and to walk humbly with your God.

MICAH 6:8

Contents

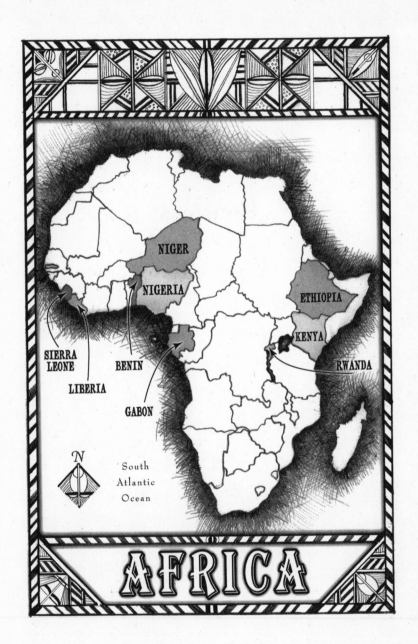

NIGER

NIGERIA

ETHIOPIA

KENYA

RWANDA

SIERRA
LEONE

BENIN

LIBERIA

GABON

N

South
Atlantic
Ocean

AFRICA

Say You're One of Them

An Ex-mas Feast

Now that my eldest sister, Maisha, was twelve, none of us knew how to relate to her anymore. She had never forgiven our parents for not being rich enough to send her to school. She had been behaving like a cat that was going feral: she came home less and less frequently, staying only to change her clothes and give me some money to pass on to our parents. When home, she avoided them as best she could, as if their presence reminded her of too many things in our lives that needed money. Though she would snap at Baba occasionally, she never said anything to Mama. Sometimes Mama went out of her way to provoke her. "*Malaya!* Whore! You don't even have breasts yet!" she'd say. Maisha would ignore her.

Maisha shared her thoughts with Naema, our ten-year-old sister, more than she did with the rest of us combined, mostly talking about the dos and don'ts of a street girl. Maisha let Naema try on her high heels, showed her how to doll up her face, how to use toothpaste and a brush. She told her to run away from any man who beat her, no matter how much money he offered her, and that she would treat Naema like Mama if she grew up to have too many children. She told Naema that it was better to starve to death than go out with any man without a condom.

When she was at work, though, she ignored Naema, perhaps because Naema reminded her of home or because she didn't want Naema to see that her big sister wasn't as cool and chic as she made herself out to be. She tolerated me more outside than inside. I could chat her up on the pavement no matter what rags I was wearing. An eight-year-old boy wouldn't get in the way when she was waiting for a customer. We knew how to pretend we were strangers — just a street kid and a prostitute talking.

Yet our *machokosh* family was lucky. Unlike most, our street family had stayed together — at least until that Ex-mas season.

THE SUN HAD GONE down on Ex-mas evening. Bad weather had stormed the seasons out of order, and Nairobi sat in a low flood, the light December rain droning on our tarpaulin roof. I was sitting on the floor of our shack, which stood on a cement slab at the end of an alley, leaning against the back of an old brick shop. Occasional winds swelled the brown polythene walls. The floor was nested with cushions that I had scavenged from a dump on Biashara Street. At night, we rolled up the edge of the tarpaulin to let in the glow of the shop's security lights. A board, which served as our door, lay by the shop wall.

A clap of thunder woke Mama. She got up sluggishly, pulling her hands away from Maisha's trunk, which she had held on to while she slept. It was navy blue, with brass linings and rollers, and it took up a good part of our living space. Panicking, Mama groped her way from wall to wall, frisking my two-year-old twin brother and sister, Otieno and Atieno, and Baba; all three were sleeping, tangled together like puppies. She was looking for Baby. Mama's white T-shirt, which she had been given three months back, when she delivered Baby, had a pair of milk stains on the front. Then she must have remembered that he was with Maisha and Naema. She relaxed and stretched in a yawn, hitting a rafter of cork. One of the stones that weighted our roof fell down outside.

Now Mama put her hands under her *shuka* and retied the strings of the money purse around her waist; sleep and alcohol had swung it out of place. She dug through our family carton, scooping out clothes, shoes, and my new school uniform, wrapped in useless documents that Baba had picked from people's pockets. Mama dug on, and the contents of the carton piled up on Baba and the twins. Then she unearthed a tin of New Suntan shoe glue. The glue was our Ex-mas gift from the children of a *machokosh* that lived nearby.

Mama smiled at the glue and winked at me, pushing her tongue through the holes left by her missing teeth. She snapped the tin's top expertly, and the shack swelled with the smell of a shoemaker's stall. I watched her decant the *kabire* into my plastic "feeding bottle." It glowed warm and yellow in the dull light. Though she still appeared drunk from last night's party, her hands were so steady that her large tinsel Ex-mas bangles, a gift from a church Ex-mas party, did not even sway. When she had poured enough, she cut the flow of the glue by tilting the tin up. The last stream of the gum entering the bottle weakened and braided itself before tapering in midair like an icicle. She covered the plastic with her palm, to retain the glue's power. Sniffing it would kill my hunger in case Maisha did not return with an Ex-mas feast for us.

Mama turned to Baba, shoving his body with her foot. "Wake up, you never work for days!" Baba turned and groaned. His feet were poking outside the shack, under the waterproof wall. His toes had broken free of his wet tennis shoes. Mama shoved him again, and he began to wriggle his legs as if he were walking in his sleep.

Our dog growled outside. Mama snapped her fingers, and the dog came in, her ripe pregnancy swaying like heavy wash in the wind. For a month and a half, Mama, who was good at spotting dog pregnancies, had baited her with tenderness and food until she became ours; Mama hoped to sell the puppies to raise money for my textbooks. Now the dog licked Atieno's face. Mama probed the dog's stomach with crooked fingers, like a native midwife. "Oh, Simba, childbirth is chasing you," she whispered into her ears. "Like school is chasing my son." She pushed the dog outside. Simba lay down, covering Baba's feet with her warmth. Occasionally, she barked to keep the other dogs from tampering with our mobile kitchen, which was leaning against the wall of the store.

"Jigana, did you do well last night with Baby?" Mama asked me suddenly.

"I made a bit," I assured her, and passed her a handful of coins and notes. She pushed the money under her *shuka;* the zip of the purse released two crisp farts.

Though people were more generous to beggars at Ex-mas, our real bait was Baby. We took turns pushing him in the faces of passersby.

"*Aii!* Son, you never see Ex-mas like this year." Her face widened in a grin. "We shall pay school fees next year. No more *randa*-meandering around. No more *chomaring* your brain with glue, boy. You going back to school! Did the rain beat you and Baby?"

"Rain caught me here," I said.

"And Baby? Who is carrying him?"

"Naema," I said.

"And Maisha? Where is she to do her time with the child?"

"Mama, she is very angry."

"That gal is beat-beating my head. Three months now she is not greeting me. What insects are eating her brain?" Sometimes Mama's words came out like a yawn because the holes between her teeth were wide. "Eh, now that she shakes-shakes her body to moneymen, she thinks she has passed me? Tell me, why did she refuse to stay with Baby?"

"She says it's child abuse."

"Child abuse? Is she now NGO worker? She likes being a prostitute better than begging with Baby?"

"Me, I don't know. She just went with the *ma*-men tourists. Today, real white people, *musungu*. With monkey."

Mama spat through the doorway. "*Puu,* those ones are useless. I know them. They don't ever pay the Ex-mas rate—and then they even let their *ma*-monkey fuck her. Jigana, talk with that gal. Or don't you want to complete school? She can't just give you uniform only."

I nodded. I had already tried on the uniform eight times in two days, anxious to resume school. The green-and-white-checked shirt and olive-green shorts had become wrinkled. Now I reached into the carton and stroked a piece of the uniform that stuck out of the jumble.

"Why are you messing with this beautiful uniform?" Mama said. "Patience, boy. School is just around the corner." She dug to the bottom of the carton and buried the package. "Maisha likes your face," she whispered. "Please, Jigana, tell her you need more—shoes,

PTA fee, prep fee. We must to save all Ex-mas rate to educate you, first son. Tell her she must stop buying those *fuunny fuunny* designer clothes, those clothes smelling of dead white people, and give us the money."

As she said this, she started to pound angrily on the trunk. The trunk was a big obstruction. It was the only piece of furniture we had with a solid and definite shape. Maisha had brought it home a year ago and always ordered us to leave the shack before she would open it. None of us knew what its secret contents were, except for a lingering perfume. It held for us both suspense and consolation, and these feelings grew each time Maisha came back with new things. Sometimes, when Maisha did not come back for a long time, our anxiety turned the trunk into an assurance of her return.

"*Malaya!* Prostitute! She doesn't come and I break the box tonight," Mama hissed, spitting on the combination lock and shaking the trunk until we could hear its contents knocking about. She always took her anger out on the trunk in Maisha's absence. I reached out to grab her hands.

"You pimp!" she growled. "You support the *malaya*."

"It's not her fault. It's *musungu* tourists."

"You better begin school before she runs away."

"I must to report you to her."

"I must to bury you and your motormouth in this box."

We struggled. Her long nails slashed my forehead, and blood trickled down. But she was still shaking the trunk. Turning around, I charged at her and bit her right thigh. I could not draw blood because I had lost my front milk teeth. She let go and reeled into the bodies of our sleeping family. Atieno let out one short, eerie scream, as if in a nightmare, then went back to sleep. Baba groaned and said he did not like his family members fighting during Ex-mas. "You bite my wife because of that whore?" he groaned. "The cane will discipline you in the morning. I must to personally ask your headmaster to get a big cane for you."

A welt had fruited up on Mama's thigh. She rolled up her dress and started massaging it, her lips moving in silent curses. Then, to punish me, she took the *kabire* she had poured for me and applied it to the swelling. She pushed the mouth of the bottle against it, expecting the fumes to ease the hurt.

When Mama had finished nursing herself, she returned the bottle to me. Since it was still potent *kabire,* I did not sniff it straight but put my lips around the mouth of the bottle and smoked slowly, as if it were an oversized joint of bhang, Indian hemp. First it felt as if I had no saliva in my mouth, and then the fumes began to numb my tongue. The heat climbed steadily into my throat, tickling my nostrils like an aborted sneeze. I cooled off a bit and blew away the vapor. Then I sucked at it again and swallowed. My eyes watered, my head began to spin, and I dropped the bottle.

When I looked up, Mama had poured some *kabire* for herself and was sniffing it. She and Baba hardly ever took *kabire.* "Kabire is for children only," Baba's late father used to admonish them whenever he caught them eyeing our glue. This Ex-mas we were not too desperate for food. In addition to the money that begging with Baby had brought us, Baba had managed to steal some wrapped gifts from a party given for *machokosh* families by an NGO whose organizers were so stingy that they served fruit juice like shots of hard liquor. He had dashed to another charity party and traded in the useless gifts — plastic cutlery, picture frames, paperweights, insecticide — for three cups of rice and zebra intestines, which a tourist hotel had donated. We'd had these for dinner on Ex-mas Eve.

"Happee, happee Ex-mas, *tarling!*" Mama toasted me after a while, rubbing my head.

"You too, Mama."

"Now, where are these daughters? Don't they want to do Ex-mas prayer?" She sniffed the bottle until her eyes receded, her face pinched like the face of a mad cow. "And the govament banned this sweet thing. Say thanks to the neighbors, boy. Where did they find this hunger killer?" Sometimes she released her lips from the bottle with a smacking sound. As the night thickened, her face began to swell, and she kept pouting and biting her lips to check the numbness. They turned red — they looked like Maisha's when she had on lipstick — and puffed up.

"Mama? So, what can we give the neighbors for Ex-mas?" I asked, remembering that we had not bought anything for our friends.

My question jerked her back. "Petrol . . . we will buy them a half liter of petrol," she said, and belched. Her breath smelled of carbide, then of sour wine. When she looked up again, our eyes met, and I lowered mine in embarrassment. In our *machokosh* culture, petrol was not as valuable as glue. Any self-respecting street kid should always have his own stock of *kabire*. "OK, son, next year . . . we get better things. I don't want police business this year — so don't start having ideas."

We heard two drunks stumbling toward our home. Mama hid the bottle. They stood outside announcing that they had come to wish us a merry Ex-mas. "My husband is not here!" Mama lied. I recognized the voices. It was Bwana Marcos Wako and his wife,

Cecilia. Baba had owed them money for four years. They came whenever they smelled money, then Baba had to take off for a few days. When Baby was born, we pawned three-quarters of his clothing to defray the debts. A week before Ex-mas, the couple had raided us, confiscating Baba's work clothes in the name of debt servicing.

I quickly covered the trunk with rags and reached into my pocket, tightening my grip around the rusty penknife I carried about.

Mama and I stood by the door. Bwana Wako wore his trousers belted across his forehead; the legs, flailing behind him, were tied in knots and stuffed with *ugali* flour, which he must have gotten from a street party. Cecilia wore only her jacket and her rain boots.

"Ah, Mama Jigana-*ni* Ex-mas!" the husband said. "Forget the money. Happee Ex-mas!"

"We hear Jigana is going to school," the wife said.

"Who told you?" Mama said warily. "Me, I don't like rumors." They turned to me. "Happee to resume school, boy?"

"Me am not going to school," I lied, to spare my tuition money.

"*Kai,* like mama like son!" the wife said. "You must to know you are the hope of your family."

"Mama Jigana, listen," the man said. "Maisha came to us last week. Good, responsible gal. She begged us to let bygone be bygone so Jigana can go to school. We say forget the money — our Ex-mas gift to your family."

"You must to go far with education, Jigana," the wife said, handing me a new pen and pencil. "*Mpaka* university!"

Mama laughed, jumping into the flooded alley. She hugged them and allowed them to come closer to our shack. They staggered to our door, swaying like masqueraders on stilts.

"*Asante sana!*" I thanked them. I uncorked the pen and wrote all over my palms and smelled the tart scent of the Hero HB pencil. Mama wedged herself between them and the shack to ensure that they did not pull it down. Baba whispered to us from inside, ready to slip away, "Ha, they told me the same thing last year. You watch and see, tomorrow they come looking for me. Make them sign paper this time." Mama quickly got them some paper and they signed, using my back as a table. Then they staggered away, the stuffed trousers bouncing along behind them.

Mama began to sing Maisha's praises and promised never to pound on her trunk again. Recently, Maisha had taken the twins to the barber, and Baby to Kenyatta National Hospital for a checkup. Now she had gotten our debt canceled. I felt like running out to search for her in the streets. I wanted to hug her and laugh until the moon dissolved. I wanted to buy her Coke and chapati, for sometimes she forgot to eat. But when Mama saw me combing my hair, she said nobody was allowed to leave until we had finished saying the Ex-mas prayer.

I HUNG OUT WITH Maisha some nights on the street, and we talked about fine cars and lovely Nairobi suburbs. We'd imagine what it would be like to visit the Masai Mara Game Reserve or to eat roasted ostrich or crocodile at the Carnivore, like tourists.

"You beautiful!" I had told Maisha one night on Koinange Street, months before that fateful Ex-mas.

"Ah, no, me am not." She laughed, straightening her jean miniskirt. "Stop lying."

"See your face?"

"*Kai,* who sent you?"

"And you bounce like models."

"Yah, yah, yah. Not tall. Nose? Too short and big. No lean face or full lips. No firsthand designer clothes. Not daring or beautiful like Naema. Perfume and mascara are not everything."

"*Haki,* you? Beautiful woman," I said, snapping my fingers. "You will be tall tomorrow."

"You are asking me out?" she said in jest, and struck a pose. She made faces as if she were playing with the twins and said, "Be a man, do it the right way."

I shrugged and laughed.

"Me, I have no shilling, big gal."

"I will discount you, guy."

"Stop it."

"Oh, come on," she said, and pulled me into a hug.

Giggling, we began walking, our strides softened by laughter. Everything became funny. We couldn't stop laughing at ourselves, at the people around us. When my sides began to ache and I stopped, she tickled my ribs.

We laughed at the gangs of street kids massed together in sound sleep. Some gangs slept in graded symmetry. Others slept freestyle. Some had a huge tarp above their piles to protect them from the elements. Others had nothing. We laughed at a group of city taxi drivers huddled together, warming themselves with cups of *chai* and fiery political banter while waiting for the Akamba buses to arrive with passengers from Tanzania and Uganda. Occasionally we'd see the anxious faces of these visitors in the old taxis, bracing for what would be the most dangerous twenty minutes of their twelve-hour journeys, fearful of being robbed whenever the taxis slowed down.

We were not afraid of the city at night. It was our playground. At times like this, it was as if Maisha had forgotten her job, and all she wanted to do was laugh and playact.

"You? Nice guy," Maisha said.

"Lie."

I pulled at her handbag.

"You will be a big man tomorrow . . ."

She dashed past me suddenly to wave down a chauffeured Volvo. It stopped right in front of her, the window rolling down. A man in the backseat inspected her and shook his bald head. He beckoned a taller girl from the cluster jostling behind her, trying to fit their faces in the window. Maisha ran to a silver Mercedes-Benz wagon, but the owner picked a shorter girl.

"Someday, I must to find a real job," Maisha said, sighing, when she came back.

"What job, gal?"

"I want to try full-time."

"*Wapi?*"

She shrugged. "Mombasa? Dar?"

I shook my head. "Bad news, big gal. How long?"

"I don't know. *Ni maisha yangu,* guy, it's my life. I'm thinking, full time will allow me to pay your fees and also save for myself. I will send money through the church for you. I'll quit the brothel when I save a bit. I don't want to stand on the road forever. Me myself must to go to school one day . . ."

The words died in her throat. She pursed her lips, folded her hands across her chest, and rocked from side to side. She did not rush to any more cars.

"We won't see you again?" I said. "No, thanks. If you enter brothel, me I won't go to school."

"Then I get to keep my money, ha-ha. Without you, they won't see my shilling in that house. Never." She saw my face, stopped suddenly, then burst into giggles. "I was kidding you, guy, about the brothel. Just kidding, OK?"

She tickled me, pulling me toward Moi Avenue. I held her hand tightly. Prostitutes fluttered about under streetlights, dressed like winged termites.

"Maisha, our parents —"

She turned sharply, her fists balled.

"Shut up! You shame me, you rat. Leave me alone. Me am not your mate. You can't afford me!"

Other girls turned and stared at us, giggling. Maisha strode away. It had been a mistake to mention our parents in front of the other girls, to let them know that we were related. And I shouldn't have called her by her real name. I cried all the way home because I had hurt her. She ignored me for weeks.

AFTER MAMA STOPPED CELEBRATING the end of our debt, she fished out two little waterproof Uchumi Supermarket bags from the carton and smoothed them out as if they were rumpled socks. She put them over her canvas shoes, tying the handles around her ankles in little bows. Then she walked out into the flood, her winged galoshes scooping the water like a duck's feet. She started to untie our bag of utensils and food, which was leaning against the shop, her eyes searching for a dry spot to set up the stove, to warm some food for the twins. But the rain was coming down too heavily now, and after a while she gave up.

"Jigana, so did you see those Maisha's *ma*-men?" she asked.

"There were three white men, plus driver. Tall, old men in knickers and tennis shoes. I shook hands with them. Beautiful-beautiful motorcar. . . . I even pinched that monkey."

"Motorcar? They had a motorcar? *Imachine* a motorcar to pick up my daughter." She stretched forward and held my arms, smiling. "You mean my daughter is big like that?"

Otieno woke up with a start. He stood groggily on the cushions, then he climbed over Mama's legs, levered himself over me with his hand on my head, and landed in the flood outside the shack in a crouch. He began to lower thin spools of shit into the water, whiffs of heat unwrapping into the night, the cheeks of his buttocks rouged by the cold.

When Otieno returned to the shack, he sat on Mama's legs and brought out her breast and sucked noisily. With one hand, he grabbed a toy Maisha had bought for him, rattling its maracas on Mama's bony face. She was still looking ragged and underweight, even though she'd stayed in the hospital to have her diet monitored after Baby graduated from the incubator.

Mama took out our family Bible, which we had inherited from Baba's father, to begin our Ex-mas worship. The front cover had peeled off, leaving a dirty page full of our relatives' names, dead and living. She read them out. Baba's late father had insisted that all the names of our family be included, in recognition of the instability of street life. She began with her father, who had been killed by cattle rustlers, before she ran away to Nairobi and started living with Baba. She called out Baba's mother, who came to Nairobi when her village was razed because some politicians wanted to redraw tribal boundaries. One day she disappeared forever into the city with her walking stick. Mama invoked the names of our cousins Jackie and Solo, who settled in another village and wrote to us through our church, asking our parents to send them school fees. I looked forward to telling them about the lit parks and the beautiful cars of Nairobi as soon as my teachers taught me how to write letters. She called out her brother, Uncle Peter, who had shown me how to shower in the city fountains without being whipped by the officials. He was shot by the police in a case of mistaken identity; the mortuary gave his corpse to a medical school because we could not pay the bill. She called Baba's second cousin Mercy, the only secondary school graduate among our folks. She had not written to us since she fell in love with a Honolulu tourist and eloped with him. Mama called Baba's sister, Auntie Mama, who, until she died two years ago of a heart attack, had told us stories and taught us songs about our ancestral lands every evening, in a sweet, nostalgic voice.

The sky rumbled.

"*Bwana,* I hope Naema put clothes on Baby before she left," Mama said to me, the middle of her sentence wobbling because Otieno had bitten her.

"She put Baby in waterproof paper bags. Then sweater."

Otieno, having satisfied himself, woke up Atieno, who took over the other breast, for they had divided things up evenly between them. Atieno sucked until she slept again, and Mama placed her gently near Otieno and began to shake Baba until he opened one eye. His weak voice vibrated because his face was jammed into the wall: "Food."

"No food, tarling," Mama told him. "We must to finish to call the names of our people."

"You'll be calling my name if I don't eat."

"Here is food—New Suntan shoe *kabire*." She reached out and collected the plastic bottle from me. "It can kill your stomach till next week."

"All the children are here?"

"Baby and Naema still out. Last shift . . . and Maisha."

"Ah, there is hope. Maisha will bring Ex-mas feast for us."

"Ex-mas is school fees, remember?"

Mama groped inside the carton again. She unearthed a dirty candle, pocked by grains of sand. She lit the candle and cemented it to the trunk with its wax. Taking the Bible, she began to read a psalm in Kiswahili, thanking God for the gift of Baby and the twins after two miscarriages. She praised God for blessing Maisha with white clients at Ex-mas. Then she prayed for Fuunny Eyes, the name we had given to the young Japanese volunteer who unfailingly dropped shillings in our begging plate. She wore Masai tire sandals and *ekarawa* necklaces that held her neck like a noose, and never replied to our greetings or let her eyes meet ours. Mama prayed for our former landlord in the Kibera slums, who evicted us but hadn't seized anything when we could not pay the rent. Now she asked God to bless Simba with many puppies. "Christ, you Ex-mas son, give Jigana a big, intelligent head in school!" she concluded.

"Have mercy on us," I said.

"Holy Mary, Mama Ex-mas . . ."

"Pray for us."

IT WAS DRIZZLING AGAIN when Naema returned with Baby. He was asleep. Naema's jeans, *mutumba* loafers, and braided hair dribbled water, her big eyes red from crying. Usually she sauntered in singing a Brenda Fassie song, but tonight she plodded in deflated.

She handed the money over to Mama, who quickly banked it in her purse. She also gave Mama a packet of pasteurized milk. It was half full, and Naema explained that she'd had to buy it to keep Baby from crying. Mama nodded. The milk pack was soggy and looked as if it would disintegrate. Mama took it carefully in her hands, like one receiving a diploma. When Naema brought out a half-eaten turkey drumstick, Mama grabbed her ears, thinking that she had bought it with the money she'd earned begging. Naema quickly explained that her new boyfriend had given it to her. This boy was a big shot in the street gang that controlled our area, a dreaded figure. Maisha and I detested him, but he loved Naema like his own tongue.

Now Naema wriggled and fitted her lithe frame into the tangle on the floor and began to weep silently. Mama pulled the blanket from the others and covered the girl's feet, which had become wrinkled in the rain.

"Maisha is moving out tomorrow," Naema said. "Full time."

Mama's face froze. No matter how rootless and cheap street life might be, you could still be broken by departures. I went outside and lay on the row of empty paint containers we had lined up along the shop's wall, hiding my face in the crook of my arm.

Guilt began to build in my gut. Maybe if I had joined a street gang, Maisha would not have wanted to leave. I wouldn't have needed money for school fees, and perhaps there would have been peace between Maisha and my parents. But my anger was directed at the *musungu* men, for they were the visible faces of my sister's temptation. I wished I were as powerful as Naema's boyfriend or that I could recruit him. We could burn their Jaguar. We could tie them up and give them the beating of their lives and take away all their papers. We could strip those *musungu* naked, as I had seen Naema's friend do to someone who had hurt a member of his gang. Or we could at least kill and eat that monkey or just cut off his *mboro* so he could never fuck anybody's sister again. I removed my knife from my pocket and examined the blade carefully. The fact that it was very blunt and had dents did not worry me. I knew that if I stabbed with all my energy, I would draw blood.

After a while, my plans began to unravel. I realized that I would never be able to enlist Naema's boyfriend. Naema herself would block the plan. In fact, until that night she had been taunting Maisha to move out, saying that if she were as old as Maisha she would have left home long ago. Besides, even if I fled to the Kibera slums, as soon as we touched the tourists, the police would come and arrest my parents and dismantle our shack. They would take away Maisha's trunk and steal her treasures.

BABA STARTED AWAKE, as if a loud noise had hit him.

"Is that Maisha?" he asked, closing his eyes again.

"No, Maisha is working," Mama said. "My Maisha commands *musungu* and motorcars!" she said, her good mood returning.

"What? What *musungu,* tarling?" Baba asked, sitting up immediately, rubbing sleep and hunger from his eyes with the base of his palms.

"White tourists," Mama said.

"Uh? They must to pay *ma*-dollar or euros. Me am family head. You hear me, woman?"

"Yes."

"And no Honolulu business. What kind of motorcar were they driving?"

"Jaguar," I answered. "With driver. Baba, we should not allow Maisha to leave—"

"Nobody is leaving, nobody. And shut up your animal mouth! You have wounded my wife! Until I break your teeth tomorrow, no opinion from you. No nothing. Did you thank the *ma*-men for me?"

"No," I said.

"Aiiee! Jigana, where are your manners? Did you ask where they were going? Motorcar number?"

"No, Baba."

"So if they take her to Honolulu, what do I do? Maybe we should send you to a street gang. Boy, have you not learned to grab opportunities? Is this how you will waste school fees in January? Poor Maisha."

He squinted incredulously, and lines of doubt kinked up his massive forehead. He pursed his lips, and anger quickened his breath. But that night I stood my ground.

"I don't want school anymore, Baba," I said.

"Coward, shut up. That one is a finished matter."

"No."

"What do you mean by no? You want to be a pocket thief like me, . . . my son? My first son? You can't be useless as the gals. *Wallai!*"

"Me, I don't want school."

"Your mind is too young to think. As we say, 'The teeth that come first are not used in chewing.' As long as you live here, your Baba says school."

"*La hasha.*"

"You telling me *never?* Jigana!" He looked at Mama. "He doesn't want school? Saint Jude Thaddaeus!"

"*Bwana,* this boy has grown strong-head," Mama said. "See how he is looking at our eyes. Insult!"

Baba stood up suddenly, his hands shaking. I didn't cover my cheeks with my hands to protect myself from his slap or spittle, as I usually did when he was angry. I was ready for him to kill me. My family was breaking up because of me. He stood there, trembling with anger, confused.

Mama patted his shoulders to calm him down. He brushed her aside and went out to cool off. I monitored him through a hole in the wall. Soon he was cursing himself aloud for drinking too much and sleeping through Ex-mas Day and missing the chance to meet the tourists. As his mind turned to Maisha's good fortune, he began to sing "A Jaguar is a Jaguar is a Jaguar" to the night, leaping from stone to stone, tracing the loose cobbles that studded the floodwater like the heads of stalking crocodiles in a river. In the sky, some of the tall city buildings were branded by lights left on by forgetful employees, and a few shopping centers wore the glitter of Ex-mas; flashing lights ascended and descended like angels on Jacob's dream ladder. The long city buses, Baba's hunting grounds, had stopped for the night. As the streets became emptier, cars drove faster through the floods, kicking up walls of water, which collapsed on our shack.

Back inside, Baba plucked his half-used *miraa* stick from the rafter and started chewing. He fixed his eyes on the trunk. A mysterious smile dribbled out of the corners of his mouth. Eventually, the long stick of *miraa* subsided into a formless sponge. His spitting was sharp and arced across the room and out the door. Suddenly, his face brightened. *"Hakuna matata!"* he said. Then he dipped into the carton and came up with a roll of wire and started lashing the wheels of the trunk to the props of our shack. For a moment, it seemed he might be able to stop Maisha from going away.

Mama tried to discourage him from tying down the trunk. *"Bwanaaa . . .* stop it! She will leave if she finds you *manga-mangaring* with her things."

"Woman, leave this business to me," he said, rebuking her. "I'm not going to sit here and let any Honolulus run away with our daughter. They must marry her properly."

"You should talk," Mama said. "Did you come to my father's house for my hand?"

"Nobody pays for trouble," Baba said. "You're trouble. If I just touch you, you get pregnant. If I even look at you — twins, just like that. Too, too ripe."

"Me am always the problem," Mama said, her voice rising.

"All me am saying is we must to treat the tourist well."

Atieno was shivering; her hand was poking out of the shack.

Baba yanked it back in and stuck her head through the biggest hole in the middle of our blanket. That was our way of ensuring that the family member who most needed warmth maintained his place in the center of the blanket. Baba grabbed Otieno's legs and pushed them through two holes on the fringe. "Children of Jaguar," he whispered into their ears. "Ex-mas *ya* Jag-uar." He tried to tuck Atieno and Otieno properly into the blanket, turning them this way and that, without success. Then he became impatient and rolled them toward each other like a badly wrapped meat roll, their feet in each other's face, their knees folded and tucked into each other's body — a blanket womb.

Mama reminded him to wedge the door, but he refused. He wanted us to wait for Maisha. He winked at me as if I were the cosentry of our fortune. Mama handed Baby to me and lay down. I sat there sniffing *kabire* until I became drunk. My head swelled, and the roof relaxed and shook, then melted into the sky.

I was floating. My bones were inflammable. My thoughts went out like electric currents into the night, their counter-currents running into each other, and, in a flash of sparks, I was hanging on the door of the city bus, going to school. I hid my uniform in my bag so that I could ride free, like other street children. Numbers and letters of the alphabet jumped at me, scurrying across the page as if they had something to say. The flares came faster and faster, blackboards burned brighter and brighter. In the beams of sunlight leaking through the holes in the school roof, I saw the teacher writing around the cracks and patches on the blackboard like a skillful *matatu* driver threading his way through our pothole-ridden roads. Then I raced down our bald, lopsided field with an orange for a rugby ball, jumping the gullies and breaking tackles. I was already the oldest kid in my class.

Mama touched my shoulders and relieved me of the infant. She stripped Baby of the plastic rompers, cleaned him up, and put him in a nappy for the night. With a cushion wrested from Naema, who was sleeping, Mama padded the top of the carton into a cot. After placing Baby in it, she straightened the four corners of the carton and then folded up our mosquito net and hung it over them. It had been donated by an NGO, and Baba had not had a chance to pawn it yet. Then Mama wrapped her frame around the carton and slept.

I WOKE UP BABA when Maisha returned, before dawn. He had been stroking his rosary beads, dozing and tilting until his head upset the mosquito netting. Mama had to continually elbow or kick him off. And each time, he opened his eyes with a practiced smile, thinking the Jaguar hour had arrived. The rain had stopped, but clouds kept the night dark. The city had gorged itself on the floods, and its skin had swelled and burst in places. The makeshift tables and stalls of street markets littered the landscape, torn and broken, as if there had been a bar fight. Garbage had spread all over the road: dried fish, stationery, trinkets, wilted green vegetables, plastic plates, wood carvings, underwear. Without the usual press of people, the ill-lit streets sounded hollow, amplifying the smallest of sounds. Long after a police car had passed, it could be heard negotiating potholes, the officers extorting their bribes—their Ex-mas *kitu kidogo*—from the people who could not afford to go to their up-country villages for the holidays.

Maisha returned in an old Renault 16 taxi. She slouched in the
back while the driver got out. Kneeling and applying pliers to
open the back door, the driver let her out of the car. Baba's sighs
of disappointment were as loud as the muezzin who had begun to
call Nairobi to prayer. My sister stepped out, then leaned on the
car, exhausted. There were bags of food on the seat.

She gestured at Baba to go away. He ignored her.

"So where is *our* Jaguar and *musungu*?" Baba asked the taxi
driver, peering into the shabby car as if it might be transformed
at any moment.

"What Jaguar? What *musungu*?" the driver asked, monitoring
Maisha's movements.

"The *nini* Jaguar.... Where is my daughter coming from?"
Baba asked him.

"Me, I can't answer you that question," he told Baba, and
pointed to his passenger.

She bent in front of the only functioning headlamp to count
out the fare. Her trousers were so tight that they had crinkled on
her thighs and pockets; she struggled to get to the notes without
breaking her artificial nails, which curved inward like talons.
Yesterday, her hair had been low cut, gold, wavy, and crisp from
a fresh perm. Now it stood up in places and lay flat in others, revealing patches of her scalp, which was bruised from the chemi-
cals. It was hard to distinguish peeling face powder from damaged
skin. To rid herself of an early outbreak of adolescent pimples,
she had bleached her face into an uneven lightness. Her eyelids
and the skin under her eyes had reacted the worst to the assorted
creams she was applying, and tonight her fatigue seemed to have
seeped under the burns, swelling her eyes.

The driver could not easily roll up the window. He extended his arm to guard the food bags, his collateral. Baba brought out a six-inch nail and went for the worn tires. "What *dawa* have you given my daughter? She always comes home strong."

The driver crumpled immediately, his pleas laden with fright. "*Mzee,* my name is Karume. Paul Kinyanjui wa Karume. . . . Me, I be an upright Kenyan. I fear God."

"And you want to steal my daughter's bags?"

"No. Please, take the bags. Please," the man begged, trying to restrain Baba from bursting his tires.

"*Aiie,* Baba. You shame me. Shut up," Maisha said weakly, pushing the money toward the driver.

Baba collected the bags and strolled from the road, his nose full of good smells, until he suddenly broke into a run, to untie the trunk before Maisha reached the shack.

The driver got into his car and was about to put the money into his breast pocket when he started frisking himself. Baba stood watching from the door of the shack. Soon it was as if the driver had soldier ants in his clothes. He unzipped his pockets, then zipped them again quickly, as if the thief were still lurking. He removed his coat, then his shirt, and searched them. He recounted his itinerary to the skies with eyes closed, his index finger wagging at invisible stars. He searched his socks, then he got down on all fours, scouring the wet ground. He dabbed at the sweat, or tears, running down his face. "Where is my money?" he said to Maisha, finally finding his voice. "*Haki,* it was in my pocket now, now."

Maisha charged forward and screeched at Baba until his stern face crumbled into a sheepish grin. He returned the fat wad of notes, giggling like the twins. The driver thanked her curtly, brushing his clothes with trembling hands. As soon as he'd reconnected the ignition wires to start the car, he creaked off, his horn blaring, his headlamp pointing up and to the left like an unblinking eye.

MAISHA STAGGERED INTO THE shack, holding her perilously high heels over her shoulders. Mama had made room for her and the bags and had sprayed our home with insecticide to discourage mosquitoes. My siblings inside started to cough. As Maisha came in, Mama stood aside like a maid, wringing her hands. I could not look Maisha in the eye and did not know what to say.

"Good night, Maisha," I blurted out.

She stopped, her tired body seized by shock. She searched my parents' faces before tracing the voice to me.

"Who told you to talk?" she said.

"You leave full time, I run away. No school."

"You are going to school," Maisha said. "Tuition is ready."

"Run away? Jigana, shut up," Baba said. "You think you are family head now? 'All are leaders' causes riots. Stupid, *mtu dufu!* Nobody is leaving."

Maisha glared at us, and we all turned our backs to her as she opened the trunk to take out a blanket. The sweet smell of her Jaguar adventures filled the shack, overpowering the heavy scent of insecticide. Though her arrivals always reminded us that life could be better, tonight I hated the perfume.

"Me and your mama don't want full time, Maisha," Baba said, picking his nails. "We refuse."

"Our daughter, things will get better," Mama said. "Thanks for canceling our debt!"

"You are welcome, Mama," Maisha said.

Mama's face lit up with surprise; she was so used to being ignored. She opened her mouth to say something, but nothing came out. Finally, she sobbed the words "*Asante,* Maisha, *asante* for everything!" and bowed repeatedly, her hands held before her, as if in prayer. The women looked into each other's eyes in a way I had never seen before. They hugged and held on as if their hands were ropes that tied their two bodies together. In spite of the cold, beads of sweat broke out on Mama's forehead, and her fingers trembled as she helped Maisha undo her earrings and necklace. Mama gently laid her down.

I believed that Mama might have been able to persuade her to stay, but then Baba signaled to Mama to keep quiet so that he could be the negotiator.

"Our daughter," Baba said, "you need to rest and think carefully. As our people say, north *ama* south, east *ama* west, home the best . . ."

"Maisha, no school for me!" I said. "I told Mama and Baba. They will return fee to you."

"Jigana, please, please, don't argue," Maisha said. "Even you. You cannot even pity me this night? Just for a few hours?"

MY PARENTS SAT OUTSIDE, on the paint containers. I stood by the wall, away from them. I wanted to see Maisha one more time before she disappeared.

Fog brought the dew down, thickening the darkness and turning the security lights into distant halos. We could hear Maisha twist and turn on the floor, cursing the limbs of her siblings and swatting at the mosquitoes. It was as if we were keeping a vigil of her last night with us. We were restless, the silence too heavy for us. Baba mumbled, blaming himself for not going more often to sweep the church premises. He agreed with Mama that if he had swept daily, instead of every other day, Saint Joseph the Worker would have bettered our lot. Mama snapped at him, because Baba had always told her that he was not interested in Saint Joseph's favor but in a clean place for people to worship. Then Baba blamed her for no longer attending the KANU slum rallies to earn a few shillings.

The night degenerated into growls and hisses. I preferred the distraction of the quarrel to the sound of Maisha's uneasy breathing. When Maisha clapped one more time and turned over, Mama couldn't stand it anymore. She rushed inside, took the mosquito net off the carton, and tied it to the rafters so that my sister was inside it. She sprayed the place again and brought Baby out to breast-feed. The coughing got worse. Baba tore down some of the walls to let in air, but, since the wind had subsided, it was of no use. He picked up the door and used it as a big fan to whip air into the shack.

IN THE MORNING, ATIENO and Otieno came out first. They looked tired and were sniffling from the insecticide. They stood before us, spraying the morning with yellow urine, sneezing and whimpering.

The streets began to fill. The street kids were up and had scattered into the day, like chickens feeding. Some moved about groggily, already drunk on *kabire*. One recounted his dreams to others at the top of his voice, gesticulating maniacally. Another was kneeling and trembling with prayer, his eyes shut as if he would never open them again. One man screamed and pointed at two kids, who were holding his wallet. No one was interested. His pocket was ripped to the zipper, leaving a square hole in the front of his trousers. He pulled out his shirt to hide his nakedness, then hurried away, an awkward smile straining his face. There was no sun, only a slow ripening of the sky.

The twins started to wail and to attack Mama's breasts. Baba spanked them hard. They sat on the ground with pent-up tears they were afraid to shed. Naema broke the spell. She came out and sat with me on the containers, grabbed my hands, and tried to cheer me up. "You are too sad, Jigana," she said. "You want to marry the gal? Remember, it's your turn to take Baby out."

"Leave me alone."

"Marry me, then — me am still here." She stuck out her tongue at me. "I'm your sister too — more beautiful. Guy, do me photo trick . . . smile." She was well rested and had slept off her initial shock at Maisha's departure. Now she was herself again, taunting and talkative, her dimples deep and perfect. "You all must to let Maisha go."

"And you?" I said. "You only listen to Maisha."

"I'm big gal now, guy. Breadwinner. If you want school, I pay for you!"

She blew me a kiss in the wind. Maisha's creams were already lightening her ebony face.

Before I could say anything, Naema erupted with mad laughter and ran into the shack. She almost knocked Baba down as she burst out with the bags of food we had forgotten. She placed them on the ground and tore into them, filling the morning with hope, beckoning all of us on. Baba bit into a chicken wing. Mama took a leg. The rest of us dug into the sour rice, mashed potatoes, salad, hamburgers, pizza, spaghetti, and sausages. We drank dead Coke and melted ice cream all mixed up. With her teeth, Naema opened bottles of Tusker and Castle beer. At first, we feasted in silence, on our knees, looking up frequently, like squirrels, to monitor one another's intake. None of us thought to inflate the balloons or open the cards that Maisha had brought.

Then the twins fell over on their backs, laughing and vomiting. As soon as they were done, they went straight back to eating, their mouths pink and white and green from ice cream and beer. We could not get them to keep quiet. A taxi pulled up and Maisha came out of the shack, dragging her trunk behind her. Our parents paused as the driver helped her put it into the car. My mother began to cry. Baba shouted at the streets.

I sneaked inside and poured myself some fresh *kabire* and sniffed. I got my exercise book from the carton and ripped it into shreds. I brought my pen and pencil together and snapped them, the ink spurting into my palms like blue blood. I got out my only pair of trousers and two shirts and put them on, over my clothes.

I avoided the uniform package. Sitting where the trunk had been, I wept. It was like a newly dug grave. I sniffed hastily, tilting the bottle up and down until the *kabire* came close to my nostrils.

As the car pulled away with Maisha, our mourning attracted kids from the gangs. They circled the food, and I threw away the bottle and joined my family again. We struggled to stuff the food into our mouths, to stuff the bags back inside the shack, but the kids made off with the balloons and the cards.

I hid among a group of retreating kids and slipped away. I ran through traffic, scaled the road divider, and disappeared into Nairobi. My last memory of my family was of the twins burping and giggling.

Fattening for Gabon

Selling your child or nephew could be more difficult than selling other kids. You had to keep a calm head or be as ruthless as the Badagry-Seme immigration people. If not, it could bring trouble to the family. What kept our family secret from the world in the three months Fofo Kpee planned to sell us were his sense of humor and the smuggler's instinct he had developed as an *agbero,* a tout, at the border. My sister Yewa was five, and I was ten.

Fofo Kpee was a smallish, hardworking man. Before the Gabon deal, as a simple *agbero,* he made a living getting people across the border without papers or just roughing them up for money. He also hired himself out in the harmattan season to harvest coconuts in the many plantations along the coast. He had his fair share of misfortune over the years, falling from trees and getting into scuffles at the border. Yet the man was upbeat about life. He seemed to smile at everything, partly because of a facial wound sustained in a fight when he was learning to be an *agbero.* Ridged and glossy, the scar ran down his left cheek and stopped at his upper lip, which was constricted; his mouth never fully closed. Though he tried to cover the scar with a big mustache, it shone like a bulb on a Christmas tree. His left eye looked bigger than the right because the lower eyelid came up short, pinched by the scar. Because of all this, sometimes people called him Smiley Kpee.

A two-tone, blue silver 125cc Nanfang motorcycle was the last major purchase Fofo Kpee made that month when our lifestyle took an upswing and the Gabon plot thickened. He planned to use it to ferry people across the border between Benin and Nigeria to boost our family's income.

I could never forget that windy Tuesday evening when a wiry man brought him back on the new bike to our two-room home that faced the sea. I rushed out from behind the house, where I was cooking Abakaliki rice, to greet Fofo Kpee. His laugh was louder than the soft hum of the new machine. Our house was set back from the busy dirt road; a narrow sandy path connected them. On either side of the path and around our home was a cassava farm, a low wedge in between the tall, thick bushes, clumps of banana and plantain trees, and our abode. Our nearest neighbors lived a half kilometer down the road.

I was bare-chested and barefoot, wearing the sea-green khaki shorts Fofo had just bought for me, and my feet were dusty from playing soccer. Yewa had been building sand castles under the mango tree in front of our house when the bike arrived.

"Smiley Kpee, only two?" the man who brought Fofo exclaimed, disappointed. "No way, *iro o!* Where oders?"

"Ah *non,* Big Guy, you go see oders . . . *beaucoup,*" said Fofo, a chuckle escaping his pinched mouth. He turned to us: "*Mes enfants,* hey, *una* no go greet Big Guy?"

"Good evening, *monsieur!*" we said, and prostrated ourselves on the ground.

The man turned away, ignoring us, his large eyes searching the road, his narrow forehead set in wrinkles. He had a small pointy nose. Although his head was clean shaven, his high cheekbones lay under a thin beard. He was in a tight pair of jeans, sandals, and an oversized, dirty-white corduroy shirt that hung on his lean frame like a furled sail, in spite of the wind. If not for his commanding height and presence, he could have been any other *agbero* at the border.

"My friend, make we go inside, *abeg,*" Fofo Kpee pleaded with him. "Sit down and drink someting. Heineken, Star, Guinness?" He turned to me: "Kotchikpa, *va acheter* him de drink."

"*Rien* . . . notting!" Big Guy said slowly and firmly, barely audible above the sea murmuring in the distance.

Apart from the invitation to drink, we didn't understand what they were talking about. But this didn't worry us. Having an *agbero* as an uncle, we were used to people coming to harass him for various things at all hours of the day. So we knew he would laugh his way out of the man's harassment now.

"We never said two, but five," Big Guy said, waving his fingers, some of which ended in dead nails, before Fofo. "Where de oder children now?"

Fofo stepped away from the fingers, saying, "You know my arrangement wid your people?"

"*Quel peuple?*" Big Guy taunted.

"Your boss," Fofo Kpee said.

"But *tu dois* deal wid me—*directement!*"

"Ah *non, abeg,* make we celebrate first. *Gbòjé* . . . relax."

"No, I dey very serious. *Just moi.*"

"You? You want do me open eye?"

"I no want frighten or cheat you. We *dey* do dis kind business like dis. . . . I *dey* warn you *o. Abi,* you want play wid fire?"

"We *dey* dis deal togeder," Fofo begged him. "No fear. Everyting go *dey* fine."

Big Guy shrugged and surveyed our surroundings, his eyes as suspicious as those of a traveler who has been duped at the border. He cast a disgusted glance at me and my sister and looked away. In the distance, the sun was a ball of gold in the foliage of the coconut plantation that guarded the approach to the Atlantic Ocean. The water that could take us abroad frothed gray and wild, resisting the sun's gold brushes, and on this canvas of water, the coconut vistas cast their swaying grids. The wind from the sea blew at the land in a mild, endless breath.

"Big Guy, calm down, look at me, *o jare* . . . you worry too much."

Big Guy shrugged and said, "No, Big Guy no *dey* worry. *Na* you *dey* worry."

We could tell that Big Guy was disappointed. He pursed his lips so hard that we saw a bit of the red of his nostrils, embers of the anger he was fighting to control. As I said, I didn't worry because I had seen Fofo in more difficult situations, and I was confident he would calm the man.

"What about de house?" Fofo Kpee said, gesturing at our house.

"What about it?" Big Guy said, without even giving our house a look, though Fofo continued to encourage him.

Its zinc roof was completely covered with rust, and the two rooms had no ceilings. The walls were made of mud and plastered with cement, and in the narrow veranda, there were mounds on either side of the door, for sitting, which is where Fofo wanted Big Guy to be if he didn't want to enter the house. The eaves were supported by pillars made of coconut wood.

"You like it?" Fofo asked.

"Your house *dey* OK for de business for now," Big Guy said. "I want leave."

"You see, you see," Fofo told him, chuckling. "At least I do one ting well."

"Well, after, we go build de one *wey* better *pass* dis one . . . bigger."

"*Ça ira, ça ira* . . . Tings go work out."

Big Guy walked away, the disappointment still in his eyes.

"Of course, only dead people *dey* owe us!" he said. "Only dead people."

"I sure say nobody go die. . . . Well, as de Annang people *dey* say, de dead no *dey* block de way, de killer no *dey* live forever," Fofo Kpee called out to him, laughing. "See you tomorrow, *á demain o*. And make you greet *ta famille pour* me *o*."

We didn't know what to make of the motorcycle when Big Guy left. We stood around it quietly, as if a long lost member of our family had returned. Fofo Kpee stared at our faces, as if he had given us a puzzle and wanted to see the first sparks of our comprehension.

"Nanfang!" Yewa exclaimed, breaking the spell. "*Zokeke* . . . *zokeke!*"

"Who owns it?" I gasped.

"Us *o*," Fofo said, and chuckled. "*Finalement*, we get *zokeke!*"

Uwem Akpan

"Us? *Zokeke?*" I said.

"*Oui o,* Kotchikpa, my son."

Yewa began to circle the bike in silence, like a voodoo priest at his shrine, her hands held out but afraid to make contact. She had large brown eyes that now shone out from her lean face, as if the machine's aura forbade them to blink. Her hair was short, like a boy's, and she wore only pink underpants, her stomach bloated. Her legs stepped lightly, her feet in socks of dust. My palms, dirtied from stoking the cooking fire with wood and making sure the pot of Abakaliki rice didn't fall off our stone tripod behind the house, began to sweat. I held my hands away from the bike and away from my shorts, rubbing my fingers against my palms.

"We belong to you," Yewa chanted in a whisper to the machine. "You belong to us, we belong to you."

"Yeah, daughter," said Fofo, enjoying our bewilderment. "God done reward our faitfulness. . . . *Nous irons* to be rich, ha-ha!"

The sudden merriment in his voice stopped Yewa. She looked at my face, then at Fofo's, as if we had conspired to trick her. Fofo Kpee opened his portmanteau, which he carried to the border every day, and pulled out the invoice for the bike from Cotonou City. It was too much for us. I started clapping, but Fofo stopped me, saying he didn't have enough drinks yet to offer people who might be attracted by the noise. I held my hands apart, palms facing each other as if they were of two opposing magnetic poles, my desire to clap repelled by Fofo's warning. Then a wave of happiness rose within me, and I ran inside, washed my hands, and put on a shirt and my flip,-flops, as if an important visitor had descended on us. When I came out, Fofo had opened our door and pushed the thing into our parlor-cum-bedroom. He lit a kerosene lantern and put it on a stand near the door to the inner room. The lantern's rays played above the Nanfang's fuel tank, outshining its two-tone design like the glow of a setting sun over the waves of the Atlantic.

To lock the front door, Fofo pulled out a plank of wood from under our bed and placed it snugly on the metal latches. Tonight, he tested the lock's strength, putting his left shoulder on the bar and carefully applying his weight. He sighed and nodded, beaming contentedly at the bike.

"We must buy new doors for de house," Fofo Kpee said.

"Windows also," Yewa blurted out, her attention still wrapped around the Nanfang as if the windows were part of it.

"Yeah, *pas du problem,*" he said, and started locking up the two little square wooden windows on either side of the door. "We go change *les choses lopa lopa,* many tings, I tell you."

There were two six-spring beds on either side of the room and a low wooden table in between. I slept with Yewa in one bed, while Fofo had the other bed to himself. Our clothes were in cartons under the beds, but Fofo's important clothes hung at one corner of the room, from a *bambu* pole suspended from the rafters by two ropes. Because the room was small, the bike stood, poking its handlebars and front tire into the wardrobe, like a cow whose head is lost in the tall grass it's eating. In the evenings, when we gazed into the roof, its rusty texture looked like stagnant brown clouds, no matter the brilliance of our lantern. On very hot days we could hear the roof expand with little knocking sounds.

Now we drew closer and gawked, and smelled and felt the Nanfang's body. Fofo had to shout at me twice to warn me about bringing the lantern too close to the machine. The smell of newness overpowered the stuffiness of the room. Yewa pulled at the clear plastic that covered the seats and lights and mudguards, until Fofo warned her not to remove them.

"I get someting for *vous*," Fofo Kpee said to calm us down. He sank into his bed and dug into the portmanteau and offered us little cones of peanuts and half-melted toffees from his pocket, which we chewed in the wrappers. That night Fofo didn't tell us stories about which he laughed louder than we did. He brought out a bottle of Niyya guava juice and poured us a drink. "Hey, *temps de celebration*," Fofo Kpee said. "We tank God!"

"We bless his name!" we responded.

He raised his cup. "Ah, we no create poverty. . . . Cheers *à la* Nanfang!"

"Cheers!" we responded, tipping our cups.

It had been a long time since we had fruit juice. Yewa drank hers immediately, in one long endless gulp, tilting the cup so quickly that the juice poured from both sides of her face and dribbled onto her belly, thick red teardrops. I took one gulp and stopped, thinking it would be better to save the juice until dinner, and went to set my cup down on a safe spot between the lantern stand and the wall.

The excitement of that night was such that when we finally descended on the Abakaliki rice and stew of onions, *kpomo*, and palm oil, we didn't mind if we found little pebbles in the rice. No matter how thoroughly you picked the rice for stones, you couldn't get rid of all of them. Now, occasionally, we cracked a pebble, held our jaws, and washed down the half-chewed food with juice. Though Fofo Kpee used to scold me each time he bit into a pebble, because it was my job to pick the rice, that night he didn't. We were celebrating our Nanfang. And with my stingy sips of juice, I could stand any amount of sand in the rice that night.

When I got down to the last gulp, I stopped and saved it. I had water instead and ate and drank until my stomach filled up, the palm oil in the stew yellowing my lips. Then I downed the rest of the juice so the taste would remain in my mouth until I went to bed.

"KOTCHIKPA, MY BOY, QUICK quick, go prepare de inner room for de Nanfang!" Fofo Kpee told me after dinner.

"Yes, Fofo Kpee," I said.

"Let the Nanfang stay here!" Yewa appealed to him. She was still jumping up and down, celebrating.

"Ah *non,* my gal," Fofo said. "Next room for Nanfang."

"I shall sleep inside, then," my sister said, bowing her head to her chest and looking sad. "With Nanfang."

"*Je dis non,* Yewa," Fofo insisted, and tried to change the subject: "I go buy tree new book for you. Your teacher go *dey* happy well well for you now, yes?"

"I don't want books," Yewa said.

"Hmmm, you no want book?" he asked. "*D'accord,* new *crayons?* Pencils?"

She shook her head. "I want to sleep *avec* Nanfang . . ."

"*Haba!*" Fofo Kpee shut her up.

Yewa sat down on the floor in protest, facing the machine, her back to us. Fofo went over and squatted behind her and caressed her shoulders, while she shrugged and tried to push him off.

"Ah, *mon* Yewa, *mon* Yewa," he sweet-talked her, "you go learn how to write. You be future professor!"

"No," Yewa said, shaking her head vigorously, as if a bug had just entered her nostril. Yewa was like that when she set her mind on something, stubborn and saying little.

"Ah *non,* you no want be *agbero* like me, *oui?*"

"Leave me alone."

Fofo leaned over to pour more juice into her cup, but she refused.

"Why you no want be good gal today?" he said. "Well, Kotchikpa no go write for you. Everyone must learn to write. Education *est* one person, one vote."

Yewa was silent.

"Yewa, *tu es toujours un bébé!*" I said, trying to coax her out of her stubbornness. "Crybaby!"

"Leave me alone."

"*Oya,* I go buy you sandal for school" Fofo Kpee begged her. She still didn't get up, so Fofo stood, shrugged, and came and sat on his bed and faced me. "Kotchikpa, *je t'acheterai* two textbook plus an exercise book, *d'accord?*"

"Books for me?" I said, excited. "When?"

"Tomorrow. You no go borrow book again for school. Since you like to read, you go *dey* read every night."

"Thanks, Fofo Kpee," I said, and glanced at the new bike, as if to acknowledge that without it coming into our lives I wouldn't have had what I needed for school.

"Witout education, you children, *comme moi,* go just rot for dis town, where danger full everywhere. No, I go try make sure *say una* go *dey* rich. I go even make sure *say una* go come be like de children of our politicians and leaders. *Una* go go school *sef* for abroad." He paused, then turned sharply to Yewa. "Hey, *mon bébé,* no problem if you no want be professor. *Abi,* you want become international businesswoman, yes? Anyway, you go *dey* cross dis ocean to Gabon, go come, go come, as if you *dey* go toilet," he said, snapping his fingers and pointing in the direction of the ocean.

"Give us a ride on the Nanfang," Yewa said suddenly, in a petulant voice. I felt she wanted to be granted this, since she couldn't sleep in the same room with the Nanfang.

"Easy, *pourquoi pas?*" our uncle said, going over to pour her more juice. "*C'est tout?*"

"Yes, take us out, Fofo, please," said Yewa, turning around. She was struggling not to smile, trying to remain angry, as if she still had all the power.

"Oh no, me I be responsible man," Fofo Kpee said in a cooing voice, and smiled a large smile. His face creased and lessened the tension on his left eye, making the scar on his cheek look artificial. "How me go come risk *una* life when I never *sabi* how to drive de *zokeke* yet? Gimme time . . . I go carry you go anywhere. . . . *Bois . . . bois.* Drink . . . drink."

"*Allons* Braffe! To see Papa and Mama!" I said.

My sister quickly unstuck her mouth from the cup, swallowed, and said breathlessly, "Yes, yes, to Braffe . . . to Braffe!"

"*Absolutement,*" Fofo said.

"Tomorrow," Yewa said.

"No . . . impossible."

"Mr. Big Guy will ride us," I said.

Fofo shook his head. "Ah *non,* you want shame me, *mes enfants?* How me go arrive for Braffe village when I never fit drive my *zokeke?* No, make we wait small. I go learn fast. . . . Even *sef,* I never get enough money to visit Braffe now."

"Papa and Mama will be happy to see us and the Nanfang," Yewa said, and got up and came to sit on the bed with me.

"Grandpapa will give you many handshakes. Grandmama will dance," I said. "Hey, let's go on Monday."

"Kotchikpa, Monday?" Fofo Kpee said incredulously. "No, I go first come your school to pay school fees on Monday. . . . School before pleasure, right, *mon peuple,* right?"

"Yes, Fofo," I said. When I looked at my sister, happiness had taken over her face. She started babbling about our family in the village.

We hadn't seen them for one and a half years, since Fofo came to the village to take us to live with him. Papa, a short chubby man with a stern face, was bedridden, tended by our dutiful and teary grandmother. Mama, a mountain of a woman, with an everlasting smile and restless energy, had already lost her bulk, become emaciated, and couldn't walk to the farm without resting two or three times under the *ore* trees by the roadside. No matter how many times we asked, nobody volunteered any information about our parents' sickness. Our relatives talked in hushed voices about it, a big family secret. However, by eavesdropping, I learned that my parents had AIDS, though I didn't know what it meant then.

Before we left home, our relatives gathered in our parents' living room, and Papa and Mama told us to be obedient to Fofo Kpee, not to disgrace them by being ungrateful to him at the border town to which he was taking us. They said he would henceforth be our father and mother and that I was to show a good example to Yewa and to protect the name of our family at all costs. I promised everyone I would be good. Fofo said he was happy to take care of his brother's children and said he would bring us back to the village to visit our parents and our older siblings, Ezin and Esse and Idossou, whenever time and resources allowed. My grandpapa, the gentle patriarch of our extended family, prayed over us that morning before we left on the Glazoué-Cotonou Road. Grandmama sobbed silently beside Papa, who had turned his face to the wall to cry. I remember our siblings and a host of relatives waving to us until our bus turned the corner, heading south.

Now, whenever we asked Fofo about our parents, he always said that they were recovering. He said they were eager to see us and we would soon go back to visit, but it was more important that we got used to our new home and studied hard in school. That Nanfang night, in my excitement, I was already thinking of the celebration that would sweep through our family when we rode in on the motorcycle, and everyone saw that one of theirs had brought home something better than a Raleigh bicycle. I figured once we got off the machine, Ezin and Esse and Idossou would be the first to get a ride. I could imagine Mama and our aunties cooking up pots of *obe aossin,* melon soup; *iketi,* cornmeal; and mounds of *egun,* pounded yam; and Papa and his brothers making sure there was plenty of *chapalo,* local beer. I looked forward to seeing all our friends and cousins, telling them about the beauty of the ocean and all the border hassles. We might even arrange a soccer match between all the boys in our extended family and another family in the village.

FOFO KPEE PULLED OUT a bag from under his bed and rested it on his lap like a baby, feeling for something inside without looking, until he grabbed and pulled out an old green four-angle schnapps bottle. It was half filled with *payó*. He shook it and opened it, the local gin's pungency briefly overpowering the scent of the new bike. He sipped slowly from the bottle, his eyes glittering in the heat of the drink, his left eye shining more because it was bigger, the scar looking like a large tear flowing down his cheek.

"*S'il vous plaît,*" Yewa whined again, gawking at the drink, "I want to sleep with my Nanfang tonight. Just tonight." Her little bony face was upturned, the yellow lantern light washing over one side like a half moon. Tears shone from the lighted part of her face.

"If you want small *payó,* say it," Fofo Kpee said. But Yewa pretended not to hear what he said. "Gal, you go be big-time businesswoman for Gabon. You be hard bargainer!"

"*Please,*" Yewa said.

Fofo Kpee gave up and poured some gin into the silver top of the bottle and then into Yewa's mouth. Yewa swallowed, cleared her throat, and smacked her lips contentedly. She didn't say anything else, but just stroked the spokes of the motorcycle gently as if they were the strings of some beloved musical instrument.

"Finish de room for de *zokeke,* den I go give you your drink," Fofo told me. "*Payó* head no good for Nanfang!"

I entered the inner room, which was smaller than the first, and began to move things around to make space for the machine. The room had become our treasure store and had been filling up recently, with the sudden change in our lifestyle. I picked up packets of roof nails and gaskets and placed them on the pile of second-hand corrugated roofing sheets by the far wall, near the back door. There were two huge black plastic water vats, neither of which needed to be moved, in opposite corners of the room, and five bags of Dangote cement, stacked by the near wall below the window, that kept shedding a fine gray dust. After I began to move things, a stuffy thickness filled the air. My nostrils felt itchy, and I sneezed three times. If we swept the room, even with the two windows open, the dust whirled up and beclouded everything like the harmattan haze. I began to work the bolt on one window to let in the humid ocean air.

"No open de window *o!*" Fofo said from the parlor, his voice raspy from the gin. "You want expose my *zokeke* to tieves, huh? *A yón* cost of Nanfang?"

"I'm sorry," I said.

"You better be—*nuluno!*"

I went on to rearrange the corner of the room where our food and utensils were. On a big upturned wooden mortar, I put a wicker basket of plates and cutlery. The long black pestle was leaning in the corner, its head white and cracked by use. I stacked up three empty pots, careful not to touch their soot, careful not to touch our pot of *egusi* soup, which I had already warmed for the night. Stirring it would make it sour before morning. Soon, Fofo, in a solemn procession, brought in the machine and stood it at the center of the room, like a giant bearing down on everything, an athlete poised at the starting line.

That night, the bike followed me into the land of my dreams.

I rejected Suzuki, Honda, and Kawasaki and chose a Nanfang and became rich forever. I used it to climb the coconut trees, learned to park on the palms, and used coconut milk for gas. I rode it across the ocean, creating a huge wake behind me. I flew it like a helicopter to distant places and landed it many times in my father's compound in Braffe. At school, all my classmates had Nanfangs, and we played soccer riding them, like in polo. I rode my Nanfang until I grew old, but the Nanfang neither aged nor needed repairs. At the end of my life, my people buried me atop it, and I rode that Nanfang straight to heaven's gate, where Saint Peter gave me an automatic pass.

FOR FOUR DAYS, WE watched Big Guy teach Fofo Kpee how to ride along the strips of grass in the coconut plantation. From our house, we could see Fofo perched on the bike, his face split in two by his trademark laugh. He looked like a pantomime because we couldn't hear him or the bike over the sound of the ocean. Big Guy's shaven head was so oiled that it reflected the sun. Both of them seemed to be having fun, and on the horizon, a ship heading to or leaving Porto Novo dragged a black funnel of smoke across the sky.

The next Sunday, we got ready for church. Fofo had informed the pastor that we were going to have our first Family Thanksgiving, which was what some well-to-do families did every Sunday.

At dawn, Fofo Kpee woke up and took the Nanfang behind the house and propped it on our bathing stone. He undressed it of its plastic covers as gingerly as one would remove stitches from a wound. He poured Omo detergent into a bucket of water and swirled and rattled the water until it foamed. Gently, he sponged the frame and scrubbed the tires, as if they would never touch the ground again. After rinsing the Nanfang, he wiped it with the towel the three of us shared. During our own bath, he squatted and soaked our feet and scrubbed them with a new *kankan,* a native sponge, for the big occasion. He held the *kankan* like a shoe brush and worked on our soles until their natural color returned, until the fissures disappeared.

Later, Fofo Kpee rode us to church, wearing a new *agbada* and huge sunglasses, which gave him a bug-eyed look. The wind pumped up the flanks of his *agbada* like malformed wings. It was our first ride: Yewa was on the gas tank, clutching our family Bible, sporting her flowery dress and new baseball cap. In a pair a of corduroys and a green T-shirt, I was crushed in between Fofo and two acquaintances of his. The woman behind me was dangling a big squawking red rooster by its tied legs on one side of the machine. She was a large woman and her big headgear hovered over me like a multicolored umbrella. The man at the end of the bike carried on his head a basket with three yams, pineapples, oranges, a bag of *amala* flour, and five rolls of toilet paper.

A triumphant midmorning sun filled the day, and a clear blue sky beckoned us. The road was crowded with churchgoers. Fofo Kpee sped off, tooting his horn nonstop, flashing the lights to clear the road ahead of us. The crowd parted before us like the Red Sea before Moses's rod. Some people waved and cheered us on. My chest swelled with pride, and my eyes welled up with tears, which the wind swept onto my earlobes.

When we got to Our Redeemer Pentecostal Church, Big Guy was waiting by the entrance, smiling at us like an usher. He had shaved his beard, and in his gray suit and loafers, he looked even taller and more intimidating. He stood as straight as one of the thin pillars that adorned the church's entrance. The church was a big, uncompleted rectangular structure. The new roof shone in the bright sun, but the church had no doors or windows yet, and the walls hadn't been plastered. You could hear hundreds of shoes shuffling on what we called the "German floor" as worshippers walked in and found their places among the pews, which, for now, were planks set on blocks.

Fofo parked the bike under a guava tree, although not before he had felt the ground around the stand with his right foot to see whether it was safe to do so. He unfolded a big tarp and covered the Nanfang, in case it rained, however unlikely that was.

"Ah, *mon ami,* good morning *o!*" Fofo greeted Big Guy, grabbing his hand when we got to the door.

"I tell you say I no go miss dis one," Big Guy said, and pulled us aside, away from the doorway. "Somehow, I been tink *say* you go bring de oder children to church."

Fofo Kpee froze. "*Wetin?* Which children, Big Guy?" he said.

Big Guy looked away. "You know *wetin* I *dey* talk, Smiley Kpee, you know."

Big Guy wasn't as agitated or angry as he had been when he brought the Nanfang and said he expected to see *five* children. Now, there was an uneasy silence between the two men. The four of us looked like an island in the river of people entering the church.

"OK, God bless you," Fofo Kpee said, and nudged him on the side. "Make we talk about dis matter *oso.*"

"Tomorrow never come," Big Guy said, his voice rising in seriousness.

"You loser! Who send you come spoil my Family Tanksgiving?"

Because of the way Fofo sounded, some people turned and stared at Big Guy. Two ushers started wading through the crowd toward us, as if they anticipated a quarrel.

"Just joking," Big Guy said, and let out a nervous laugh.

"I hope you *dey* joke," Fofo said, chuckling, and people went back to minding their business.

Big Guy turned to us immediately and squatted before Yewa, touching her cap and holding our hands. In spite of his bad nails, his palms were soft and gentle. "Oh, our children are so beautiful!" he said.

"Thank you, *monsieur*," we said.

"Wow, Fofo *dey* treat you well *o*."

"Yes, he does, *monsieur*."

"*Abeg o. Appellez-moi* Big Guy. Just Big Guy, deal?"

"Yes, Big Guy," my sister said, nodding.

"And you?" Big Guy said, turning to me.

"Yes, Big Guy . . . *monsieur*," I said.

"Oh, no, no," he said, clucking his tongue disapprovingly. "*N'est pas* difficult. Big Guy, just Big Guy. Your kid sister done master de ting." He turned again to Yewa: "You must be smart for school, *abi?*"

"Yes, Big Guy," Yewa said, licking her lips excitedly.

"No worry, Kotchikpa go master de name too," Fofo said, coming to my defense as Big Guy rose to his feet. "Give de boy time, man . . . right Kotchikpa?"

"Yes, Fofo," I said.

"Dere you are," Fofo Kpee said to Big Guy, and shook his hand again, while folding the wings of his *agbada* onto his shoulders. His smile was so wide that the tension between his lip and left eyelid eased, and his eyes looked the same size. "*Etẹ n'gan dọ? Na* our family turn for Tanksgiving. *Abeg,* join us in peace."

"*Pourquoi pas?*" Big Guy said, shrugging. "You know say our God no be poor God. . . . He bring me and you togeder for better ting."

"Yeah, you know, as our people say, man be God to man," Fofo said. "Hunger *o,* disease *o,* bad luck *o,* empty pockets *o* — our heavenly *baba* go banish all of dem from us today. God done already shame Satan."

"If you *dey* poor, know dat because you be sinner. Someting *dey* wrong wid you. And God *dey* punish you," Big Guy said.

IN CHURCH, THE FOUR of us sat in the front pew. When it was time for Thanksgiving proper, we went to the back. Fofo went outside and rolled the Nanfang up to the church. Two ushers helped him lift it over the three stairs at the front.

Like two acolytes, Yewa and I stood at the head of the procession, our dance steps at once shy and excited, not completely in sync with the heavy drums and singing. Then came Fofo and Nanfang. He held the bike majestically, like a bride. Still, from time to time Fofo Kpee managed to stoop low and gyrate and flap and gather his *agbada.* The trumpets were so loud that even if the rooster we brought, which was held by someone deep in the procession, was still squawking, nobody heard.

When there was a lull in the trumpeting, someone behind us filled the church with a loud yodeling. When I turned around, I saw it was Big Guy. He loomed behind us like a pillar of cloud. His dance was elegant and unique: he didn't bend down like Fofo but was very erect, as if his suit refused him permission to stoop or spread out his long legs. Instead, he simply shook and threw his legs and arms gingerly, like a daddy longlegs.

Behind him, the crowd of well-wishers swelled the aisle with dancing, bringing up the gifts of yam, fruit, *amala* flour, and toilet paper we had brought from home. In this flux, the ushers stood like statues, holding out baskets into which we tossed naira and cefa bills. When we had gathered in front of the sanctuary, Pastor Concord Adeyemi, short, thin, and bearded, came before us. His suit was charcoal black, and a sizable cross dangled from a chain around his neck over his tie. He wore jheri curls.

"Now, bring out your offering and raise it to the Lord to be blessed . . . Amen!" he thundered into the microphone.

"Amen!" the church responded.

People began digging in their pockets for money. Yewa and I brought out our twenty-naira bills, which Fofo Kpee had given to us solely for this purpose. Fofo had said it was important today we held up N20 bills instead of the N1 coins we had held during other people's Thanksgivings. Today wasn't the day for us to be ashamed, he had said. Now, when I looked behind, Fofo was holding up a N100 bill. The roof of the church looked littered with naira and cefa bills, suspended in the air by hundreds of hands.

"Raise it higher to the Lord," the pastor said. "And be blessed in Jesus' name!"

"Amen."

"Higher, I say. . . . You get from the Lord what you give. We need to finish building this church, Amen?"

"Amen."

"Don't curse yourself today. . . . Add more to the Lord. This is your salvation Sunday, your breakthrough Sunday. You, that man, don't spoil it for the Lord by offering so little." He pointed somewhere in the back and everybody turned to look in that direction. "If you change your ways, tomorrow the Lord could bless you too, with a Nanfang. Poverty is a curse from Satan. . . . The Lord is ready to break that curse. Do you believe?"

"Yes, we believe."

Some people substituted their bills for a higher denomination.

"And do not spoil it for Smiley Kpee either. He has been a faithful Christian over the years, OK. Don't bring bad luck to his Nanfang."

"God forbid, God forbid!" the church hollered.

"Don't spoil it for these two children of his!" He reached out and touched Yewa and then me. "May the Lord bless you with infinite goodness. May you always be lucky, Amen?"

"Amen."

"And you can bless your neighbor too," he said to the church. "What is your neighbor holding up?" There was a low murmur as people spoke to their neighbors, some teasing others to bring out more money. Big Guy whispered something into Fofo Kpee's ear, gave him a CFA10,000 bill and took away the N100 bill, and both men smiled. Fofo was so happy, there were tears in his eyes. "Our God is a rich God, not a pauper," the pastor said.

"Amen."

"And make sure your neighbor is not tempted to put back in his pocket what has been shown to the Lord. Amen?"

"Amen."

He signaled to the choir, which intoned "The Lord Will Bless Someone Today."

The Lord will bless someone today
The Lord will bless someone today
The Lord will bless someone today
The Lord will bless someone today

It could be me
It could be you
It could be someone by your side

The Lord will bless someone today
The Lord will bless someone today

As we sang along, our gift baskets were passed over the sanctuary rails to the assisting pastors, two wives of Pastor Adeyemi. After the wives had finished putting the gifts behind the sanctuary, they came out and joined in the blessing—two tall, elegant figures making their way through the praying crowd, placing their hands on the abdomens of the pregnant, whispering, "*Omo ni iyin oluwa,* . . . Children are the greatness of God."

Then, as the pastor came down to bless the Nanfang, he asked us again to lift our money higher. He prayed that God should bless our household forever and that He should protect Fofo from Satan. Then his composure disintegrated as he bent down and grabbed the handlebars of the machine and launched into the "Holy Spirit, Fire!" benediction. His jheri curls flew everywhere, his cross jangled against the gas tank. He shook the Nanfang hard, to banish ill luck, until the faces of Fofo Kpee and Big Guy became clouded with fear. Eager to protect the bike, they reached out and held on to it with all their might while the pastor rained blessings on it. Soon the pastor placed his hands on our heads, and then people dropped their money into a collection basket, watching one another to keep cheats from substituting lower denominations or stuffing it back into their pockets.

THAT AFTERNOON, BACK AT our house, Fofo had rented white plastic chairs and a multicolored tarpaulin canopy for a party. Women, whom Fofo had hired to cook, brought the food in *coolas* and ladled it out to our guests. Though it wasn't a big crowd, Fofo had gotten the dirt road in front of our house blocked, to give the impression of a large, overflowing party. In our part of the world, if a party didn't disrupt traffic, it wasn't a party.

Fofo Kpee stood up when he got a chance and said in his comedian voice, "My people, my neighbors, *honton se lé,* family *se,* dis de day de Lord has made . . ."

"Make we rejoice and be glad!" we all replied, laughing.

He cleared his throat and shouted, "Alleluuu . . ."

"Alleluuuia!" screamed the crowd.

"You see my broda and his wife who live abroad send me dis *zokeke!*" He pointed to the Nanfang, which was standing under the mango tree, alone, as if on exhibition. "You see, I no go die poor man," he continued. "I can't be *agbero*ing all my life. I must do someting to get rich. Like carrying *una* good people on my *zokeke* and making money. You must patronize me *o.* You no go just come here to eat my rice for notting *o.*"

"You go carry us till you tire!" someone said. "Smiley Kpee, *na* true talk!"

"I mean, look my face."

He touched his scar and pulled at his lip and people began to laugh.

"Scarecrow!" one woman shouted, her mouth full of rice.

"No worry, when I get money well well, I go do surgery . . . my face no go smile like dis all de time again. *N'dǫ na dǫ* face *se*, military face. Den *una* no go know again wheder I *dey* vex *o*, wheder I *dey* sad *o*, wheder I *dey* lie *o*. . . . I mean, even now, who tell *una* say I *dey* happy wid *una?*"

More laughter. "*Agbero!* Nanfang*agbero!*"

He paused and pointed directly at Big Guy, then wagged his finger. "Make sure you no be like dis, my new friend, who want disgrace me before my Tanksgiving!"

People laughed and Big Guy shook his head in jest, stood up, and said to the people, "*Mon peuple*, I no dance well for church dis morning?"

"You dance well well," the crowd said, supporting him.

"*Mais, il est un bon homme*. Very good man," Fofo Kpee said. "*Na* my new friend. . . . Dem just post *am* to dis area. You go know *am* better later. . . . For now make you just *dey* enjoy me, *dugbe se to ayawhenume se*. Once I become rich, my dogs no go even let *una* come near my gate *o, comme* Lazarus."

"Den make you remain *agbero* till dy kingdom come!" someone said.

He waited out the laughs, then said, "*Kai,* you better start looking for anoder monkey man to harvest your coconuts. . . . Anyway, on a serious note: joy full my belly today because my broder and wife done rewarded me, say I do deir children well well."

"Make God *dey* bless dem *o!*" someone said.

Fofo Kpee pointed to us, and all the attention shifted our way.

Yewa and I stopped stuffing ourselves with rice and looked at each other. I felt lost because I knew my parents were in the village, not abroad. It was as if I didn't hear Fofo well. Did Big Guy bring the bike from my parents in Braffe? No, that couldn't be true. My parents weren't that rich even when they enjoyed full health. Again I thought maybe he said they had recovered, and this party was also in their honor. So I stuffed myself with more food. With my bare hands, I ate my whole mound of jollof rice; the hired cooks used Uncle Ben's rice, which we could consume fast, without fear of pebbles. I saved a piece of fried *zebra* fish, sliced as thin as a plantain chip, for last. I didn't give what Fofo had said another thought.

"When my broder and his wife and oder children come to see us," Fofo Kpee continued, "you go even eat better better tings. . . . Alleluuu . . . !"

"Alleluuuia!" the people said, and he sat down.

That evening, the visitors danced to music coming from our recently bought, used Sony boom box. Big Guy stood up and took off his jacket to reveal an immaculate white shirt. He pulled his trousers up to his waist to give his long legs room and showed us how to dance *makossa*. He moved his arms and legs, as if his suit now gave him permission to do so. He rolled his hips and gyrated to the electric guitar and heavy drums. With his smooth moves, he was a spectacle to behold. We began to like him. He reminded Yewa that she was an intelligent girl. He picked her up and tossed her repeatedly into the air and caught her. Many kids gathered around him, asking him to toss them too. He got sweaty, his shirt got dirty, his loafers became covered with dust, but he didn't care. We had so much fun that the next day we had diarrhea and a temperature. We didn't go to school.

ONE WEEK LATER, FOFO Kpee came back early from work and sat on his bed, wringing his hands. He was so preoccupied with what he wanted to say that he didn't change his work clothes or bathe for the night. Then he leaned forward and said, "You *dey* enjoy school dese days, wid your new book?"

"I like my books!" Yewa said.

"The teachers like us now," I said. "We share our books with our friends."

"Good," he said, wriggling into the bed until his back touched the wall. Above his head was a big old 1994 World Cup calendar that featured pictures of the thirty-two national soccer teams that had made the finals. The lantern's rays mapped out patches of light and shadow on it, because the wall was uneven.

He pulled Yewa in between his legs and tugged at her cheeks playfully. The bedspring squeaked, sending a wall gecko scrambling from under the calendar. It went up the wall and rested on the wide space between the wall and the roof, its tail on the bicycle chain that held them together.

"Your godparents go happy say you *dey* enjoy school," Fofo said suddenly. "Be grateful to dem *o. E jẹ dọ mi ni d'ope na yé*."

"Godparents?" I asked, sitting up on our bed.

He looked at me carefully and nodded. "Oh yes, you two *dey* lucky to have godparents, you know."

"From Braffe?" Yewa asked. "When did they come?"

"*Non, pas comme ça,*" Fofo giggled. "Ah, no, you no know dese ones."

"Does Big Guy know them?" she asked. "I want to dance with Big Guy. He can go with us to Braffe and teach Ezin, Esse, and Idossou to dance *makossa.* You promised to take us to Braffe."

"We go go dere . . . for sure. But I want introduce you to your godparents first. Dat man and woman done give us many many tings. Nanfang. Sony. Drugs for your parents. Uncountable tings. *Onú ḷopa ḷopa lé.* Your parents like dem *beaucoup.* Your godparents want help our whole family, beginning wid your education. . . . We be deir adoptees. *Comprenez* de meaning of *adoptee?*"

"No," we said.

"When stranger come take a child like him own . . . *Mais,* listen *o,* we must tell people de godparents be our real relatives *o.*"

"Our relatives?" I asked.

"You lie, Fofo," Yewa said. "You go go hell. You lie."

"Oh, young people, you no *dey* understand de Bible!" he exclaimed. "I know say dis one go hard to explain. Dat's why I no boder to shower or *na yi changer nú se lé* before talking to you. If you tell a good good lie, you no go enter hell. Only de bad lies go put you for hell, *mes enfants.* As your Sunday-school teacher *dey* teach *una,* in Genesis twelve, ten to sixteen, Abraham, de fader of faith *meme-lui,* come tell de Egyptians good lie dat his wife Sarah be his sister to spare his life. Also, Jacob and Rebekah come deceive Isaac to claim Esau's inheritance in Genesis twenty-seven, one to tirty-tree, remember?"

"Please, Fofo, tell us that story again," Yewa pleaded as we drew closer to him. "Tell us about Abraham . . ."

"Quiet! No distract me *o*," he snapped. "Just *dey* listen now because I *dey* preach."

"Yes, Fofo," she said.

"And *dans la Nouvelle Testament*," he continued with renewed fervor, "make you no forget how de tree wise men come trick Herod to save de Baby Jesus in Matthew two, tree to sixteen. So like dese Bible people, we must protect our fortune. We must say dat your godparents be our relatives; oderwise, people go start to bring deir own children to dem or start being jealous.... *Vous comprenez un peu, oui?*"

"Yes, we understand," we said.

"In any case, your godparents want it like dat. You two go understand well well when you grow up. My children, dis world *est dangereux*. Make you no trust anybody *o*. No tell anybody about our blessings, *d'accord?* Or you want make armed robbers come visit us from Lagos? You want make dem spoil *am* for us?"

"No, no, Fofo."

We shook our heads.

"Very good, den, my children.... Because of dis family meeting, I quick come from work. I want tell *una* de whole trud about everyting, *d'accord?*"

"OK."

"Your godparents are NGO people."

"NGO?" I asked.

"Yes, NGO people," he repeated. "Nongovermental organization . . . repeat after me . . ."

"Nongovernmental organization," we said.

"*Encore?*"

"Nongovernmental organization."

"*Bon! Très bien! C'est une groupe* of people who *dey* help poor children all over de world. NGO are good people and travel *partout.*"

He smiled at us and looked as relieved as one who has broken a piece of difficult news. He stood up and took off his clothes, beginning with his cowboy boots, then his blue suit. He put on his shorts.

He was the best-dressed Nanfang motorcyclist I had ever met. Since we had become richer, he went to work in *okrika* suits and shoes from Europe, which he bought in the open market that surrounded the no-man's-land. There was an unkempt look to him because the clothes were rumpled, and we had no iron or electricity yet. We had new school uniforms, and when he rode us to school in the morning, we looked smart and well fed. And our classmates wanted to hear about our "abroad" parents.

"Is that why you said during the party our parents sent you Nanfang?" I asked.

"Yes, my boy . . . *ça c'est très correcte!*"

"Now I understand."

"You *dey trop* intelligent for *ton âge. A nọ flin nú ganji.* You remember well. Ah *non,* you cannot just tell everybody about your plans, you know. De book of Jeremiah, chapter nine, verse four, say, No trust your friend *o* . . . every friend *na* slanderer. So make *una* no tell your schoolmates or your friends for church about dis, *d'accord?*"

"OK."

I nodded alone.

"Yewa?" he asked.

"I know how to keep quiet," she said.

He came and sat down, reached under his bed for his *payó* bottle, and poured himself a drink. He tossed the full content of the shot into his mouth, as if he were pouring it into a bucket. He had two more shots, cleared his throat, and stretched out on his bed. "Come, you know what to call your godparents?"

"No," my sister said.

"Godpapa? Godmama?" I said, guessing.

"No," he said. "Godmama, Godpapa, *dey* sound too *okrika!* Make you try again."

"Mom . . . Dad?" I said.

"No, *juste* Papa and Mama . . . *efó!*"

"Papa? Mama? No!" Yewa protested.

"*Hén,*" Fofo said, dragging out the word *yes.*

"My papa and mama are in Braffe," Yewa said.

"We know dat," he said.

"Let's call them Mom and Dad, then, to avoid confusion," I suggested.

"No, it's better to address dem exactly as you *dey* address your parents. *Ils sont* your godparents. Godparents. Godparents, you know?"

I shrugged and gave up and looked at Yewa, who was staring down stubbornly.

"Does Big Guy know our godparents?" I asked.

"*Absolutement,*" Fofo said.

"But you said we should not tell our friends," I said. "Did you tell Big Guy?"

Yewa looked up sharply, sensing the contradiction. Fofo didn't reply immediately. Instead, his face split into a long mischievous smile as he nodded and sipped his *payó.*

"Kotchikpa," he said finally, "you be bright, bright *garçon*."

"Thank you, Fofo," I said.

"But we must make sure your intelligence no *dey* lead you in de wrong direction *o*. Remember, *na* only de fly witout direction dat go follow de corpse enter grave. You understand?"

"No, Fofo," I said.

"Use your head well. . . . Big Guy done become my trusted friend—de only person I invite sit wid us for our Tanksgiving, remember?"

Now he laughed a short laugh and winked at us, as if to say, "I have defeated you finally." I laughed with him because he was funny and because I thought I should have figured this out my-self. Then Yewa laughed too.

When we stopped laughing, he tickled us. We laughed even more, but he laughed the hardest, as if some invisible hands were tickling him. Yewa started throwing her pillow at me, and we got into a pillow fight. Fofo, who normally wouldn't let us fight, didn't stop us. It seemed to amuse him. He sat there cheering us on, moving his hands, ducking each time one of us hit the other with a pillow. He coached Yewa to climb on the bed to get an advantage over me. Yewa was excited, the springs of the bed squeaking with each blow she landed. I wanted to climb on the bed too, but Fofo said no. He even asked me to allow my kid sister to win the pillow fight. Suddenly, like a crazy man, he stood up and started playing with the lantern wick. The flame fluttered. We became very excited, giggling hard, trying to figure out what he wanted to do.

He lowered the wick, and we fought in darkness. When one of us fell, he increased the flame to be sure nobody was hurt. When one of us screamed in the darkness, he laughed before giving us light. We were having fun and played until we scattered everything. The two mattresses were on the floor; most of Fofo's clothes fell from his wardrobe. The bed frame stood at awkward angles. Our cartons of clothes were out from under the beds, their contents all over the place. What finally exhausted us wasn't the energy we used playing but the toll of endless laughter on our ribs.

"ANYWAY, YOUR PAPA AND Mama—your godparents—go visit you soon," Fofo Kpee said later that night, after we had tidied up everything. "Dem go bring oder children dem *dey* help so dat *una* go all meet. Maybe dem go carry all of *una* go abroad for studies. Across de sea."

My heart leaped, and I sat up.

"Us? Abroad?" I said.

"Of course, de children who *dey* study abroad no get two head."

"What about me?" my sister asked. "You don't like me?"

"My very own, what? You want abandon your *fofo, bébé*?"

"Yes, Fofo is a big man. If Kotchikpa goes, I must go . . ."

"*Kai,* you *na* real bargainer . . . lawyer! You go *voyager* togeder, *d'accord*? Oder lucky children go even travel wid you—God bless your godparents."

After our night prayer, during which Fofo thanked God profusely for sending us our benefactors, then spoke in tongues like Pastor Adeyemi, I lay on my bed and thought about our godparents. What did they look like? Where did they live? Or did they simply travel from country to country to save children? I tried to imagine the faces of such goodness. I wanted to meet them as soon as possible. No matter how much I tried to picture them, it was the images of my parents that filled my mind.

I began to imagine my parents back in good health, my mother going to the farms in the morning, my father riding his bicycle to Korofo Market. I thought of how relieved my grandparents would feel now; out of our thirteen *fofos* and aunts, my parents were their favorites, so their sickness was a hard blow. They took care of our parents, and before we left home they fasted so much that they became almost as emaciated as the sick. I thanked God that my parents' sickness was gone. I thanked God for sending our godparents to buy drugs for our parents. With all they had already done for us, calling them Mama and Papa wasn't too much to ask. I was sure my parents back home wouldn't mind this good man and woman being addressed like this. I began to miss my parents a lot that night and looked forward to visiting home and spending time with them. I also began to miss our godparents whom I hadn't met, because I was already a beneficiary of their goodness; they were like a second pair of parents in a world where sickness had almost robbed me of the first. I even began to long to see the other children our godparents were helping. The bounds of my family extended and began to grow that night as I listened to the snoring of Fofo and the gentle breathing of Yewa beside me.

I begged God to give us the brains to do well in school so that we wouldn't disappoint our godparents and Fofo and our parents. Having spoken French and Idaatcha all our lives, I thanked God for helping us pick up English very well and even come to understand a bit of Egun in the year and a half we had spent on the border. I hoped that wherever our godparents took us we would exhibit the same flair. Remembering my promise to our parents and grandparents, I promised God again tonight, as I did every night, to be always obedient to Fofo. I told God I would do everything to support him. I asked God to guide Yewa's thinking so that she wouldn't embarrass or be difficult with our godparents when they visited us.

THE FIRST VISIT FROM our godparents and our new siblings was low-key. The three of us had sat outside on the veranda mounds, facing the sea, before they arrived.

Now Fofo brought out the lantern and placed it on the floor beside us. It stood there, its lone flame fluttering in the wind. Yewa and I were chatting and thinking about what lay at the other side of the water. Both of us were wearing green T-shirts and black shorts. We had showered that evening, and our faces glowed with AZ petroleum jelly, and we kept sneezing because our uncle had rubbed too much camphor, which he called "poor-man perfume," on our clothes.

Fofo was nervous. He kept crossing and uncrossing his legs, folding and unfolding his arms across his chest.

"Yewa, *wetin* you go call your godparents?" he quizzed her suddenly.

"Papa and Mama," she said.

"Good gal. *Gbòjé poun,* everyting go *dey* fine fine."

"Fofo, I am relaxed," Yewa said.

"And make you no forget to tank dem for school fees when you see dem. Even God *dey* like grateful creatures."

"We won't forget, Fofo," I said.

"I'm hungry," Yewa said. "Are we going to eat tonight?"

"Hungry?" He turned and glared at her. "I told you dem go bring food! Like picnic. Just be patient, *ole*. Look at your long mout. You want drink *garri* now? You and your broder, you no *dey* listen to me for dis place. Remember *wetin* your fader talk de day I bring you come here? Remember *wetin* your grandparents talk? One more *wahala* from any of you, I go cancel my plan wid your godparents. . . . I go even return you to Braffe!"

Yewa said, "I'm sorry, Fofo Kpee."

"Shut up, you *onu ylankan* . . . ugly ting. I no know where your mama carry you bastards from come my broder's house! One more word from you den . . ."

We sat in silence until dark. Fofo became more and more anxious, sucking his lips in and out. He sat erect, his back flat against the wall, his head against the closed window.

The fishermen at sea spangled the water with their lanterns, like stars. Yet there was no sea, no sky, no land, only points of light dangling in a black chasm. The night had eaten the coconut vistas too, except when the canoe lanterns, moving, were periodically blotted out behind the trees. The sea blew a strong kiss of breeze, warm and unrelenting, through our neighborhood. In the distance, we could hear the hum from the no-man's-land market fizzling out for the night. We could also hear the semitrailers and trucks coming and going from the border, backing up or parking. Sometimes, from where we sat, we saw the beams of their headlights sweeping the skies of neighboring villages, like searchlights. Fofo had told us the trucks carried assorted goods from one part of West Africa to another.

Suddenly, we heard the sound of a vehicle coming down our dirt road. As soon as it turned into our compound, the engine and the lights died out. The car swished silently toward our house, checked by our sandy pathway. A woman was the first to come down. She ran toward us on the veranda, squatted, and quietly swept us into a hug, as if the moment were too tender for words. "I'm Mama!" she said softly. Yewa seemed indifferent to her presence, her attention focused on the vehicle, but I wanted to hold her forever.

"Mama . . . welcome, M-mama," I stammered.

"Thank you, good children," she said, pulling us even closer. "How sweet of you!"

After a while, she brought the lantern nearer to see our faces. She was a tall, beautiful black woman, with deep gentle eyes and full lips and a smooth face. She was in a pair of jeans, a T-shirt, and tennis shoes, her hair gathered in a sun hat of many colors, as if she were going on a picnic. She was gracious, and her perfume was sweet, like the smell of fresh frangipani flowers. When she held us, she made sure her long painted nails didn't dig into our skin. She smiled as easily as she breathed.

"Big Guy!" Yewa shouted, the scream cutting into the gathering silence of the neighborhood. She tapped me on the shoulder, then struggled to break free from Mama, pointing to the profile of a man who had just stepped out of the driver's seat. "Look . . . Big Guy."

"Big Guy?" I mumbled. "No. Where? He's not the one."

"It's him!" Yewa insisted, still trying to break free. "He's the driver of the car . . ."

"Shh . . . shh . . . quiet, quiet!" Mama said, holding on to us tightly.

When she had calmed us, Mama broke into a beautiful smile again that softened her hug. Then she let go of me and lifted up Yewa—whose eyes were still set on the vehicle and the man by it—and brought their cheeks together. She kissed her and rubbed her head.

"There's no need to shout, honey," she whispered. "Forget Big Guy for now. You'll get a chance to greet him, OK?"

"Yes, Mama," Yewa said, her attention slowly turning to the woman.

"My daughter, I have looked forward to seeing you. I have heard so many good things about you two. Big Guy told me you're a great dancer. Do you want to dance with Big Guy later?"

"Yes, Mama," Yewa said, her eyes lit up.

"And I want to see your beautiful baseball cap too."

My sister nodded. I thought the fact that Mama knew Big Guy had taught us how to dance had a profound effect on Yewa. She began to pay the woman more attention and seemed to feel more comfortable with her.

"Good then, dear. We'll arrange that. I dance well too." She turned to Fofo Kpee, who had been watching us with fear. "Such lovely angels. . . . You go and bring the others into the house. Everything is OK."

"*Merci, madame,*" he said, and bowed slightly. "*Merci beaucoup.*"

He walked over to the car. Big Guy opened the back door for Papa and two children while Mama herded the two of us into the house, carrying in the lantern as well. After closing the door, she sat on our bed, with Yewa on her lap, leaning against her breasts.

It was as if she were our real mother. She had won Yewa over in no time. I began to feel relaxed, knowing that my sister wasn't going to spoil the evening for everybody by being stubborn.

I was also touched by Mama's gentleness. I began to think of how kind she must be to her own children, if she could be so motherly to us on our first meeting. Though she looked far richer than our mother, she acted every bit like her, and, though by now we knew her house must have been more beautiful, she appeared comfortable in our place. She looked around as if she knew what was in the next room. She was the first visitor to come into our house without my feeling embarrassed or out of place.

She was my first contact with an NGO. Her presence confirmed for me what Fofo had said: they were a group of smiling, caring people going around the world helping children like us. I couldn't stop thanking God in my heart for bringing such a woman to us. I watched her closely, the way she doted on my sister, the way she held her and spoke softly in her ears, the way she threw her head back when she paused in her speech, the way she gestured with her right hand, bejeweled with bracelets, when she spoke. I was so comfortable around her that I no longer smelled the camphor on my clothes; her perfume took over the room the way the scent of the Nanfang had when it arrived.

"I heard you danced so well in church," she said to Yewa in particular, which made me jealous.

"Yes, Mama," she said, nestling closer to her.

"I dance too," I said.

"Nice," Mama said, and returned to my sister. "You like church then?"

"Yes."

"Me too," the woman said. "I like to sing and dance and pray with others. You know, I and my husband feel God has been good to us, and we should be good to others, especially children."

Mama simply held on to my sister and closed her eyes, as if in gratitude to God. I wanted her to hold me too, but I didn't know what to say or do. I stopped watching them and kept my gaze on the floor.

THE PEOPLE OUTSIDE FINALLY came to the veranda, but they didn't come in. I couldn't tell how many were there, but I knew the voices of Big Guy and Fofo Kpee. And I suspected that the third voice, a deep voice, belonged to Papa.

"Nice kids, very nice kids . . . Kpee's children," Big Guy said, as if he were looking at chickens in Badagry open market. "Monsieur Ahouagnivo, you go see when you go inside."

"Beautiful," Papa said.

"We tank God," our uncle said.

"Unfortunately, Monsieur Ahouagnivo, as I come explain to you de oder day, Kpee no deliver completely," Big Guy said. "Where de oders, Kpee?"

"Village," Fofo Kpee said curtly. "I go bring dem to you."

"When . . . *quand?*" Big Guy asked. "You *dey* make my job difficult *o*. De agreement *na* for five children. Give us de children."

"Soon, soon," my uncle said. "I *dey* go Braffe soon. My oder nephews and niece *dey* village."

"Just bring dem and stop wasting our time . . ."

"You're distracting all of us in here!" Mama screamed to the men on the veranda.

"Gentlemen, stop, stop!" Papa said. "This is neither the place nor time for this conversation! We're here to celebrate, not to harass Kpee and these children. . . . Kpee's other children will have their chance to come to Gabon and enjoy the good things of life there, OK? And, Big Guy, always remember, you work for us, not the other way round. Give Kpee time to organize things carefully. Things will work out."

"*Monsieur,* I *dey* sorry, *monsieur,*" Big Guy said, and they stopped arguing.

The images of Ezin, Esse, and Idossou flashed through my mind. The idea that they would come with us to Gabon excited me to no end. I was sure they were preparing in Braffe to come over to the border, to go with us. It became clear to me why Big Guy was angry the day they brought home the Nanfang, and what "five" meant when he received us in front of the church that Thanksgiving Sunday. From what Fofo had said about our godparents, I knew their generosity had already extended to other members of my family, like my parents. And, though I felt that someday they might help my older siblings back home, I never knew the help would come in this form. If only Big Guy would be patient so that we could go home and get my siblings. I didn't like the fact that he had almost turned our godparents against Fofo.

I wanted to scream into Yewa's ear what I had just pieced together about our siblings, but I checked myself. I was jealous that she had Mama's full attention, so I resisted sharing anything with her.

A rush of confused feelings went through my heart. Mama's presence was everywhere, yet I couldn't get enough of it. I was grateful to Big Guy for bringing our godparents to our house but upset with him for trying to make Fofo look bad in front of Papa.

What did we do for the Lord that He brought the goodness of this NGO to us? We weren't the poorest of children in that border village. Yet from all the children in our school and neighborhood, I felt that God had chosen us. I remembered the conversation Fofo had with Big Guy in front of Our Redeemer Pentecostal Church that happy Sunday, which Pastor Adeyemi later confirmed during his blessing. For them the issue was simple: you're poor because your ways aren't straight before the Lord; if you do good, then your Heavenly Father, who is rich, will make you rich.

Yet that night, sitting there across from this wonderful woman, I didn't see what good I had done. Worse still, Yewa had actually become more stubborn and mischievous than she had been a year and a half ago in Braffe. I began to think that maybe what we children did or didn't do didn't count before the Lord. So I put my faith in Fofo Kpee: he must have done something big, something marvelous, for the Lord to bring this good luck to us. Maybe Fofo was no longer smuggling at the border; maybe he no longer duped strangers for their money. Maybe he was climbing coconut trees free for people. In my heart I began to sing "The Lord Will Bless Someone Today" as I watched Mama cuddle Yewa.

BEFORE LONG, YEWA FELL into a deep sleep on Mama. She hadn't been able to do that since our mother fell very ill in the village. Even our grandparents knew Yewa was troublesome and allowed her to come with me only after Fofo had assured them he would do everything to take care of his niece.

"Hey, Pascal, how was school today?" said Mama, looking down on the sleeping Yewa like the Madonna on her Child.

The name startled me. I looked around the room for another person. There was nobody. Who was Pascal? The front door and windows were still closed.

In the silence, Mama lifted her face to me in a wide smile, and I felt at home again, though I didn't know what to say. It sounded as if the question was directed to someone on the veranda. I could hear Big Guy and Fofo Kpee and Papa chuckling outside like people who had hit a jackpot. They seemed content to stay out there.

"Pascal . . . ?" she said again, and reached across the center table to hold my hand.

"I'm Kotchikpa," I politely corrected her, looking down.

"Yes, that's right, sweetie. Big Guy told us. . . . Kotchikpa?"

"Yes, Mama."

"Please, may we call you Pascal? With time, I'm sure we'll be more conversant with Kotchikpa. You know, with all the children in our care, from different tribes and countries, it's a bit difficult at first. Pascal is such a sweet name. Memorable. Please? Pascal?"

"Yes, Mama."

I nodded.

"Sure?"

I nodded again. "Yes, yes. It's fine."

She was still looking at me. I felt I needed to say something more, but I didn't know what. I felt better now because she had given me a bit of attention, and I hoped my sister would sleep all night.

"Thanks, Mama, for paying our fees," I blurted out.

"Oh, you're welcome, sweetie." She blew me a kiss. "So understanding, so grateful. We hear you're very bright in your school. You're the best. Oh, come over, sit with us. Don't be too far away."

She reached out for me, her bracelets jangling. I held her hand and came around the table. She hooked me into a hug and kissed my head, all the while making endearing sounds as if I were her precious, vulnerable pet. When she noticed Yewa had begun to sweat, she pulled off her colorful hat and fanned her.

"Big Guy, good evening!" I said cheerfully, as he entered the house, bringing food from the car and bowing before Mama. But he didn't answer. It was as if he didn't even see me. Mama looked at him and then at me. She squeezed my hand in a way that made me feel I should ignore him.

This evening, he was a different man. This was the third time we'd seen him, and it seemed he had changed each time. Tonight, he wore an immigration officer's outfit. In the glare of our lantern, the beret on his shaven head looked like a coxcomb haircut, and his long sleeves had stripes. He looked bigger than usual because his shirt was bloated, pumped up by cassava starch, and his trousers had two hard lines like sharp blades. His shoes glowed, and when he moved, the legs of his trousers rustled against each other with his military gait. He carried himself about with the stiffness of a bodyguard around foreign royalty.

When he came back in, Mama rebuked him. "Pascal *dey* greet you just now! *Jamais,* never ignore my children!"

He stopped and stood very erect, as if before a national flag. "Oh, I'm sorry, Madame Ahouagnivo. *Je suis très desolé. . . .*"

"Just *dey* answer the boy, *jo o.* It's not about me."

"My apologies. . . . *Bon soir,* Kotchikpa . . ."

"No, Pascal," Mama corrected him.

He bowed and said, "Beautiful name, huh."

"Good evening," I greeted him again.

Before long, he had filled our table with all kinds of food: crab soup, mounds of *akasa* wrapped in fresh leaves, macaroni, couscous, and stew. A pot of pepper soup was studded with chunks of bushmeat, each held together with white string, some of the meat still carrying the pellets that had brought down the animal, which was the kind of stuff our people liked a lot. You eat it carefully and slowly, partly because of the pepper, partly because you could bite into a pellet.

Big Guy staggered in with two *coolas,* and a draft of cold, icy air stabbed the room when he opened them. He brought out Coke, Maltina, La Place beer, and Chivita orange juice and placed them on the table. Each time he came in from outside, I expected to see the car's other passengers. From time to time, when my attention strayed from Mama and the food, I wondered what Fofo Kpee was doing with the others outside.

When our center table was full, Big Guy brought out two fold-up stands from the car. I had never seen so much food in my life except in raw form in the open market. Yet Big Guy kept bringing more. The good smell swallowed up Mama's perfume, and I was so overwhelmed that I was no longer hungry.

Though I didn't sleep like my sister, I was in my own world, a foretaste of what I thought Gabon would be like. I remembered Fofo saying we were going to be rich and start eating well. Things had moved very fast for our family, and, comforted by the care of Mama that night, I had no reason to doubt that we were coming into better times. It wasn't difficult for me to imagine that our godparents were important people, since Big Guy, an immigration officer, drove them around and served them. Thinking about Gabon as the land of opportunity now came to me naturally, and my mind began to pine for it. I imagined my sister and me being driven to school in a car. Now, even thinking about riding to school on our Nanfang felt sort of beneath me.

"Sweetie, I'll just call you Mary, OK?" Mama said to my sister, gently shaking her awake. "Good morning, Mary, sleepyhead . . ."

Yewa rubbed her eyes and her gaze wandered from me to Mama, before coming to rest on the assorted food. Her eyes widened slowly until they almost popped with shock.

"Would you like to be called Mary, or do you want another name, sweetie?" Mama said to her.

"Wake up, Yewa!" I said.

She didn't say anything but scratched her head and yawned. Then she reached out to touch the Coke nearest her.

"Your brother likes Pascal, you know," Mama tried again, winking at me. "He is now Pascal."

Yewa looked at me, a flash of understanding touching her face.

"Pascal?" she said.

"Yes, my new name is Pascal," I said, shrugging and smiling shyly. "It's OK, Yewa."

She shook her head. "My name is Yewa Mandabou!"

"When Mama gives you a name," I said quickly, "she remembers you because she has lots of children to care for. You're still Yewa, I'm still Kotchikpa . . ."

"Yes and no, Pascal," Mama interjected in the softest of voices. "It's best if we just use one name so that there's no confusion. I'm sure your sister will understand."

"Yes, Mama." I nodded.

I felt I had overreached in my attempt to help matters. A pang of remorse settled in my stomach, and I shifted on the bed and held on to the bedpost to hide my embarrassment.

"Mary?" Mama said to her, testing out the name, her smile at its widest.

Yewa nodded awkwardly, still staring at me. I nodded vigorously, partly to make up for my bad explanation earlier, partly to assure Yewa it was OK. "Mary is a beautiful name," I said. "Beautiful."

"You're so so cute," Mama told her. "Oh, so obedient, respectful of your older brother. . . . I'm sorry I had to wake you up for dinner. Is that OK, Mary?"

"I don't know," Yewa said, and shifted her attention to the food.

"She can be stubborn," I told Mama. "She needs a bit of time."

"I don't think she's stubborn," she said. "She's a good girl, and we have time."

With her forefinger, Yewa traced the Coca-Cola logo on the
can. She was about to lick the finger when Mama grabbed her
hand. "Oh, no, Mary!" she said, shaking her head. "You can have
whatever you want . . ."

"Yes, Mama," she said.

"Everything is for you, sweetie. OK, Mary?"

"Yes, Mama. . . . Could I have Coke, please?"

Mama opened the Coke immediately, as if Yewa would reject
her new name if she wasted time, and poured it into my sister's
mouth. Yewa's face was upturned like a suckling lamb's. The
bubbly drink filled her open mouth slowly, her throat releasing
loud gulps into her stomach.

Mama stopped abruptly.

"Do you want more, Mary?" she asked.

Yewa was panting. "Yes, Mama."

WHEN THE OTHERS FINALLY came into the room, it felt crowded,
with everyone sitting on the beds. Apart from the three men,
there was a boy and a girl. Mama had scooped a plateful of couscous and stew and was spooning it into Yewa's mouth. She ate
like a hungry dog, her gaze following every movement of the
spoon. It was hot inside, and though Big Guy asked Fofo Kpee to
open the two windows, the room still swelled with steamy appe-
tizing smells.

"So how are you, my children?" Papa's voice boomed out, and
Mama proudly told him our new names and nudged me toward
him to shake his outstretched hand. "Hello, Pascal," he said, taking my hand.

"Welcome, sir," I said.

"I'm Monsieur Ahouagnivo."

"Nice to meet you, *monsieur*."

Papa looked far older than Mama, as if he were her father. He was big, as tall as Big Guy, and he was very black. His skin was darker than his hair, and the lower part of his face dissolved into a thick, groomed beard. His nostrils had some gray hair. If not for his white T-shirt, which caught the glow of the lantern, it would have been difficult to see the rest of his body because of the depth of his blackness. He smiled often, staining the dimness with a set of fine teeth. He wore shorts and flip-flops, as if he were on his way to some night beach.

"Hello there, Mary!" he said, waving to Yewa, who was too busy with her food to respond.

Fofo Kpee, who was leaning by the door that led into the inner room, opened his mouth, as if to prompt Yewa. His face wore embarrassment.

"No say anyting!" Big Guy hissed to him. "Leave de gal alone."

Fofo nodded and put his hands behind him like a servant.

I had hoped he would crack jokes and ring with laughter the whole evening, to entertain everyone. Though he was tense as we awaited our godparents' arrival, I had hoped he would start acting the fool, the way he did during the party after the Nanfang Thanksgiving. But he didn't. We were in his house, but he didn't even welcome the guests or introduce them to us. Now, he stood around like a new servant who had to rely on an older one, Big Guy, to know his bearing. I didn't like it when Fofo lost his sense of humor. But tonight, I thought maybe he was dazed by

the generosity of our godparents or was afraid we might let
him down by not making a good impression.

Then Papa stood up and gestured to the other children.
"Oh, before we forget, Pascal and Mary, please, here are your
siblings . . . Antoinette from Togo and Paul from northern
Nigeria."

I smiled and turned to Antoinette, who was closer to me. But
she ignored me, stood up, and started scooping the pepper soup
into a bowl. She was short and big-boned, with a round face, little
flat nose, and big mouth that later on that night would gobble up
everything, irrespective of the food combination. Her little eyes
were restless, taking in our poor surroundings with disgust.

"Antoinette, stop and greet your brother!" Mama snapped at her.

"Mama, I don't like this hut!" she responded, and bit into a
piece of meat.

Mama glared at her. "What did you say?"

"Yes, Mama, yes, Mama," Antoinette said, and turned toward
me and gave me a peck on each cheek, the pepper in her breath
fanning my eyes.

"Good girl," Mama said, her face back in creases of smile.
"That's how we ladies greet men in Gabon!" Mama turned to
me. "I'm sure she is just teasing you. Go ahead, say hello to
Paul."

"Hello, Paul," I said, putting forward my hand.

"Hi," he said, and gave me a limp handshake.

Paul's eyes were red and teary. A tall frail-looking boy, he sat at
the edge of Fofo Kpee's bed and was as silent and unmoving as a
statue. His skin had rashes, and the lotion he used had a pungent
smell. He had a wide forehead and a sharp chin, which made his

face look like a big cone. All evening, he hung his head as if it were too heavy for his neck to carry.

"And what would you like to eat, Paul?" Papa asked.

"Nothing," he said.

"Nothing? Nothing at all?" Papa begged.

"I want to go home," Paul said.

"My son, it's OK to miss home," Papa said. "You'll get used to the coast. All our children miss home for a while. But this is for your good. We'll do everything to help you."

"Hey, honey, you must eat something," Mama said, handing Mary over to Papa and moving to Paul's side. "You need the energy, please. We know it's been difficult for you, but everything will be OK. Dear, what would you like to eat?"

The boy pointed to beans and *dodo,* and Mama served him and started feeding him. Paul began to cry even though he was older than me. Mama put the food aside, held him close, and caressed and rocked him.

Antoinette looked this way, that way, edged nearer, and whispered into my ear, "They brought many of them in a fish truck from northern Nigeria . . . desert, six days ago. I don't like him. I wish he wouldn't come to Gabon with us! I came four days ago. I'm better than him—"

"Shut up, Antoinette!" Papa said, and gave her a stern look. "Don't be rude. In Gabon, we don't whisper about people in their presence."

Antoinette sat up immediately, afraid for the first time. "I'm sorry, Papa."

"You better be!" the man said. "Good behavior is important, very important."

"It's OK, darling," Mama told Papa, handing him a bottle of La Place beer and a bowl of pepper soup. "Just relax. Don't you think you are overreacting? You, eat something too, otherwise these children will drive you nuts. Children are like that. They'll get along eventually. . . . Kpee, eat something, please. Big Guy, come on. Everybody, please, feel at home."

Our uncle began with the pepper soup and rice, but the movement of his jaws was very deliberate, as if he expected to bite into a pellet. Big Guy unwrapped two mounds of *akasa* onto a plate, poured crab soup over them, and paused to suck at a bottle of Gulder beer as if on a feeding bottle. I went for Maltina and a mixture of beans and rice and stew. Everybody was laughing at Antoinette, who had mixed pineapple juice with Maltina and Coke and was asking Papa now whether he could pour a bit of his beer into the mix. Yewa was nibbling on a chicken breast in a way that suggested she was already full. She looked tired from eating but wasn't able to say no to anything that was pushed her way.

SUDDENLY, A GUST OF wind rolled in off the sea, and we could hear it press on the door. It smashed the windows shut. Paul, who was now sitting alone, retched, bent over, and vomited. Papa rushed forward and grabbed him. Mama and the men gathered around him.

"Oh, seasickness again," Mama grumbled, and looked helplessly at Papa.

"I hope it's not as bad as yesterday," Papa said. "We didn't bring any spirits, darling, or did we?"

"I'm afraid I forgot," she said, looking beaten for the first time that evening.

"No worry," Fofo Kpee said, and exchanged a telling glance with Big Guy. "No *wahala*, no *wahala*."

He quickly produced a bottle of *payó* from under the bed, opened it, and poured it into a bowl. He soaked a piece of cloth in the gin, wrung it out, and placed it on Paul's face. Mama, who by now was already carrying the boy, held it in place. Fofo cleaned up the vomit. Paul was so weak that no matter what Mama did to hold him, he unwrapped and sprawled, their bodies in an easy tangle, mother snake sand-bathing with her baby.

"You see what I said about Paul?" Antoinette whispered to me.

"He'll be OK," I said, to keep her quiet.

"He's such a baby . . . ," she began, but stopped when Big Guy lashed her with an angry stare.

Everybody returned to their seats, and in the uneasy quiet that followed, Big Guy turned on our boom box at a low volume, and Alpha Blondy began to croon in the background. Antoinette left her food, giggled, and started dancing near Fofo's wardrobe. Her hands kept thrashing into the clothes because there wasn't much space. Then she pulled me up and asked me for a dance, and everybody cheered us on. Yewa joined us at Mama's suggestion. She stood there unable to wriggle her small waist as Big Guy taught us, because of too much food. Mama said she would have come to dance with us if not for Paul, who was still lying down. Big Guy sat there, following the heavy rhythm with his head, as if our place was too small to contain his height and dance wizardry. Fofo just watched quietly, still not comfortable with this crowd.

Later, against the lantern light, Papa checked our exercise books and praised us for being bright students. Fofo had never looked at our exercise books, so we were excited.

"You two should be given the best education possible in this world!" Papa concluded, embracing Yewa and giving me a rigorous handshake.

"We're intelligent too!" Antoinette announced to everybody, pouting.

"Yes, I should say you two are as bright as Paul and Antoinette. Right, Paul?"

Paul was still staring at the floor and didn't say anything, the cloth covering half his face like a medical mask.

When he finished looking at our books, I said, "Thank you, Monsieur Ahouagnivo!"

"No, no . . . Papa, just Papa!" Big Guy said suddenly, shaking his head and sighing and giving Fofo a bad look. "If you no remember well, just be quiet like dis *aje*-butter boy." He pointed at Paul.

"Thank you, Papa," I corrected myself. "I'm sorry, Papa."

"It's OK, Pascal," the man said.

"*N ma plón wé ya?*" Fofo Kpee fumed at me. "How come *ta soeur dey* behave better dan you *egbé*, Kotchikpa . . . ?"

"Oh, no, his name is Pascal," Mama corrected Fofo, who stiffened up like someone who has touched a live wire. "Pascal," she said again. "See how easy it is to make these mistakes? Do we expect too much from these children in one night?"

"Sorry, *madame, je voulais dire* Pascal," Fofo Kpee said, a hangdog smile straining his face.

Papa and Mama began to show us pictures of Gabon and some

of their property in that land and in Nigeria and Benin and Côte d'Ivoire. They showed us pictures of the inside of some of the ships we saw crossing the water and pumping smoke into the horizon every day. They were all very beautiful. They showed us pictures of some of the children they had helped, doing different things—studying, playing, eating, singing, even sleeping. Some were as young as Yewa. These pictures were shown hurriedly, and Antoinette commented on each of them excitedly, as if she had already been to Gabon and knew all these children. She seemed to know many of them by name.

"And, by the way," Mama said, "make sure the children remain in good health for the trip, OK?"

"Sure, *madame*," Fofo Kpee said.

"Make you buy mosquito net for dem, you hear? I mean prepare de children well well *o*."

"No worry, *madame*. Everyting go *dey* fine fine."

"And Big Guy no go worry you again about de oder children, OK," Papa said, standing up to leave.

"Tank you, *monsieur!*" our uncle said, and bowed.

"We no go take back anyting from you," Papa continued. "Just *dey* do your best. But if someting bad happen to dese two children, we go hold you responsible *o*."

Everybody laughed. Fofo gave him his assurances and winked at me and rubbed Yewa's head. He cracked a few jokes and pulled at his lip, and everybody laughed, even Paul. It seemed to me that for the first time during that long night he had come into his usual confident self. He must have sensed the visit he had dreaded was coming to an end on a good note.

"All right, then," Papa said suddenly, putting the pictures away,

"Big Guy, begin *dey* pack up. We still get two places to go. It's a long night."

"No, four places . . . seven children," Big Guy corrected him, and started packing up the food and returning everything to the car.

My heart started to sink as they packed away the food. I had nursed the secret wish that they would leave the buffet for us. I had thought about pouring out the *ogbono* soup that filled our biggest pot, to accommodate the food. I had also thought about converting our aluminum bathing bucket into a temporary pot. Instead of letting anything go to waste, we could have poured everything into these two containers and stirred. As Fofo used to say whenever anyone was eating too many things at the same time, "Dem all *dey* enter de same stomach." I could warm the food two or three times a day.

Yet I calmed myself down when Mama hugged me and said she would miss us, and Papa advised us to be studious and said that this evening was the beginning of good things to come. As Big Guy drove them away, I thought about the good work our parents were doing all over Africa.

I began to feel guilty for being greedy and wanting to keep all the food, when they needed to feed other children. I was ready to cooperate with Papa and Mama, to be as cheerful about our prospects as Antoinette was. I didn't like the trouble Paul was giving our benefactors and hoped that he wouldn't vomit at their next stop. I didn't understand that it was natural for someone from the desert to react that way to the sea, and I was upset that he had embarrassed our parents. I thought even Yewa, the youngest of us children, comported herself better than he did.

That night, it wasn't too strange when Fofo Kpee started calling us Pascal and Mary. The next day, he came to our school and changed our names in the school register to Pascal and Mary Ahouagnivo. And, remembering how much Mama loved the names, we became impatient with our schoolmates who kept using our old ones. Yewa bit the ear of one girl who taunted her with her old name, and, though the teacher thrashed my sister with *koboko,* the point had been made.

THE NEXT DAY, AFTER Big Guy came with a photographer to take our pictures for our passports, Fofo brought in people to change our wooden doors and windows to metal. He said because of our changing lifestyle and his Nanfang, it was important that our home be as secure as possible.

The workers painted the metal doors and windows tar black, and they stood out in our gray cement-plastered walls like the eyes of black pea beans. He bought huge padlocks and dog chains and added the padlock keys to his Nanfang key bunch. But the new keys were too long and threatened to tear holes in his trouser pockets, so he threaded them on a chain that he wore around his neck like a metallic talisman.

One Saturday, he stayed home instead of carrying people across the border, and dug a pit behind our house and extracted clayey sand. With water and a bit of cement, he and I mixed it, put it on a tray, then began to seal the space between our roof and the walls of the parlor. He stood on a chair inside, and I passed up the tray of the mix to him again and again while Yewa played outside, molding mini clay people. Our activity startled the lizards, geckos, and rats, and they kept scrambling out of their resting places and fleeing outside until I was no longer surprised. Fofo whistled and hummed songs most of the time. After each round of filling, we went outside, and Fofo got on a chair and worked on the outer wall, kneading the mud with his knuckles and smoothing it with wet palms.

"Fofo, why are you leaving those openings?" I asked when I saw that he had left an opening on each wall.

"Because I no want kill anybody wid heat," he said. "*E hun miawo hugan*."

"Heat? What about the windows?"

"No need to open window wid de holes. You *dey* ask *beaucoup de questions,* son . . . even de holes too big. *Abeg,* give me mix."

I passed him the mix, and he reduced each opening to the size of a man's foot. Standing on the floor inside, we couldn't see the outside through the holes, not just because they were too high but because they were close to the roof. It was impossible for sunlight to come into the room through them.

"But, Fofo, when are we going to use the roofing sheets? Are you going to change the roof soon?"

Yewa came into the parlor and stood silently behind us, but we didn't pay her any attention. My uncle's fast and furious pace dictated the work, and our conversation seemed to only whet his appetite for speed.

"Don't worry, de sheets are for our *ohò yóyó*," Fofo Kpee said.

"New house?" I asked.

"Papa and Mama want build new house for us . . . cement house. Real *ohò dagbe*."

"When are we going to see Papa and Mama?" Yewa cut in.

We stopped talking and turned to her for a while. She had come to show us her creations, which had fallen and broken. She carried the mess close to her heart, in open palms, like shattered pieces of a jewel. She said it was supposed to be a rider and a passenger on a Nanfang.

"In a few days we *dey* go Braffe . . . ," Fofo Kpee said.

"No, I mean Papa and Mama of Gabon," Yewa insisted. "I wanted to give this toy to Mama when she comes."

"No worry, Mary," said Fofo Kpee. "*Yi bayi dogó,* and no let dem break again. . . . Mama and Papa of Gabon *reviennent* soon."

WHEN WE FINISHED, FOFO swept the parlor and gathered the wet mix that had fallen near the walls. I swept everything outside. Then Fofo sent me to buy huge quantities of *amala* and *ewedu* from the market. But when I came back and we sat down and began eating, Yewa refused to join us.

"I want Gabon food!" she announced, and stood up from the bed, her face twisted in defiance. Before anyone could respond, she walked to the threshold and slumped in annoyance. She started sobbing because she had hit her head on the new metal door frame. She sat there, in the open doorway, back to us, facing the ocean.

"Gabon food?" Fofo said, looking at me, scratching his head with his pinky because the rest of the fingers were soaked with *ewedu.* "*Wetin* be Gabon food, Mary?"

"Mama brought Gabon food," Yewa cried. "I want Mama, I want Coke, I want macaroni. I am tired of *ewedu* and *amala.*"

"But de woman also bring pepper soup and *akasa* and crab soup," Fofo argued. "Dem be Gabon food too?"

"She brought those ones for you and Big Guy," Yewa said.

"Not true . . . Antoinette ate them too," I said. "I ate them too."

"*Kai*, we now get rich people problem," Fofo said. "*Auparavant*, before now you *dey* eat everyting I give you, like a good goat. Now you want select?"

"Fofo Kpee, she's not hungry," I said, cupping *amala* into my fingers.

"I want Gabon food," Yewa said, and shuffled her legs on the ground.

I continued to eat, paying no attention to her. But when I looked up at Fofo, I could see he was listening to her. "No way!" I said, wriggling deeper into the bed. "I'm not going anywhere!" I said this because I knew that if Fofo agreed with her, I would have to run back to the market to get the food for her. "You spoiled girl, get up from there," I shouted. "Look at your head like Gabon food!"

"You're stupid!" Yewa told me.

"Who's stupid? Me?" I snarled.

Yewa spun around and bared her teeth, ready to bite me, which was what she did each time I hit her for being naughty. Even against the brighter background outside, I could see her smirk. I rushed toward her, but Fofo hooked the seat of my shorts with his fingers and yanked me back. I stumbled and kicked in his grasp. Yewa stood her ground and kept calling me names until Fofo told her to stop or she wouldn't go to Gabon.

Yewa refused to come in or go out. Her eyes were swollen with unshed tears, which soon came flushing down her cheeks. The combination of her desire for what she called Gabon food and the threat that she might not go to Gabon upset her. She cried like she did when she had malaria and the quack doctor came to give her an injection in her bottom. Fofo started begging me not to beat her up, and when he saw that I had calmed down he released my shorts. He picked up Yewa, brought her into the parlor, and carried and nursed her as Mama had done that night.

"I don't want to go back to the market," I said quietly. "Why didn't this monkey say this when I was going to the market?"

"Who want send you back to market *sef?*" Fofo said. "Make you no scold your sister again. You know de gal *dey* too light. We must fatten her for de trip. Oderwise, she go embarrass Mama and Papa. And, Pascal, you suppose be glad de gal done begin like Gabon food before you reach de place."

"She has to be more considerate, Fofo Kpee," I said, and went outside to sit on the mound and sulk.

"Anyway, no *wahala,*" Fofo said. "I *dey* go market myself, den."

He carried Yewa on his back, went into the inner room, and wheeled out the Nanfang. He set it outside, smiled at it. In those difficult months, it seemed the machine was a source of stability for him, something he could always be proud of, something he would still have when we left for Gabon. He looked at himself many times in the side mirrors, smiling and mumbling to the machine, as if it could hear and answer him. Now, he swung Yewa from his back onto the gas tank, sat on the bike, and rode out to the market. He didn't come back as soon as he should have, because, as he said later on, he wanted to give Yewa a longer ride. When he came back, he put the Nanfang back as majestically as he had brought it out. We were going to eat and drink inside as usual, but Yewa complained that the smell of the wet mix was nauseating. We went outside and ate under the mango tree, like we were having a picnic.

Later that afternoon, we went back to work, this time trying to seal off the inner room. It was more difficult to work in there because it was crowded with things. Fofo wasn't in the business of letting the Nanfang stand in the sun or even in the parlor. So now he took his time and moved the Nanfang to the center of the room and covered it with our bedspread and tarp. It was as if he were dressing up a big pet. I wanted to take the other things out of the room or push them out of the way.

"Where you want put dese tings?" he asked me.

"Outside," I said.

"No . . . you no get head, boy? You want expose my riches to everybody?"

"What about the parlor?" I asked, bending down to close the pots of soup in the corner and drape old newspapers over them.

"And if person *dey* come, *wetin* we go do? You see me invite anybody to help me in dis work? No move anyting *o*," he said, pushing the mortar away from the wall to make room for the chair on which he would stand to do the job.

WE WORKED HARD AND fast. Fofo wasn't talking or whistling or humming, as he had when we worked in the parlor. He left no holes in the walls here. He seemed so focused on the job that in some ways it felt as if he was uncomfortable with what he was doing now. He had no time for finesse anymore. Even though the cement fell on all the signs of the better life we had come into, he didn't care. And when I wanted to stop to wipe off the mix, he glared at me.

"Fofo, you are leaving no holes in this room?" I asked, offering him the cement mix.

"So what?" he said.

"We need air in here."

"*Dis moi,* you sleep in dis room before?"

"No."

"Your sister *nko?*"

"No."

"You *dey* cry for de Nanfang, *abi?* Just *dey* work and stop interrogating me."

As we filled in the space at the top of the walls, the room became darker and darker because he wouldn't even open a window. I could only see his profile. Down where I stood, since we didn't move anything out of the room, it wasn't only dark but crowded. It was afternoon outside but night in our home. I wanted to light the lantern, but Fofo warned me that if his Nanfang caught fire, we would lose everything. We started sweating, and Yewa refused to come inside, saying it was getting too hot. With the lack of air, the smell of the cement mix hung heavily in the room.

"I no need dis, *un ma jlo ehe!*" Fofo Kpee cursed suddenly, and slapped the wall. "Dis no go work."

"Are you talking to me?" I asked.

"You? Why I go talk to you? Can't a man just talk about dis stupid riches? Must you answer everyting, huh? I say *ma so* question *mi ba!*"

It was the first time I saw him show frustration or doubt about our new life. Seeing how tense he was and hearing his continual sighs, I kept quiet. He was so distraught by whatever was worrying him that we abandoned the outside walls. After a while he got so angry that in one final rush of work, he closed up every-thing. And darkness descended on the room.

I prayed that his outburst had nothing to do with our going to Gabon. Since he wasn't comfortable with opening the door of the inner room, I couldn't clean the place very well. I made do with wiping the surfaces in the dark. The Nanfang was the only pos-session that was spared the dirt from our work.

That evening he drove away, still muttering to himself, to meet with Big Guy. He came back more agitated than before, with three silver-colored padlocks and black latches. While the Nan-fang stood outside, he asked me to bring the lantern into the in-ner room so he could see what he was doing. With hammer and nails, he attached the latches to the windows and back door. He padlocked the two windows and the door from inside and added the keys to his bunch. He was left with spare keys. "I buy tripli-cate, but I done give one set to Big Guy," he mumbled, his eyes scanning for a hiding place for them.

"Is he coming to live with us?" Yewa asked.

"Not really," he said. "De man *na* my best friend."

"He's our friend too!" my sister continued, delighted. "We'll play with him every day."

When Fofo Kpee couldn't find a good place, he took the keys to the parlor and put them in the breast pocket of the olive green corduroy coat in his wardrobe. He only wore it on important occasions.

THAT NIGHT, OUR HOME began to feel like an oven. We couldn't sleep, even though we took off all our clothes.

Once we locked up, a massive heat swallowed the rooms, and the walls became warm. Yewa, who always slept between me and the wall, cried, and Fofo asked me to switch places with her. We sweat until our bed felt like one of us had wet it. Though we could hear the wind coming in from the ocean, sweeping through the banana and plantain trees, we couldn't feel it. It was like standing by a stream but dying of thirst. It was stuffy, and the three of us tossed and turned. We got up and tried to sleep on the cement floor, but it felt like sandpaper, the sand and dust sticking to our wet bodies. It was useless. And when our fatigue finally plunged us into sleep, the mosquitoes, which must have survived from the previous nights, descended, and we woke up one another as we swatted them. Fofo Kpee kept cursing and blaming potential thieves for forcing us to close the rafter spaces.

Several times he went out for fresh air. When we asked him whether we could go with him, he said no and said we should get used to a bit of discomfort so that if Gabon had little discomforts, our benefactors wouldn't blame him for not preparing us.

"My children, just manage," Fofo Kpee said the second night, after dabbing our bodies with a wet towel. "Sometimes, de vessel to Gabon hot *pass* dis place . . . just manage."

The lantern by the corner pulsed with a weak flame. It revealed our wet bodies, and there was a pinch of smoke in the air that worried our eyes.

"Hotter than this? But the ships our parents showed us were beautiful and airy," I said.

"Very beautiful," Yewa said.

"You *dey* argue too much. *Attention, mì preparez mide dayi na la plus mauvaise situation.* Me I no enjoy dis *o,* so no tink I *dey* do dis for fun. You must be ready. Remember, even de Israelites, chosen people, suffer for desert, and de lazy ones *dey* suffer snakebites. So stop interrogating me for my house. When I *dey* your age I no query my parents like dis *o*. . . . Just *dey* remember: as you *dey* move your mout like scissors, no tell anybody our plans *o*. No gossip gossip, notting."

"We don't gossip," I said.

In one movement, Fofo yanked off our bedsheet and gave it to me. He took our center table and placed it on our bed, creating some space. He spread the sheet on the ground and asked us to lie down, said that it was better that way. We didn't feel the sand, so in that sense it was better, and it was cooler than the bed. But still we couldn't sleep, because of the hard floor.

"OK, good children . . . now make we talk happy tings," he said, and sat on the edge of his bed. "Since we can't sleep make we do someting else. We must be happy no matter what. So, *wetin* you go buy for me for Gabon? No matter how rich you be for dat place, no forget me *o*."

"I'll buy you Nido and Uncle Ben's rice and Nanfang, Fofo Kpee," said Yewa in a weak, sleepy voice. "I'll give you money, and you'll be able to marry many wives."

We laughed at her.

"Oh yeah . . . really?" Fofo said.

"Yes," she said.

"How many wife you want gimme?"

"Fofo, two wives, like Pastor Adeyemi. . . . They must work for NGO!"

"Only two?" he said.

"OK, five? You'll get more children."

"Children? You go help me educate dem?"

"Mama of Gabon will train them," I chimed in.

Fofo laughed and sat squarely in his bed, relishing the conversation.

"*Kai,* I tank God you two *dey* already *dey* tink like rich Gabon people."

Though we were all laughing that night, it was a struggle. Our laughter was weak, like a toy whose battery was running down. The light was dim, but the heat in the room made it feel as if that flame were the source of our hell.

Fofo Kpee opened the door to go out for fresh air, and a breath of it washed over us before he closed the door and locked it from outside. I picked up his towel and started dabbing Yewa and myself, but suddenly Fofo came back in as if a demon were pursuing him. He was a restless man: he couldn't be inside; he couldn't be outside. He took the towel from me and started to dab himself, as if the cool air had made him even hotter.

"School time," Fofo Kpee announced suddenly, like a headmaster, and went to adjust the lantern wick, making it burn brighter. He was unclad except for the piece of *wrappa* tied around his waist. Against the light, his sweaty torso glistened. He was no longer the smallish man we knew. He had gained weight, and his stomach muscles were weakening, allowing his belly to bulge like that of a newly pregnant woman. I doubted he would still be able to climb coconut trees. "We must learn someting, *mes enfants.* . . . Sit up!" he said, opening a neatly folded piece of paper.

"What are we learning?" my sister asked.

"You see, if person want go America, for example, he go need tips for de *owhèntiton*..."

"Ah, Fofo, do you want to teach us about Gabon?" I said hurriedly.

"*Mówe*... you must learn certain tings in case *l'immigration* or navy people worry your ship, you know. Our government is corrupt. We no want make dem spoil tings for us." Then he lowered his voice to an eerie whisper and pointed a frightening finger at us, saying, "Dese bad people can steal children like *you* for high sea!"

"They can?" we whispered.

"Yes, but, *mes enfants,* no fear. You go defeat dem... you get luck say Big Guy *na* your friend. Dat's why I give *am* de keys. He *na* good immigration man. He know his people."

At the mention of Big Guy we began to relax again. My sister nodded and smiled to herself.

"Is he coming with us, then?" I asked.

"Yeah, Big Guy will teach us all their tricks," my sister said confidently.

We no longer thought about the heat. Fofo was silent for a while, with the towel draped around his neck. "So ready?"

"Yes," we said, sitting up and watching his mouth attentively.

"Well, repeat after me," he said, his eyes squinting in the low light as he stammered to read: "'Mama is younger than Papa because Papa married late.'"

"Mama is younger than Papa because Papa married late," we said.

"*D'accord*... one by one... Mary?"

"Mama is younger than Papa because Papa married late," she said.

"*Bon* . . . Pascal?"

"Mama is younger than Papa because he married late," I said.

"No change anyting, stupid boy!"

"Mama is younger than Papa because *Papa* married late," I said.

"Not good enough. You suppose *dey* smile as you *dey* talk dese tings . . . just like Mary *dey* do." He went to Yewa and wiped off the sweat from her forehead and fanned her a bit with the towel before going back to the lantern. "Good gal, good gal," he praised her.

"Just do like me," Yewa said, and tapped my shoulder. I repeated the lines and smiled, to the satisfaction of both of them. Fofo fidgeted with the wick of the lantern, trying to boost the failing flame. I went into the inner room and brought out our jerrican of kerosene.

"Ah, *merci beaucoup,* my son," he said. "Who go show us how to forget poverty?" He was referring to those days, before our Nanfang, when we used to ration our kerosene from a Lucozade bottle and rushed through our homework before the flame died on us. Now, he poured the fuel into the lantern tank until the flame began to twinkle, sputtered, and grew to a good size. As he poured the kerosene, Yewa and I held our hands under the lantern, catching a few drops, their momentary coolness a balm against the heat.

"OK, make we continue school," Fofo Kpee said. " 'We live at Rue de Franceville, *nombre douze,* Port-Gentil, Gabon.' "

"We live at Rue de Franceville, *nombre douze,* Port-Gentil, Gabon," we said, then repeated one after the other.

" 'Our parents run a small NGO, Grace Earth.' "

"Our parents run a small NGO, Grace Earth," we said.

"What's de name of de NGO, *mes enfants?*"

"Grace Earth," we said.

" 'We're four children in our family. . . . We were all born in Port-Gentil. . . . Some of our *fofos* live in Benin and Nigeria. . . . We went to see them. . . . We had a good visit with them. We go every year.' "

We repeated these lines again and again until we began to doze off in spite of the heat. Fofo was satisfied and declared the lesson done. It was like the medicine we needed to sleep.

In school the next morning, we were drowsy and dull and our noses ran as if we had catarrh. Even on the soccer field, I was so slow and jittery that Monsieur Abraham, our games master, benched me as a creative midfielder, and my friends threatened to stop calling me Jay Jay Okocha. After the game, Monsieur Abraham, who was a tall, cheerful, athletic fellow, questioned me seriously about the cause of my lack of stamina. He wanted to know whether Fofo Kpee was treating me well at home and whether I was getting enough sleep and eating well. I refused to tell him, but he didn't give up. He kept an eye on me, maintaining that I was very important to his team, and in time he said he noticed the same thing was happening to my sister. He smiled at us often, and my sister came to like his beautiful teeth. Every afternoon, he brought us together and gave us some glucose to boost our energy. We wondered what we had done to get such special attention.

AT NIGHT, FOFO KPEE chewed lots of kola nuts to induce insomnia so he could oversee our progress. He kept questioning us about Gabon, and we mastered the answers. Sometimes he would fall asleep, but the next morning he looked drowsy and grumpy. His lips were stained red, with kola residue at the corners.

Some mornings, we didn't need to shower to go to school because he was constantly dabbing us with a wet towel. One time we couldn't even go to school, because rashes broke out all over us like a fine spray of goose bumps, and Fofo Kpee got us *efun,* the local calamine chalk, soaked it in water, and poured it all over our bodies. We moved around the house like little masqueraders. During the day, Fofo encouraged us to play outside the house, saying it would make the infection heal faster. Yet at night, when we needed air the most, he would sigh, lock us in, and tell us that men who would succeed in life knew how to take pain.

"'Papa has three younger brothers,'" he read to us one night. "'Vincent, Marcus, and Pierre, and two sisters, Cecile and Michelle. . . . ' Repeat after me."

"Papa has three younger brothers, Vincent, Marcus, and Pierre, and two sisters, Cecile and Michelle," I said.

"Papa has three younger brothers, Vincent, Marcus, and Pierre, and two sisters, Cecile and Michelle," Yewa said.

"Hey, what do your parents do?" he said suddenly, pointing at my sister.

"Our parents run a small NGO," she said.

"*Bon.* De name of de NGO?"

"Grace Earth!" she answered.

"Good gal . . . Repeat after me, you two. . . . 'Our father's father, Matthew, died two years ago.'"

"Our father's father, Matthew, died two years ago," we said.

" 'When he died, Tantine Cecile cried for two days.... Our grandmama, Martha, refused to talk to anyone.' "

"When he died, Tantine Cecile cried for two days," we said. "Our grandmama, Martha, refused to talk to anyone."

" 'Grandmama Martha died earlier this year and was buried beside Grandpapa Matthew.' "

"Grandmama Martha died earlier this year and was buried beside Grandpapa Matthew."

"Where do you live in Gabon, Pascal?"

"Rue du Franceville, *nombre douze,* Port-Gentil, Gabon," I said.

"Good boy."

" '*Fofos* live in Libreville, Makokou, and Bitam' . . . repeat."

"*Fofos* live in Libreville, Makokou, and Bitam," we said.

" 'Tantine Cecile is married to Fofo David and has two children, Yves and Jules.' "

"Tantine Cecile is married to Fofo David and has two children, Yves and Jules."

"OK, break time," he said.

"No break," Yewa protested.

"I say I done tire," he said, sitting down and throwing the piece of paper on the table. "According to our elders, even de piper *dey* stop for break." We grabbed the paper and looked at it, as if we had stumbled on our exam questions shortly before the test. It wasn't his handwriting. I attempted to read what I had seen to my sister, but she wanted to see the letters that formed each word. We pushed and pulled until we almost tore the paper. Fofo, seeing how close our faces were to the hot dome of the lantern, reached out and took it away from us.

"Come, go inside and bring de pot of beans here," he said to me.

"But we were going to eat it with *ogi*," I said, "in the morning, for breakfast."

"The vulture eats between his meals" — my sister started singing a nursery rhyme — "and that's the reason why. His head is bald, his neck is long . . ."

"*Na* you be vulture, no be me," Fofo Kpee said, and laughed. "OK, when he bring de Gabon *núdùdú*, you no go eat. I hope beans no be *Gabon food!* Pascal, just bring de ting out."

I went to the inner room and brought out the beans, holding the pot with old papers to avoid the soot. The food was cold, and the palm oil had solidified on top like a layer of brown icing. Fofo said it was too risky to go outside and make a fire then. I scooped the servings, which were as firm as cake slices, onto three plates. We filtered the *garri* and divided it into three bowls. Fofo Kpee added salt to his *garri*. I added sugar, Nido powdered milk, and Ovaltine to mine, and Yewa added salt and sugar and Nido and Ovaltine to hers. Fofo teased that we had already become children of the spoiled generation, drinking *garri* with milk and sugar. He ate fast so that his *garri* wouldn't soak up all the water and congeal. But Yewa and I drank our *garri* slowly, intentionally. Whenever the *garri* soaked up all the water, we poured in more and added the flavorings.

"Look at dese Gabon vultures!" Fofo Kpee taunted, and made faces at us. We laughed and ate and made merry, as we would for many nights after this.

When we resumed the rehearsal that night, we were too full to sit properly. Yewa tried lying on the cement floor to lessen the heat, but it was too hard for her bloated stomach. We climbed onto the bed. I lay on my side, Yewa on her back. My mind was in

Gabon. I saw myself in my godparents' mansion. I thought about having my own room and being driven to school daily. I thought about wearing shoes to school and about coming home to Mama's great food. The more I thought about these things, the more I laughed, and the more funny faces Fofo Kpee made. I was no longer tired that night, and for a while it seemed as if I could live without fresh air and suffer anything without becoming frustrated.

"*Non,* DIS ONE CANNOT defeat me!" Fofo Kpee shouted one evening during a nap, which he had insisted on, to ease his fatigue before giving us lessons. "*Mes enfants* no *dey* go anywhere! *Pas du tout.*"

Yewa and I looked up from our books and exchanged glances.

"*N'dọ ye ma jeyi ofidé!*" Fofo Kpee repeated in Egun, this time his body moving with the force of his voice. Yewa held on to me and opened her mouth, but I put my hand over it and pushed her behind me. Our uncle turned and twisted as if he were fighting a lion. When he almost fell out of his bed, he awoke and sat up, hurriedly rearranging his loincloth around his waist. Though we were all sweating, his now came down in waves. He had never spoken in his sleep before, so his words caught us off guard. Though I didn't say anything, I was afraid and confused and folded my hands in front of me.

"I'm OK, *pas de problem,*" he said when he recovered and caught us staring at him. "Why you *dey* look me like dat?"

"You spoke in your dream," I said.

"No be me," he denied. His voice wore a touch of anger. "Make we do school, *d'accord?* Mary, why you *dey* hide behind him to look me like say I *dey* talk Wolof?"

"I don't know," Yewa said, shrugging.

"Sure? Or you no want study tonight?"

"We want to study tonight," I said. "Maybe she's frightened by your dream."

Fofo stood up and stretched.

"My dream? Which dream?" He laughed a stern laugh and sighed. "No fear."

I couldn't tell whether he knew what he had said in his dream or not. And because of the anger in his voice now, I didn't ask him. He tried to act normal, yet he couldn't shake off the fright in which he had awakened. He kept shutting his eyes tight and opening them wide as if that would wipe away his dread. Then he started pinching his scar and shaking his head. He was more nervous and restless than he was the night our godparents came to see us. I was afraid, but I pretended to be strong so as not to frighten my sister. The nightmare should have served as a warning to me that our dream could unravel.

"You have not eaten anything," I said gently as I placed a bowl of food before him.

"Who told you I want to *manger?*" he said, pushing the bowl aside. He brought his gin out from under the bed and took two long gulps straight from the bottle and cleared his throat. "*Peut-être,* maybe *je veux* go Gabon *aussi.*" He chuckled an empty chuckle. "Maybe I should come take care of you. . . . Ah *non, il faut que* man be strong!"

"You are going to miss us?" my sister said, her voice as abrupt as a town crier's.

"Oui, c'est ça," he conceded, and shrugged, without looking us in the face. The liquor had cleansed his voice of anger. Now the more he drank the steadier his demeanor became, though it didn't stop the sweat. "Yeah, make I no worry, I suppose."

Yewa went over and placed herself in between his legs.

"We'll miss you too. Won't we, Pascal?" my sister said.

"We will," I said. "Fofo, don't worry. We'll be OK with Mama."

He didn't say anything. He just sat there, looking down, hugging Yewa, and stroking her head like Mama did. My sister climbed up to sit on his lap, and the silence seemed to last an eternity. The sweat from Fofo's face dripped on my sister, but it didn't matter. We were getting used to the heat and the perspiration that came with it. All I could think about was how he would miss us. I began to think seriously for the first time about missing him too. I started to miss his jokes and his care for us.

Some indescribable guilt arose within me, and I saw myself as an ingrate for wanting to go away. I couldn't look at Fofo's face, and he couldn't look at our faces. I wished Yewa would say something or do something crazy to shatter the silence. But she just sat there with a sad look, and the fact that she didn't disrupt this silence deepened my guilt. Who would Fofo talk to when he came back from work? Who would cook for him or wash his dishes? How should we pay him back for his care and for finding these godparents who had helped our parents in Braffe and would send our other siblings to Gabon? I made up my mind to tell our parents everything Fofo had done for us since we arrived here. And when he had children, I promised myself, I would do all I could to show love to my cousins. I started thinking about how we would insist that our godparents allow us to come back to visit him. I would write him letters every week, telling him about our lives. Maybe he would be able to visit us.

"But you can come with us," Yewa suggested, relieving me of my shame. "Mama will not mind. Maybe you can live with Fofo Vincent or Fofo Marcus or Fofo Pierre."

"Or Fofo David and Tantine Cecile," I said eagerly.

"We can take the Nanfang along," my sister said. "Once you buy a car in Gabon, you can sell it."

"No, I'll learn to ride it there," I said.

"But if you don't come with us," she said, "it's OK. I'll buy you a Lexus and Benz. . . . I'll send you money too."

Fofo Kpee looked at her sorrowfully and dipped his finger into the bucket of water by his bed and flicked a drop in my face. "Will you miss me, Pascal?" he taunted me.

"Yes, Fofo Kpee, yes," I said, nodding. "I'll build you big houses like those in our godparents' pictures."

"*Non,* I go come Gabon! Wid you."

Nobody said anything. The three of us looked at each other, and then we began to laugh until we cried. Though we were chatting now, it felt very surreal, solemn. Fofo opened his mouth as if to say something but gave up. He snatched his bottle from the table and poured gin into his mouth as though he needed a big gulp to drown whatever he had wanted to say in his stomach.

Then he poured the drink into our cups in large doses and said we needed to celebrate his coming to Gabon. We drank gleefully, until our eyes sparkled and the *payó* bit our guts. A boost of energy swept through my body, my sister became very talkative, and sleep went very far away from us.

WHEN WE THOUGHT HE was going to begin the lesson that night, he got up slowly, as if he had been taken over by voodoo, and went to the lantern, where he always stood to prepare us for our trip. He removed his *wrappa* and threw it over the table onto the floor. He was stark naked, like us. At first, we wondered if maybe it was an accident. Then we thought maybe he was drunk, though we had never seen him drunk before. But when he didn't pick up the loincloth, we became concerned. He looked like a man who had stolen from the open market and was about to be stoned. My sister had both hands over her mouth, to keep herself from letting out a sound, her eyes wide and unfocused. In embarrassment, I began to look up at the roof.

Fofo Kpee poured water into a bucket and started dabbing himself with his towel. The sight of him cooling himself with very little water, like camel riders crossing the Sahara, was unbearable. His lightheartedness was gone, and the room became very quiet except for the wind outside and the sound of him putting the towel into the water bucket and wringing it. He kept babbling and had become oblivious to our presence.

We were scared, and Yewa drew close to me. Fofo looked like a man in pain, a man who couldn't take the heat anymore. I began to wonder why he couldn't stay outside, where there was fresh air. Do the people of Gabon walk around naked and sleep in airtight rooms? Is it so hot there that we have to learn to behave like this? But when I remembered the beautiful beaches and houses in the pictures our godparents showed us, I convinced myself that that wasn't the case. Since he was now coming with us to Gabon, did he have to be this dramatic to catch up with our preparation? The whole thing was like a bad dream from which we must quickly awake.

"Hey, children," he said, finally looking at us, sounding funny again, "*j'espère que* shame no *dey* catch you to see Fofo *comme çi*." He left the lantern and came toward us. "When *una* dey small, *una* no shower wid your parents for Braffe?"

"We did," we said, still trying to look away.

"So why you *dey* behave like small chicken now? Person who fit cross de sea done become big man *o*. . . . In de boat *il faut qu'* everybody *dey* mix wid everybody, *vous comprenez?* Even dat your sister, Antoinette, if she *dey* remove her dress make sure confusion no enter your head *o*."

"She's going to be naked?" my sister asked, alarmed.

"Impossible!" I said.

"Not really," Fofo said. "But if you see her change her dress, *na* one of dose tings."

"No," she said.

"When you get sister for family, *na* like dat . . . but we be family, *oui?*" We nodded reluctantly without saying anything. "And no shame if *una* see your godparents' nakedness. No big difference *dey* between *omẹnnọtọ lẹ.* Naked people *nulopo lọ wé yé yin . . . partout.* Your godparents dey run a world organization. You go see all kind of people for Gabon. You go see white people, colored people, tourists who support de work of your godparents. Do whatever dem want — go beach wid dem, go hotel wid dem . . . if dem want take *una* go Europe, follow dem. Even if *una* no like dem, *soiyez patience,* no condition *dey* permanent . . ."

"But you're coming with us," I cut in, uncomfortable with what he was saying. Yewa was shaking her head in disagreement.

"Whatever de case," Fofo said, "make good use of *l'opportunité*. Don't worry. No big deal for all dis . . . *gbòjé!*"

The dread that had hung around him since he awoke from his nightmare went away now. Apart from his nakedness, he looked very normal. His whole body glowed with sweat except his bushy pubic hair, out of which hung a limp penis, its head smooth like mango skin, its body wearing a tube of tiny rings of flesh, like the neck of an *oba* in an *odigba*.

Suddenly, Fofo Kpee parted his legs and grabbed his genitals as if to push them back into the bush.

"You naked, I naked, why you fear?" he said like one reciting a poem. "You have it, I have it. My own big, your own small, right? Say '*hén,* Fofo,' *s'il vous plaît!*"

"Yes, Fofo," we stammered, and nodded.

"Let talk about sex, *mes bébés,*" he began to sing, and wriggled like a madman. "Let talk about *vous* and *moi.*" He balled one hand into a microphone, the other still grabbing his genitals. He skulked around the room as if he were on stage; he jumped onto the table, then jumped down. He moonwalked until his back grazed the clothes in the wardrobe. He stopped suddenly, with one leg raised in frozen posture. "You know de song?"

"No," we said.

"You want touch my ting? Come on, do it, *allez, touchez moi.*"

He was now coming toward us.

"No, no!" I said, and we backed away.

My sister was silent. She never spoke again that night but shielded her privates with her hands and moved behind me.

"Oh, you want touch your ting, *mes enfants?*"

"No," I said.

I felt a numbness around my groin, and my heart began to pound. I didn't feel the heat anymore, though I noticed more sweat was pouring from my body. My penis seemed to have shrunk completely, and my balls became one hard nut. I knew immediately this was different from my *fofo*'s ordinary clowning. I was afraid.

"Or you want touch white man, Mary, huh?" he said.

Yewa shook her head.

When he turned his gaze on me, I said, "Maybe we should not go to Gabon . . ."

"Shut up, bastard!" he exploded, and shook his head and downed more *payó*. "You want drink, *abi?*"

"No."

"You want woman?"

"No."

"Just don't disgrace me for foreign land *o* . . . you hear?"

"No."

"*Non?*"

"Yes, Fofo."

We stared at each other for a while. "Good, at least," he said, "you no *dey* hide your face anymore. *Gbòjé, gbòjé!*"

He held the cap of his penis by his fingertips and stretched it downward until the rings of flesh disappeared. He spun and released it like a cone. It didn't turn but returned weakly to its perch on the balls. He continued to do this until his penis began to get bigger. He giggled and tied his *wrappa* around his waist again and sat on the bed.

"Would you like some food?" he said.

"No," I said.

"Sure, Mary? Some Gabon food, cornflakes, Nido, huh?"

"I want to sleep," she whispered.

That night I tried to convince myself that I was drunk, that none of this had really happened. In spite of the heat, I put on my shorts and turned my back toward Fofo and lay with my hands between my legs, trying to protect myself even in sleep. My sister simply wrapped herself up in the bedspread. I was repulsed by thoughts of traveling to Gabon. I no longer felt at home in our place. It was as if every piece of furniture had been stained by Fofo's performance that night. My mind sank deeper into shame and fear as I remembered all the things we had bought since we started thinking of going to Gabon. For instance, I hated the very shorts I was wearing and thought of taking them off, but I couldn't bring myself to sleep naked that night. I hated the Nanfang and vowed never to ride on it again.

For the first time, I sympathized with Paul—and wished I could have vomited, like him, all the good food I had ever eaten in the past few months. I wondered how he and Antoinette were doing. Did they know something we didn't know? Did they go through their orientation before visiting us? Who would be giving them *this* lesson? Big Guy?

I wasn't interested in traveling anymore, though somehow my mind refused to associate my godparents with what had happened that night. I felt better thinking they didn't know, and took solace in the memory of their visit. Though I no longer felt like following them, I didn't think they meant us any harm. And though Fofo apologized to us the next morning and said he overdid things just a bit in case life became difficult abroad, I started thinking of how to escape and run back to Braffe with my sister.

ONE DAY FOFO RUSHED back from work unexpectedly, like in his pre-Nanfang days when he had duped someone at the border and needed to go underground. He jumped off his bike and stormed into the parlor. He quickly locked the door behind him and leaned against it, breathing like one who had escaped from a lion. Uncharacteristically, Fofo had abandoned the Nanfang outside. He didn't respond to our greetings. He mumbled something about protecting us from evil and started unbolting the windows. A humid gust of wind drifted in and flushed the room of the stuffiness that had filled the place since we sealed the house three weeks before.

"Yes, if dem want kill me, *ye ni hù mì*," he said to no one in particular. He had his arms akimbo and seemed very proud of this single action of opening the windows. Then he removed his coat and sat down heavily on the bed.

"Fofo, who wants to kill you?" Yewa asked quietly, not moving closer to him.

Since that night when he went naked before us, we were scared to get close to him and said very little to him. He said little to us too. Silence grew between us like yeast, and the room felt smaller, while his presence seemed to expand. We looked forward to his leaving the house, and when he was home, sometimes we pretended to be asleep.

Now I began to speak to him from our bed: "Fofo, are you . . . ?"

"Leave me alone!" he warned, holding his forehead in his palms. "*Vous pensez que* I *dey* craze, huh?"

"No, no, Fofo," I pleaded.

"I *dey* OK . . . notting *dey* wrong wid me."

Yewa didn't say anything. Now she hid behind me, as she did that bad night. The fresh wind filled the room, and we listened to it and the distant wash of the ocean on the beach. After a while, she whispered in my ear that we should go outside, but when I grabbed her hand and wanted to leave the room, he ordered us to sit on the bed. My sister began to sob.

Fofo Kpee went outside to bring the Nanfang into the inner room. He pushed the bike forcefully, like a police officer arresting a difficult criminal. "If I must sell you to be free," he said to the Nanfang, slapping the backseat, "I shall!"

When we saw him slapping the machine, we expected him to blow up at us at any moment. Then we heard him rummaging in the inner room, his anger evident in the way he threw things out of the way. He was searching for something. He came out with an iron bar we hadn't seen in a long time.

He went to work with all his energy, climbing on a chair in our parlor-bedroom and chipping the cement mix we had put up a few weeks back, driven by a fury we couldn't understand. He didn't bother to move anything or to ask me for help. The brittle fill came flying down in bits and pieces. It was as if the whole place would come crashing down. The whiff of dust streaked the fresh air. And when I coughed, he ordered us to get out of his sight.

We went outside. The late-afternoon sun had gone past the center of the sky and hit the earth at an angle, pouring out of

the clear skies without restraint. Looking down the long path
to the road, we could see people going about their business, on
foot and on bikes, in either direction. We sat quietly under the
mango tree, facing the house. I sat on the ground with my back
against the tree, my legs straight out before me, Yewa sitting on
them, her head on my chest. Its shade wide and cool, the mango
foliage wore a two-tone look, like our Nanfang. Some parts of
the tree were in bloom, the new fruit and bright-green leaves
contrasting with the old. The scent of the fruit, fresh and warm
in the sun, filled the air, and the ground around us was sprayed
with fine light-green pollen.

"Is he angry with Nanfang?" Yewa whispered to me when
we could no longer hear him working inside.

"I don't know," I said.

"When we buy him a car, he won't be angry again."

"We're not going to Gabon!"

"We're not?" she said, turning to face me. "Why, huh?"

"Did you like what Fofo Kpee said the night he danced naked? You liked what he did?"

"No. But he said sorry to us the next day." She closed her eyes
in defiance and turned her back to me. "OK, I'll go alone, with
Mama and Papa!"

It was no use arguing with her.

Under that mango tree, my mind went back to thoughts of
running away. Though I had no concrete plans and didn't know
whether it would be possible, the very idea of leaving lifted my
mood that afternoon.

I was no longer sure about escaping to Braffe. Suppose I got
there and my extended family was as fixated on Gabon as Yewa

was and no one understood my change of mind? Who would believe me if I told them what Fofo had done that bad night? Or what if our siblings had been put through this already and didn't complain? Again, I was concerned about how to escape with Yewa. How could I convince her to follow me when she was still excited about traveling?

For a moment, I thought about telling Monsieur Abraham that our uncle had gone crazy, about the late-night lessons and my plans to escape. But I was too ashamed to do that. What would he think of me? What if my classmates got wind of my uncle's craziness?

I hated our house now and felt we could have sat out there forever, without wanting to go back in. The front door and the windows were open like the petals of a trap that would slam shut once the prey stepped inside. The angular sun shaved some of the shade off the veranda, catching one of the open windows, its metal gleaming like bait.

"Let's not argue with him, so he won't be mad at us," I said to my sister. "Let's go inside."

"I want Mama."

"Get up!" I said, and pushed her off my thighs.

We tiptoed to the door and peered in. Fofo lay sprawled out on the bed, like a monster dragged ashore by fishermen. His eyes weren't completely shut. The scar on his cheek looked like a worm journeying from his eye to his mouth, or vice versa, eating his good humor. We sneaked into our bed and lay there, looking up at the roof. Though he had worked very hard all afternoon, he only succeeded in making gaping holes near the roof. They were many and ugly, rough and dreadful, like an unfinished haircut. It was worse than the space we used to have before we sealed it. Our walls now had long cracks, as if Fofo Kpee had made a mural of lightning on them. In some places, the plaster that covered the mud wall had come off, revealing a moldy interior. The smell of crushed stone lingered.

From the way he was sleeping now, we knew he would never have the energy to tackle the inner room. He didn't talk to us when he woke up, and his face was subdued. He seemed even beyond the babble that had occasionally become his lot in those days.

I made food for myself and my sister because he refused to eat or drink. We ate quickly without talking. He just lay on his bed and stared at the holes he had created, as if whatever was upsetting him would reach in through them to hurt us. He lay faceup, his hands clasped under his head, his elbows up, his legs crossed. One moment he was as still as a corpse, and the next he startled at any sound.

That night we slept better than we had in a long time because of the holes he had made. We didn't have any lessons.

BIG GUY VISITED US the following day. He appeared unceremoniously, storming in without knocking. Fofo was lying on his bed. Big Guy came in ordinary clothes and looked unkempt and worried. As if he had been expecting him, Fofo didn't stand up to receive him or even look at him. Actually, once he saw Big Guy, he sprawled out so the man couldn't sit on his bed. Our visitor ignored him too, turning his attention to us.

"*Mes amis,* hey, how you *dey* today?" he said, slipping into a big smile, flashing us a thumbs-up.

"Fine," we said.

He sat on our bed, in between us.

"I can see Fofo *dey* feed you well well."

He plucked at my sister's cheeks playfully. I hated the fact that what he was saying was true. We looked well fed these days. Our faces had become rounder, our cheeks had filled out, our ribs had disappeared, and our tummies had lost their bloatedness.

"I get good news for you *o*," Big Guy said. "We go travel next week." He rubbed his palms against each other as if he were praying to us. He pointed at Fofo, who shot him a wicked look, then glanced away. "We *dey* almost ready, OK . . . or, Mary, you want travel quick quick?"

"Today!" she said.

"Talk *am* again, bright gal!" Big Guy exclaimed, giving Yewa a high five. "You know better ting."

Fofo turned and glared at us, and Yewa turned to me, uncertainty clipping her earlier abandon.

"Pascal . . . today?" Big Guy said, turning to me.

I pretended I didn't hear him. An awkward silence filled the room.

"See, de children *dey* ready," Big Guy announced to Fofo Kpee gleefully. "No disappoint dem now *o*. It too late. No be so, Mary?"

"Yes."

"Who be the wife of Fofo David?"

"Tantine Cecile."

"Any children?"

"Yves and Jules."

"Your city for Gabon?"

"Port-Gentil."

"Excellent. Pascal, you *dey* too quiet today. Mama *dey* like your maturity. And Tantine Cecile *dey* look forward to see you. . . . Say something, *abeg,* son. . . . Antoinette and Paul *dey* greet you. . . . You no want travel today like your sister?"

I didn't want to talk to him. Once he mentioned my Gabon siblings, I became angry and imagined him dancing naked before them. It was my strongest memory of our preparations. I was as uncomfortable as if he were sitting naked with us. Though I didn't know that Fofo had come to detest the Gabon deal, I secretly enjoyed the cold shoulder he was giving Big Guy. And though I knew that Big Guy was just teasing us about leaving that day, I couldn't bring myself to share in the joke. I prayed that Fofo would just tell him to go to hell with his plans.

But both men's eyes were fixed on my face. Fofo's face was solemn, pained, and the other face had a frozen smile that seemed to need my reaction to thaw into a full one. I didn't know where to look. My throat felt like sandpaper, and my lungs burned as if they had no air. The room seemed to shrink, and I dug my fingers into our mattress. I tried to smile to hide my feelings, but I didn't know whether my face cooperated or not.

"Yes, he would like to travel today," Yewa answered for me.

Fofo looked at her sharply. Big Guy broke into a full smile. I breathed again, my forehead moist with sweat.

"Your *fofo* like Gabon, *oui?*" Big Guy asked her, as if to score an added point against Fofo, having won the standoff.

She nodded. "Yes."

Big Guy began to tickle her, making her snicker as if she had water in her throat. He explained that we would soon begin

school in Port-Gentil. He said schools in Gabon were as beautiful as schools in France, that we would catch up with classes as
soon as we got there. Though he tried to be friendly, plying us
with sweets and rubbing our heads and dancing to entertain us,
there was something hollow about his performance that day. He
wasn't wearing his immigration uniform, but the stiffness I had
seen in him when he came with our godparents hung over him.
After a while, even Yewa didn't like his exaggerated excitement
anymore. Though she kept answering his questions, she did so
with single-word answers, as if she had intentionally struck a
compromise between Fofo's discomfort and Big Guy's need to fill
up his awkward visit with chatter.

Then Big Guy resorted to laughing a big laugh, as if the whole
world had suddenly become funny. Yewa only smiled at him,
without a sound. He laughed until his frame buckled over, and he
sat on the floor; he laughed until he began to sound unnatural.
He made funny faces and rolled his tongue to keep Yewa's interest. It was as if Big Guy was learning to be a clown, like Fofo,
while Fofo was learning to be serious, like Big Guy. It was a badly
acted play, and we sat there, a captive audience. Though he turned
on the boom box and Lagbaja's "Konko Below" battered the
room, Fofo lay there, unmoving, like a fallen statue.

After a while, Big Guy yawned and went to sit with Fofo
Kpee. Fofo sat up abruptly, as if he needed to protect himself. Big
Guy put his arm around his neck.

"Smiley, *mon ami,* you *dey* take tings too serious."

"I done make up my mind," Fofo said, his face tight like a
rock, his pinched lips like its eroded precipice. "*Efó!*"

"*Non, abeg,* no talk *comme ça o,*" Big Guy said. "I only *dey* joke yesterday. . . . I mean, if you no want work for our NGO anymore, it's OK. Be fair to yourself, *au moins*. We no reach point of no return yet, so you still fit change your mind. But, no rush your decision."

Fofo looked at him without saying anything for a while. "*Peut-être,* we should suspend de plan for now."

"You're bound to feel like dis at de beginning. *Moi aussi,* I no like de plan at de beginning. It be like say you *dey* exploit de young, but actually you *dey* help dem. Dem go get plenty chance abroad. Already, we *dey* give dem food tree times daily . . . clothes, shoes, books . . . are dese bad tings for dem?"

"Maybe."

"You no get *liva o* . . . coward, huh?"

"Show me person who no go fear?"

"*Mais pourquoi?* Why?" Big Guy patted him on the back. "*Abeg, courage, oui?*"

"*Hén,* what? Leave me alone. . . . I no want teach dem new lesson."

"Ah no *o.* We still get at-sea orientation for dem *o. Na* last lesson."

Big Guy looked up at the space between the walls and the roof and nodded, smiling as if he had just noticed the change. "I see, I see. You done change de place, huh. . . . Even de windows *dey* open."

"*Na* my place. *N'gan bayi onú de jlo mi.* Or you want make I suffocate my children for my house?"

"*Ecoute,* if I be you," Big Guy said, winking at us and pulling Fofo so close that they almost fell over, "I go just *dey* follow de plan and *dey* teach dese children. No dash deir hope for notting *o.*"

The bedsprings squeaked, and they regained their balance. Fofo smiled a sad smile but didn't answer him. "You just *dey* fear fear, Kpee." Big Guy stood up. "Make we go talk outside."

"Talk?"

"I get small matter I want tell you. Make we go."

"Impossible," Fofo said calmly, his elbows on his thighs, his fists together supporting his chin. "I go pay you back. I *dey* make some money wid Nanfang. Just gimme time, *na mi tán*."

"Dis ting no be about money but helping our children. We can even give you *plus argent*. Come outside. Remember, *na* you be our point man for dis area?"

"Take de Nanfang, *abeg*."

"No way," he said, and shrugged a big shrug. "Keep de machine. Dat *na* wicked ting. We no go take your daily bread. You go destroy yourself if you negotiate like dis."

Since he wouldn't leave Fofo in peace, our uncle followed him outside.

"No come out *o, mes amis*," Big Guy said to us in a voice that betrayed a grain of anxiety. "Remain inside." We nodded. He opened the door for Fofo and closed it behind him as if our house were his.

Once their footsteps waned, we rushed to the window and watched them through the worn blinds. They walked until they reached the road and stopped. Fofo was facing us. We couldn't hear them. The plantations and sea loomed behind the road, and sometimes it looked as if the plantations were on the sea or as if the people on the road were walking on water, like Jesus.

The two men argued loudly, raising their hands. Sometimes people who knew them startled them with greetings, and you could see them stop momentarily, flash empty smiles, then go back to business as if to make up for lost time. Fofo kept shaking his head, as if he were saying a big no to whatever his friend was saying. And each time I saw the *no* shape in his mouth, I felt like clapping for him. It became very predictable, and naturally I started shaking my head too, and my mouth formed many silent *no*s. I held tight to the window frame. I was praying for Fofo to stand firm.

Then Big Guy seized Fofo by the shoulders and shook him until Fofo spun and broke free, staggered and regained his balance. He didn't move away from Big Guy but stood his ground.

"He's going to beat up Fofo Kpee," Yewa whispered. "Big Guy is mean. Is he a bully?"

"I don't know."

"Big Guy is a bad man." Her voice began to crack with emotion. "I won't dance with him anymore. And he won't follow us to Gabon! I'll report him to Mama and Papa."

"Shhh, don't cry now, OK? Fofo is strong."

Suddenly, four police officers showed up and surrounded Fofo; they came in twos from either direction, as if they had expected Fofo to try to escape. They wielded *koboko* whips, and their waists bulged with pistols and batons. All of them were screaming at Fofo, with Big Guy getting more and more manic. Fofo Kpee's mouth was shut, and he stood very still, like a man in the presence of unfriendly dogs. After watching the scene for a while, I knew that Big Guy was determined to get Fofo to agree with him. But Fofo folded his hands in front of him and shook his head periodically, very slowly. Whenever they looked in our direction, I ducked and dunked Yewa's head under the window too.

It was quite a scene, because in all of Fofo's years of being a tout, the police had never visited our place or harassed him for duping people. Yewa held my hand tightly. We didn't know whether to lock ourselves inside or to run out toward the pool of bystanders that had gathered around and blocked our view.

The police tried to disperse the bystanders, but the people simply gave them a wide berth and kept watching. At the end Big Guy stormed away as abruptly as he had arrived, and the police went in different directions, their sudden departure startling the onlookers. Fofo stood there smiling at everybody as if the whole thing were a joke. We couldn't hear what he was telling them, but from the way he was gesticulating and their periodic laughter, it was clear that his humor had returned. It was a relief; he was once again the *fofo* we knew. In a little while, the crowd lost interest and disappeared into the evening, leaving him there by the road, looking out at the sea and waving to people who waved to him.

Yewa broke free from my grasp, opened the door, and ran toward him, stumbling and shouting, "Fofo, Fofo!" He turned suddenly on hearing her and opened his mouth, but before he could speak Yewa came to a complete stop. With one sharp hand gesture, he sent her back to the house. She walked in sobbing while Fofo Kpee continued to look at the sea and the road.

When he finally turned and walked toward home, his strides were weak, his face down, his hands behind him as if in handcuffs. He walked slowly, as if he didn't quite want to reach home. It must have been more difficult to come back to us that evening than it had been dealing with Big Guy and the police. He walked like a student who had committed a big offense and was afraid of being expelled.

That night he told us we should no longer go to school. It didn't seem like a good time to ask questions, so we hushed.

FOFO KPEE NEVER MENTIONED Big Guy or Gabon in our presence again. And since Gabon had become the talk of our family and our impending departure the collective dream, its absence from our conversation created a vacuum in our lives. Fofo brooded and didn't go to work. He didn't say much to us. He seemed to be struggling even to get out of bed. He was no longer drinking. He read the Bible nonstop and prayed a lot—alone, never inviting us to join him as in the old days. His pride in his Nanfang dissipated, and he no longer washed it daily, nor tooted the horn nonstop nor rode it to church. Even his manner of dress became something else. He stopped wearing his jackets and beautiful shoes and went back to his flip-flops and rugged jeans, his pre-Nanfang clothes, whenever he left the house.

All our stuff in the inner room meant nothing to him now. In fact, it seemed he couldn't bear going in there at all. He covered the bike completely, like we did the day we cemented the inner room. Even Yewa knew better than to talk about or play with the Nanfang. In those empty days, we expected Fofo to finish removing the mortar in the parlor to let in more air and to begin working in the other room. But he never did. And, though Fofo gazed at it nonstop when he lay on his bed, it was as if he lacked the willpower or interest to carry through with the project. Instead, he put all his energy into watching us and warning us not to follow or talk to anybody without his permission.

"Be careful," he said to us the second day after Big Guy's visit, "bad people *dey* mess wid oder people children!" It was the longest sentence we had heard from him since Big Guy roughed him up. I swallowed my reaction, because I didn't want him to know what I was thinking.

He bought a machete and put it under his bed, where he could reach it in an instant. He carried a dagger in his pocket, even when we went to church. If we went outside to play, he came and sat on the mound, watching us without blinking, like a statue. Many times daily he walked around the compound, checking this and that, like a security man. If we went to the outhouse, we came out and saw him waiting, like the people who run commercial toilets in Ojota. If we wasted time, he came and knocked and asked whether we had fallen into the pit latrine. If he went out, he locked us up.

Seeing that he was ready to defend us by all means, I abandoned my plan to escape. I sensed he wasn't going to let any harm come to us. When we walked to church, he held our hands, and when people asked him about the bike he said it was sick. We entered the church with the humility of our pre-Nanfang days. One Sunday, Fofo gave some money to Pastor Adeyemi to say a special prayer for him. When the man pressed him for details of his predicament, he said he had a little family problem.

THAT AFTERNOON, WHILE YEWA was asleep, Fofo Kpee stood staring out of the window. "We must escape, Kotchikpa," he whispered.

"Yes, Fofo!" I said, leaving my bed, moving toward him. I knew he was serious because he used my native name. Shocked by my response, he turned sharply from the window and came and sat on the edge of the table, facing me. I was bursting with excitement.

He wrung his hands, searching for words like a penitent: "I know say you want go dis Gabon well well . . ."

"I don't want to go, Fofo, I do not!"

"Sofly, sofly," he calmed me, batting down the air with both hands and then holding my hands like a supplicant. A nervous smile crossed his sad face. "Ah, we no want wake her. . . . I no fit sell you and Yewa to anybody, like de slaves of de Badagry slave-trade tales. *Iro o,* I no fit allow dem ship you across dis ocean to Gabon. If you reach dat central African country, *c'est fini.* You no go smell dis West Africa soil again. . . . When Big Guy visit us last, I tell him say I no gree again. Riches no be everyting — I no want lose you. *Mais,* he *dey* very angry."

"Just one question . . ."

"Yes?"

"Do our godparents know what Big Guy is doing to us?"

"Yes . . . *complétement.*"

He let go of my hands and looked away again, embarrassed. His answer managed to hit me hard, when it shouldn't have. Since that night when I lost interest in Gabon, I had directed my anger toward Fofo and Big Guy only. And, though the pieces of the puzzle were coming together, I had refused to accept that the man and woman who were so nice to us and gave us an unforgettable buffet were bad people. But now, the shame in Fofo's eyes squashed my doubts. I was angry with them.

"Can we run away now?" I asked.

"No . . . in de dark. *Egbé.*"

"Tonight?" I looked around, elated.

"Braffe . . . *din*. Gabon trip *na* one week from today. We go abandon everyting. No tell your sister anyting, *d'accord?* She no go understand."

"Yes, yes."

"I done tell de people who know us say we *dey* relocate to Braffe."

THAT EVENING, I WAS so anxious to leave and so disgusted by my surroundings that I couldn't eat or even drink water. I saw my godparents in everything around me and heard their murmurings in the wind and distant voices. I looked out of the window often and wished I could blow out the sun like a candle or turn the world upside down so that the waters of our ocean could drown it. I begged God to send us the darkest of nights.

Unfortunately, when night came, it brought a miserly, disappointing darkness. Fofo emptied our water vats and threw away our soups. I woke up my sister and dressed her, though she was still half asleep. All of us wore our everyday clothes. Apart from our books, which Fofo stuffed into his bag and strung on the handlebars of the Nanfang, we didn't take much. From the bulges in Fofo's back pockets and shirt pockets, I believed he had taken all the money we had.

The stars were out, and a full moon hung low and bright, shining through a spray of dirty clouds. It was so bright that the mango tree and the bushes grew blurry shadows around them, and we could see as far as the sea, the coconut trees looking like an endless sheer dress. When Fofo rolled the Nanfang outside, the moon cast a dull shine on the gas tank. Though I had come to hate all our Gabon riches, that night I hoped that bike would take us to safety.

There was a lot of wind. It hurled the hoots of an owl against the night, an unmistakable refrain amid a cacophony of insects and the sough of coconut foliage. Suddenly the wind choked and broke off, the trees, which had been pushed in one direction, jerking back past their normal postures. A coconut trunk snapped and crashed, and the night creatures hushed for a while.

Fofo locked the door with a chain and a big padlock. He didn't allow Yewa to sit in her usual place, on the tank, since she wasn't fully awake. Instead she was sandwiched between us. I guided my sister's feet with mine so they would stay on the footrests. There wasn't much room. Fofo didn't rev the bike as he normally did. Like the escapees from Sodom and Gomorrah, I didn't look back but straight ahead. Our headlight was dim, and we traveled very slowly because of all the potholes. The soft whir of the Nanfang broke up the silent night, steady and consoling. Fofo knew the road well, since he used it every day, and went from one side to the other, effortlessly avoiding the potholes. The road took us away from the ocean, toward the cluster of homes nearest our place. The houses looked deserted in the moonlight, and in front of them, the long empty tables and stalls where villagers sold their wares during the day looked like the skeletons of prehistoric animals.

After a while, I glanced back and saw two bright dots of light behind us. They were very far away and seemed to be moving all over the road, as if two children were playing with flashlights. Fofo looked into the side mirror, then back, and the bike wobbled. When he steadied the Nanfang, he sped up a bit.

"Let's go fast," said my sister, who was now wide-awake.

"Road no good," Fofo said. "You get eyes? *Soit patient* till we reach Cotonou-Ouidah Road."

"Where are we going?" my sister said.

"Home," I said.

"Braffe?" she said, giggling. She tried to see my face but couldn't, because our sitting arrangement was tight.

We rode through a small town. Some shops were still open and solitary silhouettes of people darted here and there. There was a smell of burned flesh in the air. At the far end of the town, a bonfire blazed by the roadside, lacerating the moonlight's beauty. On reaching it, I noticed that the flames were billowing from a pile of tires in front of an eatery. Three goats or sheep were being roasted over the flames, and two men, all muscles and sweat, clad only in underwear, stoked and turned the animals with long stakes.

"Pascal, did you bring my things?" Yewa shouted to be heard. "I want to show my books to our parents and grandparents. . . ."

"Your books *dey* here," shouted Fofo, tapping on the bag. "I go buy you new dress for Braffe."

"You will?"

"*Mówe,* yes."

I looked back again. The two lights were closer, and from the way the beams jumped up and down, it became clear that those riders didn't care about the bad road. Though Fofo tried to speed up, they kept gaining on us.

Now, they split up, one to either side. I became afraid and pressed closer to my sister. I looked back often, and each time my sight was gouged by the lights. My stomach swelled with the urge to pee. The thought of many Big Guys coming after us over-whelmed me.

Fofo didn't stop or say anything. The bike on the right was now running neck and neck with us. Fofo sped up, but the other rider was more aggressive. He tried to overtake us and cut in front us, but Fofo dodged to the left. The bike on the other side almost hit our number plate and was forced to slow down. Each rider had one passenger.

One bike passed us and forced Fofo off the smooth track of the bad road, and now we were heaving into one pothole after another.

"Stop, quick quick . . . *arretez*," the passenger said.

We slowed down.

"*D'accord,* I *dey* stop," Fofo said, putting one foot on the ground and rolling to the edge of the road; he kept the engine idling. "*Abeg,* no harm us," he pleaded.

"Shame on you!" the passenger yelled from across the road, getting off the bike, slowly and confidently, while the rider sat there with the engine running. "Why you *dey* run?" the passenger snarled, then pulled a cell phone from his pocket and started assuring the person at the other end that things were under control. Then he said to Fofo, "You no know say we *dey* watch you? You no know you done reach point of no return for dis deal?"

"I *dey* sorry," Fofo said.

"Sorry? Turn off your lights, stupid man!" someone on the other bike commanded him, and Fofo obeyed. I turned quickly because I thought the voice sounded familiar, but I couldn't see his face.

This straight stretch of road was canyoned by tall lush bushes, an outcrop of jungle on the seacoast. The bushes on the left blocked the light of the moon and cast a gloomy shadow on the lower reaches of the road's right side, while above all was bathed in moonlight.

Fofo whispered to us, "No come down, you hear?"

"Yes," we whispered back.

"Hold de machine well well."

It was as if the people on the other two bikes were so desperate to manhandle us that they forgot to ride up to where we were. Instead they jumped off their machines and bounded toward us. My eyes still smarted from the headlights as the giant silhouettes hurtled in our direction. Suddenly, Fofo kicked his Nanfang into gear, and we took off. I felt someone's eager hand on my back and ducked before he could grab my shirt. Fofo hit his high beam and accelerated.

They were right behind us. The gap between us was as narrow as the space between our beds back home. I resented the fact that my back was their closest target and kept pressing into my sister and holding tighter to the machine. I stiffened my body; the gusts of wind lapping my clothes felt like hundreds of fingers trying to grab me. Yet my back was getting warm, as if their headlights would roast me.

We pulled away from them, Fofo crouching a bit, his head pushed forward like that of a dog in flight. And, since our bike was still new, whenever it hit a pothole, the impact was like the muffled sound of two cymbals clashing. My sister had her right cheek pressed firmly against Fofo's back as if to listen to his heart. I leaned forward beyond Yewa and tied my hands around Fofo's stomach so we wouldn't fall off, even if the bike got into the deepest pothole or jumped the highest bump.

"Hold tight!" Fofo shouted, his voice shredded by the wind, just before the Nanfang hit a big pothole. The machine went up, then landed hard and heaved, but we hung on. "You *dey* OK?" Fofo said.

"Yes," I said, though my right foot had just lost its flip-flop.

I repositioned myself and my sister. My bare foot felt better on the rest; it had more grip. My fingers were sweaty, so I retied my hands around Fofo's stomach and put my chin on Yewa's head. It felt better to have the glare of the headlights a bit farther from my back. But when I tried to discard the other flip-flop, I lost my footing. My left leg dangled, and I fought to regain my balance but couldn't. The effort pulled the bike to one side. Fofo threw his body the other way to compensate and held it there momentarily.

"We're falling!" Yewa said, like in a dream.

My fingers slipped from Fofo's, and I was now holding on to my sister and bleating like a ram. Once my knee touched the ground, the machine crashed.

When I came to, I had a headache and was lying facedown, my body on the road, my head in the grass. My knee was bleeding, but the cut wasn't deep. Yewa stood in the shrubs screaming and fighting off a man who held her wrists in one hand. The other three descended on Fofo with sticks. The blows rained on him until he fell, his hands wrapped around his head, which was almost in between his legs. He writhed and took the beating without a sound, except for an occasional groan. Yewa and I did the crying.

I was the last to be rounded up; a man grabbed my hands and cuffed them behind me with huge rough hands. I didn't resist, hoping that they wouldn't kill Fofo.

"If you shout again, we go kill dis *magomago* man!" one of the men warned us.

"Please, don't kill him," I said, sobbing.

"You children thought you could skip school without telling anybody," the familiar voice said behind me.

It was Monsieur Abraham, our games master. I turned and looked him straight in the face. In the moonlight, he was smiling, his white teeth gleaming. He wore a T-shirt and a track suit, as if he were coaching us in soccer.

Disappointment filled my heart. I remembered the glucose he used to give us those first days when we couldn't sleep well at night and got to school tired. I felt stupid for being duped and falling into such a well-orchestrated plot.

"Please, *monsieur,* don't kill him," I begged Monsieur Abraham, as Yewa continued to wail. "We won't run again."

"Really?" he said.

"We shall go to Gabon, I promise."

"Of course."

"*Monsieur,* we'll do anything you want in Gabon."

"Maybe you begin by telling this princess to shut up."

"Yewa, they won't kill him," I explained, and freed one hand to place on her mouth. But she wasn't looking at me. Her sight was trained on Fofo. "He's not dead," I said. "He'll be OK."

As I spoke to my sister, Fofo Kpee tried to get up but fell. They didn't allow us near him. His face was bloody and one eye was swollen. His clothes were torn, his pockets empty, cefa and naira notes scattered everywhere, like donations littering an important shrine. One man was fidgeting with his phone, and when he couldn't make a call he cussed his network.

The men started preparing to leave, picking up the money and turning the bikes around, in the direction we had come from. Two men bundled Fofo atop one bike, and Yewa and I were sandwiched between two men on the other. We began the journey back to the house from which we thought we had escaped.

WHEN WE GOT HOME it was still dark. Monsieur Abraham collected the keys from Fofo's neck and opened the door and shoved us inside. They threw Fofo on the floor.

"You're never permitted to speak to the children again!" our games master said, as Fofo writhed and twisted, unable to get up. They didn't let us touch him, so we sat on our bed like orphans at a parent's wake while two men searched the inner room with flashlights and another searched around outside the house. We couldn't see Fofo well, so we listened eagerly for his heavy breathing.

When they had finished the search and reorganized the inner room to their liking, they moved our bed and carton of clothes there.

"Get in there!" Monsieur Abraham said, not looking us in the eye. "You'll stay there till further notice. One of us shall stay here to make sure no one tries to run away again."

"Yes, *monsieur*," I said. "We won't disappoint you again."

"Fofo Kpee, Fofo Kpee," my sister cried, and pointed at the body on the floor as I dragged her into the room.

"Little one," the teacher said, "if you behave well, he'll be OK."

"Please, tell Big Guy we are sorry," I said. "Tell Monsieur and Madame Ahouagnivo we are sorry."

"I think they'd be happy to know that," he said. "It's not nice to betray friends. Not nice."

He locked us in the inner room. It was darker than we thought. We were restless and disoriented because they had moved things around. I felt like I was going to bump into something. With one hand I held on to Yewa's dress to keep track of her; I used the other to shield my wounded knee. We stayed near the door, trying to hear Fofo. Now, the bikes outside revved up and departed, their noise momentarily drowning out Fofo's breathing.

We heard the front door close and footsteps approach the door to our room. We backed away, stumbling over things, and I lost Yewa in the darkness. I reached the wall and squatted, then lay atop the pile of cement bags, hoping to blend in. There was a jangle of keys. When the door opened, our room brightened, and fresh air came in.

A man's profile filled the doorway as if trying to deny us the little light we were getting now. A giant of a man, he didn't attempt to enter the room. From the position of his hands, I could see he was carrying things. Uncertain what he might do to us, I peered around, trying to find my sister.

"Where you *dey?*" he called out, his voice full of menace. I said nothing. "No joke wid me *o*. I warn you."

"I am h-here," I stammered, getting up and standing with the bed between me and him.

"Come, take dis," he said. "Where you *dey?*"

"I'm sorry, I'm here."

"You must cooperate, *d'accord?*"

I inched around the bed, feeling my way toward him, craning to see Fofo, to no avail.

"*Mangez* . . . your food," he said, and pushed something warm and heavy against me.

"Thanks," I said, grabbing two plastic containers.

"You must finish everyting we give you. . . ."

"Yes, *monsieur.* We will."

"*Bon garçon,*" he said, lightening up at my false enthusiasm. "If you behave well, I go *dey* nice to you. If not, you go see for your-self. I no be bad man. Also, me I be fader; I get my own children. I no want sell anoder man children. I just *dey* do my work *o.*"

The food inside the containers was warm, and the lids were so tight that I couldn't smell what it was. I put them on the bed and then turned to the big man.

"What of Fofo?" I said.

"I done bring am food too."

"We can feed him, please. He's very sick."

"Impossible, no, just forget *am* for now. . . . And dis *na* your toilet." He pushed something else against me. "*Faites attention.* Some water *dey* inside."

"God bless you, *monsieur!*" I said, and collected it from him. It was a big plastic pail filled quarter way with water. There was a stack of old newspapers on the lid.

"Use it well *o,*" he laughed. "And make you put the paper in de pail. I go come get dem tomorrow."

"Yes, *monsieur.*"

"Everyting go *dey* fine. I like de way you *dey* behave, old boy. I no care wheder dem sell you or not. As I talk before, I just *dey* do my job."

"Thank you, *monsieur.*"

"You no fear anyting. You get courage *pass* your *fofo.* If you behave well, I go treat you well, you know. . . . Where your sister?"

"Yewa," I called out, and looked around the darkness. "Maybe she's asleep," I lied.

"Already? Yewa!" he called out, his voice filling the room like a trumpet. "Where you *dey?*"

Silence.

"I told you she's asleep," I said. "She's tired."

"Well, make sure she eat later," he said lightheartedly. "I go see you dis evening. Trust me, your *fofo* go *dey* fine."

He turned and walked out of the room, closing and locking the door from the parlor. A bit of my fear went away with him. I listened to his footsteps, then heard the bed creak as it received his body.

Though our situation had gone from bad to worse in the course of one night, I found some solace in the fact that I could make him believe I liked him. I would thank him for any little kindness toward us, I thought. I felt I had a bit of control over how things might turn out. Maybe if we behaved really well, the man would allow us into the parlor to see Fofo. Maybe he would even open the windows or at least leave the door open. My imagination began to run wild with the good things that might happen if we behaved well. I wasn't thinking of going to Braffe anymore. My desire now was to please this man, and that Fofo would get well.

I WISHED YEWA WOULD give up her pranks and come out when the man left the room. But I didn't hear her move. I whispered her name into the darkness, but there was no response. I stood there and turned slowly in a full circle, but I couldn't see a thing. I didn't know how to begin looking for her without stumbling.

I started feeling for everything in the small room with my feet and hands. My knees came to rest on the mortar in the corner, and I extended my arms and brought them slowly together, hoping to catch Yewa but hugging myself instead, because she wasn't there. I turned to head toward the next corner, but my thigh hit a pot, which toppled over. I tried to catch it, wedging it with my hip, gritting my teeth, relieved that it didn't crash to the floor. Though I couldn't see, I knew immediately that my hands and body were full of soot. I found a spot on the floor for the pot and gently set it down, bottom up, so that we wouldn't accidentally step in it. "Yewa, Yewa," I whispered, but again no answer. I went toward the cement bags where I had lain before, but she wasn't there.

Desperate, I stopped and sat on the bed, wanting to scream her name to the heavens. I took the food containers and placed them at the foot of the bed. The thing farthest from my mind at that point was food. I lay in a fetal position and buried my head in a pillow. I was beginning to lose my sense of time.

I couldn't lie still and heard only Fofo's groans. Then I began to hear someone walking quietly around our house. I sat up and listened. The footsteps were too light to be those of our guard. I also knew it wasn't my sister because I didn't think she could have gotten out. I began to suspect that we had more than one guard. But the outside didn't hold my interest for long. It occurred to me that I hadn't searched under the bed.

I stood up slowly and tiptoed toward the parlor door. Hoping to surprise her, I turned around, lay on the ground, stretched out to my full length, and rolled under the bed, risking my wounded knee, so as not to give her any chance to dodge my contact. I slid out the other side and came to rest against the stack of second-hand roofing sheets. As I got up, a beacon of hope rose in my heart because I realized Yewa might be resting on top of those sheets. Carefully, to avoid cutting my hands on the sharp edges where nails had been pulled, I worked the surface with my fingers. I found only our cutlery basket, the work tools that Fofo and I had used to cement the rooms, and our carton of clothes.

Disappointed, I went to lean on the door, where I had been with her last, before we scrambled for safety. I imagined my sister's eyes everywhere and longed for her to laugh or tease me. It was the first time in my life I didn't know where Yewa was, and I felt lost without her. My preoccupation with Fofo's well-being disappeared because at least he was breathing. Tears ran down my face, and I wished to hell for a ray of light in that darkness.

"Yewa! Yewa!" I finally shouted, and stamped my feet.

"Yes, yes," she said in a strange fearful voice.

"*Wetin dey* happen for dere?" the guard said from the other room.

"Ah, nothing, *monsieur,*" I said, relieved to hear my sister's voice, and then turned my attention to her: "Where are you?"

I moved away from the door toward the right corner but kicked a plastic crate and stopped. The joy of hearing Yewa's voice helped me ignore the pain.

"Notting?" the guard said. "You *dey* talk to me?"

"No, I meant Yewa," I said, and forced a giggle.

"Just make sure you no wound yourself *o*. . . . I want sleep; *n' jlo na gbòjé.*"

"We're sorry to disturb you, *monsieur.*"

I climbed over the crate and closed in on the corner, listening intently. When I reached our plastic water vat, which was as high as my chest and wider than my arms were long, I thought she was standing on top of the lid, leaning against the wall. So I tapped the side of the vat and whispered, "Just come down, please."

But the lid sprang open, and I caught it before it made a sound. She had been hiding inside the vat all along. "I'm here," she whispered, standing up.

"Just come out, OK?"

I tried to pull her out, but she pushed my hands away. "Leave me alone. You are with them."

"Me?"

"Yes, yes."

"No, I'm not."

"You are."

"Shh!"

"Don't lie to me. You were laughing with him right now . . . you like them. You and Fofo Kpee didn't tell me you were going to sell me. You're no longer my brother."

"Come out first, please," I said, and turned around, offering her my back and leaning into the vat. "Climb on. I'll explain later. You have to come out so he sees us when he opens the door. Otherwise . . ."

"I don't want to see anybody."

I stepped back a bit and kept quiet, partly because I didn't know what to say anymore and partly because I was afraid of waking the guard. Dealing with my sister in such darkness was like arguing or fighting with a faceless enemy who could strike at any time. I would have given anything to see her face. Maybe my tears would have convinced her of my innocence. Now her defiance came out in her agitated breathing.

"They'll kill Fofo if you don't cooperate," I resumed.

"They won't. He's one of them, like you. Leave me alone."

"Won't you eat something?"

"Never."

I couldn't persuade her, so I resorted to force. But she ducked down, squatting in the vat, locking her knees and elbows and raising her shoulders to her ears so I had no place to hold. I reached in to tickle her to soften her up, then I heard her mouth open with a crack. Her teeth hit my wrist, unable to bite. She started giggling, a rubbery sonority muffled by her body. It was as if she was mocking me or perhaps mocking all child traffickers of this world. I left my sister and went to lie on the bed, falling asleep.

WHEN I WOKE UP, I had a headache and was very hungry. Yawning and stretching, I was surprised to find Yewa snoring beside me. Fofo Kpee's groan had mellowed. My knee hurt and felt swollen.

I found my way to the toilet pail and urinated, hitting the sides to muffle the sound. Then I picked up a food container and started to eat, stuffing myself with my hands. It was to be a breakfast of *akara,* bean cake, and *ogi,* pap. The balls of *akara* that sat atop the *ogi* were cold and soggy in parts. I sensed that water had condensed in the container. I was thirsty, so I raised it to my mouth and turned it gently until water droplets trickled onto my tongue. I chewed the *akara* quickly, the cold fried oil clogging the inside of my mouth. When I came to the last ball, I noticed there was a small plastic bag in the container. I untied it and found four sugar cubes, which I figured were for the *ogi*. But the *ogi* had caked over, and there was no way I could mix the sugar into it. So I tossed one of the cubes into my mouth and chewed noisily, then began to eat chunks of *ogi*.

When I finished, my headache was gone. But I wasn't satisfied, and my mouth was parched. I was tempted to take some of Yewa's portion, but as I put down my empty container, I discovered other containers. My heart jumped. There were two more containers of food and two bottles of water. I knew immediately that the guard had come into the room while we were sleeping. I drank quickly, holding up the bottle so the water gurgled into my mouth.

"Who *dey* drink water like dat?" the guard said from the parlor. "You want choke? Is dat you, boy?"

I paused and said, "Yes, *monsieur*."

"Why you ask your sister to sleep for water container?"

"I didn't put her there."

"Who put her dere? No mess wid me *o!*"

"I swear I did not put her there."

"*Ecoutez,* tomorrow morning, we want take your *fofo* go hospital. He get high fever. And make you warn dat gal say make she no sleep for dat container again. We no want anoder high fever patient *o.* . . . How come you no eat your breakfast? Dis night you get notting."

"I have eaten it. . . . The food is nice. Thanks."

"Just finish your breakfast and lunch. And make sure your sister follow eat. Oderwise, I go come put de fear of Gabon into her."

"Yes, *monsieur.*"

It dawned on me that it was night and that it was the guard who brought Yewa to our bed. In one gulp, I finished off the bottle of water, then I sorted out the food and shook her awake.

She climbed out of bed and disappeared into the darkness, stumbled and fell down hard. Her scream shredded the silence. It seemed like a flash of light because it let me know precisely where she was. The guard came in, quick and furious, sweeping the room with his huge flashlight. Yewa lost her voice and tried to run back to me for refuge, but the man seized her by her dress.

"*Qu'est-ce que c'est?*" he asked, dragging her toward the bed. "Sit and *tait-toi! Comprends?* Shut up."

"Yes, *monsieur,*" Yewa said, sitting down.

"Eat de food *din din!*" he commanded her.

The light was close to Yewa's face. She shut her eyes and shielded her head, as if she expected to be hit. There was a dash of dried blood on her elbow, I guessed because of the crash.

"I say *manger* . . . begin," the man shouted.

"Yewa, please, eat," I said, opening up the lunch of spaghetti and stew for her.

"No feed her *o!*" the man warned me, and turned to her: "Did your broder tell you no sleep for dat container, huh?" My sister nodded yes. "*Respond-moi!*"

"I'm sorry."

"*Ajuka vi,* you want sleep for container, you no want *chop* food, I go kill you today."

"Please, no kill her," Fofo said suddenly from the parlor, his voice weak and his speech slurred. My heart skipped on hearing Fofo's voice.

"Silence, silence, *yeye* man!" the guard scolded him. "Never talk to dem . . . *jamais*."

Yewa was shaken and ate her food hurriedly between sobs. She ate with both hands and slurped and sucked the dripping stew. She didn't pause to chew but swallowed as soon as she could. The lower part of her face was gleaming with oil, and the front of her dress was soiled. The man, looking satisfied, nodded and left the room.

While Yewa ate, I used some of the water from her bottle to wash off the blood from her elbow and wiped it with the bed-sheet. When she finished the food, she asked for more. I handed her my container of spaghetti and stew, and she ate without slowing down. Afraid the food would choke her, I told her to take it easy, to no avail. I couldn't tell whether she was afraid the guard might be watching her, or whether his tyranny had awakened in her an insatiable hunger.

Immediately after she finished, she said she needed to use the toilet. I guided her to the pail, and soon the stink of her shit thickened the stuffiness in the room. When she finished, I tore a large piece of newspaper, crumpled it, and gave it to her to clean up with.

I offered her her portion of *akara* and *ogi,* but she said she was full, so I quickly ate it.

"*REVEILLEZ, REVEILLEZ!*" THE GUARD screamed into our ears the following morning. "You too *dey* sleep."

I blocked the glare of the flashlight with my hands and stood up. He told us Fofo had been hospitalized and then put the jug of water he was carrying on the floor. He set down the flashlight so its beam poured up into the roof in a wide V. He wore a native long-sleeve shirt, blue with bright red flowers. A hulk of a man, he was as tall as Big Guy but heavier. His hair was big and as black as our godfather's. His tight trousers accentuated his bulk because his thighs looked swollen, like those of local wrestlers. He moved away from the light and came toward our bed to lean on the roofing sheets.

Lit, the room looked much smaller than I remembered, and the silver padlocks on the windows and door gleamed.

"You container rat, *núdùdú lọ yón na wé ya?*" he taunted Yewa.

"Yes, I like the food," she said.

"*Wetin* be your Gabon name?"

"Me?" my sister said, and looked at me as if for direction.

"Mary," I said. "I am Pascal, she's Mary."

"*E yón.* You be good children. I no promise I go *dey* nice to you if you behave well well?"

"You did," I said.

By now he was sweating profusely. He started unbuttoning his beautiful shirt and blew twice at his chest and kept wiping his brow with his hands. I thought he was going to drink the water he had brought, to cool himself. But he didn't touch the jug. Instead he stood up and moved around the room like a teacher pacing in front of his class. I exchanged glances with my sister and braced for another orientation session.

My eyes, already used to the extremes of total darkness and

bright flashes of light, hovered over the flowers on his shirt like butterflies dancing around bougainvilleas. In the dark part of the room, where he moved, the flowers on his shirt weren't as bright, and I wished he would walk back into the light.

"Fofo and Big Guy give you lessons?" he said, turning around.

"Yes, *monsieur,*" we said.

"*D'accord,* Mary, how many *fofos et tantines Gabonaises as tu?*"

"I have three uncles and two aunties," she said.

"Names?"

"Vincent, Marcus, and Pierre, and Cecile and Michelle."

"Good, good gal . . . Pascal, talk about your grandfader, *din din.*"

"My grandpa Matthew died two years ago," I said. "Auntie Cecile cried for two days. Grandma Martha refused to talk to anyone. . . ."

"Excellent, boy, excellent," he said. "Now I go teach you *nouvelles leçons?*"

He paused and looked expectantly at us.

"Yes, *monsieur,*" we said.

"We *dey* almost ready for de *voyage,*" he said, "and Fofo done prepare you well well. *Pour example,* I *dey* sweat like hell here, but you done adjust to de heat finish. *Na* only God know why your *yeye* uncle come fear and want abscond." He brought out a piece of paper from his pocket and studied the content carefully and said, "No *wahala* . . . *repetez après moi:* 'We were rescued from the water by a caring crew. . . .'"

"We were rescued from the water by a caring crew," we said.

" 'We were more than these, but some are dead.' "

"We were more than these, but some are dead."

" 'We were tossed into the sea, and many of us died.' "

"We were tossed into the sea, and many of us died."

" 'We had been at sea for three days before the sailors told us we were at risk.' "

"We had been at sea for three days before the sailors told us we were at risk."

" 'We were heading for Côte d'Ivoire before the mishap.' "

"We were heading for Côte d'Ivoire before the mishap."

Satisfied, he asked me to stand up and go get him two cups. I went over to the cutlery basket and pulled two out.

"Make we do someting interesting," he said. "Dis *na* just some water and salt. Don't be afraid. Ready?"

"Yes," we said.

He carefully poured the water from the jug into the cups. He took a sip from each cup and licked his lips with his tongue as if it were a tasty drink. He offered the cups to us and we drank the salty thing.

"At-sea Orientation be de name. . . . Dis in case drinking water come finish for vessel . . . at least you go survive for one day."

"Yes, *monsieur.*"

"Also in case dem *dey* toss you overboard . . ."

"Overboard?" I said, surprised.

"Just for short time . . . but maybe dem go give you life jacket or big plank which many of you go hold for inside water. We *dey* do dat sometimes if navy — bad-bad government people — come harass us for sea at night, OK? Dem *dey* tie de plank to ship, so no fear. Just to hide you for water while dem *dey* search our ship. You no go sink. . . . We no want risk anyting."

"It's good to be prepared," I said.

"For de few days we get here, you go take de salt water twice a day. I go bring de water wid de *manger et* fresh water, OK?"

"Yes, *monsieur.*"

He started to leave the room but stopped and said, "Ah, one more ting — new plan. In three days, we *dey* bring oder children to live here wid you. We go take everyting out of dis room. We need space. You go show dem how to be good children."

"Yes, *monsieur.*"

"Any question? *Ou bien, wetin* you need?"

Yewa and I exchanged glances.

"Please, do you know Antoinette and Paul?" I said. "Are they coming to stay with us?"

"Are dese de children Fofo promised Big Guy?" he said excitedly, searching our faces. "Tell me de trud."

"No," I said, happy that our uncle changed his mind before he brought my other siblings into this evil plot.

"So who be dese?" he said.

"Big Guy knows them," Yewa said. "Mama and Papa brought them to our place a long time ago."

The man sighed, and his body settled into the ease of disappointment. "Well, if Big Guy know dem, trust me, dem done reach Gabon *déjà*. . . . No, you no know dis group *qui arrive ici* . . . but *ils sont des bon* kids . . . eager to travel."

"So when are we traveling?" I asked.

"Immediately de children arrive. Dis *na* your batch."

"What about Fofo Kpee?" my sister asked.

"Fofo Kpee?" the man said ruefully, as if he didn't know whom we were talking about. "What about him?"

"We will see him before we go?" I said.

"Ah, I go tell you about Fofo tomorrow," he said, and quickly switched off his flashlight before I could see his face. He left the room.

Late into that night, I didn't sleep. Everything was quiet outside. I kept thinking about what the guard would tell us the following day. I wanted to know how Fofo was doing in the hospital, and, if he was feeling bad about our trip, to tell him it was OK. It was clear to me now that he had sealed the inner room to house children until they could be shipped to Gabon. I remembered how Big Guy looked at our house when they brought the Nanfang and said it was OK for the meantime. Now I understood that Fofo and Big Guy were planning to build some bigger depot with the roofing sheets and cement.

I woke up with a start that night to the sound of a bike riding into our compound. Another one rode in and stopped, and there were brisk footsteps that got louder as they came around the house, toward the back. Slowly I stood up and looked into the darkness, then went and put my ear to the window. My breath quickened as I imagined them surrounding the house. I thought they were going to ship us to Gabon that night, and I resigned myself to my fate.

When they went past the window, I stole across the room to the back door. They went to work immediately. I heard thuds hitting the ground; I suspected they were digging. The rhythm was uneven and faster than what one man could have managed alone, so I guessed there were at least two diggers. They worked fast and hard in silence. Their tools sometimes crashed into hard objects. It sounded like they were digging beyond where we normally cooked outside, beside the bath-room. The spray of sand hitting the grass and leaves was unmis-takable.

"Deep enough?" someone said after a while.

"Too shallow," Big Guy said. "Bring your spade; continue."

I bit my lip when I recognized his voice, knowing we were in for it. I didn't want to meet him again in this life, but there he was, so close to me. It was as if he were already in the room with me, hiding under the bed or the sheets, waiting for the right time to hurt us. I could only think of the last time Big Guy came into our house, when Fofo told him the Gabon deal was dead.

"*MAIS,* YOU NO WANT pay us?" said the first speaker, and some-one stopped working. I knew because now I heard just one spade hitting the ground and spraying the sand in a neat, measured fall.

"Finish first," Big Guy said.

"I done tire," the man whined again.

I pressed my ear harder into the back door until it hurt.

"Tire? You kidding," Big Guy said.

"I *dey* go *o!* I no want work for you anymore."

"No, no, here *na* safe place."

"Dis no be de plan before," the man bargained with Big Guy. "We gree say we go dig one — not two — remember?"

"We had to abandon de oder place and run. No be *ma faute.* I no know people go surprise us for dat hour on dat road. . . . I go pay well."

"*Combien?* How much?"

"Hey, no shout," Big Guy said, laughing. "People *dey* sleep in dis house."

"Oh yeah?" the other man said, and stopped digging too. "If dem catch us *nko?* You no tell us de risk big like dis *o.*"

"Oh, just children," Big Guy assured them. "Dem *dey* sleep."

"I say I no want work again," said the first.

"We must finish before daybreak. . . . *D'accord,* how much you want?"

He managed another short laugh, that short soothing laugh that told you everything was all right when it wasn't. I remembered him laughing that way when Fofo introduced him to the party crowd after the Nanfang Thanksgiving. I could imagine his sinister eyes now, cool and quick in the dark, as he tried to renegotiate with these men.

"*Plus argent,*" one of the men said.

"More money?" Big Guy replied. "You go accept a used Nan-fang?"

"You want give us a Nanfang?" the man said, his voice rising in excitement.

"Excellent!" the other man said, tapping on the metal of his tool, as if to honor the moment.

"*La* Nanfang, *c'est* very very decent," Big Guy said softly, as the diggers got back to work, tearing the earth apart with gusto. "But if you tell anyone, I go kill you."

"We understand," one digger said. "How deep you want dis?"

"Deep enough to bury Smiley Kpee *complétement,*" Big Guy said.

My heart skipped a beat. I became weak and dropped to my knees. The stuffy air now felt like fumes in my nostrils. I tried to stand up, but my legs wouldn't support me. I sat down, my back against the door, my knees hoisted up to support my bowed head, my arms wrapped around my shins. I closed my eyes, clenched my fists, and pressed my mouth against my knees to keep from wailing. I stiffened my toes and wanted to be numb. I held my breath until I became dizzy and couldn't do it anymore.

My mind started racing: did he die in the hospital, or did they kill him? Even if he died in the hospital, I thought, they still killed him, because if they hadn't beaten him he'd be alive. I felt betrayed now because I had promised them that my sister and I would go to Gabon anyway, to protect Fofo. What would I tell my grandparents back home? What would I say to *fofos* and aunts in Braffe? What would I say to my parents?

Guilt filled my heart. I held myself responsible for his death, although I didn't know what I could have done to stop it. Maybe I should have been the one who was beaten, instead of Fofo. I hated myself and began to consider myself as bad as Big Guy and our godparents and our games master. I felt I had learned evil from them. I had learned to smile and be angry at the same time. My little pretenses before the guard worried me, and I felt my uncle would still be alive if I hadn't encouraged him to flee that night.

Tears rolled down my face, hot and fast. I heaved my weight off the door, because I was trembling and was afraid the vibration might draw attention. My heartbeat seemed louder than the thuds of the shovels outside, and after a while I couldn't even hear the digging.

My anger grew until I felt choked. I reached out and grabbed the wickers of the cutlery basket so hard that one of them snapped, and Yewa turned in her sleep. I wanted to break Big Guy's neck like that wicker for trying to bury Fofo somewhere on the road.

I took a knife from the basket and kept it by my side in case I needed to defend myself. As bad as the digging was, I wished it could have lasted forever, to delay Fofo's interment. Each time the diggers paused to catch their breath, a wave of panic crashed over me and I balled my fists.

"*ÇA SUFFIT,*" BIG GUY said. "Dat's enough for dat cheat!"

Something in his voice, the callousness, I think, emboldened me, and I felt I needed to confront Big Guy. I quickly wiped my tears and willed that he would not make me cry anymore. I tried to stand up but was still too weak, so I knelt and again put my ear to the door.

"Stop," Big Guy said. "Come out! I done promise you de Nanfang. *Wetin* you want again, huh? A new Nanfang?"

"Thank you, sir," they said, scrambling out of the grave. I heard brisk footsteps going toward the front of the house. When they returned, they were slower and shuffling, I think because of Fofo's weight. I tried to figure out how they were carrying him but couldn't. When they dropped him into the grave with a thud, I pressed against the door—and decided then that I would rather die than go to Gabon. I thought it would be better to be killed by Big Guy than to be sold over Fofo's dead body. I would drown before they hauled me onto that ship.

As they filled the grave, I heard my sister get up. I rushed over to her and covered her mouth with my hand. I whispered that we needed to lie down again, that day hadn't yet broken, and went with her back to bed. I put the knife under the mattress, right under the pillow. I lay there and thought about how best to flee from Big Guy and his people, until the guard came in the morning.

After the guard had cleared the toilet pail, he set down his big flashlight and gave us some food and a jug of salt water. My sister ate heartily.

"So how you *dey, mes enfants?*" he said, full of false pity, inspecting our faces. "*Bien dormi?*"

"Yes, we slept well," Yewa said, her mouth stuffed with yam and beans.

"You dream?"

"No dream," she said.

"You *dey* too quiet, Pascal. . . . Your eyes *dey* red, your face *dey* swollen. You no sleep?"

"I did," I said quietly.

"And you no want *chop?*" He came to the bed, lifted the pillow, and sat down beside me. He sat close to the knife. "Eat someting, *abeg,* boy, *chop o.*"

I managed a smile and poured a bit of the salt water from the jug and sipped. "I've no appetite now. I'll eat later."

"*A ma sé nude din wę ya?*" the guard said suddenly.

Yewa shrugged. "No, I didn't hear anything last night."

"And you, big boy? No look so sad, *abeg.*"

The word *big* cut into my disguise, and the picture of Big Guy loomed in my mind. I wanted to tell the guard that, yes, I knew they had killed Fofo Kpee and buried him behind the house last night. I wanted to tell him to go to hell. I thought about pulling out the knife and stabbing him. But I wasn't sure I could kill him instantly. And if I didn't kill him with the first blow, he would overpower me.

I decided to abandon the knife option and exploit his sympathy. Maybe if I begged him he would let us go into the parlor. And if we got there, I might be able to get the keys from the pocket of Fofo's olive-green corduroy coat.

"You no hear anyting?" he asked again, seeing, I guessed, my hesitation.

"No, nothing," I denied. "Did something happen, *monsieur?*"

"Oh, no, no, notting. Just Big Guy messing around for night."

"No!" Yewa said.

"Calm down," the man said. "I just de ask weder he disturb you."

"Please, how is Fofo Kpee," I said, looking down, hiding my pain.

"Well, he *dey* make progress for hospital. Dem go keep *am* for hospital for a while."

"How long?" I asked.

"He go come home small time. . . . I visit him last night."

Yewa stopped eating, looked up, and said, "You did?"

"He say make I greet *vous deux* . . . and, Pascal, he get message for you."

"Message? What message?" I said.

"*Na* you be family head while he *dey* hospital. . . . Take care of dis small gal."

He reached around me and patted my sister on the shoulder.

"Did you bring his clothes to him?" I said, hoping against hope that he hadn't touched anything in the next room, especially that olive-green coat.

"*L'hospital* always get dress for de patients. No need to bring dem from house."

I was happy that things were going my way. It was important that I keep my composure; it was important that I court the guard's sympathy. With Fofo dead, I felt I needed to beat them at their own game. I felt I had the right to be an even worse human being than Big Guy.

"Thanks for the message from Fofo Kpee," I said.

"*C'est rien,*" he answered. "Kpee be good man ... only dat he come misbehave."

"And thanks for the food, water, toilet ... everything. God has brought you to us."

"But what am I?" Yewa suddenly asked in a tiny whiny voice.

"*Wetin* you be?" the man asked, looking at me.

We both looked at Yewa, trying to understand her.

She said, "Did Fofo Kpee give you any message for me ... ?"

"No!" said the man, imitating Yewa's manner of saying no, then giggled.

I managed a fake laugh.

"I'm sure he did," Yewa insisted, and took a gulp of salt water.

"Oh, *dis-nous,* what message he give you?" the guard teased.

"That I'm Pascal's assistant ... Pascal, right? I'm not a small girl."

"Yes, you're my assistant," I said.

"Wow, Mary, *c'est vrai!*" the man said. "*Na* true *o*. Fofo say you must assist Pascal for everyting. Like assistant class prefect, *hén?*"

"Yes, *monsieur,*" she said, happy with herself.

While they chatted, I opened my food and began to nibble on the yam without any desire to swallow. I tried to smile when they laughed, but memories of the sound of earth falling on Fofo flooded me, bringing tears to my eyes. But when I imagined Big Guy's short laugh, I fought the tears and scooped hot beans into my mouth, knowing Yewa and the guard would think that was what was making my eyes teary.

"Could we at least go into the other room . . . please, please?" I asked suddenly.

"No *wahala*," he said, and shrugged. "Gimme time."

I looked away, to hide my excitement. Even Yewa seemed to feel the extra friendliness that morning. She picked up the flashlight and aimed it around the room playfully, drawing and painting intricate designs with the beam, shining it into all the crannies. It was her toy, and she behaved in that brief time like one who had the power to bathe the world in light or darkness. Sometimes she tried to use her hands to cover the face of the flashlight. Her fingers got red, but light still poured into the room. She aimed the flashlight at her belly and pushed it into her skin until there was very little light, just an eclipse on her stomach.

"*Attention, attention,* Madame Assistant Family Head, we need light *o*," the guard said, reaching out for the flashlight. He was uncomfortable. "*Na* you be prisoner, not me!"

"But we can still see," Yewa laughed, and pushed it harder

into her stomach, trying to smother the light altogether without success. The man leaped forward and took the flashlight from her.

"When are the other children coming again?" I asked.

"Tomorrow *nuit*," the man said. "We go clear de room tomorrow morning."

"Please, could we just go into the other room and sit for a while?" I said.

"Ah . . ."

"You don't need to open the door or windows . . . just let us step out of here."

"*Je comprend*, you want take a break from dis prison. We can have one lesson dere."

He led us into the parlor and cracked open a window. Though the room was dim, it was very bright for my eyes and felt colder because of the fresh air. My eyes went straight to the wardrobe, and I scanned the clothes until I saw the green coat. I was relieved that it was still there. I had no reason to think someone had tampered with it. My heart began to race, but I held on. I pretended to pay attention to Yewa, who was peering into the old soccer calendar and calling out the names of players. Without our bed, the room felt lopsided and wider.

I sat on the center table, which was closer to the wardrobe, while the guard and Yewa sat on Fofo's bed. She was understandably uplifted by being in the parlor and hummed many a Christian chorus, something she had not done since we tried to escape. She smiled at us often and peered at everything as if she were seeing it for the first time.

The door to our room was ajar. I kept looking at the floor where they had put Fofo Kpee the night they ambushed us. It was the last place I had seen him.

"HAVE YOU EVER GONE to Gabon, *monsieur?*" I asked him.

"No," he said.

"Hey, we will be in Gabon before you!" my sister said.

"No *wahala,* I go come later," he said.

"Do you think it's a good idea?" I said, looking down.

"Yes, Pascal," he said. "*Hén,* Assistant Family Head?"

"Yes," she said.

"Make we just *dey* call you AFH, why not?" the man said. "*Yinkǫ dagbe!*"

Yewa nodded, pompously.

"I miss our Nanfang," I said. "AFH always went with Fofo Kpee for a ride."

"Good machine," the guard said. "Right now, de ting *dey* mechanic shop for servicing."

I nodded as if I didn't know that Big Guy had probably handed over the machine to the grave diggers by now.

"Do you think Big Guy would allow Fofo Kpee to own the Nanfang again?" I said, and looked down suddenly.

"Of course," he said, "de *zokeke na* him property. . . . Why you *dey* look down?"

I jumped in my seat, feigning surprise.

"You *dey* OK? *Wetin* be dat?"

"I saw something."

I got up and moved away from the table, backing toward the

wardrobe. Yewa quickly pulled her feet onto the bed in fright, which was good for my ruse. She wanted to cling to the man, but he got up and asked her not to leave the bed.

"Someting? Like what?" the guard said. "*Wetin* you see?"

"Rats," I said, and kept backing toward the wardrobe.

"Dat's why you *dey* look down? You people *dey* lucky for dat prison where everyting *dey* sealed and de windows *dey* close. I *dey* see rat here every day *o*. Don't worry, I go kill dem."

I was within arm's reach of the coat, and my hands extended behind me, as if I were preparing to fall into the wardrobe. My fingers were restless. The guard had taken off one of his shoes to use as a weapon and was searching under the bed and around the room with the flashlight. He pulled out Fofo Kpee's carton of shoes and emptied it but saw nothing. I kept inching back toward the wardrobe. "Look at the other corner!" I said, prodding him. "I hope the rat hasn't entered our room."

As soon as I reached the coat, I grabbed the keys from the breast pocket and slid them into the pocket of my shorts. He was turning around at that point, but I pretended to fall, pulling many clothes down with me.

"I'm sorry, *monsieur,*" I said.

"Well, *na* just rat," he laughed, calling off the hunt. "You be woman? You too fear! If de rat worry you tonight in your room, just call me, you hear?"

"Yes, *monsieur,*" we said.

Now my insides were rising and falling with joy. I began to fantasize about our escape. Our best bet was to run in the middle of the night, while he was asleep. I hadn't thought about where we would run, but it didn't bother me. My joy now was that freedom was within our reach. I just needed to manage my excitement until then. Again, like on the day Fofo tried to run away with us, I thought it was important for me not to tell Yewa anything until we were ready to leave. I didn't want to risk it.

The guard again reviewed our lessons about being lost at sea and told us why we needed to drink salt water. We were comfortable around him.

WHEN WE WERE PUT back in the room, I was excited and jumpy and kept smiling in the dark. Against my fingers, the keys felt cold and warm at the same time. Each was half the length of my forefinger and felt light. Though I had no holes in my pocket, I was afraid of losing the keys in the dark. I kept putting my hand into my pocket to caress them and got to know all of their contours. Yewa chatted nonstop about the guard and the parlor, as if we had just returned from a picnic.

Finally, I wore myself out from excitement and I told Yewa I needed to sleep. I wanted to rest and prepare for the flight at night. First, I lay with the keys against the mattress. Then I turned so they faced up. Then I put my hand into the pocket and held on to the keys. Then I took them out of my pocket.

That night, when Yewa's and the guard's breathing had steadied in sleep, I got up and sneaked toward the back door. But when I remembered that the door always squeaked, I made for the window.

I climbed onto the bags of cement, and with shaky hands, I pulled one of the keys out of my pocket and grabbed the padlock. I trembled and fidgeted until I was able to find the keyhole. But it was the wrong key. I pulled it out and left it atop the cement bag.

When the second key didn't work either, I set it aside. I was shaking, afraid that the third might not work, so I paused and tried to calm myself. The guard sneezed and his bed squeaked. I leaned against the window frame and wrestled with a sinking feeling that we might not escape after all. I waited a few minutes, to give the guard a chance to fall back into a deep sleep.

Finally, I thrust in the third key and turned it. There was a snap as the lock was released. When I was sure nobody had heard me, I removed the padlock and put both it and the key in my pocket. I nudged the window slowly until it opened and freshness washed over my face.

It was a cold, beautiful night, and dull moonlight poured into the room. Everything was quiet and peaceful. I closed the window and crept back to the bed. I tapped Yewa on the shoulder, gently, until she sat up, scratching herself. "Kotchikpa," she said dreamily.

"Yes," I whispered. "No noise."

"Are we going to the parlor again? Where's the guard?"

"We're running away . . . lower your voice!"

"Voice?"

I gave her a firm shake.

"We're going to visit Fofo Kpee in the hospital," I lied, leading her gently away from the bed.

"Now?"

I lifted her onto the cement bags, opened the window, and asked her to climb, hoping to go after her. I pushed her head through the open window. When the wind whipped her face, a scream escaped from her mouth. She was wide-awake now and got down from the bags and retreated to the bed. I dragged her toward the window, but she fought me.

"You *dey* fight for night?" the guard said, already struggling with the door.

"Yewa . . . use the window, jump!" I screamed. "He's going to kill us!"

"Stop, stop!" the guard shouted, bursting into the room.

I pushed Yewa out of the way, toward the cutlery basket, and dove headlong through the window, breaking the fall with my hands. I ran toward Fofo Kpee's grave, but my mind was so full of Yewa's keening and its echo from the sea that I forgot to look at it.

I ran into the bush, blades of elephant grass slashing my body, thorns and rough earth piercing my feet. I took the key and padlock from my pocket and flung them into the bush. I ran and I ran, though I knew I would never outrun my sister's wailing.

What Language Is That?

Best Friend said she liked your little eyes and lean face and walk and the way you spoke your English. Her name was Selam. You said you liked her dimples and long legs and handwriting. You both liked to eat Smiling Cow toffees. She was the last child in her family; you were an only child. The world was only big enough for the two of you, and your secret language was an endless giggle, which made the other kids jealous. Selam lived in a flat in a red two-story building in Bahminya. You lived in a brown two-story building across the street.

Some days, after school, you and Selam stood together on the balcony of one of the buildings and watched Selam's two brothers and their friends on the hilly streets with their homemade kites, running and screaming until their heels kicked up puffs of Ethiopian dust. The boys ran into traders hawking CDs they carried in wide metal trays on their heads, or into horse-drawn buggies and donkeys burdened by goods, slowing down traffic. They avoided the next street, which had a mosque, because the imam would curse them if the kites entangled the minaret. He had already made it known to their parents that flying kites was foreign, blaming them for exposing their children to strange ways.

But Best Friend's parents told your parents that they had told the imam that he should not try to tell them how to raise their children in a free Ethiopia. So, many afternoons, you watched the kites rising against the distant coffee fields, then the beautiful hills, and then cupped your hands over your eyes as the kites climbed into the wide, low blue skies.

Some days, there was no need to go to one or the other's house to be together. No, you and Best Friend stood on your own balconies and screamed your kindergarten rhymes to each other across the street, over the brown birds sitting on the electric and phone wires. The wires were cluttered with dead kites, trapped like butterflies in giant cobwebs. Your mommy didn't mind your loud recitations because she said you were only children. Your daddy was OK with it but didn't want you to shout when he was taking his siesta, after which he would sometimes drive you around in his white car. Selam's parents weren't very OK with the shouts, but what could they do?

Some Saturdays, your mommy or Emaye Selam would walk both of you two streets down, behind the church, for your hair to be braided. Like twins, you always chose the same style. Some days, you went to her place and watched the Disney channel, and sometimes she came over to your place and you played Snakes and Ladders and ate *doro wot* and spaghetti.

One Sunday, after church, which Selam attended with your family because her parents traveled, Daddy drove you two to Hoteela Federalawi to eat. You read out all the billboards on the long, beautiful Haile Selassie Arada: Selam the ones on the right, you the ones on the left. In Hoteela Federalawi, Daddy picked a table outside, under a big canopy, and you sat down. You read to each other from the menu while he looked on proudly. You both ordered pizza, while Daddy got a big dish of *mahberawi.*

"Is hamburger pork?" Selam asked, and tossed a piece of mushroom into her mouth.

"Hey, who said so?" Daddy said.

"Hadiya," she said.

"I told you not to talk to Hadiya!" you said, dropping your fork. "She's not our friend."

"I didn't talk to her."

"I won't talk to you again."

"I'm sorry."

You stood up and moved your chair away from hers.

"Oh no, *ai,*" Daddy said, pushing your chair back toward Best Friend's. "Come on, *ai,* ladies. Best friends don't quarrel, *eshie?*"

"Yes, Daddy," you said. "But she spoke to Hadiya. She promised me never to speak to Hadiya, Daddy."

"I did not speak to her. She just came up to me and said I follow Christians and eat pork at Hoteela Federalawi, and ran away. I say I'm sorry. I am sorry, OK?" Tears came into her eyes. "I won't talk to you again either!" Selam shouted at you. "And I won't even hug you."

"Oh no, Selam," Daddy said, coming in between the two of you. "She's kidding. She'll talk with you, she'll sit with you." He turned to you: "Sweetheart, don't be mean to Best Friend."

Other people stared at you, and children celebrating someone's birthday under a canopy giggled. Selam heaved with sobs. Daddy loosened his tie and held her and dabbed her tears with a handkerchief. Your waitress, a lady with a silver nose ring, came over and taunted you, saying that such sweet sisters should not be quarreling and embarrassing their dad in public, after church.

Daddy said to you, "You must make up with Selam or we go home now . . . *tolo!*"

"OK, Selam, I'm sorry," you said. "I'll speak to you. Best friends . . . hugzee, hugzee?"

She nodded. "OK, best friends . . . hugzee."

You hugged. The waitress clapped and cheered and pushed your chairs back together.

"Well, my Selam, I want to say this before we continue eating," Daddy said apologetically. "You're always free to eat what you're comfortable with, *aw?*"

"Yes. Already, my daddy said I could eat pork if I wanted."

"Did he?" he asked, sounding relieved.

"Yes."

"Because this evening I was going to ask your dad to talk to you. I'm going with him to Cinima Bahminya to watch Premiereship football."

"I was just trying to tell Best Friend what Hadiya said."

"That's why I like your dad," he said, and rubbed her head. "Open-minded . . . nice man."

You sat down and began to eat, sipping fresh pomegranate juice with long red and white straws. You talked about the games you would play together when you got home and how much you looked forward to school the next day.

THEN ONE DAY, after you and your family and Best Friend's family had gone to watch the Jimma Bicycle Race in the next town, you didn't wake up in your bed but in Mommy and Daddy's bed. The flat was full of a burning smell. The streets were almost empty. Daddy said there was no school that day.

All morning, your parents didn't leave your side. Their bedroom didn't have windows that faced Selam's flat. They sat with you and watched cartoons and later told you about their childhood and the *Yelijoch Gizay* TV show they watched long ago in Addis Ababa. Daddy, acting the part of Ababa Tesfaye, told you many children's stories; Mommy played Tirufeet, assisting and fleshing out the stories.

Mommy allowed you to spend a lot of time in the bath and brought your clothes to their room. Daddy made you read all your books aloud for him and recited church prayers. They didn't hurry to go to work; they didn't hurry to go anywhere. The house help didn't show up.

You yawned and jumped out of bed.

"I'm going to see Best Friend."

"Come and sit down for a minute," Mommy said, patting the space on the bed between her and Daddy. You went and sat down. She looked at Daddy, who was looking at the wall.

He cleared his throat and said, "Honey, we don't want you to play with that girl anymore."

"What girl?"

"That Muslim girl," Mommy said, moving her huge body close to you.

"Best Friend?"

Silence.

You looked at Mommy, then Daddy. They couldn't be serious, you thought, and waited for them to say it was a joke. "No big deal," Daddy said, shrugging. "There were riots last night. Houses were burned in our neighborhood."

"Selam's flat?"

"No," he said.

"Could I go talk with her . . . ?"

"We say *ai*," Mommy said, looking you straight in the face.

"No? I just want to hug her. Please?"

"We understand how you feel," Daddy said. "We really do. . . . At six you're a bit too young to understand these things."

"Listen up, sweetie," she said, "you're our only child . . . our only child."

"But I really miss her."

"Do you know her parents have also told her to keep away from you?" she said.

"They did? Emaye Selam? Abaye Selam said that? Who'll play with me?"

"We'll play with you," Mommy said.

Daddy rubbed your back and translated what Mommy said: "*Kanchi gara mechawet iwedallehu.*"

"Who'll play with Selam?"

"Hadiya," he said.

"Hadiya?"

"Her brothers, then," he said. "You don't worry about that."

"But I don't want Hadiya to play with her. I don't like her."

You threw the remote control on the floor and ran to your room before they could hold you back. You opened the big window's blinds and looked at Selam's house. A part of her building was burned, but not Selam's flat. The building was now red and black because of the fire. Some of the burned flats looked like empty black shells, the rock-hewn blocks as solid as ever. With the blinds and windows gone, you saw inner walls and parts of singed furniture.

But Selam's flat was fine, and the blinds were closed. It looked lonely because of the fire. Looking around, you saw black smoke still rising from other houses. The sky was dirty. The donkeys and horses were gone, and a cluster of damaged buggies stood by the street corner like unwashed dishes in a sink. Even the birds were absent from the wires.

You wanted Selam to come out onto the balcony. You wanted to see her face. Your heart began to beat faster because you imagined her standing there behind the blinds, waiting for you. You imagined her sitting on her bed with her parents. You imagined her being told she would now have to pick a new best friend. You saw her playing with Hadiya. You saw them going to braid their hair and heard them giggling. Hearing them addressing each other as Best Friend, you balled your fists and wanted Selam to run onto the balcony.

"A part of our house has been burned too," Daddy said, squatting behind you, holding your shoulders. "If you open the window, the smoke will come in. . . . It's bad out there."

"Your daddy's Peugeot has been vandalized," Mommy said, sitting on your bed.

"Where's Selam?"

"They're fine, *dehna nachew,*" she said, and Daddy pulled you away from the window back to your bed. "Your daddy and her daddy spoke this morning about you two. There's tension between us and them."

"Did you quarrel with Emaye Selam?"

"*Ai,* no, she's a sweet woman," she said.

Daddy was quiet, fidgeting with the broken remote and the batteries. On the wall of your room, you saw the world map your teacher, Etiye Mulu, had taught you to trace in school. Your eyes came to "Africa, Our Continent," which Best Friend had penned on the map in her sweet handwriting, and you fought back tears.

Mommy hugged you.

"Daddy, did you quarrel with Abaye Selam?"

"Not 'us' as in *us*," Daddy said.

"It's not personal," Mommy said. "You know they're Muslims?"

"Yes."

"Faith differences," he said. "Just faith differences."

"Faith?"

"It's complex," she said.

"It's a difficult time," he said, nodding.

"Are they bad people?"

"No, not really," she said.

"OK," you said, though you understood nothing. "Are we going to school tomorrow?"

"Not tomorrow, *nega atihedjeem*," Daddy said.

"Soon, baby, soon," Mommy said.

That evening, lights came on in Selam's flat. You rushed and opened your blinds and looked. Her blinds were also open, but nobody was there. You pinched yourself for not being there when the blinds parted. You waited there in silence, hoping for someone, a shadow, to walk by the window. Nothing.

For the next two days, when Mommy left the house, Daddy stayed with you. When Daddy left the house, Mommy stayed with you. Though the streets were filling up again, and the birds had returned to the wires, your house help didn't return.

You dreamed bad dreams of Selam, even in your afternoon naps. In one dream she turned her face away from you and would not answer your greetings. When she looked at you, she wore a scowl, which burst her dimples. On her balcony, she recited the multiplication tables with Hadiya and taught her the beautiful handwriting and shared her Smiling Cow toffees with her. Hadiya's English became better than yours. While Hadiya's face became leaner and prettier and Selam liked her walk, you became ugly and twisted like the old coffee trees of Jimma. You felt so bad you sobbed, and Hadiya came to hug you. She told you that it wasn't Selam's fault, that her parents wanted her to avoid you because you weren't one of them. You cried all the more because it was Hadiya who was hugging you, not Best Friend.

IN THE AFTERNOON, YOU pretended to be reading in your room so that you could watch Selam's flat from behind your blinds, in spite of the dreams. You were sure she would not come onto the balcony. But you kept vigil because you wanted to see if Hadiya would visit her.

But suddenly, Selam tiptoed onto the balcony. Against the burned-out flats, she looked like a ghost. Her face was pale against the afternoon sun and seemed to have deep wrinkles, like the top of *hambasha* bread. She looked skinny and even shorter in the few days you hadn't seen her. Her *shama,* a gauzelike white material covering her from head to foot, fluttered in the wind. Would she run back if you appeared? If you disobeyed Mommy and Daddy and spoke to her, would she disobey her mommy and daddy and respond? Or would she report you to her parents, who might come to your parents? Would she snub you, like in the dreams? Afraid, you hid and poured your gaze on her like the sun on a cold day. Selam stared at your flat, but you didn't move. She grabbed the balcony rail and looked down into the streets, this way, that way, and you tried to follow her gaze, in case she was expecting Hadiya.

At dinner Mommy and Daddy told you to cheer up. They told you not to nibble your food. They chatted excitedly, like Selam and Hadiya did in your dreams, and poured you more and more Coke.

"Tomorrow afternoon," Mommy said, "we'll travel to Addis, to see our relatives."

"When are we coming back?"

"We've not even left yet!" Daddy said. "What's wrong with you these days? You broke the remote the other day. Get over it."

"Darling, it's OK," she said, calming him down. Then she turned to you: "We'll be back in a week. Bahminya is too tense now. *Kezeeh mewtat allebin—*"

"I don't want to go."

"Hey, what language is that?" she said, tapping on the *mesab,* our handmade, wicker hourglass-shaped table. "And it's rude to interrupt when another person is speaking!"

You closed your mouth so they would not scold you. You started eating up, since they were now waiting for you. You cut a big piece of *injera* and poured the meat sauce and a clot of vegetables onto it. You rolled it and turned up one end of the flat spongy bread so the vegetables and sauce wouldn't leak, and began to chew from the other end, hurriedly. You drank the Coke, drank water, and thanked them. You returned to your room, while they talked about how the government had kept the *complex thing* from the news, and how it had done the same thing when Muslim radicals suddenly slaughtered Christians in Jimma churches two years back.

The next afternoon you came onto the balcony. Selam also appeared, on her balcony. You looked at each other without words. You followed each other's gaze, to the coffee fields, to the hills, to the sun. The sky was cloudy. The streets emitted a low buzz below, and two donkeys brayed in the distance. The winds came in from the hills, fresh and steady. The birds lined the wires, some facing you and others facing her, in silence, as if they were awaiting the beginning of a race.

Slowly, Selam lifted her hand and waved to you as if the hand belonged to another person. You waved back slowly too. She opened her mouth slowly and mimed to you, and you mimed back, "I can't hear you." She waved with two hands, and you waved with two hands. She smiled at you. Her dimples were perfect, little dark cups in her cheeks. You opened your mouth and smiled, flashing all your teeth. "Hugzee, hugzee," you mimed to her. There was a puzzled look on her face. You embraced the wind with both hands and gave an imaginary friend a peck. She immediately hugged herself, blowing you a kiss.

She looked back furtively, gave you a signal to disappear, and rushed inside herself. You retreated too, behind the blinds. Emaye Selam surfaced, her angry face framed by a scarf. She looked at your flat and scanned the streets, then went back in.

You smiled because you had discovered a new language. You went to Mommy and Daddy and asked them when you were leaving for Addis.

"Addis will be fun!" Mommy said, and continued packing. "You'll make new friends there."

"Yes, Mommy."

Daddy paused from sipping his beer. "Good girl . . . I'll buy a new remote."

Luxurious Hearses

---

*Argue not with the People of the Book
unless it be in a better way, except with
such of them as do wrong; and say: "We
believe in that which has been revealed
to us and revealed to you; our God and
your God is One, and to God do we
surrender."*

KORAN 29:46

It was late afternoon. It was before the new democratic government placed a ban on mass transportation of corpses from one end of the country to the other. Jubril had worked so hard to forget the previous two days that his mind was in turmoil as he waited to travel south with the crowd at the motor park on the outskirts of Lupa. He knew that even if people were stacked up like yam or cassava tubers in a basket, most would still be left behind. Fortunately, he had paid for a seat on the only bus left.

To the north, the road skipped over the low hills and flattened out, straight, in the savannah toward Khamfi, Jubril's city, then into Niger. To the south, it turned a series of corners, slipping toward River Niger, toward Onyera and Port Harcourt, then into the Atlantic.

Though he was still a teenager, Jubril looked mature for his age. He was fair-skinned and wore a blue oversized long-sleeved shirt. His brown jean trousers were dirty and hung like curtains on his willowy frame. A worn Marian medal dangled from his neck, and his cowherd feet were crammed into undersized canvas shoes — their laces missing, their tongues jutting out like those of goats being roasted. Jubril had pulled down his baseball cap so that it covered most of his youthful face and hid the brilliance of his big eyes and his sharp nose. A Muslim, he had done a good job disguising himself as a Christian fleeing south. And, in any case, because of the religious conflict in the country, nobody would expect a northerner or Muslim to risk traveling with Christians to the south or the delta.

The bus was the type his compatriots simply called Luxurious Bus, a seventy-seat monster and secondhand import from Latin America that dominated the roads. In times of peace, these buses made cross-country travel easy. The hundreds of police checkpoints never stopped the buses to search them or to harass their drivers for money because the bus companies made enough to settle with the national police command monthly. The radio, television, and print media had a lot of ads about these buses. The fares were within the reach of many, and, with the country's aviation industry being so unreliable, the best of the buses were gaining the confidence of the elite. When suddenly these vehicles started offering long-distance night travel, many jumped for it. Businesspeople went to sleep on the bus in the evening, then woke up and continued their business the next morning on the other side of the country.

Jubril had neither seen nor been in a Luxurious Bus before. The very conservative brand of Islam practiced in his neighborhood in multireligious Khamfi had made it impossible for him to listen to the radio or watch any form of TV or pay attention to newspapers. With his state of mind now, he had forgotten the only thing he had heard about these buses from his friends: they had a constant supply of electricity, unlike what NEPA was providing to the rest of the country. But now that peace had deserted the land, and Nigeria was on a war footing, the myth of the Luxurious Bus meant nothing to Jubril or the crowd at Lupa Motor Park.

Their only worry now was the disappearance of the bus driver into Lupa City, which was a couple of miles away. He had been gone the whole day, scouting for black-market fuel for the long journey ahead, and the conductors had kept the Luxurious Bus locked since morning. Fuel had become a scarce commodity in the country. Cars had to line up for days on end at the pumps.

The crowd, restless and growing in size, milled around the bus, whose red window blinds were drawn. Its dark three-tone facade was a dying glow as the harmattan haze began to shut out the sun even before it dropped below the horizon. The motor park was ringed by a semicircle of stores and restaurants; some of them were running out of provisions, and others had simply closed for fear of looting. Some travelers sat, gloomy and tired, on their verandas, too discouraged or hungry to wait near the bus. The park was unpaved and uneven, the wide potholes as sandy as the bed of a seasonal river in the dry months.

Beyond this, the savannah, clothed in the reddish harmattan dust, extended in every direction, like an endless ocean, with Lupa City and a few villages and towns dotting it like little islands. Though the savannah had a few tall evergreen trees, for the most part it was full of short, stout trees. And even those stood far apart, as if they hated each other's company. Their leaves gone, the branches pointed at the sky like a thousand crooked fingers. Between the trees were shrubs and grass that had been singed by the dry season, and dark expanses of scorched undergrowth, where villagers had undertaken their annual bush-burning craze.

Jubril had tried to take in the Babel of languages that were being spoken at the motor park. He had heard many languages being spoken in one place before, but today they only emphasized his estrangement from the group. Somehow, even when he knew that there were no Hausa-Fulani in the park and that no Hausa would be spoken, he still yearned for it. He listened hard, longing to hear it as he did at Bawara Market in Khamfi, where the more than two hundred languages of his country seemed represented. But here he could mainly hear the Ibo language because of the many Ibos fleeing to their homes in the southeast. He could also hear the minority languages of the delta tribes and even those of the northern minorities, who were retreating to whatever places had been their ancestral homes. Those who spoke English did so with accents peculiar to their tribes — all of them unlike Jubril's accent. The more he paid attention to the noisy crowd, the more convinced he became that the best way to disguise himself was to speak as little as possible.

To ease his feelings of estrangement, he dug into his bag and pulled out the piece of paper on which had been written the name of the village in the delta where his father was born. He read the name silently many times. He knew that if he had to say it out loud, his accent would betray him, which was why he got Mallam Abdullahi, the Good Samaritan who helped him make this trip, to write it out clearly for him.

Many years back, Jubril's mother, as if goaded by some uncanny ability to read the future, had insisted, against Jubril's protestations, that his father came from an oil-producing village in the delta region and that his father's relatives would always protect him. Even now he knew nothing about the place. But with this paper, he felt like one on the verge of discovering something very important, something that could give him the identity his troubled nation had failed to provide. This feeling of adventure would have been enough for his mind to handle in peaceful times, but during this flight it felt like an added burden. He wished he had traveled there before now.

All day he had pined for the bus's departure, like a prisoner anticipating his release from jail. He had waited with the crowd, aware that he was not one of them, knowing that he was an easy target for the sporadic violence that had seized the land, that a simple thing like his accent could give him away. He was one of those who had lost their families in the Sharia crisis in Khamfi. And many times during this journey the weight of the tragedy had shocked him out of proper recollection of the events that had precipitated it. He knew this bus was his only way to safety and had tried everything to forget what had happened to him, including the two-day hunger that was sinking its jaws into his stomach. Yet now and then, his despair broke through his control, and he bit his thin dry lips. Sometimes, in a last-ditch effort to suppress his tears, he shut his eyes tight.

Though he was exhausted, he hovered around the bus, not wanting to sit on the verandas of the stores and restaurants, as many of his compatriots were doing, or even on the bare earth, succumbing to fatigue. To him, his fellow travelers looked like drowning men, grabbing on to whatever they could before they were swept away by the crisis that had overtaken their country. Some were with their children and spouses. Some had lost everything, even their sanity.

FOR THE FIRST TIME in Jubril's life, it did not infuriate him that there were women all over the place. He had been in the crowd a long time before he became aware, not just of them, but of the fact that he did not react to them in any way. Only three days before, this would not have been possible. He would have preferred to trek a thousand miles on foot rather than sit in the same vehicle as a woman. In his part of Khamfi it was not even permissible for a man to give his wife, daughter, or sister a ride on his *okada* or bicycle. Now it felt as if he were experiencing the immediacy of these women in a dream, one in which he could commit any sin and not be held accountable by his conscience or the *hisbah,* the Sharia police.

Suddenly, it seemed the women were everywhere. Because of the crowd, some were pressing in on him. Many of them wore trousers and shorts, and some did not cover their heads. The voices of the younger girls floated in the harmattan wind like a strange, sweet melody.

Then his dispassionate attitude toward these Christian women shifted to humor, then irony. To Jubril, they looked funny in their makeup and tight-fitting trousers. He caught himself thinking about all the *hijab* and *niqab* and *abaya* that would be needed to cover them and shrugged. He imagined himself laughing at them, and a tinge of good feeling came over him, not so much from the sight of the women but because he had reacted well to the situation and did not give himself away. He became more certain that he could survive this journey, if only he could maintain his ability to secretly poke fun at some of the inconveniences. This novelty provided his first lighthearted moment since his flight from Khamfi, a real relief from the angst that had fretted his soul.

He soaked up this antidote with every pore of his body, scanning the crowd with quick darting eyes, as if he needed to see more women and girls to be happy or to be sure of a safe trip. Soon he did not have to fight back tears. He wanted to laugh out loud like a madman, but he controlled himself. If these Christians asked him why he was laughing, what would he say? No, *haba,* he was not going to lose control of himself because of women. He thought it would be awful if, after having disguised himself successfully and survived the journey thus far, he let a bunch of hell-destined women do him in. He prayed that when push came to shove Allah would give him the grace to see the lifestyles that challenged him as laughable rather than as sources of irritation and temptation.

Jubril was still watching the women, paying special attention to the myriad hairdos, when the bus conductors invited the passengers to board. Everybody, those with tickets and those without, swooped to the doors. Jubril took his time getting to the door and entering the vehicle. But, jostling down the aisle, he discovered that an old man had taken his seat, which was in the last quarter of the bus.

"Good evening, sa," Jubril whispered to him, covering his mouth with his hand to change his accent.

"What's the problem?" replied Chief Okpoko Ukongo.

"Notting."

"Good."

Slowly Chief Ukongo put away the packet of Cabin Biscuits he had been eating and surveyed Jubril from head to toe. Jubril looked down as a sign of respect. The chief was a gaunt man with a long bony throat. He wore a black bowler hat, the type his compatriots called Resource Control. His small head made him look more like a soldier wearing an oversized helmet. He was in a red flowing corduroy chieftaincy dress covered with black roaring-lion prints. Now and then, he fingered the three rows of royal beads around his neck, lifting one or two, then letting them clack. His eyes were tired and so sunk in, it seemed tears would never climb their steep banks to be shed.

"*Abeg,* sa, dis *na* ma seat," Jubril whispered again, bowing curtly and smiling, standing right by the chief.

"What seat . . . me?" the chief said.

Though Jubril's voice was low, even fearful, an unusual pride attended his manners—his right hand was in his pocket. It infuriated the old man to no end.

Jubril held his right arm at a conspicuous, somewhat arrogant angle. The skin of his forearm looked stiff and the muscles taut, as if he were holding on to something in his pocket. But the truth was that his right hand had been amputated at the wrist for stealing. Nobody on the bus knew this, and it was important that Jubril keep this fact hidden. If they found out, they would know he was Muslim, for they had seen people like him before. His plan to run south would unravel. So now, though his elbow kept bumping into other refugees boarding the bus, making him wince with pain, he did not change his posture. He held a black plastic bag containing his few belongings in his left hand.

Jubril looked up and said to Chief Ukongo a second time, "Ma seat, *abeg.*"

"Meee?" the chief shouted, startling the boy, who stepped back, ramming into a man. Before he regained his balance, Jubril waved and mimed an apology in the man's face, like an amateur clown. A few people turned to stare.

The bus had become rowdy, and refugees were stowing their luggage under the seats and overhead. Five seats from where Jubril stood, there were two university-age girls, Ijeoma and Tega, struggling and insulting each other over a piece of luggage. Tega, the taller of the two, was as dark as charcoal. Her dirty cornrows were decorated with a few colorful beads, which forced Jubril to keep looking at her, in spite of the dirt. She was in a pair of bell-bottom jeans and a brown sweater and clogs. Ijeoma, the other girl, had lighter skin, like Jubril. She wore an Afro and had a lean face dominated by big eyes. She wore a white blouse over a short olive-green skirt, and sandals.

Now Tega was pulling the bag out of the overhead compartment, arguing that the compartment belonged to the person sitting under it; Ijeoma was stuffing it back in, saying that, though she sat four seats away, she had the right to stow her luggage there. Nobody paid them much attention.

For a moment, there was a ruckus by the door as more people attempted to force their way onto the bus. But the two police officers who maintained security, in the tradition of Luxurious Buses, shut the door. Sighs of disappointment erupted outside.

One man who was wrapped up in a blanket, to fight a vicious fever, asked whether the driver had returned from buying fuel. Five people said no simultaneously, in voices that revealed different levels of frustration.

One of them, a stout restless man, started scolding the sick man. Emeka had a round face with little piercing eyes, and wore a red monkey coat over a white shirt and black trousers. He had just a pair of black socks on his feet because he had lost his shoes running away from the fanatic Muslims. As Emeka reproached the sick man, another man at the back started yelling at him for taking things out on someone who asked an innocent question. Soon there was a lot of shouting and cussing on the bus.

"I'M SURE YOU ARE not waiting for me," the chief said, glancing at Jubril.

"Yes."

"You want to fight like those two women? I don't know why people are always fighting in this country."

"No."

"No, no, no, you can never be talking to me." The chief shrugged. "I mean, look at me, look at you. How old are you?"

"Sixteen."

"Better speak up, boy!" the chief barked. "How old did you say you were?"

The shout attracted attention, and Jubril became quiet. He resorted to sign language: he flashed the five fingers of his left hand three times and then one finger.

"Oh, now you're dumb?" Chief Ukongo said.

"No."

The chief sighed and shook his head, his face seeming to shut down in anger. He tapped his well-polished black shoes on the floor, then reached down and picked up his walking stick from under the seat. He waved it at Jubril. "*You* can't be talking to me . . . in which world? Just because they say 'democracy, democracy,' you can't address me as you like. Who are you?"

"Sorry, sa."

"Sir? Listen, don't let the he-goat's face catch fire because of his precious beard. I don't blame you but this so-called democracy. I must be addressed properly. Chief . . . chief! I'm not your equal."

"Yes, Chief."

"Who are you?"

Jubril looked down, praying that the old man would not insist on a name.

The old man swallowed hard and lifted up his stick. "May Mami Wata drown your stupid head!" he said, and thudded the stick twice for emphasis. He returned to his Cabin Biscuits.

The teenager would have sat anywhere in the bus to avoid attention. But even the spot where he stood had been paid for. Because of the crowd outside and the need of southerners to flee the north, even the aisle was portioned out. The spot's owner, a pregnant woman with a baby son strapped to her back, was already asking him to move. For now, Jubril stepped toward the chief and leaned into his headrest so others could get to their seats. He made sure his right arm did not stick out into the aisle by wedging his plastic bag between his right hip and the chief's seat.

He seemed to have a bit of peace where he stood, because nobody bothered him, and that could have let his mind wander to the genesis of his flight, but he resisted. He started distracting himself by paying attention to the bus itself, which he had not done properly since he boarded. His eyes roamed the ceiling, from the toilet at the rear of the bus to the back of the driver's seat. It was the only open space in the vehicle, gray and clean. It felt big because everything below was so crowded. Though some of the overhead storage doors were left ajar, jutting into the ceiling space, the fluorescent lights fascinated him. With his eyes he counted the long, flat bulbs that filled the bus with soft light. It was part of the Luxurious Bus myth his friends had talked about: he could not fathom what it would be like to live with constant electricity. In fact he felt that the electricity on the bus was being wasted, since the sun had not yet set, and he did not really understand why the lights would be needed for the journey anyway. If it were his decision, he would have wanted total darkness on the bus, to reduce the possibility of fellow refugees finding him out. But he kept himself from thinking along the lines of being caught. To do so now might make him lose his composure. He turned his mind away from the fluorescent bulbs.

The next thing he noticed was the bus's two TV sets. They quickly created conflicting interests within him. Luckily, the TVs were not on. The few times he had watched television were in someone else's house, during the 1994 World Cup and the 1996 Summer Olympics, at which his national soccer team won the gold. A boy of ten in 1994, he had gone to watch with his uncle and his older brother Yusuf. The TV had to be run on a generator because NEPA could not be counted on even in such times of national pride. Their host only allowed them to watch during play and turned off the set during halftime for fear of scandalous advertisements. Of course, during the Olympics two years later events like women's gymnastics and track and field were off-limits. Now, the presence of the TVs in the bus worried Jubril and made his heart beat faster, for he had heard of their incredible powers of corruption. And, he reasoned, one never knew what these Christians would watch. So, while he was impressed by the fact that the bus would not lose electricity, he was uncomfortable at the prospect of the TVs being turned on.

He did not know what to think of the fact that he found the TVs more intimidating than the presence of women. He would rather watch the women than TV. He tried to make fun of the very idea of television, just as he had done about his physical proximity to women, but he was not successful. He could not come up with a theology that would allow him to intentionally watch TV without feeling like he was pushing himself into a bottomless pit of temptation and sin. He tried to calm down, arguing that the women on TV might not be much different from the ones around him. But another voice within him countered: What if the TVs show pictures of naked women? What if they show pictures of people drinking alcohol? What if Prophet Muhammad is cursed on TV? Maybe these two things in the bus are not even TV sets. Have you been on a bus like this before? What if they just look like TVs? Confused, Jubril shifted his attention to the safer diversion of woman-watching.

Ijeoma and Tega had stopped fighting about storage and returned to their seats. Ijeoma had lost and now held her bag on her lap. She was still scolding Tega in an endless mumble. Jubril watched her intently, paying close attention to her long beautiful legs. He wanted to see her feet but could not because the bus was so crowded. His eyes zoomed in on her fingers, which were laced together over her bag. He admired her fingers for a while before it dawned on him that what actually held his attention was her crimson nail polish. He looked at the fingernails of his left hand; they were dirty and jagged, for he had bit them during the flight. Anxious to know whether she had painted her toenails too, he craned his neck and leaned over but could not see. He looked at Tega, the object of Ijeoma's venom. She sat there quietly, as if winning a battle about overhead storage on a bus were a big accomplishment. Though her nails had their natural color, they were too glossy to be real; he also noticed that her nails were longer. Jubril wondered how a woman could cook for her husband or do laundry with such talons. He did not like her, though he could not keep his eyes from the colorful beads in her dirty hair. All of this led him to compare the different hairstyles on the bus. He did not know their names and wondered what they were called. Some were attractive, he had to admit. Some were ugly, some were newly braided, some were old. Some were unkempt, and some were wild, as if the violence of the previous two days emanated from there.

When he ran out of hairdos to compare, Jubril figured there might be more women on the bus than men and started counting them. He even looked outside one of the windows and counted the women he could see. He was like a person addicted: the more women he counted or watched, the more women he needed to assuage his TV anxieties. But there were only so many women on the bus. He closed his eyes momentarily and attempted a prayer, yet the urge to look at the TVs hit him like a bout of diarrhea. Again, his mind started coming up with reasons why he should look at the TVs. Well, they were not yet turned on, he rationalized. Maybe this was one more temptation Allah had sent to make him strong. It was as if he had gotten so close to Satan himself that he could not help but peer at the hoofed feet, long tail, and horns.

THE TVs WERE SUSPENDED from the ceiling by iron cages, their brown, untidily welded rods contrasting with the smooth ash black of the TV sets. One was directly behind the driver's seat; the other was in the middle of the bus. Jubril gulped down the details in a hurry, as if the TVs would come alive any moment, at which point he would be forced to look away or shut his eyes.

The feverish man whom Emeka had scolded suddenly began to cry, and Jubril's attention came back to his immediate surroundings. The man was now slung across his seat, pulling his blanket ever tighter, which reminded Jubril of some of the bodies he had seen as he fled Khamfi. The people around the man were trying to do something about his sickness. Emeka took out three doses of Fansidar from his pocket. "This should take care of your malaria," he said as he handed the drugs to the man. "We don't need a dead man in here!"

"Three doses?" said Madam Aniema, an old woman. "Usually, it's one dose of three tablets. You will kill him with nine tablets!"

She wore a green lace blouse and a beautiful *wrappa*. She had no head tie, and her wrinkled face was framed by bushy white hair and a pair of glasses. She sat in the same row as Emeka but at the window.

"By the grace of God, nothing will happen to him," Emeka said.

"It's overdose," she argued.

"Maybe you are not a believer, then," he said.

"That's beside the point here."

"You must belong to one of those old, dead Churches."

Emeka had more supporters, including the patient himself. They all argued that the sick man needed a bit of an overdose to "balance" his severe fever.

Madam Aniema brought out a little bottle of water from her handbag and helped the man take the drugs. She stayed close to him. Jubril was impressed by this kindness and looked favorably on the lady. He did not stare at her or laugh secretly at her uncovered hair. Her matronly carriage reminded him of his mother, though the latter was not that old. Actually, he had not noticed her all this while and had probably left Madam Aniema out of his census. He was a bit taken aback by his reaction to this woman. Before now, he had never thought he could feel that way toward any woman but his mother. As long as they were women, he just put them in one category in his mind — it was easier that way. Yet he could not see what was so special about Madam Aniema. It was not his first time meeting an old woman or seeing a woman being charitable.

"I'm not sure this man can make it!" Emeka said, bringing Jubril's mind back to the sick person.

The man was shaking hard, and when he attempted to speak his voice shook too. Yet, as malarial patients are wont to do, he was sweating profusely. Madam Aniema held him like a child.

"He no go die," Tega said. "Satan *na* liar!"

"*Na* you be riar!" Ijeoma said to her, her large eyes seeming to cover her whole face. "Go wash your stupid hair *jo o!*"

"By de grace of God, your head no correct!" Tega told her. "Because I no allow you steal my space."

"By de special glace of God, *na* your head no collect!" she retorted.

"Maybe we gave him too much Fansidah," Madam Aniema said.

"He needed a big jolt," Emeka said.

"It was too much," Madam Aniema insisted, pulling her patient closer. "And we did not even know whether he had eaten anything."

"Once it is well with the soul, it's well with the body."

Having said that, Emeka removed his monkey coat and, with Madam Aniema, struggled to rid the man of his blanket, which they thought was the cause of the sweating. But he held on. Finally Emeka took it away from him and suggested that people give him a space in the aisle. Other sympathizers pushed and argued until some in the aisle volunteered to share their space with the sick man. Emeka spread the blanket on the floor and laid him down on his back, with many passengers pressing against him and stepping over him. The space was so tight that they arranged his hands on his chest as if he were in a coffin too narrow for his body. The people agreed that an old man from the aisle should take the sick person's seat until he was strong enough to sit up.

The chief gave Jubril a bad look, as if to say, If you had behaved well you would have been the one to benefit from that seat. Jubril had watched the drama from a distance, with a mixture of pity and jealousy and then repulsion. When the sick man had struggled with Emeka for the blanket, Jubril felt like helping Emeka. But he did not know what to do. How could he have helped with one hand? How could he have dared to speak with his Hausa accent? He had prayed for the man silently and wished that Allah would keep death far from him, at least until he got to his destination.

Jubril began to feel a strange affinity for the sick man: the malaria had twisted his tongue, making him babble, and Jubril had to speak as little as possible and feign an accent for the sake of his disguise. He watched the people watching the man, and on their sympathetic faces he could see that the man might not make it home alive. The spike in his fever had put a chill on the struggle for space in the bus, and the refugees now spoke in hushed voices. Jubril really admired how Emeka had rallied to help the sick man and talked people out of their spaces for him.

Yet, seeing how one man got the sympathy of the whole bus, Jubril began to feel jealous. What could he do to endear himself to these people? How could he get everybody to arrange for a place for him to sit or ask the chief to give him back his seat, without giving himself away? And then he could not bear to look at the sick man on the floor. He reminded him of so many corpses he had seen on the way here. In his mind Jubril tried to distinguish the dead from those who were in the process of dying, like this man. He could not.

He kept looking at the ceiling of the bus. Now his revulsion for the sick man was so strong that he preferred to look at the TV sets. They were not as frightening as before, though when he looked at them his sensibilities were not as unguarded as when he looked at the women. He paid attention to the knobs and the rings around the knobs. He wished the darkness of the TV screens would descend on his recent memories, and he wished those memories, which kept pressing to be recognized, were fastened and caged like the TVs.

"Well, if he die," Tega said, pointing to the sick man, "we must decide quick quick *wetin* we go do wid de corpse, *chebi?*"

"You want steal de corpse or de dead man space too?" Ijeoma said.

"We must take the corpse home," Emeka said.

"No, I tink we must give his space to anoder person!" Tega said.

"It's our tradition to be laid to rest in our ancestral land," Emeka said.

"No need to carry dead body home when so many *dey* stranded," Tega insisted.

"But he has paid his fare," Madam Aniema said.

"And the Luxurious Bus insurance covers his burial, you know," Emeka said.

"Who go claim de body *sef* dis *wahala* time? *Na* major crisis we *dey* now."

"I'm sure you be Musrim," Ijeoma said. "Dat's why you want buly *am* quick quick."

The bus was silent.

The word *Muslim* formed in many mouths, but nobody had the will to say it aloud. Instead they turned and looked at Tega carefully and then examined their neighbors. It was as if a sacrilegious word had been uttered in the holy of holies. Jubril looked down and bit his lip. He felt that all eyes were on him but kept telling himself they were not talking about him. In his ears, the silence was like an eternity. He closed his eyes and waited for blows to land on him.

"You want incite dem to kill me, *abi*?" Tega said, finally finding her voice. She was breathing hard and pulling at her cornrows as if she intended to tear out the beads. Her eyes met the dangerous stares in the bus with credulity.

"She is not a Muslim!" Emeka announced, and the whole

bus was behind him, scolding Ijeoma for calling Tega a Muslim. They told her a fight over storage space was too small a matter to elicit such bad will toward a fellow Christian. They berated her for ingratitude to God, for she was seated, when others would have to stand for hundreds of miles during the journey home. The cacophony seemed unending, with some insisting that Ijeoma must apologize to Tega and to the whole bus.

"My people, my people," Chief Ukongo said, standing up and thudding his stick repeatedly to calm the situation. When everybody kept quiet, the old man cleared his throat. "This matter is getting out of hand. Let no one say *Muslim* or *Islam* again on this bus. We have suffered too much already at the hands of Muslims. . . . If the man dies we shall take him home, period."

"Yes, good talk!" one man concurred.

"Chief, you go live forever!" another said.

"Make nobody mention anyting *wey* be against God's children!"

"Yes, let's watch what we say on this bus," Madam Aniema said.

As the conversation reverted to the bus's insurance policy, Jubril began to breathe again. He did not know how he had managed to remain on his feet at the mention of the word *Muslim* or when people had searched the faces of their neighbors. Though he had looked down immediately, he had expected someone to grab him and tell him he was a fraud. He expected someone to pull his arm out of his pocket. It was as if his mind had stopped, for he did not hear Tega protesting her innocence or the chief diffusing the people's anger toward Ijeoma. The point at which he started hearing again was when someone said, "Yes, good talk!"

Now Jubril wedged the bag between his knees and used his left hand to wipe the sweat that trickled down his forehead. It was not enough, so he pulled a shirt from his bag and mopped his face and neck and tried to pay attention to the conversation around him. When he returned the shirt to his bag, he felt the piece of paper that bore the name of his father's village. It was like an energy boost. He thought of taking it out and looking at it but decided against that. He wriggled his toes in the canvas shoes to be sure they were not numb and shifted his weight from one leg to the other. He looked about the bus and even smiled at the chief, who did not smile back.

He listened to the chatter around him as one might a fairy tale, both hopeful and afraid of the awesome possibilities. He was surprised that a bus company could insure its passengers against injury, accident, or cost of burial, whereas the politicians who promised the people better health care never delivered. It was as if this bus and its company existed in a dream world. Since the motor park he had run to was already south of Khamfi, in his mind Jubril began to associate all the new things he had experienced so far with the myth of the south. In his imagination, he saw the south as more developed than the north, even if it was inhabited by infidels. He saw well-paved roads and functional hospitals. He saw huge markets and big motor parks full of Luxurious Buses. He thought about big schools with colorful buildings and well-fed children. He believed this was precisely the sort of place to escape to. He needed a place to hide and to heal, and from the little he had heard from these Christians he did not think he had made a mistake by running south.

THE MORE JUBRIL LABORED to suppress thoughts of his journey so he could focus on maintaining his disguise, the more his mind revolted. When he was not dwelling on the circumstances of his escape, his mind wandered further back into his past, to some distant event that was tangled up in his flight from Khamfi.

For example, the dread of each stage of the journey, not knowing if he would make it to the next stop, had forced him, in the past two days, especially in Khamfi, to harbor thoughts he had never considered important and that he even would have considered heretical. Though he had no recollection of his home in the south—or of his infant baptism there—and would probably never have thought about his father's ancestral home if not for the crisis, his heart pined for it now. Yet, the prospect of being both a Christian and a Muslim still felt like an aberration to him. If someone had told him a month ago that he would be standing here, trying to blend in with a crowd of southern Christians, he would have considered it an insult or a curse and called down Allah's condemnation on the fellow.

Like his multireligious, multiethnic country, Jubril's life story was more complicated than what one tribe or religion could claim. He had lived all his life in Khamfi and was at home with his mother's people, the Hausa-Fulanis. He had always seen himself as a Muslim and a northerner. Looking at his skin color, he had no problem believing he would fit in where he was going. There were many on the bus who were fairer than he was. He could have been from any ethnic group in the country. What worried him was that he did not know enough about Christianity to survive in this crowd. It seemed like an insurmountable obstacle. So many times, he cleared his throat and grabbed his Marian medal with his fingers and stroked it, his whole attention focused on it, as if the Muslim in him now shared the same Catholic adoration he had considered idolatrous in Khamfi. Though Mary was accorded a lot of respect in his religion, he had always thought the Catholics went too far by making thousands of sacramentals about her and setting up shrines. The advice of Mallam Abdullahi, the man who gave Jubril the medal, flashed across his mind: Don't feel too bad wearing the medal, as Maryam in the Koran was the mother of Prophet Isa, Jesus. Though Jubril would rather not have been wearing the medal, this theology was good enough for him—and, besides, his rescuer had assured him that all Christians who saw him wearing it would think he was Catholic and let him be.

JUBRIL'S MOTHER, AISHA, a sad willowy figure, like Jubril, had told him a long time ago that he was born in his father's village, Ukhemehi, in the delta. His father, Bartholomew, a short taciturn man, used to be a fisherman and farmer. Jubril's maternal grandfather, Shehu, was a cowherd who had migrated with his cattle from Khamfi in the north, away from the widening Sahara, to the rain forests of the delta. One thing had led to another, and Bartholomew fell in love with Aisha. Their relationship soon became a community concern, not because the two friends were doing anything wrong but because no one in that area would dream of having a serious friendship with a Muslim lady, much less marry her. Shehu agreed with the villagers: he did not want his daughter to marry in the south or to change her faith. The Ukhemehi people were fine with allowing Shehu and his family to cultivate the land and graze their cows, but the prospect of this beautiful girl and handsome young man coming together unnerved the community, and people were already gossiping about them as if they had been caught sleeping together.

Bartholomew was a chorister in his village church, Saint Andrew's Church, and a member of three pious societies, Saint Anthony of Padua, Legion of Mary, and the Block Rosary, in addition to being a member of the Catholic Youth Organization, to which every youth in the church belonged. So, naturally, when he started getting close to Aisha, pressure came from all these affiliations. But he could not stop. Things came to a head when the two rebelled against the jingoism of the community and started running away from home for days on end to Sapele and Warri and Port Harcourt.

When Father Paul McBride, an optimistic, outgoing Irishman, noticed that his church was heading for a major scandal, he called on the two and counseled them. When he was sure of the depth of their love, he spoke to their parents. It was not long before they married. Though Aisha's people were staunch Muslims, their tradition did not consider a woman converting to the "People of the Book," as Jews and Christians are known in the Koran, apostasy. Aisha converted to Catholicism and was christened Mary. Jubril was the second child of this marriage.

And, just as at his brother's infant baptism three years before, when Father McBride insisted on Yusuf (Joseph), a saint's name—something, according to him, without the traces of paganism the missionaries associated with native names—at Jubril's baptism, he picked Gabriel. He entrusted the child to the patronage of Saint Gabriel, the archangel.

They were a model family, a point of reference for intertribal and mixed marriage. In fact, in his homily at the wedding, Father McBride had reminded the congregation that the couple was a symbol of unity in a country where ethnic and religious hate simmered beneath every national issue, and he challenged the whole village to emulate the couple's openness. Perhaps the myriad tribes and religions in the country could be welded together by the love within such marriages, Father McBride thought, and the respect accorded in-laws would at least instill tolerance. He did everything to support the marriage. Because Bartholomew and Mary were poor, Father McBride begged money from the white tycoons of nearby multinational oil companies to help celebrate the diversity of this marriage, building them a house and supporting their needs.

But these were hard times. Due to decades of oil drilling, the soil was losing its fertility. Rivers no longer had fish, and, worse still, repeated oil fires annihilated hundreds of people each time. Shehu, fearing for his cows, moved away from the oil-rich villages to other parts of the south soon after the wedding.

When ancestral worshippers began asking people to bring animals to sacrifice to Mami Wata and other deities whose terrains were supposedly desecrated, Father McBride told his faithful to forget the pagans. The problem deepened when little children began to develop respiratory diseases, and strange rashes attacked their bodies, and the natives started running away to the big cities.

One day, without warning, Aisha escaped with the children to Khamfi, her father's original home. Yusuf was five and Jubril two years and three months. Bartholomew was crushed, and his resulting depression left him open to the taunts of the community. To protect their Catholic marriage, Father McBride advised Bartholomew to follow his wife to Khamfi, offering to foot the bill and arranging for a nearby Catholic parish to hire him as a laborer. But Bartholomew refused to go for fear of recurring religious and ethnic cleansing in the north. His only hope was that the children would come back when they were old enough to ask about their roots. He remarried promptly, even after Father McBride told him his wife's action was not sufficient reason to annul the marriage; he became a member of Deeper Life Bible Church.

Yusuf and Jubril grew up in Khamfi's sprawling Muslim-only Meta Nadum neighborhood and lost contact with their father and Ukhemehi. Their mother went back to Islam, and the brothers went to the mosque with their uncles. But Yusuf kept asking about his father and remembered a few things about his childhood in Ukhemehi and never quite felt comfortable in the mosque. Over the years, while Yusuf indulged in the snippets of their family history that often spilled out of their mother on her bad days, when she bemoaned her misfortunes, Jubril was the opposite. While his brother pulled closer to his mother to hear these stories, Jubril was distant. He blocked them out because they embarrassed him, and a measure of enmity came between the two boys as a result. Aisha was afraid for Yusuf because she could see he was in danger of apostasy.

This was Yusuf's situation when one day neighborhood

friends called him a bastard. The following month he decided to go back to Ukhemehi to search for his father. In spite of Aisha's plea and his uncles' threats, Yusuf ran away. Having been gone barely four months, he came back, surprising everyone, as a firebrand Deeper Lifer. It was from him that Jubril first heard about the supposed freedom of the south and the fantastic notions of a better life and how the whole village and the Deeper Life community welcomed him like the Prodigal Son. When Yusuf started insisting that his name was Joseph, instead of Yusuf, in Meta Nadum, Aisha could not sleep at night. Yusuf was not deterred by the antagonism this created between him and his brother or by the cold shoulder he was getting from his extended family. Seeing that he was determined, Aisha did not ask him to abandon Christianity altogether, but sneaked out to the nearest Catholic parish and recounted her ordeal to the priest. She wanted Yusuf to return to the Catholic Church because she knew that way his risk of being killed would be less than as a Deeper Lifer.

Back home she sat Yusuf down and gently told him that he was not a Deeper Lifer but a Catholic because of his infant baptism. She explained to him that, according to Catholic theology, baptism leaves an indelible mark on a person's soul—and whatever religion a person may choose later can not affect that Catholic mark. She told him that, in that sense, his Islamic faith and recent Deeper Life faith were nullified. She explained that though the Catholic Church, unlike Islam, would not force anybody to be loyal, the belief was that wherever you went you remained Catholic. But Yusuf refused to honor the appointment she had set up for him with the priest and continued to express his Deeper Life evangelism. Not only did he carry a Bible around Meta Nadum and recite the verses aloud, he set about trying to proselytize his neighbors, à la a Jehovah's Witness, insisting that it was the duty of every born-again Christian. In tears, his mother had turned to Jubril, pleading with him not to have anything to do with his brother's blood. But he too said he had to protect the honor of his family, neighborhood, and Islamic faith.

It was not long after this that Yusuf was mobbed by some relatives and neighbors and stoned to death, like Saint Stephen, for apostasy. Though Jubril did not join in the killing of his brother, he was close enough to hear him pray in tongues as the stones rained down on him.

STANDING IN THE BUS, these were some of the thoughts that swamped Jubril's mind. Losing material things — like the dozens of cows in his care, which his Khamfi attackers would have destroyed or claimed since his flight — did not bother him. And it was beyond him at this point to think about the national consequences of the crisis. He did not want to think about all his former friends who helped rout him out of Khamfi. He did not want to remember his childhood years of racing down the dusty unpaved streets of Meta Nadum, or the afternoons spent planting carrots and cabbage in the wide valley of the seasonal river that bordered one side of the neighborhood. It was best now to forget these things. He did not want to recall their conversations as they poured out of the mosque after Friday *Jummat,* all in long gowns, *babarigas* and *jhalabias,* the epitome of friendship in that celebratory throng, or how they stopped by each other's houses to eat and drink *zobo.* He

did not want to consider the years spent together in the outskirts of
Khamfi tending cows, or the times they fretted together about the
health of some calf and one of them had to carry it home on his
shoulders, like a good shepherd, or the times they made forays into
the Christian areas during riots to firebomb churches.

They had held Jubril as a true Muslim for not allowing family
loyalties to come between him and his religion when Yusuf was
given his just deserts, and Meta Nadum had rallied around him
when he had readily submitted his hand to be chopped off as
punishment for stealing someone's goat. When a few hard-
nosed journalists interviewed him later, he had exuded unparal-
leled confidence in his faith, although he did not allow them to
take his picture. He even pleaded with them to tell the human-
rights group that had taken his case to the supreme court not to
bother. Somehow he had become a hero. A rich man even
entrusted him with the care of his cows.

Now, he just wanted to cry for his mother, who had disappeared in this crisis, consoling himself that maybe she had been
merely displaced, like him, not killed. He wanted to apologize to
her for the enmity between him and Yusuf. For Jubril to begin
thinking in depth about his brother's death now, after his friends
betrayed him, would have shattered him. So Jubril tried to think
of Yusuf only in relation to his mother's grief. He could not imagine life without her. He preferred to imagine her back home in
the walled compound on the fringe of the neighborhood, where
they lived with his maternal uncles. He imagined her moving
from room to room, stroking her *tasbih,* prayer beads, and crying
for him until her eyes became as red and dry as the mud walls of
the local silos in the square courtyard. He could see her, her tall

frame bent by the loss of a son, coming out into the courtyard as if her sorrow had filled the rooms and now overflowed.

Once the riots broke out, he imagined his cousins and uncles standing guard with guns and machetes, to forestall the maddening mob of *almajeris*—Koranic-school pupils, some of whom had turned wild from years of begging on the streets—from plundering their home. He could see the faces of some of these *almajeris*. He could see the streets swarming with mobs, and endless clouds of dust rising as high as the minarets that jutted out of many private mosques in the neighborhood. He could not feel anything for these Muslims, nor for the Christians with whom he was fleeing. He could not be sure whether his Khamfi relatives would defend him, nor was he ready to entrust his life to anyone as he had done in the past.

That fateful afternoon, when Khamfi exploded, Jubril was coming back from grazing his cows. He ambled along behind the beasts, which filled the dirt road that connected the fields to his home, and placed his stick on his shoulder. When he heard two sharp shouts coming from the direction of the city, he thought nothing of it.

The blue sky had been bleached by the harmattan dust. The strong desert wind whipped the landscape, filling his *babariga* and drying the day's sweat. Being this close to home, he usually would have heard cars and trucks honking their horns on the major highway that passed near the town, but he heard nothing but the sound of the savannah sharpening the endless sough into a whistle.

When Jubril got to the corner, the beasts started trotting, anticipating a drink from the few pools in the valley. He jogged along with them, eager to take off his tire sandals and soak his feet in the pool while the cows drank. But as they turned to descend into the wide valley, the cows were startled by two people. Both carried leaves and were shouting to Jubril to pluck a branch from the bushes, but Jubril could not hear them clearly. Apart from the leaves, one carried a carton, the other a sack — their belongings. They ran as fast as they could into the savannah, as if they had stolen something and the owner was in hot pursuit. Jubril brought down his stick immediately and herded the animals to one side, positioning himself between them and possible danger.

When he got to the pools, it worried him that he did not find other herds and cowherds. Uncharacteristically for that time of day, the remnants of the river trickled into the pools clear and undisturbed. Even the farmers, who would normally be watering and tending their cabbage gardens at that hour, were absent. The place was deserted, and the gardens, green and fresh in the dead of the harmattan, looked like new wreaths in an old cemetery. Scouting around, Jubril discovered that the edges of the hoof-prints left on the soft ground by herds that had returned before him were jagged and tilted to the front, and that cow droppings did not stand in little hills but had poured out in crooked lines. He surmised that the animals had galloped past the pools. Quickly, he whipped his cows, and they ran toward home, and he ran after them.

A CHANTING MOB THAT suddenly swung into Jubril's path from a side road hesitated for a moment before going in the other direction. Though Jubril was far from the crossroad, the sight was so unusual that the cows panicked and stopped. They huddled together on one side of the road like schoolchildren around an *akara* seller. The mob kept pouring into the road, kicking up a haze of dust that moved like a low pillar of cloud. The people carried leaves, stones, knives, and sticks, and Jubril thought he recognized a few of them.

"*Sanu* Jubril, *sanu* Jubril!" Lukman and Musa called out from the crowd. They were Jubril's friends. They abandoned the throng and ran toward him, whistling and waving green leaves.

"*Sanu* Lukman . . . *sanu* Musa!" Jubril said, and waved back to them.

They were older than Jubril. Musa was a hulking figure, bare-chested, and had carved his beard into what the non-Muslims called "Sharia beard," which Jubril would have loved to have had if he had been blessed with thick facial hair. Lukman was thin and the taller of the two. Apart from the leaves, Musa was carrying a sword, and Lukman clutched a clear jar of gasoline that had no lid. Running toward Jubril, Lukman used the palm of his hand to stopper the container, and Jubril suspected the bulge in his breast pocket was a box of matches.

"Where your leap?" Lukman said to Jubril, panting and pointing at Musa's leaves.

"My friend, *wetin dey* haffen?" Jubril said, moving away from the cows to meet them. "*Kai, wetin* be de froblem dis time?"

"You no come frotest, huh?" Musa said.

"Which frotest? Gimme time," Jubril said, and tried to nudge Musa on the rib, but he dodged.

"Leave me alone," Musa said.

"Make I fark de cows pirst. I *dey* come."

"You no come frotest," Lukman repeated, glaring as Jubril tried to pat him on the shoulder. Jubril stopped dead in his tracks. "You no be good Muslim . . . ," Lukman said.

"Me?"

"Yes," Musa said.

Jubril laughed a short laugh. "*Haba!*"

"Your mama no allow you pollow us to be *almajeris* in dose days . . . ," Musa said, and looked at Lukman as if he wanted him to complete the accusation.

"You two *dey* craze *o!*" Jubril taunted them.

"She no allow make you join us kill dis Christians," Lukman said.

"My mama no be like dat," Jubril argued. "I say I *dey* come. I go join *una* now now. Ah ah, no vex now. Come, pollow me go fark dis cows, and I go join."

Jubril moved back toward his cows, but the two lunged at him menacingly. Lukman put down the jar, and Musa adjusted his sword. The tiny bells that adorned the brown sheath jangled. Jubril stopped laughing, sensing trouble. His friends were not smiling and their eyes bore hatred. He had never seen them like that before.

Remembering the two people who ran past him near the pools, Jubril jumped up and plucked some leaves from a Flame of the Forest, to show solidarity with whatever cause his friends were advancing. But his effort only alarmed them, for they thought he was trying to flee. They held him by his *babariga*.

"OK now, I be one of you," Jubril said, waving the leaves before them, dropping his stick.

"One of who?" Musa said.

"Dis no be matter of leap, you hear?" Lukman said.

"Come, *wetin* I do you?" Jubril asked them.

"*Wetin* you do us, huh?" Lukman said.

"Yes . . . why you *dey* harass me like dis?"

"OK, we no go fay you de money we owe you," Musa said.

"Which money? If you *dey* talk about de thousand naira you come borrow prom me, *na* lie *o*. You go fay me. Ha-ha, dat one no be talk at all."

"Cancel de debt now or else . . ."

"You must fay me my money. Oderwise I go refort you to de *alkali*. Dis one we go hear por Sharia court!"

With that, Jubril spun suddenly and freed himself from their grip.

"Also we go hear por court say you be pake Muslim!" Lukman said. "You be Christian . . ."

"Me? Christian?"

"Traitor, traitor!" they charged.

"Por where?" Jubril said. "You no go pit blackmail me por dis one."

"Yusup, your inpidel brother, better *fass* you," Musa said.

"Traitor, traitor," repeated Lukman.

Two men stopped and wanted to know what was going on.

Jubril still thought there was a chance they were pulling his leg. He felt he had proved that he was a devout believer. He remembered the wild celebration that swept through the north a few months back, when the Manzikan governor launched his total Sharia, arguing that common law was rooted in the Bible and Christianity. He said the Muslims had been cheated by Christians all along and that the time had come for Muslims to enjoy a legal system rooted in the Koran and Islam. He maintained that with Sharia the state would be cleansed of all the vices and immorality that plagued the people.

Jubril had joined the huge crowds chanting and brandishing the picture of their hero, the Manzikan governor. For three days, Jubril had gone out and demonstrated for the Sharia system to be established in Khamfi, though he, like most in the crowd, knew that in Khamfi there were as many Christians as there were Muslims.

It must be said, though, that for Jubril, it was not just a naive celebration — or a political rally, as the southern press had insinuated. Actually, the pro-Sharia rally swelled because people like him were ready to personally testify with their maimed limbs. Their presence had energized the rally. When Manzikan State gave single women in its employ a three-month ultimatum to get married — even if it meant being someone's third or fourth wife — or lose their job, Jubril and Musa and Lukman had gathered and cheered. They were convinced that Sharia should be extended to the whole country. Brothels and bars were shut down. When Manzikan warned that those who did not wear the Sharia beard could not bid for government contracts, barbers had long lines of devout men waiting to have their beards carved up. Jubril even accompanied Musa to the barber's shop.

Now, Jubril laughed at his friends' accusations, brought out a small picture of the hero-governor from his pocket, and held it high for everyone to see. But Lukman and Musa insisted and in fact swore that they would never fight against Christians with Jubril on their side.

"Dis boy *na* souderner," Musa said. "Inpidel."

"Enemy widin," Lukman said. "How we go pit make war wid dis barbaric Christians when one of us be one of dem?"

This was when it actually dawned on Jubril that the crowd was heading toward Kamdi Lata, the exclusive Christian quarters, and Shedun Sani, the mixed areas, to wage war with the Christians. The accusation his friends made against him became even more painful. He immediately swore by Allah that he was a real Muslim, but that was not enough. With the tension in the land, it was a terrible time to accuse someone of apostasy or of coming from the south. Jubril tried to tell the growing throng that his accusers actually owed him money and had refused to pay, which was true. But Lukman and Musa insisted that Jubril was not one of them, even though he spoke Hausa with the proper accent. Jubril wanted to talk about his brother's death, but they stopped him. He wanted to show his cut hand, but they threatened to accuse him of stealing another goat and warned him to stop the delaying tactics and to confess. Seeing how things were going, Jubril tried to explain his roots as his mother had told him, a story that he did not know well and did not care about until now.

"Jubril, dem no baftize you as small baby?" Musa asked, a mischievous smile dangling on his lips. "We know you, we know your baftism story."

"Answer quick quick," one of the bystanders said.

"We no get time to waste," another said.

Perhaps in days of peace, he would have had a chance to explain himself before a Sharia court. Perhaps he would have been tried and given a fair hearing, but these were wild days. Now, as he began to explain about the money Musa and Lukman owed him, Musa slapped him and wrestled him to the ground. They removed his *babariga* and fell upon him with clubs and stones. It was as if Musa was so angry he forgot to take out the sword, for he clubbed him with its sheath. Jubril lay on the ground, bent over, groaning, shielding his head with his hands. He did not re-act to his many wounds or wipe the blood from his body. He just lay there as his head swelled with dizziness and the earth spun around him.

Soon he did not feel the blows anymore. When he opened an eye, he saw that the circle of people who had beaten him had wid-ened, receding from him. Some of them were beginning to shep-herd the cows away. When Jubril saw Lukman going back to get the gas, he summoned all his energy, got up, and ran. They did not expect this, were caught unaware. Jubril ran toward the bushes, toward the pools, and they chased him, chanting, *"Allahu Akbar, Allahu Akbar!"*

Jubril remembered running very fast and being surprised that he could move at all, given his wounds. When he looked back, the ranks of his pursuers had swelled; even those who had left the task of burning him to Lukman and Musa had joined in. They pelted him with rocks, but he did not stop or fall. He heard some gunshots, but he kept going. He went past the pools and up the hill into the savannah. The mob spread out and thrashed the cab-bage farms. Jubril ran like a dog; he ran until his vision darkened. He remembered falling; he remembered dizziness beclouding him. . . .

Suddenly someone on the Luxurious Bus brushed past his pocketed wrist. This brought Jubril back to the more crucial busi-ness of maintaining his disguise. Instinctively, he pushed his arm deeper into his pocket. He cursed himself for dwelling on his flight. He begged Allah for strength.

When Jubril looked toward the front of the bus, he realized that two police officers had come aboard and were standing over the sick man. They were in plain clothes. Like soldiers evacuating a wounded comrade from the front, they held their rifles at the ready. They acted as if the sick man were dead, though he was still babbling. In spite of the pleas from Emeka and Madam Aniema and Tega, the police said it was better for the sick man to leave the bus, to make room for others. Hoisting him into a standing position, they frisked him and relieved him of his ticket. When the passengers murmured, the police assured them that they would put him on the next Luxurious Bus. The murmur turned to jeers as the police dragged him out and deposited him on a veranda.

More passengers came onto the bus, and Jubril had to keep moving back, still preoccupied with the image of the sick man. He left the chief's place and jostled from spot to spot in the aisle. But he was becoming more and more conspicuous, because most of the refugees in the aisle were beginning to sit down on the floor. When he looked at the chief, the chief either glared at him or looked away, as if Jubril was trying to rob him of *his* seat.

"It seems someone is in your seat," said Emeka, who was still smarting from the eviction of the sick man, when Jubril leaned against his seat.

"Yessa."

"Well, tell him to get off," Emeka said. "This is the era of democracy, young man!"

"Ah . . . yessa," Jubril said, covering his mouth with his left hand.

"Yessa *ke?* And leave my seat alone. It's one man, one vote. . . . One man, one seat!"

"*Abeg,* no halass de boy," Ijeoma said. "Cally your anger go meet de porice. No be dis boy lemove de sick man from dis bus."

"Hey, don't tell me what to do," Emeka said, folding and re-folding his monkey coat on his lap. "Is your husband a soldier?"

"You get wife yourserf?" Ijeoma said.

"Is this place not tense enough already?" Madam Aniema said.

"This is democracy," Emeka said. "I have a right to shout if I want, OK. . . . Let me tell you something, you women. This is not the military era, when people could not get what they wanted or say what they felt. This is eight months since the generals were bribed with oil-drilling licenses so they could peacefully leave power for us civilians. Remember, you could never disobey a soldier then. Don't forget that even here in the city of Lupa a soldier shot a bus driver and a bus conductor because they refused to give him twenty naira at an illegal checkpoint—"

"So what?" Ijeoma cut in, scratching her Afro, her big eyes narrow slits. "We civirians better *pass* soldiers? You *dey* talk as if you be de onry smart person for dis bus. And, what do you mean by 'you women'?"

"Yes, Mr. Man, make you no insult us for dis Luxurious Bus *o,*" Tega said. "*Na* woman *dey* cause dis *wahala* for Khamfi?"

"No mind de man, my sister," Ijeoma said. "He *dey* talk rike porygamous man!"

Emeka looked at one and then the other, surprised the two

women were now in the same camp. He began to wag his finger at them as he searched for what to say, but Madam Aniema advised him: "Don't say anything about them. If this gives them peace, so be it. Women are like that."

"As I was saying, no matter what has happened, you cannot lose hope in democracy!" Emeka said in a friendlier voice, ignoring the two women, his words rising above the commotion. "Be hopeful, be hopeful!"

"Who tell you say we done lose hope?" Tega taunted him. "*Na* person like you *wey* escape Khamfi only in socks *dey* lose hope . . . not we!"

"No mind de *yeye* man," Ijeoma said. "We say make you reave dat boy arone, you begin brame woman. No be woman born you?"

Jubril looked at Ijeoma and Tega, his countenance appealing to them not to argue with Emeka. He had been happy that the conversation had moved away from him, but now he was afraid it was coming back. He wished he could have asked the women to shut up, or that they would have known on their own that it was wrong to argue with men in public.

Sensing that more people were standing at the back of the bus, Jubril moved there to make himself less visible. But he had only stood in his new spot for a few minutes when someone asked him whether he was in the toilet line. He shrugged and shook his head no. But when the person in front of him and the one behind him said they were in the toilet line and were not offended that Jubril had cut ahead, he nodded and smiled sheepishly. Jubril craned his neck and was then able to discern the line snaking through the aisle around the passengers sitting on the floor. It seemed like the only stable part of a space fretted by anxiety and movement. The line stopped right in front of the toilet door, with the chest of the person who was next resting against it. Though Jubril had never used a toilet before and had no urge to use one now, he did not quit the line. He appreciated it, because he noticed that people who had bought the aisle spaces were tolerant and considerate. He wished the line would last forever, that refugees would take longer and longer in the restroom.

When he looked up front to see where the chief was, he discovered that he was sitting only three seats away and still eating his Cabin Biscuits, his cheeks plumped out like those of a Hausa-Fulani trumpeter.

JUBRIL WAS GLANCING PERIODICALLY at the chief, silently irritated with him, when suddenly the TV sets came on. The images hit him like lightning, driving his face in another direction. He shut his eyes. But he had already seen the images, and, as they say, what the eye has seen it cannot unsee. He felt violated. He could not process the pictures right away.

The noise from the TVs replaced the din of the bus, as everybody hushed and turned their attention to the screens. Everyone in the toilet line looked back to catch the action — except Jubril, who had reopened his eyes and was thinking about how to overcome this latest hurdle. He wanted so much to be part of the crowd in every way. It was no longer about whether Allah would punish him for watching TV. It was just that his conservatism stiffened his neck, and he kept his back to the screen. Jubril wanted to relax and let his guard down. But, now, wherever he looked he seemed to be confronted by faces. It was like driving against traffic. He tried to look at the ceiling but could not even manage that. Feeling that his predicament was written all over his face and that it might draw attention to him, Jubril stared at his canvas shoes. He looked so hard that he could have counted each tiny thread, but he did not actually see anything. Fear rose and spread over him like goose bumps. The fingers of his left hand became sweaty and trembled. His cut wrist was numb, and he tried to move his elbow into a more comfortable position.

When he tried to turn around to face the TVs, he could only make it halfway, like a clogged wheel, and found himself looking out a window, a welcome distraction. He poured his gaze into it.

The sun had gone down. The crowd outside the bus was not as restless as before. More refugees had crowded onto the few verandas. Some people sat wherever there was space in the park, clutching their belongings, expecting other buses. Everybody looked tired, and even the chatter was subdued.

Out on the savannah, as if in a dream, some of the evergreen trees seemed to swell as they let out gentle sprays of bats into the twilight. High in the sky the bats mixed and mingled and flew in one direction, toward the park, as if blown by the wind. It looked like a giant shapeless figure with many legs atop the evergreen trees. They gradually filled up the sky. After a while, it was like a big black wave, stretched out, bobbing, shrieking through the dusk.

Someone tapped Jubril on the legs. He looked down, then quickly away. It was the pregnant lady, seated on the floor, breastfeeding her baby. Her name was Monica. She had escaped with just her baby. Her big eyes were red from crying, and her face was

swollen with sleeplessness. She held on to her infant with all tenderness. She was wearing a long white dress that someone had
given her in the course of her flight. Two sizes too big, it seemed
to provide the extra cloth she needed to nurse in.

"*Haba,* my broder, you no fit even watch TV?" Monica teased
Jubril, an uneasy smile washing over her face.

"Me?" Jubril mumbled like the chief, pretending to watch the
bats outside.

"You alone *dey* suffer for dis riot? Or you want tell me say your
situation bad *pass* de sick man *wey* police *comot* for dis bus?"

Jubril nodded. "Yes."

Though he had resigned himself to being in close proximity
to women on this journey, the sight of a woman breast-feeding
did not settle well with him. He did not like the fact that she
was smiling at him or talking to him while doing this. He could
not look down, for that would mean seeing her breasts. He did
not want to talk with her, return the smile, or do anything to
encourage her attention. Yet he tried to be gentle in his response.
This woman had to be handled more carefully than the TV, he
thought, because she was directing her attention to him and
demanding a reply.

He wanted to move away, but where could he go? He looked
back, making a conscious effort not to look at the TV, to search
for Madam Aniema. He held his left hand like a visor over his
eyes, to shield them from the TV's images. The sight of Madam
Aniema's white hair and the memory of her kindness countered
the discomfort that was beginning to build in his heart because of
Monica and Tega and Ijeoma.

"Ah ah, which kind *shakara* be dis now," Monica continued,

and touched his leg again. "You *dey* cover your face as if sun *dey* for Luxurious Bus. You too proud. *Abi,* sadness *dey* do you like dis? Your situation no bad *pass* my situation *o.* Dem done burn my house; and my husband and my two children, I no see dem *o.* Only dis baby remain. But I no lose hope. But why I no go smile? Why I no go watch TV? Look at you: I *dey* talk to you, but you no even want look my face? You alone want go toilet?"

"No," Jubril said, embarrassed, the word escaping from his mouth before he could stop it.

Monica chuckled, happy that at least she could get a rise out of him. "I see, maybe you get dysentery."

"Mmmh," Jubril groaned.

"Na wa for you *o!"*

The passengers seemed relieved to watch TV, and a certain peacefulness and order reigned: almost everybody was looking in the same direction. It was the first sign of unity Jubril had witnessed since he boarded the bus. Now, he could hear Emeka whispering sharply at people to bend or get out of the way so he could see the TV properly.

"No worry, de toilet line *dey* move like snail," Monica whispered to Jubril. "At least, make de TV *dey* entertain you. You *dey* too serious for dis trip. . . . See, even my baby *dey* suck breast and *dey* watch TV. . . . Cheer up."

"Mmmh."

"No mind dis *chakara* boy!" Tega whispered to Monica. "Forget him. See how he *dey* pose wid one hand for pocket?"

Once the comment about his hand was made, Jubril turned and faced the TV sets, like everybody else—but with eyes closed. His pocketed wrist was hidden from the view of the women, and he pretended that he did not hear the comment about it. He shut his eyes so tight that there were wrinkles on his face. Closing his eyes was a split-second decision, a compromise that gave him peace. He was reassured that no one else would bother him for not looking in the right direction. A bit of his alienation from the others melted, and he felt more connected to his surroundings. The fact that the women did not bug him again was proof enough of that.

"Yes, now you *dey* act like a human being," Monica said after a while, thinking that he was watching TV. She moved the baby from one breast to the other.

"Stop whispering over there!" Emeka said.

"Who make you crass plefect for dis bus?" Ijeoma hissed, as if she had been waiting to do so. "*Yeye* man, you no get TV for house? You be de dliver? *Abi,* conductor? *Abi,* you want brame women again?"

If Jubril had opened his eyes, he would have seen the TVs beaming beautiful foreign images. The clips they were watching could have been from one of those huge multinational TV empires. But since the logo had been wiped off—pirated pictures, you would say—by the local or national channels that broadcast them, you could not really tell.

Jubril could hear his fellow passengers laughing and making comments about the pictures. Emeka had been silenced, so people reacted freely. They hummed along with the jingles and were connected to the global village of advertisements, sports, fashion, and news. These images washed away, or washed over, the sadness and tension and anxiety of the refugees. It was like fresh air, and, though Jubril could not see the pictures, he could feel the good mood growing around him, like mushrooms in the dark;

he knew people were being entertained, like Monica was saying. Though he forced himself to wear a stock smile, his eyes were still closed. The more relaxed he felt, the greater the temptation to open his eyes became. He did not give in. He closed his eyes so tight that a dizziness swam before them, then a dull pain pressed against them. He was like the blind and used his ears to decipher the situation around him. The voice of Monica stood out, annoying and too close for comfort.

He thanked Allah for the reprieve that closing his eyes had brought him. He had found a way to avoid Monica. There was no limit to what he could endure, he thought. While others found peace in things external, his own came from deep within: the triumph of finding a way to maintain his tradition, his uniqueness, in a strange world. Now, if only he could get the chief to leave his seat, he thought, he could put his forehead on the headrest and pretend to sleep until the bus moved, until the bus reached his father's village.

Abruptly there was quiet, a deep silence that Jubril instinctively knew could only come from shock. And then four or five people read aloud what was written on the screen:

Breaking News: Religious Riots, Khamfi

The passengers became restless again, and a din rose above the TVs as everybody began to talk at the same time. Some said they knew the dead they had seen on TV and shouted their names. Others said this could not be their Khamfi — the multiethnic, multireligious city a mere two hours north of the motor park.

The Khamfi they saw that evening was the corpse capital of the world. Churches, homes, and shops were being torched. The sharp, unblinking eye of the news camera poured its images into the darkening bus, bathing the refugees in a kaleidoscope of color. Jubril could sense this effect behind his eyelids as the camera zeroed in on charred corpses sizzling in electric-blue flames. Cries of fury poured into the bus from the TV screens, heightening the agitation of the refugees. Jubril listened for the voice of the chief but did not hear him. Was he still in his seat? Was he asleep? Why did he not say anything when everybody else was talking? He turned his ears more deliberately in the chief's direction and then his eyes.

The refugees rose to their feet at the sight of hungry-looking *almajeris* running around with fuel and matches, setting things and people afire. They were much younger than Jubril's friends Musa and Lukman. In the bus, anger replaced shock and passive complaints. It was not really the sight of corpses burning — or the businesses of their southern compatriots being leveled by firebombs, or the gore when some of the kids were fried in gas before they had a chance to use it — that roused the refugees. All over the country, people had developed a tolerance of such common sights; decades of military rule, and its many terrorist plots directed at the populace, had hardened them. What riled them was the sight of free fuel in the hands of *almajeris*.

The shouts of the refugees rang out into the approaching darkness and rallied the people outside the bus. The verandas emptied, and everybody came together, milling about the bus like winged termites around a fluorescent bulb. Hearing the word *fuel* made Jubril uneasy. He remembered Lukman and his gas jar and the matches in his pocket. He remembered Musa and his sword. He remembered the crowd chasing him up the wide valley, the gunshots, the stones. It felt as if all the people around him were Lukman and Musa and would soon smoke him out. His wounds seemed to burn under his clothes. He hid his face and tried to breathe normally.

"Where's our driver?" Madam Aniema shouted, as if someone had hit her. "Is he back with the fuel yet?" The shock of hearing such anger in a sweet woman's voice almost made Jubril open his eyes.

"The driver has not come back yet!" Emeka said.

"Are those children using fuel or water?" she continued.

"Water *ke?* Fuel!" Tega said.

"Who give dem fuel to burn people when we no *fit* get fuel tlavel home?" Ijeoma said.

"Our fuel, our fuel . . . southern oil!" some of the passengers began to chant.

For a moment it sounded as if the bus would explode with anger. Finally Jubril opened his eyes.

The toilet line had melted into the crowd, because those who had been sitting on the floor were now standing. Jubril could feel Monica right behind him, her child wailing into the commotion, kicking and flailing his tiny hands. Monica, in an attempt to soothe him, kept tapping her feet to rock him, breaking the monotony of his cry. Jubril pressed against the person in front of him to make room between his back and Monica.

"Who *dey* give dis Muslim kids dis fuel?" Monica said.

"Politicians!" Emeka said. "They're using southern fuel to burn our people and businesses!"

"Nobody go touch our oil again," Monica said. "Dem *dey* use our oil money to establish Sharia, yet dem done pursue us out of de nord!"

The bus filled with loud plans about how best to stop the government and multinational oil companies from drilling for oil in the delta. Some said they would have to put this into effect as soon as they reached home and started cursing the driver for delaying their departure.

"You be against national interest . . . national security!" said one of the two police officers as he pushed his way onto the bus. He was pointing a pistol at everybody, waving it from side to side. The people pushed into the seats, some climbing on top of others to get out of his way. When he had come midway into the bus, his colleague appeared and covered him with an AK-47.

"*Na* our oil!" Monica said to the first officer.

"Who's talking?" the officer asked.

"*Na* me," she said.

She pushed forward fearlessly with the baby, even as others were backing away. She shoved Jubril aside, then handed her baby to someone. She gathered up her long dress with both hands, as if she were going to wade into a knee-deep stream. "I say, *na* our oil," she said again to the police. "We *dey* democracy now, you hear?"

All eyes had turned from the TVs to the confrontation between Monica and the police. Some were begging her to calm down. For Jubril, it was not just that he felt this was the wrong time to challenge the police; he also did not like the fact that a woman was standing up to the law. Maybe he would have taken it better if the bus were filled with only woman passengers and the officer of the law was also a woman. Monica was standing right in front of Jubril, just her body separating him from the gun. He tried to ease back into the crowd, but nobody would let him; nobody wanted to take his place. So he just stood there staring vaguely at Monica's calves and feet, holding his breath and praying that the police would not open fire.

"Who be dis woman?" said the police.

"Daughter of oil," Monica said. "And who be you?"

"You are asking me?" the officer said.

"Yes?"

"I *dey* warn you *o,* stupid woman. You done lost your mind to dis Sharia *wahala!*"

"I say you get ID?" the woman said. "Or dem done send you to kill us?"

"ID? Why should I show you my ID?"

"Come, woman, you better behave *o,*" the other officer said from the door. "Or soon you go be daughter of bullets."

"*Oya* . . . go ahead," Monica said. "If you finish killing me, then kill my baby, OK. . . . *Wetin* I get for dis world again?"

"We just *dey* enforce government order!" the police retorted. "Government order!"

"We no *dey* military government," Monica said. "We *dey* for democracy now."

"Shut up. . . . Government is government! Government oil. Federal government oil, you hear?"

The officer at the door backed out of it and fired warning shots into the night sky. The sounds of people running and scrambling outside entered the bus.

Inside, the refugees hushed, even Monica. She stood there as if she was expecting the bullets to hit her. The police asked the man holding the baby to return him to Monica. The man started trembling, as if suddenly the child had turned into a viper. Monica took her baby reluctantly from the man, not so much because of the officer's order, but because fear of the police could have caused him to drop the child. She sat down on the floor like a zombie. When the police went away, she began to cry, pacing herself with periods in which she rattled on about her dead husband and children.

THE TOILET LINE AGAIN revealed itself as most people in the aisle sat down. A few more had joined the line, pushing Jubril back several spaces, toward the front of the bus. He now stood next to the chief—who sat quietly, as if the recent turmoil had happened on another planet—facing the back of the TV set. He Jubril no longer needed to close his eyes. Everybody from the back of the bus to those a few seats from where he stood looked in his direction, inches above his head. He studied them, the colorful light from the TV dancing, an artificial beauty playing on their gloomy, misery-stained faces. He watched anxiously, sweeping the entire width of the bus with wary eyes, eager to read the true nature of what they were seeing.

Some of the refugees were crying, but others began to cheer as the TV broadcast more action-packed scenes from Khamfi. Columns of adult northerners and southerners wielding automatic rifles and machetes were battling each other. Madness whipped up the red dust of Khamfi. Many neighborhoods burned, littering the heavens with funnels of smoke.

Emeka stood up, threw his monkey coat on the floor, and started cheering. "That man with the big gun in the group to the left is my cousin!" he said. "The man with lots of rosaries and scapulars wrapped around his rifle . . ."

"Your real cousin?" Madam Aniema asked.

"Absolutely. . . . His name is Dubem Okonkwo. I am Emeka Okonkwo." He pointed again at the screen. "That one is my friend . . . Thomas Okoromadu Ikechi. . . . That bare-chested muscular one in brown trousers. We're all from Anambra."

"Oh, you come flom Anambla?" Ijeoma said.

"*Kpom kwem!*" Emeka said, his eyes fixed on the screen. "Come on, Tom, give it to them. Give it to them. . . . Blow the head off that pagan Muslim with firebombs!"

"I come flom Anambla also *o,*" Ijeoma said. "*Na* my prace *o.*"

But Emeka did not pay her any attention. "My Dubem, give them the fight of their lives. These people have to be taught a lesson."

"Yes, dis countly berong to us too!" said Ijeoma.

The fight on TV went on, at times the Christians gaining an upper hand, then the Muslims dominating. For many on the bus, perhaps Khamfi looked more like some of the towns down south, in the delta, that General Sani Abacha had sent soldiers to obliterate because the natives had asked for their land to be developed after four decades of neglect and environmental degradation by government-multinational oil companies. Government troops had stormed the delta with tanks and rocket launchers and terrorized the people. Some reporters said it was the perfect excuse for the government to rein in the increasingly rebellious oil villages of the delta. Others said it was easier to drill oil in land not cluttered by hungry, illiterate natives, who stood around begging for food, water, and medicine. Whichever the case, the few survivors had fled and become refugees in big, multiethnic cities like Lagos, Kaduna, Jos, and Khamfi.

As Emeka urged his people on, Jubril touched the chief's shoulder lightly and bent down to whisper in his ear.

"Who told you to touch a royal father?" Chief Ukongo hissed.

"Mmmh," Jubril mumbled, and stepped back.

Nobody was listening to them: they were all glued to the TV. Even those in the toilet line had turned around to watch. They inched backward each time someone got out of the toilet. It was as if nobody could afford to miss a thing.

"Wait a moment, *who* are you?" the chief asked Jubril, as if he had just noticed the boy. "Don't hang around me!"

"Yessa," Jubril said.

Some people stared at them, angry because the chief's voice had distracted them from the TV. But the old man was unfazed. He fanned himself slowly. From his demeanor and commanding voice, it was not hard to see that he once enjoyed honor and close ties to the generals. Now, though his fortunes had depreciated since the introduction of the so-called democracy and he may have even lost weight, he refused to believe that he had degenerated to the level of this dirty, arrogant teenager.

"I say, who are you?" the chief repeated. "You seat thief . . . who are you?"

The boy whispered, "No . . . Jubril . . ."

Realizing that he had given his Muslim name, Jubril straightened up immediately, his heart pounding. He looked around to see whether anybody had heard him, but nobody was paying attention. Jubril faked a smile, pulled closer to the chief, put a finger in his mouth to alter his accent, and said, "Sa, I mean Gabriel . . . G-a-b-r-i-e-l . . . angel of God!"

"I don't care about any angel of God. . . . Remove that stupid finger from your mouth. You are disgusting!"

"Just shut up, you two," Emeka said.

"Where two of *una dey* when police come here?" Ijeoma said. "Why you no talk den? Make you no disturb our cable TV *o!*"

"Cowards!" Monica spoke for the first time since the police incident. "Royal fader, my foot!"

"I say everybody shut up," Emeka said again. "I *dey* watch my people do combat! You get relative who *dey* do Schwarzenegger for cable TV before?"

"You *dey* ask me to shut up, huh?" Monica said.

"By the grace of God," Emeka said.

"Wait, you and me go wear de same trouser today!" the woman said.

"Too many madwomen in this bus today," Emeka said.

Monica carefully put the baby on the floor, got up, and tried to gather her clothes for a fight. But she found that cumbersome. She wanted to remove her long dress altogether. But her neighbors held her back and tried to talk her out of causing trouble. They admonished Emeka for calling her a madwoman. "I for teach you lesson now now!" Monica managed to say to Emeka.

Jubril was unsure about how well he had corrected his mistake. The chief's face was blank, so he started to relax again. He thanked Allah that Emeka and Monica and Ijeoma had distracted the bus the way they did. He considered this another miracle and celebrated it in the depths of his being. Actually,

Monica's action had lessened the ill will he had felt toward her. As she was challenging Emeka, he had been rooting for her to make more noise, to antagonize Emeka so the focus of attention in the bus would never come back to him and the chief.

Now Jubril allowed three people to pass him in the toilet line, just to make sure he remained behind the middle TV. He shut his eyes again. He shifted his wrist nervously in his pocket. Mentioning his real name was a close call.

JUBRIL WAS NOT USED to being called Gabriel, though it was an old, new name. He had always been ashamed of what his mother told him about his pre-Muslim, Christian roots. Now he tried to repeat "Gabriel" quietly to himself many times, as if he were reciting his *tasbih,* in a bid to get used to it. He did not want to be taken unawares again. "*Na* just a name," he said to himself. "Just a name. Jubril and Gabriel *dey* mean de same ting." He started to imagine himself in his father's village and hearing people calling him, "Gabriel, Gabriel." He imagined himself turning immediately to the source of the call. He imagined himself awaking in the morning as soon as he heard "Gabriel." He learned to spell it backward. He started to sing the name in his mind, but he was having problems with the *J* and *G*.

Before the riots, it had pained him that his personal story was not as straightforward as he would have wanted. Over the years he did everything he could not to remember the parts that he knew. If people said anything about the delta or about the Atlantic Ocean, he would quickly change the subject, because, in his mind, that was the shameful place of his birth. He equated *southerner* with *infidel,* and even when someone told him there were Muslims in the south, especially among the Yorubas of the southwest, somehow his mind had refused to accept that these southern Muslims were real or genuine. He felt privileged to be a northerner and did everything to groom that part of his identity.

When people talked about the oil wealth of the south, he would feel anger rising in him and wonder why Allah would have given the oil to the land of the infidels. So he was relieved when during the recent campaigns, some politicians started telling the crowds that the crude oil actually belonged to the north and not to the people who lived in the oil fields of the delta. Like many, Jubril was swayed by their spurious argument: that the oil deposits in the delta were the result of years of sediments being carried from the north by the River Niger; the politicians wondered why the delta people should then claim the oil as their own; they wondered why they should ask for a bigger budgetary allocation from the new, democratic government. As they spoke, Jubril, who had skipped taking the cows to graze, had applauded and roared with the crowd. Though he could not read properly, he gladly received two copies of the booklet that propagated these arguments, one for himself and the other for his mother. Other northern politicians who came to town but did not say the oil wealth belonged to the north or that they would introduce total Sharia did not get a big crowd.

Now Chief Ukongo's sarcastic "*Who* are you?" cut deep into Jubril's soul. The events of the previous two days had knifed through his Muslim identity. Running in the bush from Khamfi, Jubril's mind had become a whirlwind of questions: Allah, is it true that once a person is baptized, as my mother said I was at birth, he remains a Christian forever, never able to remove the mark from his soul? Are you punishing me for this infant baptism that I did not choose? You know that as long as I can remember, I have always felt every inch a Muslim, and to prove my steadfastness, I did challenge Yusuf's apostasy and sacrificed his brotherhood to you. . . . If the world will not accept me as a southerner-northerner, will you also condemn me as a Christian-Muslim? Though I was attacked by Musa and Lukman for being a fake Muslim, Allah, please, give me the wisdom to convince the Christians in this bus that I am truly one of them. Lead me home, merciful one, lead me to peace. . . . Allah, your religion of Islam is a religion of peace.

Suddenly there was chaos in the bus. The irresistible pull of the cable pictures was gone, replaced by grainy black-and-white pictures of refugees in a police-and-military barracks in Khamfi. The images were unsteady, as if the local cameramen were trembling with the pain of their compatriots while filming. When the pictures steadied a bit, you could see the people who had been displaced. They sat everywhere, in the fields, on the verandas, and some were still running into the barracks. Many were like the people in the bus or in Lupa Motor Park, clutching the few belongings they could escape with.

The passengers were now standing, agitated, searching around for the cause of the change in TV stations. The first person to find his voice was Emeka. He pointed at the screen and shouted, "My cousin, my cousin. . . . Let me see my cousin! Let me see my friend! Give us cable TV." Then he pointed at the police officer who had the remote control, and everyone glared at him. The officer dangled the remote from his fingers like it was the ultimate symbol of power.

"Which cousin? Shut up!" said the officer to Emeka. "Listen, dis foreign TV channels *dey* spoil de image of our country. Dese white stations *dey* make billions of dollars to sell your war and blood to de world. . . . We no bad like dis. OK, why dem no *dey* show corpses of deir white people during crisis for TV? *Abi,* people no *dey* kill for America or Europe?"

"You *dey* speak grammar!" someone shouted. "*Wetin* concern us wid America and Europe? *Abeg,* give us cable TV."

"Remove dis toilet pictures!" said another.

"So our barracks be toilet now?" the police answered. "What an insult!"

"You *na* mad mad police," Monica said.

"OK, cable TV no be for free anymore!" the police said.

"But, it's our pictures we are watching on cable TV," Madam Aniema said. "Why should we pay you to see ourselves and our people?"

The police answered, "Because government *dey* complain say cable TV *dey* misrepresent dis religious crisis."

"Officer," said Ijeoma, pointing to Emeka, "you no hear dis man talk say he done see his cousin for inside cable TV? We no go pay notting. We done pay for Ruxulious Bus arleady!"

"Government order!" the police said.

"Which order?" said Ijeoma, grabbing her Afro in frustration. "How you take hear dat order? No be you and we *dey* dis bus togeder?"

"*Amebo* woman, you understand police work? Stop interrogating us!"

"Please, show me my cousin!" Emeka said, tears running down his face. Please, return to that channel. . . . I want to see my cousin again! Is he alive?" The police did not even look at him. "Officer, I'll give you whatever you want later . . ."

"*Later?* We no *dey* do *later* for cable TV," the police said, watching Emeka's hands like a dog expecting its owner to offer something. "Give us de money now now. . . . Cable TV, life action . . . e-commerce!"

"E-commerce?" Emeka said, looking around.

"Oh yes, e-commerce no reach your side? You tink we police no *dey* current?"

"My brothers, whatever it is, I'll pay you later . . . I swear!"

"Show us de money, we show you your cousin . . . quick quick. White people call *am* e-commerce."

"Which white people?" said Monica. "*Abeg,* leave white people out of dis cable talk."

"Please, don't shout at them," Emeka begged Monica.

She laughed at him. "I no tell you before? Now you go beg me tire *o.*"

As Emeka searched in his pockets for money to give the police, many refugees intervened and begged Monica not to exact her revenge on Emeka by insulting the police.

"Please, show my cousin," Emeka said. "I know he'll never let Jesus Christ down in this battle. . . . I pleaded with him to run south with me, but he said Khamfi was the only home he knew. He was born in Khamfi . . ."

Seeing the ten-naira note he was offering them, the police laughed and asked him the last time he saw a N10 movie. He told the police he had lost everything in Khamfi. They told him to also consider his cousin and friend lost.

Emeka looked as if he had been thrown out of a film premiere and sat down. His disappointment infected the whole bus. Some cried, though nobody wanted to give the police more money. Jubril felt like giving Emeka a N50 note but did not, fearing such charity might draw attention to him.

Others prayed aloud for the day when they — the *talakawas,* the wretched people of this world, who were the subjects of such black comedy on TV — would be rich enough to watch the irresistible pictures of their pain and shame. The murmuring in the bus gathered momentum; people pounded their seats. Everybody was talking except the chief and Jubril. The chief sat tight, like most postcolonial African heads of state. Jubril realized he was the only other person who did not condemn the police publicly, so he joined the protest to be in step with the majority.

"You toilet people *dey* cause trouble for dis bus!" one policeman shouted at the line of TV-watching, backward-moving refugees.

"We no be troublemakers *o . . . biko!*" a man pleaded, turning to face the toilet.

"Shut up . . . *na* you!" the police said.

"I am sorry," the man begged. "OK, give us police state. We no want democracy again."

"Even, you too many for dat toilet line . . . it no be pit latrine. Bring two hundred naira each if you want shit now now!"

The bus became quiet. The line began to fall apart.

"Please, make we pay fifty," someone said.

"Greedy man," the police said. "How you take go from two hundred to fifty?"

"Small, small . . . I be businessman," the man said.

"OK, if you get one-fifty, enter toilet wid immediate effect," the police said. "First-class toilet. . . . *Dey* flush after four buttocks only. . . . And no wash your hand. . . . Serious water shortage *dey* Lupa!" Three refugees paid and moved ahead of those who could not pay.

After a while the police said, "Okay, if you get eighty, stand after first class. . . . If you get less than eighty, shut your buttocks and sit down!"

A refugee begged, "Officer, you fit collect twenty for fifth class?"

"Your head correct at all? OK fifty!"

With the reduced fee, some people returned to the line, including Jubril. Emeka sat there with his head in his hands, tears streaming down his cheeks. Tega stood up and made a sad speech to the police officers. She complimented them for their sense of compromise and for not shooting or beating anybody. She told the police that in spite of what was happening in the land, she was hopeful that democracy and compromise would prevail.

When the police finally left, the bus refugees were as beaten down as the hordes of grim-faced Christian and Muslim and northern and southern refugees they watched on TV. In the barracks, or sitting in the fields, in groups, they shared their tears. Some read the Koran for consolation, some the Bible. One woman brought out a little black calabash and placed it momentarily on the foreheads of each remaining member of her household. Others just sat there, too shocked to talk to any god.

Occasionally, their common grief was interrupted as the heavily guarded gates of the barracks opened to admit truckloads of more refugees. Whenever the soldiers and the police came near the refugees, the refugees cringed. Were they going to be betrayed and given out to be slaughtered? If the civilians were not safe when the soldiers ruled the land, how safe were they coming into the barracks? Some of the refugees were so afraid that without being asked, they paid the guards to ensure their protection.

JUBRIL HAD NOT EATEN since Mallam Abdullahi had given him a piece of bread. Now, his eyes began to lust for the chief's snacks, and the old man, who was watching him, offered him two Cabin Biscuits. Jubril refused at first, distrustful of his intentions.

"Take it, don't pretend!" the chief said. But when Jubril mimed his thank you to him and extended his left hand, the chief withdrew the gift. "I cannot allow you to insult my chieftaincy with your left hand!"

"I no want eat. . . . I want sit," Jubril said, lying.

"Son, I'm not bribing you. Just trying to be nice to you."

"Tanks."

In spite of the chief's taunts, Jubril could see that the man was not at peace and ate his snacks without pleasure. The wrinkled, feeding movements on his face, like a faulty light switch, happened many a fraction faster than his tottering Adam's apple moved as his jaws slowly pounded the food. The TV glare splashed on the chief's face, like a searchlight on the dark, troubled waters of his soul.

"Make sure you *dey* de right seat *o!*" the police shouted from the door.

"Yes, officers," everybody chorused.

"If you no get your ticket, we go trow you out quick quick. If you *dey* wrong place, we go charge *una* extra for loitering *o,* you hear?"

"Yes, officers."

"De bus driver *dey* come now now."

The news that the driver would soon arrive brought some relief to the bus. People whispered to their neighbors and adjusted themselves in their seats for the long-awaited trip home. Jubril fished out the Madu Motors ticket from his bag. He studied it carefully and was satisfied. *Gabriel O: #52* was scrawled on it. He tucked the ticket back into his pocket carefully, like a prized possession, and smiled to no one in particular in anticipation of the trip.

Outside, the crowd was in an uproar. They gathered around the bus as if to storm it.

"No worry, dis no be last bus," the police addressed them. "Many bus *dey* come from nord. Dem go stop to carry *una*. Dem fit arrive before we leave *sef.* . . . Last night many of dem carry people from here too."

"Lies, lies!" people shouted. "Dis bus no go leave here tonight *o!*"

The police stepped forward and fired into the air to ward off an assault. The crowd backed away.

"Why don't you sit down here?" the chief told Jubril, whom he had been studying. He pointed to a place on the floor that was already occupied by a man. The chief let out a sinister laugh, as if he were above the law in asking the owner to give up his space.

"Old man, *na* de boy's seat *dey* under your buttocks," the man quickly protested. "Your ears correct so—"

"Excuse me?" The chief cut him short. "I refuse to be addressed improperly!"

"Look, old man, stand up. . . . Tief!" a second person challenged him, and the number of people supporting Jubril grew.

"For *koro-koro* daylight, you want steal someone seat?" the first man said. "You *dey* behave like police!"

"I sure say you want all of us to call you shief," Tega said. "Shief dis, shief dat. . . . Too many shiefs for dis country. I go buy my resource-control hat too!"

"Be very, very careful how you talk to me!" The chief turned sharply to the man whose space he had wanted to give to Jubril. "Are you addressing me as *old man?* Me? Do you know who I am?"

"Christ de Son of God no like as you *dey* cheat dis small boy since."

"Are you preaching to *me?*"

"By the grace of God," the man said.

"Look, I'm not even supposed be in this bus with you," the chief said. "Look, I'm not one of *you!*"

"Den leave de Luxurious Bus," Tega said from her seat. "Who you be? Abasha man? Babangida boy!"

"As our people say, before the discovery of peanuts, people were not eating pebbles. . . . Keep your Christianity to yourself!"

"No confuse us wid proverb," Tega continued. "Maybe you be pagan . . . wizard!" A few people laughed at her comments.

"Pagan, eh?" the chief said. "How dare you call my traditional religion paganism!"

"But, Chief, you *dey* pray poritics wid dis ting," Ijeoma said. "Just reave de seat."

"If you no be Christian, *wetin* else remain?" Tega said.

"He is suffering from political correctness," Emeka said, speaking for the first time since the police changed the TV channel.

"Let me tell you," the chief said, "before the harvest of alligator pepper, the medicine man was already carrying his bag, not the other way round. . . . The religion of my ancestors is far older than yours in this country. This land belongs to us."

"*Yeye* gods!" Tega said.

"If you pagans stop sacrificing human body parts to the devil," Emeka said, "this country will be more peaceful than Switzerland."

The chief laughed a sardonic laugh, casting a telling glance at the faces of the TV refugees, in whom nobody was interested any longer. "And your imported religions are blessing this country, yes? Or, please, tell me: are we, the so-called pagans, the ones chasing these people to the barracks? Are we the ones chasing you from the north?"

"We no *dey* shed brood!" Ijeoma eagerly argued for the Christians.

"Which blood?" the chief asked. "Is the blood of goat and sheep that we use for our sacrifice to be compared to the human blood you are spilling in Khamfi?"

"You *dey* rie," Ijeoma said. "You *dey* do human saclifice and litual too."

"Be careful, my daughter!" the chief said. "A royal father does not lie. Be very careful."

"Chief, you *dey* lie, period," Monica said, and people started laughing. The chief himself could not keep a straight face and joined in. He put his stick down, rattled his necklace, and proudly ran his fingers all over the many lion prints on his dress.

"But why are you attacking my religion?" he said, finally regaining his composure.

"See now," Monica continued, "anybody who fit laugh like you fit lie." This brought more laughter. Even a few people outside hopped by the window to see what was happening.

"It's the Muslims who kill in Allah's name," Emeka said in a serious voice. "It's not a laughing matter."

"*Haba,* calm down, Cousin of Dubem, Friend of Tom," Monica argued. "We no want too much stress for dis bus. . . . You get too much tension for body."

"No, we must correct the chief's erroneous theology. By the grace of God, Christianity is pure forgiveness. Otherwise, this country would have gone up in flames by now. You pagans are like the Muslims . . ."

"It's an insult to compare my religion to that barbaric religion!" the chief said, still laughing. "I had warned you not to mention *Islam* or *Muslim* in this bus, remember?"

"Yes, we made dat rule," Tega said, and the bus was quiet for a moment, as if silence was needed to purify the air of that violation.

"*Abeg o,* we must settle my seat *wahala o,*" said the man whose space the chief wanted to give to Jubril.

"Yes, let's see the tickets," Emeka said. "Too much talk."

Everyone turned in the direction of Jubril and the chief.

Jubril immediately showed them his ticket. He brandished it as if he had a winning lottery number. At least there will be a third party to settle this case, he thought.

"So, Chief, where your ticket?" Monica asked, the question that was on everyone's mind.

"Me?" the chief said, clearing his throat.

"Of course," Ijeoma said.

"Do you think I could be sitting here without a ticket?"

Ijeoma and Emeka exchanged glances, and for some reason
nobody wanted to push Chief Ukongo to produce his ticket. Instead, the passengers were cheering for Jubril, encouraging him to
claim the seat from the chief. Jubril felt relieved. Though he knew
their cheers would die instantly if they discovered that he was a
Muslim, the mere fact that they supported him, a sixteen-year-old
boy, against a chief made him feel good. He knew that in Khamfi
nobody would ever support him over and against a royal father or
an emir, even if he were 200 percent right. It was like a foretaste of
the freedom he hoped to enjoy in the south, and all the beatific vi-
sions of the place now flooded him. It was as if he had finally
gotten the support of *his* people, the southerners. Jubril was not
bothered by the religious difference between the chief and his
Christian supporters, or even by that between his supporters and
himself anymore. He felt like singing and dancing. He had learned
in the last few days that one needed to tolerate certain things for
the sake of other things. Because of this singular gesture of support, for the first time in that bus, he could see himself letting go
and daring to look at the TV — just to show his appreciation. This
was not the time to think about Islam or Christianity or God too
much, he thought. It was a time just to be a human being and to
celebrate that. What mattered now was how to get people to lay
down their weapons and biases, how to live together.

THOUGH THE CHIEF HAD not ceded the seat to him or shown his
ticket, Jubril was still lost in happiness. In this unguarded moment,
the memories of his flight again forced themselves into his mind.
And because he felt more accepted on the bus, he let them flow.

For the first time during his wait at the motor park, he believed he could manage his inner turmoil without giving himself away.

He remembered falling and losing consciousness in the savannah as the mob, led by Musa and Lukman, pursued him, but he did not account for what happened while he was blacked out. The next thing he remembered was waking up, weak and sore, covered by mats in a dark room.

The tart smell of the mats had hung heavily in the room. He was lying on his back on the floor; the place was dead quiet. Jubril pinched himself to be sure he was alive. He was so tired that the mats felt like lead. For a moment he thought he was a body being prepared for burial. He breathed cautiously, not daring to move. He cursed the day he had met Musa and Lukman and wondered whether they had captured him. Why would they keep him alive? He could still see their triumphant faces as they beat him, and their gnarled expressions as they pursued him up the valley. He tried to accustom his eyes to the darkness. He could hear the wind ripping through the savannah as well as the faint chirping of birds. He knew he was in the country, but he could not tell how far he was from where he had fallen.

Suddenly, he heard the unimaginable: the explosive sound of Pentecostal Christians speaking in tongues. It poured out all around him, in unrelenting torrents. Jubril's heart beat faster; he had fallen into the hands of Christian fundamentalists. Some of them were praying in tongues, which reminded him of his brother Yusuf on the day of his death. The Christians were very near and seemed to fill the room. He thanked Allah that he did not move or attempt to stand up, knowing how dangerous that could have been, even if he had the energy. They prayed as if the place belonged to them, their trembling bodies ruffling the mats. He was scared and would have blocked his ears if he had not been so afraid to move.

The rapid-fire prayer flooded him with memories of Yusuf. Were they going to spare his life? Why had they brought him into their midst? How did they find him? How could Allah allow Jubril's friends to condemn him for supposedly belonging to a faith he never assented to or practiced, and hated with a passion? Disowned by Muslims and now captured by Christians, he held on to his conscience and prayed.

As the prayers filled Jubril's ears in the dark, he tried to forget the stones falling on Yusuf. He tried to forget how Yusuf screamed the names of his uncles and neighbors and pleaded with them to spare him, and how, when Yusuf realized it was no use, he resumed, with ebbing strength, praying in tongues and calling on the name of Jesus.

"Allah the Merciful, forgive me!" Jubril repeated silently to drown out the unnerving memories of Yusuf. I should have been nicer to him when he came back from the delta, he thought. I should have listened more to my mother. I should have refused to witness his stoning. "Allah, soften the hearts of these Christians and spare me," he prayed, begging with every inch of his bruised body. With what had been done to Christians in the north and the vengeance that was sweeping across the land, Jubril knew it was only Allah who could save him. "Allah, you will remember me," Jubril prayed. "Give me the strength to remember you."

AFTER WHAT FELT LIKE an eternity, Jubril heard an approaching commotion. By their shouts and songs, he was sure they were

Muslim. As the mob surrounded the house, the Pentecostals shut up like croaking toads whose ponds have been invaded. The image of Musa and Lukman loomed in his mind. He was so afraid that he could not pray anymore. He thought about standing up to flee, to deny his two friends the joy of finally killing him. But when he realized that the Christians who had prayed moments before, as if the whole earth belonged to them, did not move, even to defend themselves, he calmed down. It was just as well, because when he stretched his leg a bit he realized that he was still too weak to stand.

He waited for the door to burst open, for his fellow Muslims to rush in and kill him. He waited for their torches to fill the darkness with momentary light that would be followed by the eternal darkness of death. The mob seemed to have gone past the house and run farther into the savannah. He breathed again, and after some time he heard footsteps in what seemed to be a corridor next door. Listening hard, he picked up the low but unrelenting whispers of Hail Marys. They actually sounded closer to him now than the earlier ecstatic prayers had. He thanked Allah again that he had not moved when he first heard the Muslims. Who knew what these whispering Christians would have done to him?

He was still trying to figure out where he was when the mob came back, its chants louder and its numbers greater than before. When the leaders demanded to see the owner of the house, Jubril almost fainted.

"Quick quick, bring out de inpidels!" someone commanded the man. "You *dey* hide dem por your house."

"I get no stranger for my house," the man said.

"One last time, we say bring dem out *o*."

"I say I no get visitor for house."

"Some feople say you *dey* hide feople por your house. Dem tell us say you do de same ting during de last riots, two years ago."

"I be Mallam Yohanna Abdullahi," he said. "I be teacher, serious Muslim."

"We know."

"So why I go hide infidel for house?"

"Because some of us Muslims be traitors."

"Some of us *dey* helf dis souderners escafe when Allah done give dem to us to wife out," said another man.

"Dis Igbo feofle," said another, "dis delta feofle, dis Yoruba feofle, de whole menace prom soud, all of dem must die!"

"Dem no like us Hausa feofle," said yet another.

The *mallam* said, "Me, I be Hausa man too. . . . How can I protect anybody who no like my tribe, you understand?"

"Well, if we see dem por your house we go kill you *o*."

Jubril could not believe what he had heard. It shocked him that his host was a Hausa Muslim. It sounded like a play, and he waited for him to crack under the pressure. They lined up his sons and warned them that their mob had already killed many Hausa Muslims who attempted to hide the infidels. But the sons of Abdullahi were all as courageous as their father and insisted that they had no strangers in their midst.

When the mob came in to search the house, they were a drove of locusts in their destructiveness. They said they were going to be rough on Mallam Abdullahi and his family because they had been informed that he had protected Christians and southerners in past riots. They searched for infidels in the kitchen, fighting

over the food; they looked for infidels in the barns, looting yams
and bags of peanuts. They hunted for infidels in the inner cham-
bers of the man's house, abusing his wives and daughters to avenge
the fact that Mallam Abdullahi had helped people in the past.
Nobody in Jubril's room could pray aloud anymore. Like Jubril,
they were all storming heaven silently, asking God to give more
courage to their host.

The door to the room burst open, and a gust of wind swept in.
But nobody entered. Mallam Abdullahi was by the door with
two men who harassed him and pushed him around. He was barefoot and wearing a jumper. Jubril could hear another group approaching, chanting war songs, and closed his eyes and waited.

"*Wetin dey* inside, *mallam?*" asked one of those with Abdullahi.

"Notting," he said.

"Sure?"

"Just some prayer mats. Yes, for my entire family. . . . You want
make I open de window for you?"

He attempted to enter the room, but they dragged him away.

It was only when they had been gone for a few minutes that
Jubril realized that he was covered in sweat and his lips were quiv-
ering. Before now he would have hunted down the infidels himself, but the betrayal by Musa and Lukman had changed him and
his outlook. The mere thought that he had been hidden beneath
other people's prayer mats was too much for him. He heard one or
two people around him sobbing, and tears ran down his face as
well. They were the first tears of joy he had shed in his life. He
would never have thought of allowing an infidel to touch his prayer
mat. He could not have asked the Abdullahi family for more, and
even if one of the family members now gave them up, it would not

have made much difference to Jubril, because of all they had sacrificed up to that point. He was filled with thanksgiving, with a mysterious pride that his fellow Muslims could risk everything for infidels. With one hand he held on to the prayer mats tenderly. He blessed Abdullahi, whose family prayer mats were holy enough for all.

THE WIND CAME IN and filled the room, and people scrambled to hold the mats in place. Then Jubril felt his mat being pulled down toward the floor on either side. He almost shouted in fear. The pressure increased gently but firmly, keeping the mats from blowing away.

"Hold the mats!" whispered a frightened Christian into Jubril's ear.

"*Abeg* . . . no kill me, *abeg*," Jubril pleaded instinctively.

As his unknown companions pulled the mats closer, he gingerly inched his pocketed wrist away from the pressure. In the darkness, he figured there must be at least five or six other praying and anxious strangers under the same mats. These other people kept calling on Jesus and Mary to save them, their supplications subsumed in the commotion of the mob outside.

"For Christ's sake, hold the mats with two hands," another neighbor admonished Jubril. "What is in your pocket that's dearer to you than your life?"

"Notting," he said to the Christians. "Just *dey* help me . . . I be one of you."

"Lazy man, hold de mats!"

As they whispered back and forth, they knew that their lives all hung in the balance and that if anyone panicked, they would all perish—including Mallam Abdullahi and his terrorized family. Still unable to secure the mats with two hands, Jubril was relieved when his neighbors reached out to help him.

This joint effort to survive and Abdullahi's courageous witness filled Jubril with hope. In that dark room, he experienced a joy he could not explain, a joy that he would feel later on informed his belief that Allah would protect him in a busload of Christians.

Lying there, he became awake to everything, like a Sufi contemplative, surrendering completely to Allah's will. In his heart, he began to invoke the divine name of his creator. He would have loved to have broken out in wild celebration, but he held his body so still that his spirit seemed to expand, celebrating Allah's grandeur.

He could feel his precious breath crawl through the hairs in his nostrils, then swell his stomach. He could feel a running sensation in his lower legs. The skin where his two knees touched, which had been numb, now had a throbbing ache. Jubril was present to the trembling in his neighbors' hands as they helped him hold his mats in place, and he could sense the heat from the bare floor entering his back. He could feel his sweat fill up his pores, tumble out, and tie his body to the floor in long watery ropes, soaking his wounds and clothes. His wounds began to hurt afresh. Saliva, which had dried in his mouth when the fanatics struck, flowed again and tasted good to him. Even the smell of the mats seemed wonderful. He was fully alive. His whole body, except his cut wrist, praised Allah silently, in the manner creation celebrates its intricacy, in ways no mortal can fully comprehend.

He felt connected to his newfound universe of diverse and unknown pilgrims, the faceless Christians. The complexity of their survival pierced his soul with a stunning insight: every life counted in Allah's plan.

THEY WERE STILL BEGGING God silently, together, in different ways, when the mob began to pour gas all over the homes in one last attempt to teach Mallam Abdullahi a lesson. Two men came and stood by the door to the room, spraying the place. The fuel fell on the mats like the first raindrops on banana leaves. Jubril and his companions stilled themselves and waited for the flick of the matches as the fuel's coldness, sharpened by the harmattan wind, stung his wounds. The raiders were so close that any movement could have given them away. Like a statue in the rain, Jubril did not blink. He felt the liquid hit his eyes. He waited for the kind of fire that he himself had set many times on the property of infidels in Khamfi . . .

Jubril felt someone tapping him on the shoulder and jumped.

"I did not mean to hurt you," Chief Ukongo apologized. The pain on Jubril's face made him look to the chief like someone who was dying to control whatever powers he hid in his pocket. "Well, son, whatever pocket juju . . ."

"Notting *dey* my pocket," Jubril said.

"You know what I have in *my* pocket?" the chief taunted him. "If you deny your juju in public, he can't defend you. I hope you know that. Anyway, yours can't overpower *mine*. . . . If you try *me,* son, I'll kill you!"

"Ah ah, Shief Resource Control," Tega said, "leave dis boy alone."

Uwem Akpan

"First, you have cheated him out of his seat," someone said. "Now you accuse him of hiding juju in his pocket."

Monica asked, "Chief, you want steal his money too?"

"What money does this little goat have?" the chief said. "I was just tapping his shoulder to show him my bus ticket. . . . It's now time for me to prove that I am not encroaching on his rightful seat. My only problem with this boy is his attitude."

"Yessa," Jubril said, nodding vigorously, for the prospect of getting his seat was close. He dug into his bag and brought out his ticket again, in case they would need to compare the two. People sat up or craned their necks to see the chief's ticket.

While searching in the bag on his lap, the chief assured them, "You'll understand me better when you see my ID . . ."

"ID? We no want any ID!" Ijeoma warned him. "Come, make you lespect yourself *o!*"

"*You* don't want to see my ID?" Chief Ukongo shouted at her, and tapped his chest repeatedly, as if his most sacred of rights had been desecrated. "Young woman, who made you the judge between a royal father and this rascal? You expect me to bring out my ticket . . . without even seeing my ID? Do you know who I am?" Having said this, he yanked out a huge talisman from his bag, plucked one feather from it, and blew it into the air. The people shouted in fright, and those who were near where the feather landed backed away. The chief broke into some incantation, his head shaking like the tail of a rattlesnake.

"Now, young woman, you can come and ask me for my ticket," he finally said. "And you, young juju man, let's see who is more powerful. Bring out what you have, and let's see!"

Jubril asked the police, who had come onto the bus when they heard all the commotion, to settle the matter once and for all. But when the officers saw the situation, they left, saying they would come back when they finished drinking their beer.

The chief laughed at Jubril and told his challengers that they would suffer when the bus reached his domain. "Do you know who has been keeping the peace in the delta?" he said. "The police recognize my status. Do you know how I got onto this bus in the first place? You'll regret inviting the police!"

But Jubril was not intimidated. He wanted justice.

"Our son, our son," Madam Aniema said, "please, beg the police not to come into the case! We have suffered enough already on this trip. Please, what is your name?"

"His name is Gabriel!" the chief said immediately.

"Ah, Gabriel, our angel," the lady continued, "are you rich enough for police intervention?"

"She's right, young man," Emeka said. "You moved too fast. You know these are extraordinary times. All of us were admiring your patience with the chief. Things would have worked themselves out, you know. You see how these policemen denied me a chance to know whether my cousin and friend died or survived the Sharia war in Khamfi. They are ruthless."

"To invite police to help you for dis country," one woman said, "is like farmer *wey* invite locust to his farm!"

"No sane parent want expose his daughter to rapists," another said.

"Gabriel, you see, for dis country," Monica said, "de police, de soldiers, no be norderners or souderners or Christians or Muslims—just plain rogues. . . . Dem no fit give you justice."

"I warned you about mentioning the word *Muslim,* did I not?" the chief said.

"I *dey* sorry," Monica apologized. "I forget."

"How come nobody listens to royal fathers anymore in this country?" the chief said. "What is wrong with us?"

Emeka stood up and went to where Jubril was, stepping carefully over the chief's feather on the way, to explain things to him. "You see, Gabriel," he whispered, "you know that, since this is a civilian government, we should try to settle our quarrels without bringing in the police or soldiers. The generals stole billions of our oil dollars during the years of military rule. . . . Now some of these generals have turned around in these democratic times to back laws that would cut off the limbs of poor chicken thieves . . ."

"If we drag dese same generals go Charia court," Tega came in, "what part of deir body we go cut? What part go remain? Still we no go recover our money. Charia cannot toush dese rish Muslims *o!* Before you know it, dem go run go Common Law court. Even de rogue governors who introduce *am* no go smell de so-called Charia court. Dem go run go ordinary court for immunity against de same Charia . . ."

"My sister, just take it easy," Emeka pleaded with her. "Just allow me to carefully explain things to Gabriel."

But she said, "My advice to all of *una* be say make we poor people *dey* learn to protect ourselves. . . . Gabriel, quick quick, go remove dis case from police hand."

But Jubril was past hearing. His mind had drifted back to his woes as they analyzed the crisis. His vacant face wore a collapsed smile. His eyes were distant, vaguely transfixed on the ceiling of the bus, away from the TVs.

How will my father receive me when I reach Ukhemehi? he thought. What will I tell him about Yusuf? Would my leaving Islam for Deeper Life placate him and the extended family? Yusuf had said some of them had remained Catholic and some relapsed into their ancestral religion. What does justice demand of me? When would I tell my father the whole truth? Yusuf must have told him I was a conservative Muslim when he visited home. What do I tell them about my hand? How long could I keep it hidden? Maybe I should lie to my people in the delta, tell them that I did not steal, that I was forced to confess, that I never in my life supported Sharia. Maybe if they knew that, they would be more sympathetic to my situation.

He reached down into his heart and found some solace: maybe a full public confession would be the right thing to do, the kind that Yusuf himself preached about in the parable of the Prodigal Son. Jubril was ready to risk any consequence, even death. His flight began to assume the mission of going back to tell his father the truth, a truth he must do everything to conceal until he reached his destination. He was very sure of his father's forgiveness and the hospitality of the village of Ukhemehi because of what Yusuf had told him.

"Gabriel doesn't hear properly," the chief said, chuckling, seeing Emeka and Ijeoma's consternation. "Sorry, I forgot to tell you. Sometimes he even uses sign language."

"Gabliel, you *dey* claze!" Ijeoma snapped, shouting so loud that the rest of the bus turned to look. "We *dey* beg you say no bling porice kill us, you *dey* smile and pose rike Gucci model . . . wid one hand for pocket." She grabbed him and shook him until his mind came back to the bus. "We say we no want porice to settle any case for dis bus!"

When Jubril looked around and saw everybody looking at him, he said, "Ah, no police again."

"You be deaf?" Emeka asked.

"No vex," Jubril said to them, bowing.

"My people, don't worry," the chief said. "I'll tell the police not to bother, OK?"

"Yes, Chief!" they said.

"Tank you, Chief. . . . So you be real chief."

"God bless you, Chief!"

Now that the police were out of the picture, the passengers relaxed again. Jubril listened to the banter in the bus about the power in the chiefs' domains. Jubril could only compare the idea of being a chief to that of being an emir in the north, though from what he was hearing, he knew the emirs had more power.

Chief Ukongo rose to his feet and cleared his throat. "My people, now you're talking . . . to me . . . your chief!" he addressed the bus. He thudded the floor with his stick and went to where the feather was. He picked it up as tenderly as possible and put it together with his talisman in his bag. "As our people say," he continued, "the world is full of gods, but the important ones are called by their names. And also, do not forget: no matter how small an idol is, it is good to carry it with two hands. You see, my people, this is a period of national crisis. You should rally around your royal fathers. . . . The north is uniting around the emirs." He asked Jubril to sit on the floor near him, where the feather had fallen. Jubril sat down immediately, near Monica. She smiled at Jubril; he ignored her.

The old man dropped some biscuits into Jubril's lap. Jubril thanked him. The refugees who supported him a few moments ago did not even look at Jubril. His loneliness and fear came back, rising like yeast. He pushed his body against the seat of the chief to keep from trembling. The more he pressed against his sore muscles, the more he aggravated the wounds under his clothes. He came back to his senses when the chief asked him why he was not eating. Chief Ukongo sounded to Jubril as if he would not only deprive him of the food but might use his magical powers to turn him into a grain of sand. He ate quickly.

SOMEWHERE IN THE CROWD outside, above the din of the bus stop, a dog barked breathlessly several times. With each effort the barks got weaker, as if the dog, like a whooping-cough patient, could not save itself from that sickening, involuntary urge.

The local TV station continued to broadcast its ugly pictures of the conflict, taking with it most of the passengers' attention as they waited for the driver and fuel. Now, without passion, they watched the pictures of the barracks, shown over and over again, listening to the same TV anchor telling them everything was OK. But Jubril was watching the chief the whole time. The old man, in spite of finally being recognized by his people, was restless. It seemed to Jubril that the momentary peace that had pervaded the bus had evaded this man. Every now and then, some indiscernible angst brought tears into the gullies of the chief's eyes. He took out his identity card, looked at it, and asked Jubril how the refugees could have refused to acknowledge his ID. "How could they refuse to see it, when I voluntarily showed it to them?" he asked.

"Sorry, Chief," said Jubril. "Sorry."

"It's OK," he said.

The chief peered at the happy, confident face he once had and wrinkled his brow as if he was trying to remember something. Another wave of tears came close to spilling onto his cheeks, but then lost steam, as if the chief lacked the energy to remember and to cry simultaneously.

"My son, Gabriel," he said, glancing sorrowfully out the window, into the dark of Lupa, "I once enjoyed this country. You know I once did?"

"No, Chief."

"I'm telling you I once did."

"Yes, Chief."

"I don't know why the god of my ancestors allowed the military to hand over power to civilians. . . . With the military in power, this Sharia war would never have taken place. We royal fathers used to go to the seat of government as the sole representatives of our people, guardians of the people's mandate. Now everybody treats us as if we are no longer important." For the first time, the chief's tears fell. "I remember how General Sani Abacha granted us royal fathers five percent of the taxes collected in our domain for saying a resounding yes to his plan to rule our country forever. He even promised us each a house in the capital city. He gave us cars, good cars . . . but I'm in this Luxurious Bus because I have hidden my cars for now. You know why?"

"No, Chief."

"Because I don't know whether these new democrats would ask the royal fathers to return them. This democracy is now destroying the country. You agree with me, yes?"

"Yes, yes, Chief."

Jubril was now leaning on him, giving him his full attention. The more the chief spoke, the more the boy came to believe that this man could probably protect him, not just in this bus but when they reached their destination in the delta. Jubril liked the fact that the chief was confiding in him, and he thought the chief was more reliable than the other passengers.

He touched a fringe of the chief's dress, the corduroy material soft on his fingers. Back in the north, he could never imagine being this close to an emir. He could not imagine traveling in the same vehicle with an emir or sitting down to talk with him face-to-face, much less such an important personality whispering to him his life's disappointments. He remembered all the times he had seen an emir. Jubril was always deep in the crowd, quiet and courteous. He could not boast of shaking an emir's hand or of being close enough to touch his turban as he was touching the chief's dress now.

He felt bad about not giving up the seat all this while, about arguing with Chief Ukongo, about inviting the police to harass him. Back in Khamfi, complete obeisance to the emir was the beginning of wisdom, and the emir's word was law in his domain. Jubril remembered the sirens and motorcades of governors, and even the presidents, paying courtesy visits to the emir of Khamfi, Alhaji Muhammad Kabir Jadodo; he remembered the politicians going to seek the emir's blessings before declaring their interest in any elected office in Khamfi. Above all, he thought about the beautiful and imposing palace in Khamfi and of all the salaried workers and all the charity Alhaji Jadodo doled out to the endless number of *talakawas* who flocked there. He remembered how these *talakawas* rose against some human-rights activists who tried to question the emir about the source of his wealth.

"For example," the old man whispered, "it wasn't necessary that you harass me for this seat as you did."

"Sorry, Chief."

"All because of tickets."

"Very sorry, Chief." Jubril felt so bad that he unearthed his ticket from his bag and offered it to the old man. "Keep. I no want again. . . . Sorry, Chief."

The old man collected it and stuffed it in his pocket and nodded. "Good boy. You see, we know what's good for this country. We, the emirs, obas, chiefs, we advised the military governments against Sharia! That's why we did not have Sharia all these years." He thumped his chest repeatedly and placed his ID on Jubril's leg.

Jubril picked it up. "Good photo . . . beautiful, Chief!"

The old man smiled. "That's right, my son. We kept this country together until this madness of democracy!" Then he became serious and began to admonish the press: "The newspapers say the generals, whether from the north or south, were rats from hell who were waging war on the central bank for decades and that we needed elected people, whom we could hold accountable! The press is to be blamed for this democracy in our country. They say the most decorated soldiers have all their children in universities in Europe and America, while the commoner's child is stuck in our rotten universities. They say even our Muslim soldiers' children drink, eat pork, and womanize freely in the white man's land, while their parents want Sharia back home. They say though the northern generals have stolen all the money in the country and have ruled this country for very long, their north is still full of wretched cowherds. But, Gabriel, the worst is they say that we, we royal fathers, are sitting on our people!" He paused and swallowed hard. "Don't these new democrats and the newspapers know that the people of England respect their royalty? They blame us . . . in spite of all we have done for the country . . ." His voice broke off, pained at the mere recall of the criticisms. Jubril nodded in sympathy.

"The generals took us very seriously . . . us, us!" the chief said. "Cordial relationship. . . . For example, they told us why we needed to send our troops to Liberia and Sierra Leone, why our sons had to die for democracy there."

"Our soldier people go Sierra Leone?" Jubril asked.

"Em . . . Gabriel, don't forget to put 'Chief' before asking your question."

"Chief, no vex, no vex, Chief."

"Yes, that's more like it. . . . And stop covering your mouth with your hand or chewing your finger when you talk! It's annoying."

"Sorry, Chief. I no brush my tood for many days. My mout *dey* smell."

"Anyway, as I was saying, if not for our soldiers, those countries would be no more! *We* and the generals gathered other West African countries under ECOMOG —"

"Hey *Chief*," interjected Monica in a whisper, pointing an accusing finger at him, "*na* you *dey* boast like dis? When did General Babangida share power wid you?"

"Woman, you don't understand," the chief said.

"*Na* lie *o*. . . . I understand dis one," she insisted. "Dat general like power too much *o*. If he no change handover date many times, if he no cancel our 1993 elections, Abacha no for become our leader. . . . *Na* de same people. Locust years. De man *dey* use you. He no share no power wid you, *abeg*."

"OK, woman, it is not exactly like I was saying. All I was trying to say was that the military respected us. May I talk now, Madam Lawyer?"

"Just make you no lie for dis young man, Chief."

The chief went back to Jubril, who did not like Monica's intervention at all.

"Gabriel, the point is, we taught those Sierra Leonean and Liberian rebels a lesson. We lost a lot of soldiers . . . for a good cause!"

"Chief, how many die for combat?"

"That's codified information, not for everybody, you know. A lizard may listen to a conversation, but he may not say something. I mean, who are you to want to know how many soldiers died in combat? Is government business your father's business that you must know about it? Or are you now the commander in chief?"

"No, Chief."

"Then stop behaving like a democrat!"

"Yes, Chief."

"I tell you, if we bring back those ECOMOG soldiers, these Sharia people in the north will think twice! Trust me, ECOMOG can keep this country one! Gabriel, don't be confused by all this talk about freedom and equality. . . . To let an old man rest on a good seat is a virtue. To let a royal father take the better seat is nothing compared to what we actually deserve—"

"Yes, Chief."

"It's rude to interrupt a royal father."

Jubril opened his mouth and quickly closed it, afraid of making another mistake. He resorted to nodding.

"Gabriel, I know you want to say something, yes?"

"Chief, pardon me. . . . I happy for ECOMOG."

"Good. If the government were this sensible, appealing to *us*, we would stop the Sharia war, you understand?"

"Chief, bring ECOMOG to Khamfi."

"Don't worry. When we arrive in the delta, I shall call up fellow royal fathers in the north. We're important. We're the repository of wisdom and history and tradition."

This little assurance about the patriotism and effectiveness of ECOMOG soldiers gave Jubril hope that someday he would return to his Khamfi. Already, he was adoring ECOMOG soldiers and fantasizing about their coming to stabilize the country. Even if things worked out with his father, Jubril decided, he must return to Khamfi to find his mother and Mallam Abdullahi, within whose house Allah had planned Jubril's miraculous escape. Jubril could only think of ECOMOG, the sacrifices they had made abroad, and what they could do for his compatriots. Maybe ECOMOG soldiers are like Mallam Abdullahi, he thought. The more the chief prattled on about ECOMOG, the more the image of Abdullahi burned in Jubril's mind. He felt better. Imagining what ECOMOG could do felt a bit like the comfort of a return ticket in his back pocket, though he had none.

He remembered the night after the mob threatened to burn down the house. He remembered the harsh wind that bit into his wounds as Mallam Abdullahi drove him and the other escapees in his Peugeot 504 pickup deep into the savannah, where he released them, one by one, like pigeons. Knowing that there were

Muslims and Christians in the group, Mallam Abdullahi had told them he was uncomfortable releasing them together. Jubril was the last to be set free, so his fellow Muslim had spoken longer with him, empathizing with him about his hand. He had advised Jubril to hide his wrist in his pocket until he reached his father's village. Repeatedly, he told Jubril that Islam was a religion of peace. "You and I," he said as he hugged Jubril, "must show this to the world. Remember, nobody has a monopoly on violence. So don't go around trying to terrorize the Christians."

Now, Jubril looked at himself, at his clothes and shoes and the Marian medal Mallam Abdullahi had given him to help him fit in with the southern crowd. The money the *mallam* had given him was not gone, even after Jubril paid the exorbitant bus fare. That night in the bush, Jubril had knelt down to thank Mallam Abdullahi for the money, but the man said he was only doing *zakat,* one of the five pillars of his religion, and bade him do the same to the next person.

"Gabriel, don't cry . . . don't cry," Chief Ukongo consoled, as the memories got the better part of Jubril. "Don't be sad about how the government has treated the royal fathers. They shall re-member us soon."

"Chief . . . I *dey* tank God for my life. Chief, you be big man like de emir?" he asked suddenly, to make the old man happy.

"Of course, yes. Glad you get the point. Finally!"

"Chief, you go help me when we reach home?"

"That's how it should be. As our elders say, the ant's hope of reaching the sacrificial food lies in the folds of the wrapping leaf. You can't hope to reach *my* place, but you're harassing me . . . the folly of youth!" The chief managed a deep hearty laugh, shifting and stirring in his seat as if on a throne. "Of course we chiefs are like emirs, but our people are a bit heady and don't give us the respect we deserve—but will in the end. You have just seen the typical behavior toward a southern chief in this bus and from this woman." He pointed at Monica, who smiled.

"For me, all you royal faders *dey* exaggerate your powers!" she said, and shrugged.

"Don't mind her," the chief told Jubril.

"Yes, Chief," he said.

"You see, the emirs never suffer this type of humiliation from their subjects," the chief continued. "I knew this when we used to visit General Abacha to plan his life presidency. God bless his soul. He understood the importance of royal fathers. After him, soldiers chickened out and handed power over to civilians, and look at our country now . . ."

Jubril felt so comfortable with the chief that he fell asleep in spite of the commotion and his aching body. He had not slept for two days, but now, with the chief keeping guard over him, as it were, he drifted off.

BY THE TIME THE driver finally came back with a drum of fuel, it was completely dark outside. With the help of the police officers and bus conductors, he refueled the bus. There was no moon, no stars. The light from the bus, framed by large windows and blinds, poured out into the darkness like long stakes. An eerie silence had descended on the land, and it seemed that the will of those outside the bus to murmur was swallowed by it. They moved about quietly, not knowing what their fate would be once the bus left. Occasionally, a gunshot rang out and drew a collective gasp from the crowd, and occasionally, the pained dog barked weakly.

When the door opened the passengers thought the driver was ready to begin the journey, but the darkness spat a lanky newcomer onto the bus. He began to pick his way forward, staggering over people sitting on the floor, searching for a space. His hair was rotten, dreadlocks, and an army beret sat like a crown of disgrace over it. A rope gathered his ragged camouflage garb at his tiny waist. He was carrying a dog. He held it gently, as if it were a two-day-old baby.

"Are you the driver?" Emeka asked.

"No."

"Then get out immediately."

"By the way," the newcomer said, "the police say the driver is too tired to begin the yourney now. He needs to eat and sleep for a while."

The passengers became uneasy and rose as one to eject him, Emeka leading the charge. They dragged him toward the door. Monica had given her child to somebody again so she could give Emeka the backing he needed. Tega and Ijeoma joined her, cussing the man in Urobho and Ibo.

But, flailing in Emeka's grip, the man managed to produce a ticket.

"The police gave me this ticket and opened the door for me. How do jou think I got onto the bus?" the man said, when Emeka dropped him. He moved on, as if the people had just finished singing a welcome song for him, searching for his place. "So why are jou harassing me?"

"Because you *dey* craze!" Tega said.

"Me?"

"Of course," Tega said.

"My name is Colonel Silas Usenetok."

"Colonel? You?" Madam Aniema said.

"Who admitted you into the army?" Emeka asked.

Colonel Usenetok halted in front of Jubril. "Get up!" he said, poking the sleeping Jubril with his dirty boot. "I say, get up!"

Jubril turned and said sleepily, "I *dey* my place."

People warned the colonel against hitting Jubril. The sympathy of the whole bus was with him. Besides, nobody wanted to travel with the colonel, for he looked like a madman. They berated the police for letting him in, and some suggested he should sit at the space allotted to the two policemen for the journey.

"Jou better wake up before I flush jou from this bus," the soldier warned Jubril again.

"Nosa."

Everyone looked at Chief Ukongo, but the old man did not say anything or even look in the direction of Jubril. His attention was fixed on his beads, which he was stroking. He clacked them against each other with measured alacrity.

"With immediate effect . . . jour ticket?" the soldier commanded Jubril. "Who are jou? We must see jour ticket now. I need to sit down because the driver is so tired. It will take a long time before we move from here."

"My newly arrived son," the chief intervened, still playing with his beads, "we shall not look at any tickets!"

"What?" the soldier exclaimed. The whole bus became quiet when the chief spoke. The soldier looked around, as if trying to understand the silence.

"Obey the wishes of the people," the chief said, still looking down. "They don't want you on this bus. . . . This is a democratic country."

"Democracy my foot," Colonel Usenetok said. "Show me the asshole's ticket . . . period!"

The chief rose up, took off his Resource Control hat to reveal a head of white hair, then put it back on. He cleared his throat and looked around. "Soldier, do you know I'm not even supposed to be on this bus? Do you know I'm supposed to be helping the government solve this national crisis . . . not being insulted by a madman!"

"Excuse me. Jou're insulting me? After all I've done for this country?" The soldier started searching in his rags for his ID. Finding the ID appeared to be so important to him that he dropped the dog and his fingers trembled. His camouflage had so many holes and slits that even he was confused about where to find things. Then he flashed his ID and announced, "Colonel Silas Usenetok . . . ECOMOG Special Forces!"

Jubril looked at the chief, then returned his gaze to the soldier. Admiration for the soldier spread on his face immediately, on the strength of what Chief Ukongo had told him about ECOMOG soldiers' self-sacrifice. Jubril stood and offered up his place, though many in the bus said he should not.

Colonel Usenetok picked up his dog.

"Gabriel, you are not giving him your place," the chief said calmly, and the other passengers concurred. Monica held Jubril down with both hands, as if she were planting a tree.

"He has insulted my chieftaincy," the chief declared, and then, turning to the soldier, said: "We don't accept IDs on this bus . . . ask anybody."

"Yeah . . . *ole* . . . no ID!" someone said.

"No mad soldierman ID!"

"Your generals done steal our money finish in de name of ECOMOG!"

"*Kai, kai, kai,* my people, forget about what the generals did!" the chief said, calling them to order, and turned to the soldier. "Let me tell you something, because you're too young to understand the history of this conflict in our country . . ."

"Which conflict, which history?" the soldier said. "Jou're talking as if jou were a living witness when God created the world."

"Very good then. Even if you *were* there when Britain arbitrarily joined the north and south together to found this country, you couldn't travel with us! Even if you were there when the British forged the Muslim-majority north and the Christian-majority south into a country, we couldn't allow you. Whether you have a ticket or not is beside the point now. . . . As a royal father, the safety of *my* people is paramount. Too many of them are already dead, and now I don't want them to be bitten by this mad dog!"

"We no want dis dog for dis bus *o!*"

"Human right before animal right!"

"Police is public enemy number one!"

Colonel Usenetok laughed at them. He held the dog closer to his heart and pecked it on the nose. Without warning, the dog jolted and convulsed in that deathly bark that the refugees had heard periodically outside. Its body was cramped, and its jaws wide open, with nothing more to vomit except a few drops of blood. While those around him squirmed and tried to push away, the colonel used his clothes to collect the blood. A foul smell filled the bus, and people tongue-lashed the ECOMOG man. Having this dog in their midst did not sit well with the bus refugees.

"The gods of our ancestors will not allow jou, Nduese, to die!" the soldier prayed for his dog. "They must protect jou till we reach home and jou get the right herbs! The gods who guarded me in the war fields of Liberia and Sierra Leone, who never allowed the RUF rebels to cut my hands or legs, won't disappoint me." With this, the ECOMOG man brought out from under his rags a wreath of assorted talismans. The refugees gasped. It was bigger and more intimidating than the collection the chief had. He plucked one talisman that looked like a necklace of cowry shells and hung it around Nduese and poured some herbal liquid down the dog's throat. A few drops trickled on Jubril. Nduese's coughing began to mellow.

On hearing the soldier's testimony of rebels cutting people's limbs, Jubril nodded, following every movement of the soldier with rapt attention and a bizarre smile, as if the ECOMOG man had hypnotized him. But while his sight was locked on the soldier, his pocketed wrist was vibrating, seemingly on its own. Unknown to all on the bus, Jubril's mind was neither on the soldier nor on whatever they thought was in his pocket, but on the day his right hand was cut. He remembered the night before that day, how he tried to sleep but could not.

Up until that last night he had been brave about it and actually walked around anticipating the event with gay abandon, a boy completely at peace with a just punishment, a sort of hero in his neighborhood. As far as he was concerned, the hand was dead. He absolutely believed that once the hand was cut off, he and others would be discouraged from stealing again. He ignored the hand and tried not to look at it and looked forward to being relieved of this source of self-hate. Jubril started using his left hand only. And just to make sure he did not mistakenly use the fingers or palm of the condemned hand, he tied a red rubber band around his right wrist as a reminder, as if to delineate a clear line between good and evil, love and hate. With this sort of clarity, he felt comfortable using his right elbow, for it was a part of the body he had not forfeited to theft. Two nights before the amputation, he had slept peacefully and even happily dreamed of the hand being cut.

But that last night, alone in the room, he lay awake. While he still accepted that his hand should be cut off and prayed loud and clear that Allah's will be done, he found himself many times, to his embarrassment, shaking hands with himself in the dark. He performed many types of handshakes and even pretended to shake hands with another person. For the last time, he used his right hand to feel the different parts of his body. He stood up and wandered around the cell, feeling the wall and the floor. He moved the fingers among themselves like a flutist or guitarist. He said good-bye to that part of him he had already sacrificed to theft, knowing that when day broke he would be wafted away by anesthesia.

THE REFUGEES, SEEING JUBRIL unnerved and uncoordinated, believed that the soldier had charmed him. They appealed to the chief to ask his fellow idol worshipper, Colonel Usenetok, to remove his spell from the boy. Chief Ukongo did not say anything, though he watched the soldier with calculating eyes. The people murmured as Jubril continued to act strangely.

"It's jou Christians and Muslims who've charmed Khamfi with jour evil politics!" Colonel Usenetok said gleefully, putting down Nduese in his excitement. His eyes were like two points of light. "Jour faiths are interlopers on this continent!"

"All soldier people are tieves . . . *ole!*" Tega said, and others booed him.

"Hey, lady," the soldier said, "I fought in Sierra Leone without pay. Government still hasn't paid me for a jear now. . . . I didn't steal jour oil money!"

"And you *dey* call yourself army colonel?" Monica said. "You be *yeye* man *o!* Why you no steal? You no be good colonel at all, at all."

"Why are you saying this?" Madam Aniema asked.

"Saying what?" Monica said.

"My sister, what has this got to do with idol worship?" Madam Aniema said. "Stealing cannot be a good thing."

"But why de soldiers from our place always *dey* stupid?" Monica said, then turned to the soldier: "You, tell us, soldierman, *wetin* you *dey* retire to now?"

"To dignity . . . conscience!" the soldier replied.

Tega was the first to break the silence. She stood up and let out a guffaw. She laughed as if someone were tickling her. Emeka joined in, and then the whole bus sounded like a room full of giggling adolescent girls. Even the police, who peered into the bus after hearing the soldier's reply, joined in the laughter. The chief sat there, looking at the soldier with an impish grin, shaking his head very slowly. It was as if the soldier were no longer a threat to the bus but a source of comic relief.

"Soldierman, listen," Monica said, motioning with her hands to the people to stop laughing. "Soldierman, you go eat dignity and drink conscience, *abi?* Your wife and children go *dey* happy well well to receive you from Sierra Leone empty-handed."

"No problem," the soldier said.

"No *wahala,* huh?" she taunted him. "We no tell you before? You be madman. . . . *Na* only crazeman who go reach colonel for army and no steal money for dis country."

"Jou're the mad people!" he said, and pulled his dog closer to himself. "I'm going back home to farm as my ancestors did before oil was discovered in my village!"

"Which farm?" Monica said. "Farmland no *dey* again for delta *o!* Mobil, Shell, Exxon, Elf. . . . All of dem done pollute every grain of sand."

"I'll fish, then."

"Fish *ke?* Dem done destroy de rivers . . . no fish."

At this point, Monica gave up, melting into laughter. She laughed long and hard until she lost her breath. Others started talking about the pollution of the delta, about how they must make sure all the oil companies moved away from there, and how the democratic government must be driven out of the area. They said the delta must secede from the country, so they would have the right to manage their resources. In time, they all stopped talking and were overcome by laughter, like laborers dropping off to sleep at the end of the day. It robbed their plans of the earlier bitterness and was no threat to the police.

Only the soldier and Jubril kept straight faces. Jubril was

Uwem Akpan

disappointed and sided with the ECOMOG soldier. He thought the soldier deserved the best, having gone out to serve the country gallantly, as the chief had said. The fact that the chief was laughing too only made matters worse for the boy. Jubril began to realize that he did not understand the old man. He wondered when the driver would wake up so they could begin their journey.

EMEKA SAID FINALLY, "IT's like you don't understand us, Colonel. We're not saying you should've stolen . . . as in stealing. Remember, it's your oil. It comes from your villages, by the grace of God! You should've made enough money out there to bid for an exploration license."

"I've no interest or expertise in oil business," the soldier said.

"You don't *need* expertise," Madam Aniema said. "Just money!"

"Jou civilians can bid for licenses if jou like."

"Foolich talk!" Tega said. "Nobody back home get dat kind money . . . except *your* superrish soldiers from oder parts of dis country . . ."

"I served this country within and abroad for thirty-two years. If not for my minority tribe, I would've been a yeneral by now!"

"Are you saying since you're not a general you didn't get a piece of the billions of dollars the country pumped into ECOMOG?"

"*Kai,* leave the generals out of this!" the chief said suddenly. "It's people like this madman we should probe . . . not generals!"

At this, Colonel Usenetok lost it. He untied the rope from his waist and wanted to flog the chief, but the people blocked him.

They told him they were free to question him because they were in a democracy. The soldier was so angry he seemed delirious and started to hop and shove people all over the aisle, like a bad spirit. Without the rope, the ragged camouflage garment flared along with his temper. More talismans were exposed. He jumped over the heads of people sitting in the aisle.

"Dis no be de savannah of Sierra Leone *o!*" a refugee said.

"You think we *dey* urban warfare for Liberia?"

"We must eject this madman."

The more they yelled at him, the more erratic his behavior became. He pulled out his hands like two machine guns and fired at people, his mouth producing the rat-a-tat. He shot at the ceiling and announced that he had brought down helicopters. He fired into the window and claimed he was keeping the RUF rebels at bay. The people called the police to come and deliver them, but they were nowhere to be found. When the colonel got to the front of the bus he stopped suddenly and said: "The government hasn't paid my arrears. I come here and you're robbing me of my seat—after six years at the war front, in the service of the fatherland? And you're talking democracy? No stupid chief talks for anyone in a true democracy!"

"No, my people," the chief said, and stood up. "This madman's worship is not the true religion of our ancestors! I know the religion of my ancestors. We don't know what mad juju he brought back from his travels. . . . We must throw the soldier out before it's too late! I repeat: Gabriel shall not surrender his seat!" Then he turned to the soldier: "As our ancestors say, you can't quarrel with God and then scale the palm tree with a broken rope. If you insist, I shall leave this bus! And this whole bus must face the consequence once you reach *my* delta! My people will ask you what you did with me . . ."

"Then *jou* shall not travel on this bus!" the soldier shouted, punching the air. "I've suffered too much for freedom in this country . . . in Africa. And jou want to eyect me from the bus because of my reliyion?"

"You must go," the chief said.

"Let me tell all of jou in this bus, none of these white countries, which brought us Christianity and democracy, came to die for the Liberians. Did any of these Arab countries peddling militant Islam in Africa send troops to Sierra Leone? I say jou all are mad, to kill each other for two foreign reliyions. We wretched ECOMOG soldiers went out there to die for democracy while the little democracy in this country is being scuttled by yenerals and politicians and chiefs . . . rogues. We saved Liberia . . . Sierra Leone. Hooray to the West African soldier! I shall kill somebody before I leave this bus today. Try me. I have learned so much from where I have been."

"My people, see what I mean?" the chief laughed. "My son, making sense doesn't depend on how many places you have visited. As our people say, if winning a race depended on one's number of legs, the millipede would beat the dog hands down . . ."

"Chief, you *dey* talk sense!" the refugees said.

"Yet get wisdom well well!"

"May you live forever *o!*"

Chief Ukongo chuckled and fanned away the sweat that was beginning to collect on his face. He thudded his stick and looked around the bus as if it were his parlor. "As I was saying, my people, we're not safe with his mad juju. . . . We must *vote* him out of this bus, since we're in a democracy. Colonel, you said you have learned democracy abroad, right? OK, let's practice it. . . . We have come to the end of campaigns and endless talk."

"But my quarrel is with this boy who has my space!" the soldier said. "And he's ready to give me my seat . . ."

"You've charmed the boy!" the chief interjected. "I'm his royal father and must protect him!"

The soldier began to shout at the top of his lungs. He was telling the bus about the rebels of Liberia and the child soldiers of Sierra Leone. He rattled on about how ruthless the child soldiers were and how he had killed many of them, how he would not spare any child who carried a gun. He talked about how he had to start taking cocaine to march at the pace of cocaine madness exhibited by the child soldiers.

The chief said his stories and boundless energy were a ploy to disrupt free and fair elections. He said his people would never be intimidated by a soldier ever again.

MADAM ANIEMA REMOVED HER thick glasses, squinting her eyes and looking around the bus as if she had finally found a solution to the soldier menace. Then she brought out the little water bottle from which the sick man had drunk. She announced to everyone that she was carrying holy water. She made a sign of the cross, stood up hastily, and went about sprinkling the place with the water, to neutralize the soldier's charms. People made way for her lean frame.

"Saint Joseph, Terror of the Devil!" she said faintly.

"Pray for us!" the bus responded.

"Sacred Heart of Jesus!"

"Have mercy on us!"

She rolled out a litany of saints to come to their aid, and gently she sprinkled the water on the colonel, who was still fuming and ranting about being cheated, and commanded the devil to leave them. The soldier calmed down, looking on in disbelief.

"Once the Church has blessed the water," she said, "the spirit of God fills that water. Now we can travel with the soldier even to Moscow." She turned to the soldier: "You find a place and sit down. You are OK. Thanks for what you have given to the country."

"I will sit down," the soldier said.

The passengers thanked her profusely, and some even asked her to preach to them. Monica begged her to sprinkle some of the water on her baby, which she did. They asked her why she did not sprinkle it on the sick man. She said that there was no need, since he had taken the pills with the holy water, and that the man would be fine wherever he was.

"We no be like all dis *nyama-nyama* churches!" one Catholic man said from the back.

"We know how to deal wid Satan!" another said.

"Because we've been in this church business for two thousand years now!"

"Colonel," Madam Aniema said, "you will be given a place—"

"You've got the real thing, woman!" the chief cut in with his congratulations. He stood up again and smiled at everybody, like a headmaster whose student has just triumphed at a debate. "Your holy water is as powerful as what those bearded Irishmen sprinkled on our ancestors to make them instant Catholics. Then, the

Church didn't waste time dipping you into a river before you got the Spirit . . ."

"*Yesss!*" the Catholics cheered.

"Just three drops of water and you knew Latin like the pope," the chief said.

"*Of courssse!*"

"I'm going to personally tell Rome to ordain you a priest . . ."

"No, no, no. . . . That's not our church!"

"Chief, we no *dey* ordain women for our church!"

A light murmur went through the bus. Some said Madam Aniema should be exempted from church tradition, while the Catholics said it was impossible to ordain women and warned outsiders to mind their own business. The soldier stood there, watching, surprised he was no longer the focus of attention. He looked at Madam Aniema intently, as if expecting her to offer him a seat.

"My Catholic children, I am sorry," the chief said. "I wasn't trying to destroy your faith, OK . . . ah . . . ah . . . but as you can see this woman's water bottle is too small for our trip. If this soldier's six years' madness returns on the way, we will run out of holy water."

"I no be against Catholic Shursh *o*," Tega said. "But Shief *dey* talk sense."

"Yes, make we *dey* look at dis situation well well," Monica said.

Madam Aniema said, "We can all find a space on this bus . . ."

"I insist he must be *voted* out, and I am speaking as a royal father!" the chief concluded.

At this, they began to contribute money for the voting, which meant bribing the police. The chief whispered something into Jubril's ear, and the boy quickly paid for both of them.

The soldier started shouting and threatening again, knowing

they would get rid of him. He lobbed imaginary grenades at people.

Jubril was perplexed; he did not know with whom to side. He knew the floor space was not his. And because of the erratic way the chief was acting, he could not bring himself to say the chief had his ticket. Jubril was uncomfortable with the way his fellow passengers were switching sides on every issue. What would happen if the chief denied that Jubril had given him his ticket and he was thrown off the bus? What chance did he have if they forced him to reveal the content of his pocket? He begged Allah to take control of his fate.

SUDDENLY EMEKA BEGAN TO tremble like the sick man had, calling on God with all his might. The bus was not afraid but happy, saying he was possessed by the Spirit. They thanked God for revealing himself in the midst of the threat they were facing from the mad soldier. Emeka threw away his monkey coat and took off his shirt. His big eyes were blinking riotously like a broken traffic light, and every inch of his short frame vibrated with fervor. Though his mouth was wide, the torrent of glossolalia flying out seemed bigger. He spoke without catching his breath. To Jubril's ears, he sounded like Yusuf. Jubril quickly hid his face from Emeka and shut his eyes, trying not to think of his brother. He tried to chant some Islamic incantations in his heart to distract himself from Emeka's speaking in tongues. But it did not work. In his mind, Emeka became Yusuf. Though he opened his eyes, he could not rid himself of thoughts of Yusuf.

"There's an enemyyy in this bus!" Emeka said. "We must

cleanse this bus spiritually . . . Jesus! Jeeesuzzz! The bloood of Jesus must disgrace you today . . ."

"In Jesus' name!" the bus resounded.

"I say, the blood, blood, blood of Jeeesuzzz must cover this journey."

"Amen!"

"Jehooovah, who deigned that Jonah be thrown into the sea . . . reveal him to us now, noww, nowww."

"Now now, Jesus! Save us, Holy Spirit!"

"Reveeeal to us the evil one on this bus."

Emeka stamped his feet and ranted on, looking up with eyes glazed, as if he were consulting the heavens, as Yusuf did the afternoon he was stoned. Emeka was out of control. Sometimes, it was as if he would fling himself out the window and disappear into the night. At the other end of the bus, the soldier was exhibiting all the madness of the war front. The two looked like the foci of a twin whirlwind, spinning close to each other but never merging. The bus was totally behind Emeka, cursing the mad colonel and drowning him out with prayers.

Now Emeka began to tremble toward Jubril.

"You've betrayed Christ!" he accused Jubril, reaching for his neck. "Who sent you to condemn God's children to a bad journey?"

The refugees were surprised and disappointed that he was taking on Jubril and not the soldier.

"No vex, *abeg o*," Jubril pleaded.

"No say anyting," Tega advised him. "Just *dey* quiet . . . *na* mistake. *Na* de soldier he want hold."

Monica said in a loud whisper, "Gabriel, no fight him *o* . . . de Spirit go correct himself. . . . We go pray for de correction."

By now Emeka had grabbed Jubril firmly by the neck and was shaking him. Some prayed that the Spirit might be inspired to rid the right person from the bus. But when they saw that Emeka was determined, they went back to advising Jubril not to say anything or to retaliate, as it would be folly engaging the Holy Spirit. Jubril appealed to the chief as Emeka dragged him toward the door, much in the way he had dealt with the soldier when he entered the bus. But the old man said nothing. Jubril, terrified, trembled as much as his possessed captor. For a while the two whirlwinds came very close and shaved into each other, as Emeka bundled Jubril past the madman, heading toward the door.

"Accept Jesus as your personal Savior!" Emeka said in Jubril's face.

"My broder," Jubril said, talking to his late brother Yusuf, "I be your blood. I be one of you."

"No, no, no, no," Emeka said, pushing him to the floor. "Kneel down. . . . You're the eneeemy!"

Jubril took the pain as his body slammed into people and then to the floor. His concern now was to make sure his right wrist did not come out of his pocket. He held it down with his left hand. "I no be enemy. . . . I be your blood broder . . . Gabriel!" he pleaded. "I accept Christ."

"Liar! Who are you?"

"Ah . . . I first Catolic! Remember Mama say dem baptize us as baby, Joseph?"

"I'm a member of the Pentecostal Explosion Ministries. We don't believe in child baptism!"

"We be one fader, one moder. Joseph, I *dey* accept you now."

To prove his identity to his brother, Jubril showed him his

Marian medal. But Emeka tore the medal and flung it out a window as if he had mistakenly picked up a red-hot coal. "Mary is an
idol in Catholic worship," he said. "And child baptism prepaaares
a child for hell. . . . I knooow you! You cannot hiiide from the
Father of Jesus Christ."

"Beg our fader to forgive," Jubril said. "You alone fit beg for me."

"You must come with me then, if you want to meet our
Father!"

"Our fader go forgive me . . . your killer?"

"Yes, yezzz! The Father is forgiveness!"

The refugees were astonished. They now thought the chief
could have been right when he accused Jubril of carrying a talisman in his pocket. They looked at each other and increased their
prayers and thanked the Lord for the miraculous powers of Emeka.
Jubril lay there on the floor of the bus as the sick man had done,
but on his side. His two wrists were latched together at the pocket
in case Emeka, who was hovering over him, attempted to pull
him up by his right arm.

"Emeka, ask him what wishcraft he use kill him broder," Tega
said.

"No tell de Spilit *wetin* he go ask," Ijeoma whispered to her.
"De Spilit no need your advice."

"Me, I want know *wetin dey* him pocket," Tega said.

Others asked them to be quiet and complained that it was already bad enough that the soldier was distracting the Spirit with
his madness. They warned the two women that they were not
in a position to judge Jubril or to intervene, and that since the
omnipotent Spirit did not attack his pocket, they would not
attempt it either. As far as they were concerned, the Spirit had

already taken over the journey. The bus rained with thanksgiving prayers for Jubril's conversion as Madam Aniema sat there quietly reading a torn copy of *The Imitation of Christ*. She behaved as if Emeka was the one to be saved from Lucifer. Occasionally, when he trembled in her direction, she sprinkled her holy water on him, without lifting her eyes. A few other Catholics who did not join Emeka's prayer session sat grim-faced, grumbling about the denigration of their baptism and the disposal of the Marian medal. They nodded in approval whenever Madam Aniema sprinkled water on Emeka. Others looked at her as if she were a miniature Satan who badly needed Emeka's cleansing.

Emeka pointed at Colonel Usenetok. "May your juju be destroyed by the bloood of Jesus!"

"Amen!" the bus agreed, more enthusiastic than they were about Jubril. The ring of people around Emeka loosened, and their attention turned to the mad soldier. Most people were standing now, ready to give the Spirit a hand if need be.

"Jesus, your blood has already covered us against the Muslims," Emeka said, coming to stand face-to-face with the soldier. The chief cleared his throat at the word *Muslim* and opened his mouth to say something, but Monica nudged him to keep quiet and told him the Spirit could do no wrong.

"Jou again?" the soldier laughed. "What have I done to jou?"

"Chut up!" Tega said to the soldier, looming behind Emeka, wielding her clog.

"Lady, why are jou against me?" the soldier said.

"No worry," she said. "De Spirit go chow you pepper."

"If this man touches me this time, I will yust kill him."

"You can't do de Spirit anyting. Who born you?"

The soldier stood there, unperturbed. He seemed more interested in the people behind Emeka than in his ranting.

"May the Muslims drown in Khamfi, like Pharaoh and his army in the Red Sea," Emeka said, as if the soldier were a Muslim fanatic. "In Jesus' name!"

"Ameeen!"

"I commaaand you, I commaaand you, Jesus, to come down, here here here, and battle this juju!"

With that, Emeka tackled the ECOMOG man, and they went down like two gladiators. Jubril wanted to join the fight on the side of Emeka, but they restrained him. Everyone backed away, saying it was a spiritual fight, and anybody who was not called by the Spirit, like Emeka, was risking his life. The fighters writhed on the floor and tore at each other's clothes and skin, bloodying the aisle. There were loud prayers that Emeka might conquer the juju soldier. The commotion was so loud that the refugees outside gathered around the bus and hopped up and down to get a glimpse of the action.

"STOP OR WE GO shoot!" The police barged into the spiritual combat, cocking their rifles.

"No way, officers!" someone said.

"Dis one no be police fight *o!*" another said.

"Officers, guns no go *fit* win dis kind war," Monica said. "Dis fight *na* for God, no be for Caesar."

"Remember, police, you too go all die," Tega said, "if you allow dis ECOMOG soldierman follow us home!"

Colonel Usenetok broke free and scrambled toward the police

for protection, with Emeka in pursuit. The officers lowered their
guns and tossed Emeka out of the bus, reprimanding him for
fighting with a soldier. They said they would never allow a civilian to disgrace a man in uniform, no matter how tattered.

Outside, the refugees who had followed what was going on
restrained Emeka, who was bent on running into the savannah to
engage whatever evil spirits lurked there. He was like a man on
drugs, his muscles still bulging with unexhausted power. This
incident brought some consolation to the park refugees. With
Emeka in their midst, some of them started thanking God for
the Spirit who would protect them, even if the government failed
to do so. Emeka had become the center of attention, and they
milled around him in the dark, some reaching out to touch him.
Then a few people switched on their flashlights; those with can-
dles lit them. The light surrounded him like a halo that was too
big for a saint and had to be shared by all who were near.

In the ghostly silence that sealed the bus, Jubril stood up and ap-
proached the door like a zombie. He said he wanted to be outside
with his brother. He said he had stood by while people killed
Joseph the first time and was not going to make that mistake again.
When people asked him who Joseph was, he pointed at Emeka and
said that he would rather return to Khamfi and die than travel
without him. There were tears in his eyes. The refugees were edi-
fied by how deep his conversion had been. Though threatened by
what the ECOMOG man would do now, they were consoled that
the Spirit had converted at least one person to Christianity.

Tega appealed to Jubril, whispering to avoid the attention of
the victorious ECOMOG man. "Gabriel, no cry. Leave everyting
for de Spirit."

"De next ting for you is proper baptism!" Monica said. "When we reach delta, we go baptize you for river like Jesus for River Jordan . . ."

"Ha-ha, where would you get a river that is not clogged by oil in the delta?" the chief said.

"Dat's why we Christians must fight de oil companies for our rivers!" Monica said. "Dis oil drilling *dey* affect our prayer life *o.*"

"Don't wolly," Ijeoma said. "When we reach home, we know *wetin* we go do to oil companies. For now, according to de Retter to de Lomans, even when we no fit play, de Spilit *dey* play for us! Dat's why de Spilit descend on Emeka." She turned to Jubril: "Gabliel, dis Emeka is flom my virrage. You want mourn *pass* me? Stop clying."

Tega invited Gabriel to take her seat, to console him. He could have sat anywhere. He was enjoying the hospitality afforded a new convert. But Chief Ukongo was not happy and said it was not a good idea to separate Jubril from him. He signaled to Tega, who was standing by Jubril, to return him to his former place. Tega said no and gave the chief a bad look. He tried to get Jubril's attention, but Monica prevailed on the chief to forget that idea.

The soldier found Nduese under one of the seats and broke into a celebratory dance, a wild gyration of worship. People backed away to give him a bit of space, still afraid of him since he had defeated the Spirit.

From his bag, the soldier pulled out an egg-shaped stone in a little container of water. He set it down, a temporary altar, and circled the spot in a seat-obstructed, jagged symmetry, calling out to Mami Wata, the goddess of the sea, in a litany of names. The soldier thanked her for leading him to war and back and for defeating Emeka. He promised her he would clean and restore her rivers in the delta to what they were before the Christians and Muslims dirtied them with sacrilege and greed for oil.

He squatted before the mobile shrine. "Mother, don't abandon me now," he said. "Remember, I performed this ritual every morning to jou in Liberia and then in Sierra Leone." He looked into the bowl of water, bringing his face closer until his reflection filled its surface, then touched it, causing it to ripple. "Mother, thank jou. . . . Jou fill the earth with jour children!" he whispered. "We all belong to jou!"

Everyone's attention was trained on the soldier, though in the background Chief Ukongo could be heard talking to his dog. He held it in his lap, stroking its bony body and whispering sweet things into its torn ears. Nduese looked at him attentively.

"Do you know that without the royal fathers our country is finished?" he asked the dog, which had begun to whine agreeably. He stuffed Nduese's mouth with biscuits. "Nobody likes the royal fathers anymore. When my great-grandfather was the chief, people listened to him. He organized the people to fight off the wicked white men, who came to enslave us. Many died fighting against white people's guns and swords because once he spoke people obeyed." Nduese began to lick the chief's hands.

"When my grandfather came to power, they listened to him too . . . even missionaries. He gave them land to build churches and hospitals and schools, which is how the south became more educated than the north. In my father's time, it was the same thing. I mean, these big oil companies consulted him regularly, which is why the oil tribes weren't killing each other, as they do today in the delta. Even the military government worked hand in hand with him. . . . But now, nobody wants to hear anything from *me* . . . not my people, not the oil companies. What kind of democracy is that, my friend?

"Do you know that two years ago, my people, I mean *my* people, burned the cars the oil companies gave me? The youths complained about the polluted land and dead rivers. I tried to talk to the oil companies, but they kept postponing my appointments to represent the people to them. The youths burned down my palace, accusing me of supporting the oil companies and military government! I tell you, if the military government had not rebuilt my palace and given me new cars, I would be homeless today. . . . How can they burn my palace, the very symbol of their existence? If this were my great-grandfather's days, he would have given all these hopeless delta youth to the white people, free. . . . The military had promised me a house in Lupa when the soldiers vacated power. . . . One day God must bring the soldiers back. I will always miss General Abacha!" He pointed at Jubril. "Then, imagine that young man . . ."

"Be quiet!" someone warned, because the chief's voice was rising.

"Let de soldier worchip," Tega said, "so we can have our peace."

"Leave dat dog to sleep *o,*" Monica said.

Now realizing that the dog was fast asleep, the chief shook it and turned its head toward Jubril. "Look at that Gabriel," he said to the dog. "He's refused to remove his hand from the pocket . . . in spite of our pleas. He and his parents are the type of useless people we would have given to the white man in those days. And we would see how he would have plowed the sugar plantations in America with one hand in his pocket. . . . Or maybe they should have sold him to the Arabs, who would have castrated him immediately."

THE SOLDIER GLANCED AROUND the bus and said he wanted something to sacrifice to his goddess, some food or drink to manifest their union. There was nothing, and the people were afraid of what he meant by *sacrifice*. Was he talking about human sacrifice? Was he going to kill someone?

But the soldier opened his mouth very wide and with it covered one of the wounds he had sustained while fighting Emeka. He sucked the blood reverently, as if it was an extension of his sacrifice at the war front. Whatever became of his life, he prayed out loud, he had done his part, and he begged Mami Wata to lead him home. In one final stamp of his foot, he praised her for defeating Jesus Christ and Muhammad in the land. He flashed a crazed smile at everyone.

"Now, who is occupying my seat?" he asked, as he began to pack up his altar. "Yust stand up before I flush jou."

"If you know you *dey* his seat," Tega quickly warned the bus, "*abeg*, stand up *o*."

"But wait a minute," the soldier said, his eyes scanning the bus. "Where is Nduese? Someone has stolen my dog. My dog or else . . ."

The refugees quickly pointed to the chief.

"Honorable soldier," Chief Ukongo said, smiling, "the beautiful dog is asleep."

"Yust give me my dog," the soldier said. "I am warning jou for the last time."

"Brave soldier, my apologies. . . . While you were saying your prayers, I took care of it for you." He stood up, carrying the dog like a bouquet of flowers to the soldier, and bowed curtly before him.

The soldier snatched Nduese from him. "Don't bow before me, jou old rogue!"

"Please, Colonel, on behalf of everyone on this bus," the chief said, "I invite you to rest your tired bones on the seat left behind by the misguided spirit-man who fought you."

"*Abeg,* our broder, make you sit dere!"

"It is a nice seat!"

"You have suffered so much for this country!"

"No, I want my seat," the soldier maintained. "My oriyinal seat."

"Just give us time, please, to sort ourselves out," the chief said. "All of us are behind you."

"Our dear colonel, be patient with us," Madam Aniema said suddenly, removing her glasses. Her voice was like a spray of cool water on the fire of anxiety that was consuming the bus. Seeing how the soldier suddenly listened to her, everyone now looked up to her. Only Jubril sat with his face buried in the headrest before him, no longer sure of what to do or whom to trust.

"Colonel, I have always supported your stay on this bus," Madam Aniema said.

"Jes, that's true," the soldier said.

"Yes, she has always supported you," the chief said. "We are not all bad."

"Shief, chut up!" Tega said. "Make dis holy woman represent us."

"Because of jou, madam," the soldier said, "I will be patient.

But I want my seat. All my life I have always made do with what is mine. I am not a thief."

Having said this, he curled up comfortably on the seat of the expelled Emeka, next to Madam Aniema, stroking his dog and looking into the darkness outside. There was an uneasy calm on the bus. It was as if the biggest worry of the refugees had been solved, and Madam Aniema went back to *The Imitation of Christ,* oblivious to the murmurs of thanks directed toward her. The Catholics held their heads up again and went back to extolling the great things their Church had done over the centuries. Even the police came back in and praised the refugees for their spirit of tolerance and dialogue, assuring them that the driver would soon finish his rest and come to take them home. They reminded the people that whoever caused trouble would be treated like Emeka.

Soon, the colonel and Nduese, to the relief of all, fell asleep. They slept as if they had not rested for the six years he had served on peacekeeping duties abroad.

OUTSIDE, IT WAS GETTING cold, seeming to deepen the darkness, and more Luxurious Buses started to arrive from the north. Their powerful headlights swept the skies and the bushes as they heaved over the low hills, and their hazard lights twinkled as they negotiated corners. They had turned their horns into sirens, blowing them nonstop. Hope filled the park, with people rushing to the roadside, waving frantically in an effort to stop the buses. Police officers tried to control the crowd and move people off the road but were unsuccessful. Most of the buses slowed down to avoid accident, but they did not stop.

When one bus finally stopped, it was swamped by the crowd. People had their money ready, waving it, eager to pay exorbitant fees to get home. The police quickly ordered them to stand in lines as the conductors started issuing tickets and collecting money. Some refugees preferred to give more money to the police than was necessary. The police then made a profit buying tickets from the conductors.

"Only de brave people go enter de bus," a police officer said, blocking the door. "No be any coward *o*."

"There's nothing we have not seen before," one lady said.

"Officer, if you want bribe, we go pay," another passenger said.

"We must reach home by all means."

When the doors opened, a low cry emanated from the crowd. What they saw jolted them, pushing them back. Apart from a few front seats, the bus was full of dead bodies, and there was blood everywhere. The seats were strewn with corpses of every shape and size: children, women, and men. The aisle was impassable, with bodies piled as high as the seats. It was as if someone had gassed a crowded bus. Most of the bodies had wounds, and some were burned. There were also body parts.

Emeka began to wail. His grief was infectious and seemed to open a dam of human emotion in the park. People were crying for the dead. Their sorrow was such that they would not allow the bus to leave, and yet they could not immediately summon the courage to enter it. They knew that these were the bodies of fellow southerners and formed a barricade in front of the bus. The police tried in vain to encourage the people to board.

Emeka asked the police if he could return to the first bus, saying he could not handle traveling in the second one. He could be heard crying and explaining to one and all what had happened to him on the first bus, but nobody was in the mood to listen to his Spirit story. It was as if the refugees, after what they had seen, had forsaken the aura and mystery of the world of the Spirit. Emeka showed the police his ticket, but they accused him of inciting the stranded refugees to block the bus and said they had suspected he was a troublemaker from the time he offered just ten naira to watch cable TV. They said they would make sure he was the last person to leave the motor park.

"Who still want travel for dis bus?" the police asked the crowd.

"Officers, give us time," one refugee said.

"De driver of dis luxurious hearse no get time to waste *o*," the police said. "Just *dey* pretend say de bodies *dey* alive or pretend say you be dead. . . . Last night, many refugees like you *dey* join de hearses. By now dem done reach home . . . or you want make we remove de dead from de bus?"

"No, we must carry our dead home," someone said.

"We shall never leave them in the north!"

The harmattan wind sniffed the land in short livid bursts, sending up a low cloud of heavy dust that stung the refugees' nostrils and eyes. They pulled whatever clothes they had tighter around themselves and gathered at the back of the bus near the heat of the exhaust pipe.

THE POLICE BUNDLED THE sick man on the veranda and brought him toward the luxurious hearse. He was no longer babbling, but weak and flailing his arms. He protested as the police dumped him on the bus.

"I don't want this bus!" the sick man shouted.

"But you be as good as dead!" a policeman shouted back. "Dem *dey* count fish, crab *dey* talk!"

"Please, let me die in the north!" he begged.

"No, you must go home!" Then the officer turned to the refugees: "See, you no go die if you enter de bus. Even dis sick man no die. He even get energy to shout."

Gradually, silently, volunteers got onto the bus and filled up the few remaining seats at the front. Some, still weeping, sat with the dead. As more people entered the bus, the space became tight. A group of men came up with a plan to maximize the space for both the living and the dead. They grabbed the corpses like logs of firewood and rearranged them, pushing them toward the back so they rose like a hill, reaching the TV set near the ceiling. Some tore their scarves or shirts into strips, which they used to blindfold their children before boarding the bus. Others argued that it was too long a journey to make in a blindfold and forced their children to gawk at the dead until they got used to the sight.

Two more buses arrived.

THOUGH THE REFUGEES IN Jubril's bus knew that Colonel Usenetok had the police on his side, they were not yet completely defeated. When they were sure the soldier and his dog were sound asleep, they began to plan their next line of attack.

"Jesus no go let de devil win for dis war!" Tega whispered to those around her.

Madam Aniema said, "My daughter, why don't we let the

sleeping dog lie, as they say? I'm sure this soldier is not going to cause any trouble on the way."

"No talk rike dat, madam," Ijeoma said. "What of Emeka?"

"We need Emeka for dis bus," Monica said.

"De man done pay for de bus," Ijeoma said. "And *wetin* I go tell my ferrow virragers who know *am?*"

Madam Aniema hushed. People began to talk about how to bring Emeka back. The bus had taken on the feel of a community whose progress had been thwarted by a temporary evil, a misfortune whose duration no one knew, but whose defeat was certain.

"My people, these days we need the hottest kind of Spirit," the chief said. He stood up, cracked his knuckles, and adjusted his beads. "The kind that possessed Emeka . . . to cleanse this country. As we say, if a ghost rat is stealing from your house, you also buy a ghost cat, not an ordinary cat. . . . I know what needs to be done!"

"De chief is making sense," Ijeoma said.

"So, Chief, *wetin* we go do?" Monica asked.

"My people, we must act fast now that the soldier is asleep. A little while ago, we taxed everybody so we could vote him out, remember?"

"Yes, yes!" they said.

"Let us contribute more money. Enough to get the soldier out, enough to bring Emeka back. I will do a quick e-commerce with the police. I know them. If we give them enough money, they won't remember who is wearing a military uniform or not."

They began to tax themselves again. The old man went out to negotiate with the police, and they let Emeka back in. The police did not throw out the mad soldier. Emeka came in looking very somber. The drunken, spiritual dazzle that had covered his face when he spoke in tongues had long since deserted him. Now, he looked like an ill-prepared *akpu* and shivered from the cold. They found a place for him to stand, away from the soldier. No matter how much the refugees tried to lift his mood, telling him how useful his spiritual powers would be for the journey, Emeka was inconsolable. He babbled nonstop about the corpses he had seen in the other bus.

THE POLICE FINALLY WOKE up the driver. A huge, muscular fellow, he shuffled to the bus, looking like he had carried the drum of diesel from Lupa to the motor park on his head. The passengers were relieved to see him and actually applauded him, the way passengers sometimes clap for a pilot when a turbulent flight has touched down safely. As he entered the bus, the refugees stranded outside screamed uncontrollably. He turned on the engine and revved it, causing echoes in the savannah. The two police officers came onto the bus and took their seats, and as the driver negotiated his way out of the park, he turned off the cabin lights.

Jubril's whole being seemed to levitate as the bus pulled away, and he welcomed the semidarkness wholeheartedly. If he could have made the darkness absolute he would have done it. It was as if it could conceal his whole history until daybreak. He sat up for the first time since he leaned forward on the headrest, still not knowing whom to trust. He surveyed the place the way he had wanted to when there was light, though now he could not see anyone's face clearly. He remembered the time he lay under the mats in Mallam Abdullahi's home, covered in darkness, and how consoling that darkness was after he learned they were prayer mats.

As he looked out into the passing savannah, the wind from the open window whipped his face. He thought of how Mallam Abdullahi had released him in the bush under the cover of darkness, how he ran in the direction the *mallam* had indicated. How in the daylight, he had slipped from tree to tree, like an eaglet too young to handle long flights, knowing he was vulnerable to attack in the open spaces between the stout savannah trees. He hid from bands of fellow refugees because he could not trust anybody. At night, he listened for signs of danger within the howls of the wind, yet he covered more distance, keeping close to the Khamfi-Lupa Road. He remembered his constant plea before Allah, his maker: "If you do not accept me and my plans to embrace my southern identity and lead me safely home, who will?"

AS THE BUS GATHERED speed, the police wished them a pleasant journey and told them not to worry about those left behind and promised to turn on the TV. The driver honked and turned on his hazard lights, like the recently arrived luxurious hearses from the north. Before long the bus was going at top speed, slipping quietly through the savannah toward the rain forests.

In spite of the circumstances of his travel, for Jubril, being on this bus was like a dream: the rush of wind in his face; the sight of the bus's headlights cutting through the darkness in an unending thrust; the feeling of being still while the dark bushes sped past, streaked by the flashing hazard lights; the gentle pull of the seat to one side as the bus took wide corners or descended into the valleys. He was thankful to Tega for giving him the seat and looked at her often as she stood beside him in the dark. By the time the police turned on the TV and went to the local channel, Jubril was so happy to be in this crowd he could no longer restrain himself from watching. Though the pictures were fuzzy, he could make out some of the images.

"Dem *dey* chow soudern towns *o!*" Tega said, as soon as the pictures became better. Jubril, who had longed to see the south since the beginning of his flight, now watched without blinking. He considered it a foretaste of where he was heading.

The magic of TV enthralled Jubril, then horrified him. He watched police and soldiers manhandling rioters in different southern cities. He watched them shoot at the mobs to quell the violence incited by the arrival of luxurious hearses from the north. He saw barracks brimming over with northerners while soldiers and police stood guard. The rioters were not retreating, in spite of the might of the security forces. He noticed that vast numbers of people were in Western clothes and that women were rioting alongside the men. Jubril saw the compact vegetation of the rain forest, creation in full bloom, which was quite different from the semidesert of Khamfi.

The south he saw that night on TV was not what he had expected. The roads were primitive, and in some places rain had washed them away completely. The military jeeps could not cope, and soldiers had to come down and chase the rioters on foot. Some primary schools had no roofs, and he could see blackboards hanging on mango and melina trees in the fields. The bald circles on the earth around trees convinced him that, just as in some parts of Khamfi, the children took their lessons outside.

After the TV had shown the military effectively chasing the rioters through the city, a reporter said that not everybody in the shell-shocked refugee crowds was from the north. The camera zoomed in on some southerners who he said were also hiding in the barracks. He said they had been chased there by the fury of their kin — for attempting to save the northerners — and added that the northerners were not comfortable with the presence of southerners, because not all of them knew why the southerners had joined them. The only difference Jubril saw between the two groups was the way they were dressed.

The reporter was still commenting when someone whispered in his ear. He stopped talking for a moment and then announced: "Because of the crisis in the country, the federal democratic government hereby bans the ferrying of corpses for burial from one part of the country to another until further notice. The government has given the military an order to intercept any bus or truck guilty of this."

THEN THE CAMERAS ZOOMED in on a man whom the reporter identified as the leader of the Hausa-Fulani community in Onyera. He was tall and lean, as black as Tega. Though he wore a bandage on his head, blood ran down his face like tears. He spoke with his eyes closed, as if the camera flashes were hurting them. This image disturbed Jubril. He would have turned away, but the memory of Mallam Abdullahi, who was also Hausa-Fulani, calmed him.

"My name is Yo . . . Yohanna Tijani," stammered the leader, into the reporter's microphone. "I've never lived in the north. . . . My great-grandfather settled here a hundred years ago, like some of your people. I was born in Onyera and grew up here. My mother was a southerner, an Ibo, and I married an Ibo woman too, because the Ibos accepted us as their own. I appeal to you, my grandparents and in-laws: spare our lives. We didn't begin the Sharia war in Khamfi. Most of us Muslims in this country are peace-loving people. . . . We who live with you here didn't kill any of these people whose corpses are now arriving in Luxurious Buses. But now we *are* killing your people . . . in self-defense. We're guilty of bloodshed. Forgive us—" The audio cut out, and the sound of static filled the bus. The police lowered the TVs' volume until all they could hear was the soft purr of the bus, the hiss of the tires on the road, and the flutter of the window blinds. Then the pictures wobbled into large screwy lines and disappeared.

"God, make you no permit soldiers intercept our bus *o!*" Ijeoma said. "We no cally any dead people *o.*"

"What sort of country be dis?" one refugee said.

During the lull, they started analyzing the impact of the government order. The general opinion was that the government had no right to stop anybody from taking the corpses of their kinsmen back home to bury. They blamed the government for not protecting them in Khamfi. They blamed the president for not sending in the military early enough, as he would have done if oil installations in the delta were under threat, and the senators for not taking a strong stand against what was happening in the land—for being paralyzed by the same religious divide that had torn the country apart. They blamed the judiciary for never dealing promptly with cases of religious fanaticism.

"It's a hopeless situation," Emeka said, regaining a bit of his former ebullience.

"You want start trouble again," the police accused him.

"Please, I'm sorry," Emeka begged. "I won't say anything more, I promise."

"Just shut up!" the police said, turning up the volume. "De TV done clear now."

". . . On behalf of our people," Yohanna Tijani was saying, "I want to thank you, Christians. If not for some of you who died hiding us and many who are here with us in the barracks, it would've been worse. . . . I want to say a special thanks to that family that hid me under their Sacred Heart altar and prayed their rosaries while Bakassi Boys stormed the house. . . . My wife, an Ibo Pentecostal Christian, who was visiting with her family, wasn't that lucky. She was killed by her people for hiding some Muslims, one of whom was our son. . . . Everybody is saying our northern generals, who have stolen your oil money, are responsible for this betrayal of nationhood, for the extreme poverty in the land. The truth is that most of us here don't know any generals and are not related to them. If we did, we too would be rich and our children would be studying abroad. We beg you, whatever the generals are doing, whatever the politicians are saying, it's within our hearts to spare each other. They're not losing wives and children. We are. Their money is safe and is reaping interest in Europe and America and Asia and the Middle East, but where shall we get money to rebuild our lives?" The sound and pictures broke up, then disappeared.

In the gloom, Jubril's heart pounded, overpowered by the man's plea and the wonder of TV. He thought he had escaped the sight of blood and killings in Khamfi. But, from what he had just seen and heard from Yohanna Tijani, the madness had spread to the south. His mind went back to the mob of Lukman and Musa, and the mob that came to Mallam Abdullahi's house. He pressed his tongue against his teeth till it began to hurt, hoping against hope that the images on TV were fabricated.

In the semidarkness, it was easy to see that, apart from the mad soldier who was asleep, the refugees were agitated. Though what the northerner had said touched them, they wanted to know the extent of the damage. Would they make it to the south? Would they be mistaken for a busload of corpses and be impounded by the military? It worried them because since the Nigeria-Biafra War their people had never retaliated against the recurring massacre of their people in the north. Everyone was afraid. It was clear to them that the local channels were not ready to show the extent of the riots in the south. They pestered the policemen for cable TV, for nobody believed the local channels would tell them much.

"No worry," the police said, "we no be luxurious hearse, OK? Dem no go intercept us."

"We want cable TV *o!*"

"When Abacha hanged Saro-Wiwa because of our oil, we saw it first on foreign TV!"

"When Abacha himself die *na* foreign press talk *am* first!"

The police instructed the driver to turn off the hazard lights and turn on the cabin lights so the bus would not be mistaken for a hearse. The driver did. The passengers' anxieties rose and fell as the bus skirted the corners, yet some were urging the driver to move faster: death by motor accident seemed more desirable to them than the forms of death meted out by the ethnic cleansers at both ends of their country.

By the time they started encountering vehicles traveling the other way — mainly tractor trailers and smaller trucks, the kinds that transport cows from the north to the south — even the police officers were eager to know the real situation in the south. All vehicles seemed to be going north, blazing with a full complement of hazard lights and horns. Luxurious hearses were also heading north.

HAVING LIVED THROUGH THE ordeal in Mallam Abdullahi's house and having just heard the testimony of Yohanna Tijani about the generous southern Christians, Jubril felt that with heroic people like this, his nation would rise above all types of divisiveness. Instinctively, in his yearning for consolation, he envisioned the different peoples of his country connecting at a deep, primordial level, where one's life was irreversibly connected to one's neighbor's, like a child's to its mother's.

THE FRIGHTENED PASSENGERS HAD now turned inward, for strength, and peace reigned among the different religions on the bus. Everybody seemed tired of screaming about their god in someone else's face. Meanwhile, the police kept flipping the foreign channels for the updates they wanted. It was not long before the truth was told:

Breaking News: Reprisal Violence in
Onyera and Port Harcourt

Both city centers were matted with corpses and gore, and the anchor said other southern cities were preparing for vengeance against the Muslims and northerners in their midst. She said buses full of southern corpses were beginning to arrive in Onyera and Port Harcourt. She said that trucks had also begun ferrying corpses of northerners killed in the southern riots back to the north, and that the country was on the verge of a north-south war. She said that what mattered in the conflicts was the fighters' tribes, insofar as external features and dressing and language could identify them. She confirmed that the government had banned the movement of corpses to check reprisal violence.

Images of the riots poured into the bus, the cameras pursuing the action as if it were a UEFA Champions League match. The southern youths were uncontrollable and spilled out with their machetes, guns, and clubs in every direction, like the lava of an erupted volcano. They killed and killed, as if in this singular madness they would avenge all the massacres of their people who lived in the north, in the past and in the future. The audio was so clear that the refugees could hear the slurp of machetes slashing into flesh and the final cries of the victims.

Then, the broadcast split into three interactive frames. One showed the reporter, who was in direct contact with the news anchor in another frame. They discussed the carnage being shown in the third. Then the third frame anticipated and zoomed in on a mosque and expanded to fill the whole screen. The golden dome sparkled in the sun like a bishop's skullcap, the corners of the mosque reaching up in four beautiful minarets, like carefully sculpted bedposts, the sky above them a rich blue canopy decorated with woolly clouds. The green and white motif of the fenced compound stood apart, like an eternal freshness, from the widening chaos of the city. Then youths with torches surrounded it, smashing doors and windows. The minarets started spewing thick black chimneys of smoke, like an industrial plant. Because there was no wind, the smoke enveloped the golden dome, which caved in before the mosque erupted in a ball of fire.

The coverage returned to Khamfi, recapping the past two days of crisis. Tempers flared again in the bus. Jubril never thought the people of the south could be capable of such violence. And no one had ever told him that there were northerners who lived in the south, whose lives could be in danger.

Suddenly, everybody on the bus stood up and cheered, even the police. They were like soccer fans, urging their teams to victory.

"We're tired of turning the other cheek!" Madam Aniema said.

"No more northerners in Igbo land!" Emeka said.

"Urhobo land for de Urhobos!" Tega said.

"De Musrims done burn my church four times in Khamfi!" Ijeoma said.

This shouting had little effect on Jubril. The sight of a mosque going up in flames had given him an instant fever, even though he himself had set churches on fire. It was too much for him, and he wept. Jubril had not cried since the gas spilled into his eyes when he lay among the Christians in Mallam Abdullahi's house. Now the tears kept coming, and with one hand he caught their watery beads. Sobs shook his body, like that of a convulsing Nduese. He twisted in his seat to shield his face from the TV, and in this valley of tears he forgot himself—and lifted his right wrist to his face.

HE TRIED TO PUT it back in his pocket, but it was too late. Those who saw it moved away from him, including Tega. Looking at the stern faces around him, Jubril knew it was no use trying to hide. The police asked him to stand up and come into the aisle. They frisked him for firebombs and guns.

His hand had been sliced off just above the wrist. It had not healed yet and could not be fully straightened. It was covered by a loose ball of dirty bandage, which had all along bulged in his pocket like a gloved fist. The police removed the bandage and threw it out the window. The wounded skin of the stump was white and taut.

Passengers were asking the driver to stop the bus and make Jubril get off. He refused, saying the road was unsafe. Looking at the others, Jubril knew that they were going to lynch him. Trembling more with fever than with fear, he did not shout or struggle against those who started to push him.

"Stop! Just hold on!" Chief Ukongo intervened. "My people, a tick that sockets itself into your skin is not removed by force. . . . A stone thrown in anger cannot kill a bird . . ."

"Old man, we no get time for proverb *o!*" the police told him.

"My people, how would our Lord Jesus react to a situation like this?"

"Pagan . . . you know Chlistianity *pass* us?" Ijeoma said.

They pulled at Jubril's shirt and tore it off, watching him the way one watches a wild animal that has just been captured. They acted slowly, deliberately, as if their anger was being bottled up somewhere inaccessible to them.

"Gabriel, please," Madam Aniema said, "don't tell me you are a northerner!"

Emeka said, "He is. Guilty . . ."

"Sssh, be quiet!" she shushed Emeka, and everybody else kept quiet as well. "You're not a Muslim, Gabriel?"

"Ah . . . ah . . . I come prom soud, but I be prom nord," he said with a Hausa accent. "I be Catolic. I do child baftism. Mama say once you be Catolic you be Catolic porever. I want remain Catolic, *abeg*."

"Are you a Muslim?" Madam Aniema asked him again.

He shook his head. "I no be Muslim again."

"I see," she said, and broke into tears. She tried to appeal to the passengers to give her more time to talk to him, but they pushed her aside. They scolded her for crying, saying she was too emotional to face the truth.

"Now, let's be serious," Chief Ukongo said. "Which north? Which south? Are you from Niger or Chad?"

"No, Chief."

"Are you a mercenary?" he continued.

"No, Chief."

"Because, my son," he said, "we know some politicians in the north have hired mercenaries from Niger and Chad to fight this Sharia war with Arab money."

"Chief, I be one of you," Jubril said. "I no collect money prom folitician." His slender body tilted a bit to the left, as if his remaining hand was weighing him down. The stump was unsteady, vibrating, as if it were the source of his fever. Its muscles kept twitching, contracting and relaxing to imaginary grips.

"I wash my hands of this boy," the chief said, shaking his head.

"My village get oil . . . Ukhemehi!" Jubril declared. He again attempted to convey the mangled story of his religious identity, but their murderous looks told him it was useless. These were not the stares of Catholics or born-agains or ancestral worshippers.

His conversion meant nothing to them. Their stares reminded him of his fundamentalist Muslim friends, Musa and Lukman.

When they started jeering at him again, it was not so much at his northern-southern claims, but at his supposed Christo-Muslim identity. They told him to lift up his cut wrist so that Muhammad would come to his help. He did not argue. He obliged them, raising the stump as straight and as high as he could.

Knowing full well that these people were not going to spare him, he returned to his God of Islam, the one he truly knew, although this journey had permanently altered his fanatic world-view. He flushed the desire to be a Christian from his soul. With all he had seen and experienced, he could not forget the sources of Allah's help during his flight. He raised his stump for Mallam Abdullahi and his family, for showing him another way. He raised it to celebrate the Christians who had held a Muslim's prayer mats for him. He raised it for those northerners who had lived their whole lives in the south, who were struggling, like him, with the unsettling prospects of going home for the first time. He raised his arm for Yusuf, who refused, when the crucial moment came, to abandon his faith; he felt one with him, though they belonged to different faiths and worlds now. He saw the stump as the testimony of his desire to follow Allah wherever he led him, of his yearning for oneness with him.

"Cut him loose . . . jou wicked RUF rebels!" growled Colonel Usenetok, finally awakened by the commotion.

The sight of an amputee had caused the soldier's fragile mind to snap again. He failed to see a distinction between a religion-prescribed amputation and limbs axed off by the RUF. He had lost his mind fighting such savagery in Sierra Leone and Liberia.

"Soldierman, you want die for dis Muslim?" the refugees warned him. "Dis no be Liberia or Sierra Leone *o!*"

"I say cut him loose . . . nowww!"

Chief Ukongo reminded him, "Colonel Usenetok, you *are* one of us! I keep telling you: respect the democracy you went to fight for . . . here. Respect our opinions!"

The colonel was not going to beg them to free Jubril. He stormed the kangaroo court and took them all on. He was a soldier fighting with honor, to save a citizen. He fought as if he alone could redeem the military's image from the untold shame and misery it had brought on the country.

The driver was forced to stop the bus. The soldier fought on, unafraid, because long before the refugees dragged him and Jubril out and slit their throats, his sacrifices abroad had prepared him for anything. They would have taken the soldier's body home if the police had not reminded them of the government warning against moving corpses.

NDUESE STOOD OVER THE two corpses and barked repeatedly into the heavens. The dog mistook the still-twitching, protesting stump as a sign of life.

My Parents' Bedroom

I'm nine years and seven months old. I'm at home playing peeka-boo in my room with my little brother, Jean. It's Saturday evening, and the sun has fallen behind the hills. There's silence outside our bungalow, but from time to time the evening wind carries a shout to us. Our parents have kept us indoors since yesterday.

Maman comes into the room and turns off the light before we see her. Jean cries in the darkness, but once she starts kissing him he begins to giggle. He reaches up to be held, but she's in a hurry.

"Don't turn on any lights tonight," she whispers to me.

I nod. "*Yego,* Maman."

"Come with your brother." I carry Jean and follow her. "And don't open the door for anybody. Your papa is not home, I'm not home, nobody is home. Do you hear me, Monique, huh?"

"*Yego,* Maman."

"Swallow all your questions now, bright daughter. When your papa and uncle return, they'll explain things to you."

Maman leads us through the corridor and into her room, where she lights a candle that she has taken from our family altar, in the parlor. She starts to undress, tossing her clothes on the floor. She tells us that she's going out for the night and that she's already late. She's panting, as if she'd been running; her body is shining with sweat. She slips into the beautiful black evening dress that Papa likes and combs out her soft hair. I help her with the zipper at the back of her dress. She paints her lips a deep red and presses them together. The sequins on her dress glitter in the candlelight as if her heart were on fire.

My mother is a very beautiful Tutsi woman. She has high cheekbones, a narrow nose, a sweet mouth, slim fingers, big eyes, and a lean frame. Her skin is so light that you can see the blue veins on the back of her hands, as you can on the hands of Le Père Mertens, our parish priest, who's from Belgium. I look like Maman, and when I grow up I'll be as tall as she is. This is why Papa and all his Hutu people call me Shenge, which means "my little one" in Kinyarwanda.

Papa looks like most Hutus, very black. He has a round face, a wide nose, and brown eyes. His lips are as full as a banana. He is a jolly, jolly man who can make you laugh till you cry. Jean looks like him.

"But, Maman, you told me that only bad women go out at night."

"Monique, no questions tonight, I told you."

She stops and stares at me. As I'm about to open my mouth, she shouts, "Quiet! Go, sit with your brother!"

Maman never shouts at me. She's strange today. Tears shine in her eyes. I pick up a bottle of Amour Bruxelles, the perfume Papa gives her because he loves her. Everybody in the neighborhood knows her by its sweet smell. When I put the bottle in her hands, she shivers, as if her mind has just returned to her. Instead of spraying it on herself, she puts it on Jean. He's excited, sniffing his hands and clothes. I beg Maman to put some on me, but she refuses.

"When they ask you," she says sternly, without looking at me, "say you're one of them, OK?"

"Who?"

"Anybody. You have to learn to take care of Jean, Monique. You just have to, huh?"

"I will, Maman."

"Promise?"

"Promise."

Maman heads for the parlor, and Jean trails after. He's whimpering to be held. I carry the candle. We sit down on our big sofa, and Maman blows the candle out. Our parlor is never totally dark, because of the crucifix in the corner, which glows yellow green. All translucent, as Papa likes to say. Jean toddles to the altar, as usual. He places his hands on the crucifix as if playing with a toy. The glow enters into his fingers, making them green, and he turns to us and laughs. In quick strides, I bring him back. I don't want him to pull down the crucifix, which leans against the wall, or the vase of bougainvillea beside it. It's part of my duty to tend to the altar. I love the crucifix; all my relatives do. Except Tonton Nzeyimana — the Wizard.

The Wizard is Papa's father's brother. He is a pagan and he is very powerful. If he doesn't like you, he can put his spell on you, until you become useless — unless you're a strong Catholic. The color of his skin is milk with a little coffee. He never married because he says he hates his skin and doesn't want to pass it on.

Sometimes he paints himself with charcoal, until the rain comes to wash away his blackness. I don't know where he got his color from. My parents say it's a complicated story about intermarriage. He's so old that he walks with a stick. His lips are long and droopy, because he uses them to blow bad luck and disease into people. He likes to frighten children with his ugly face. Whenever I see the Wizard, I run away. Papa, his own nephew, doesn't want him in our house, but Maman tolerates the Wizard. "No matter, he's our relative," she says. Tonton André, Papa's only brother, hates him even more. They .don't even greet each other on the road.

Though I'm a girl, Papa says that the crucifix will be mine when he dies, because I'm the firstborn of the family. I will carry it till I give it to my child. Some people laugh at Papa for saying that it'll come to me, a girl. Others shrug and agree with Papa, because he went to university and works in a government ministry. Sometimes when Tonton André and his wife, Tantine Annette, visit us, they praise Papa for this decision. Tantine Annette is pregnant, and I know that they would do the same if God gave them a girl first.

Without his ID, you'd never know that Tonton André is Papa's brother. He's a cross between Papa and Maman — as tall as Maman but not quite as dark as Papa. He's got a tiny beard. Tantine Annette is Maman's best friend. Though she's Tutsi, like Maman, she's as dark as Papa. Sometimes on the road, the police ask for her ID, to be sure of her roots. These days, my parents tease her that she'll give birth to six babies, because her stomach is very big. Each time she becomes pregnant, she miscarries, and everybody knows that it's the Wizard's spell. But the couple have been strong in their faith. Sometimes they kiss in public, like Belgians do on TV, and our people don't like this very much. But they don't care. Tonton André takes her to a good hospital in Kigali for checkups, and Papa and our other relatives contribute money to help them, because both of them are only poor primary school teachers. The Wizard offered to give his money too, but we don't allow him to. If he gave even one franc, his bad money would swallow all the good contributions like the sickly, hungry cows in Pharaoh's dream.

Maman stands up suddenly. "Monique, remember to lock the door behind me! Your papa will be back soon." I hear her going into the kitchen. She opens the back door and stops for a moment. Then the door slams. She's gone.

I LIGHT THE CANDLE again and go into the kitchen and lock the door. We eat rice and fish and return to our room. I dress Jean in his flannel pajamas and sing him to sleep. I change into my nightie and lie down beside him.

In a dream, I hear Tonton André's voice. He sounds as anxious as he did yesterday afternoon, when he came to call Papa away. "Shenge, Shenge, you must open the door for me!" Tonton André shouts.

"Wait, I'm coming," I try to tell him, but in my dream I have no voice, and my legs have melted like butter in the sun. There's a lot of commotion and gunshots that sound like bombs.

"Come to the front door, quick!" he shouts again.

I wake up. Tonton André is actually yelling outside our house. I go into the parlor and turn on the fluorescent lights. My eyes hurt. People are banging on our front door. I see the blades of machetes and axes stabbing through the door, making holes in the plywood. Two windows are smashed, and rifle butts and *udu-funi* are poking in. I don't know what's going on. The attackers can't get in through the windows with their guns and small hoes, because the windows are covered with metal bars. Afraid, I squat on the floor, with my hands covering my head, until the people outside stop and pull back.

I hear Tonton André's voice again, but this time it's calm and deep, as usual, and everything is quiet outside.

"Poor, sweet thing, don't be afraid," he says, now laughing confidently, like Jean. "They're gone. Your papa is here with me."

I pick my way through the broken glass and open the door. But Tonton André comes in with a group. Men and women, all armed.

"Where's Maman?" he asks me.

"Maman went out."

He looks like a madman. His hair is rough, as if he had not combed it for a year. His green shirt is unbuttoned and he's without shoes.

"*Yagiye hehe?*" someone from the mob asks, disappointed. "Where's she gone?"

"She didn't say," I answer.

"Have you seen your papa this evening?" Tonton André asks. "*Oya.*"

"No? I'll kill you," he says, his face swollen with seriousness. I scan the mob. "You told me Papa was with you. . . . Papa! Papa!"

"The coward has escaped," someone in the crowd says.

"*Nta butungane burimo!*" others shout. "Unfair!"

They look victorious, like soccer champions. I know some of them. Our church usher, Monsieur Paschal, is humming and chanting and wears a bandanna. Mademoiselle Angeline, my teacher's daughter, is dancing to the chants, as if to reggae beats. She gives a thumbs-up to Monsieur François, who is the preacher at the nearby Adventist church.

Some of them brandish their IDs, as if they were conducting a census. Others are now searching our home. Sniffing around like dogs, they've traced Maman's Amour Bruxelles to Jean and are bothering him, so he begins to cry. I run to our room and carry him back to the parlor. I can hear them all over the place, overturning beds and breaking down closets.

Suddenly, I see the Wizard by the altar. He turns and winks at me. Then he swings his stick at the crucifix, once, twice, and Christ's body breaks from the cross, crashing to the floor. Limbless, it rolls to my feet. Only bits of his hands and legs are still hanging on the cross, hollow and jagged. The cross has fallen off the altar too. The Wizard smiles at me, enjoying my frustration. When he's distracted for a moment, I grab Jesus's broken body and hide it under Jean's pajama top. I sit down on the sofa and put Jean on my lap. The Wizard now searches excitedly for the body of Jesus. He is like an overgrown kid looking for a toy.

He turns to me. "Shenge, do you have it?"

I look away. "No."

"Look at me, girl."

"I don't have it."

I hold on tighter to Jean.

The Wizard switches off the lights. Jean bursts into laughter, because now his stomach glows like Jesus. The Wizard turns the lights on again and comes toward us, smiling a bad smile. Jean is not afraid of the old man. When the Wizard reaches for Jesus, Jean fights him, bending almost double to protect his treasure. The Wizard is laughing, but Jean bites the man's fingers with his eight teeth. I wish he had iron teeth and could bite off the Wizard's whole hand, because it's not funny. But the old man teases us, dangling his tongue and making stupid faces. When he laughs, you can see his gums and all the pits left by his missing teeth. Now wheezing from too much laughter, he snatches Christ's body from Jean and puts it in his pagan pocket.

Tonton André is bitter and restless. Since I told him that my parents have gone out, he hasn't spoken to me. I'm angry at him too, because he lied to get in, and now the Wizard has destroyed my crucifix and stolen Christ's body.

When I hear noises in my parents' room, I run in there with Jean, because my parents never allow visitors in their bedroom. There are two men rummaging through their closet. One man is bald and wearing stained yellow trousers, the bottoms rolled up—no shirt, no shoes. He has a few strands of hair on his chest, and his belly is huge and firm. The other man is young, secondary-school age. His hair and beard are very neat, as if he had just come from the barber. He's bug-eyed and tall and is wearing jean overalls, a T-shirt, and dirty blue tennis shoes.

The big-bellied man asks me to hug him and looks at the younger man mischievously. Before I can say anything, he wriggles out of his yellow trousers and reaches for me. But I avoid his hands and slip under the bed with Jean. He pulls me out by my ankles. Pressing me down on the floor, the naked man grabs my two wrists with his left hand. He pushes up my nightie with the right and tears my underpants. I shout at the top of my voice. I call out to Tonton André, who is pacing in the corridor. He doesn't come. I keep screaming. I'm twisting and holding my knees together. Then I snap at the naked man with my teeth. He hits my face, this way and that, until my saliva is salted with blood. I spit in his face. Twice. He bangs my head on the floor, pinning down my neck, punching my left thigh.

"*Oya!* No! Shenge is one of us!" the Wizard tells him, rushing into the room.

"Ah . . . leave this little thing . . . to *me,*" the naked man says slowly. His short pee is pouring on my thighs and my nightie, warm and thick like baby food. I can't breathe, because he has collapsed on me with his whole weight, like a dead man. When he finally gets up, hiding his nakedness with his trousers, the Wizard bends down, peering at me, and breathes a sigh of relief.

"Shenge, can you hear me?" the Wizard says.

"Ummh."

"I say, you're all right!"

"All right."

"Bad days, girl, bad days. Be strong." He turns to my attacker and growls, "You're lucky you didn't open her womb. I would've strangled you myself!"

"Jean," I whisper. "Where's my brother?"

The overalls man finds him under the bed, curled up like a python, and drags him out. Jean lays his big head on my chest. An ache beats in my head as if the man were still banging it on the floor. My eyes show me many men in yellow trousers and overalls, many Wizards. The floor is rising and falling. I try to keep my eyes open but can't. Jean keeps feeling my busted mouth.

Someone lifts me and Jean up and takes us back to the parlor. Tonton André is sitting between two men, who are consoling him. He's got his head in his hands, and the Wizard is standing behind him, patting his shoulder gently.

As soon as Tonton André sees us, he springs to his feet. But they pull him down and scold him and tell him to get ahold of himself. He's not listening, though.

"My bastard brother and his wife are not home?" he says very slowly, as if he were coming out of a deep sleep. "He owes me this one. And I'm killing these children if I don't see him."

"My nephew," the Wizard says, thudding his stick once on the floor, "don't worry. He must pay too. Nobody can escape our wrath this time. Nobody."

"*Koko, ni impamo tuzabigira*," people start murmuring in agreement.

I don't know what Papa could owe his younger brother. Papa is richer than he is. Whatever it is, I'm sure that he'll repay him tomorrow.

The crowd calms down. People stand in groups and carry on conversations, like women at the market. I get the impression that there are more people outside. Only Monsieur François is impatient, telling the others to hurry up so that they can go elsewhere, that the government didn't buy them machetes and guns to be idle.

After a while, the Wizard leaves Tonton André and comes over to us. "Young girl," he says, "you say you don't know where your parents are?"

"I don't know," I say.

"When they return, tell them all the roads are blocked. No es-cape. And you, clever girl," the old man says, tapping me on the chest, "if you want to live, don't leave this house for anything. Ghosts are all over our land. Bad ghosts." He whisks his cane and tosses his head as if he were commanding the ghosts into existence. And then he goes out, into the flow of the crowd.

I lock up as soon as everyone has left. The flowers are crushed, the altar cloth trampled. Pieces of glass are everywhere. The draw-ers from the writing desk are hanging out, and the bookshelf has fallen over. The TV is now facing the wall, and a cold wind ruffles the window blinds. I find the cross and put it back on the altar.

I want to sleep, but fear follows me into my room. My fingers are shaking. My head feels heavy and swollen. There's a pebble in my left thigh where the naked man hit me. My mouth is still bleeding, staining the front of my nightie. I shouldn't have tricked the Wizard. What are the ghosts he summoned going to do to us? He has put his spell on Tonton André also. Jean is covered in goose bumps. I'm too afraid to tidy up our room. We huddle in one corner, on the mattress, which has been tossed onto the floor. I start to pray.

I wake to the sound of my parents and other people arguing in the parlor. There's a lot of noise. It's not yet dawn, and my whole body is sore. One side of my upper lip is swollen, as if I have a tof-fee between it and my gum. I don't see Jean.

I limp into the parlor but see only my parents and Jean. Maybe I was dreaming the other voices. My parents stop talking as soon as they see me. Maman is seated on the sofa like a statue of Marie, Mère des Douleurs, looking down. Papa stands near the altar, holding Jean and scooping hot spoonfuls of oatmeal into his mouth. Jean's eyes are dull and watery, as though he hasn't slept for days. Shaking his head, he shrieks and pushes the food away. "Eat up, kid, eat up," Papa says impatiently. "You'll need the energy."

My family isn't preparing for Mass this Sunday morning. The parlor lights are off, the furniture still scattered from last night. The doors and windows are closed, as they have been since Friday, and the dinner table is now pushed up against the front door. Our home feels haunted, as if the ghosts from the Wizard's stick were still inside.

I hurry toward my father. "Good morning, Papa!"

"Shhh . . . yeah, good morning," he whispers. He puts Jean down on the floor and squats and holds my hands. "No noise. Don't be afraid. I won't let anyone touch you again, OK?"

"*Yego,* Papa."

I want to hug him, but he blocks me with his hands. "Don't turn on any lights, and don't bother Maman now."

"The Wizard said that ghosts are—"

"No ghosts here. . . . Listen, no Mass today. Le Père Mertens went home on leave last week." He's not looking at me but peering out of the window.

I hear a sneeze from the kitchen, stifled like a sick cat's. I search my parents' faces, but they're blank. A sudden fear enters my body. Maybe I'm still dreaming, maybe not. I push closer to Papa and ask him, "Tonton André is now friends with the Wizard?"

"Don't mention André in my house anymore."

"He brought a man to tear my underpants."

"I say leave me alone!"

He goes to the window and holds on to the iron bars so that his hands are steady, but his body is trembling. His eyes are blinking fast and his face is tight. When Papa gets quiet like this, he's ready to pounce on anyone.

I go to the sofa and sit down silently. When I slide over to Maman, she pushes me away with one hand. I resist, bending like a tree in the wind, then returning to my position. Nothing interests Maman today, not even Jean, her favorite child. She doesn't say any sweet thing to him or even touch him today. She acts dumb, bewitched, like a goat that the neighborhood children have fed sorghum beer.

From the window, Papa turns and looks at me as if I'm no longer his sweet Shenge. When he sees Jean sleeping on the carpet by Maman's feet, he puts the blame on me: "Stubborn girl, have you no eyes to see that your brother needs a bed? Put him in the bedroom and stop disturbing my life."

But I circle the parlor, like an ant whose hole has been blocked. I am scared to go to my room, because of the ghosts. Papa grabs my wrist and drags me into my room. He turns on the light. Our toys litter the floor. He puts the mattress back on the bed and rearranges the room. But it's still messy. Papa is cursing the toys, destroying the special treats that he and Maman bought for us when they visited America. He kicks the teddy bear against the wall and stamps on Tweety and Mickey Mouse. Papa's hands are very dirty, the gutters around his nails swollen with black mud. When he sees me looking at him, he says, "What are you staring at?"

"I'm sorry, Papa."

"I told you not to turn on the lights. Who turned on this light?" I turn off the light. "Go get your stupid brother and put him to bed. You must love him."

"*Yego,* Papa."

I go to the parlor and hope that Maman will intervene. She doesn't, so I bring Jean back to the bed.

"And stay here, girl," Papa says. He goes back to the parlor, slamming the door.

WHEN I WAS YOUNGER, I used to ride into the hills on Papa's wide shoulders. We were always visiting Maman's family's place, in the next valley. Papa told me that when he first met Maman she was my age, and they played together in these hills. They went to the same primary school and university.

In the hills, you can see the clouds moving away, like incense in a church. Our country is full of winds, and in the hills they blow at your eyes until tears stain your cheeks. They suck through the valleys like hungry cows. The birds rise and tumble and swing, their voices mixing with the winds. When Papa laughs his jolly-jolly laugh, the winds carry his voice too. From the top of the hills, you can see that the earth is red. You can see stands of banana and plantain trees, their middle leaves rolled up, like yellow-green swords slicing the wind. You can see fields of coffee, with farmers wading through them, piggybacking their baskets. When you climb the hills in the dry season, your feet are powdered with dust. When it rains, the red earth runs like blood under a green skin. There are tendrils everywhere, and insects come out of the soil.

I walk tall and proud in our neighborhood. The bullies all know that Papa will attack anyone who messes with me. Even when he is drunk on banana beer, my tears sober him. Sometimes he even goes after Maman, for making his girl sad. He scolds his relatives when they say that it's risky that I look so much like Maman. Papa likes to tell me that he wanted to go against his people and wed Maman in our church when I was born, even though she hadn't given him a son yet. Maman wouldn't hear of it, he says. She wanted to give him a male child before they had the sacrament of matrimony. Papa tells me every-thing.

Maman's love for me is different. Sometimes she looks at me and becomes sad. She never likes going out in public with me, as she does with Jean. She is always tense, as if a lion will leap out and eat us.

"Maman, I'll always be beautiful!" I told her one day, as Papa was driving us home from a lakeside picnic. Maman was in the passenger's seat, Jean on her lap. I was in back.

"You could be beautiful in other ways, Monique," she said.

"Leave the poor girl alone," Papa told her.

"I don't understand," I said.

"You will when you grow up," she said.

THIS TIME WHEN I wake up, rays of yellow morning are leaking in through the holes in the door and the torn blinds. They riddle the gloom, and I can see dust particles dancing within them. Our neighborhood is quiet. When I go into the parlor, Papa is moving from window to window to ensure that the blinds leave no space for outsiders to peep in. Maman is standing at the table, straining her eyes as she examines two framed photographs.

One is from my parents' traditional wedding. It's ten years old. I was in Maman's belly then. All the women are elegantly dressed, the *imyitero* draping over them like Le Père Mertens's short vestment. Married women who have given birth to sons wear *urugoli* crowns. Maman got hers only last year, when Jean was born. There are some cows tethered in the background. They were part of the dowry Papa offered for Maman. But no matter what I try to focus on, my eyes go to Tonton André's smiling face. I cover it with my hand, but Maman pushes my fingers off. I look at the other picture instead, which was taken last year, after my parents' church wedding. Papa, Maman, and I are in front. I'm the flower girl, my hands gloved and a flower basket hanging down from my neck with white ribbons. Maman holds baby Jean close to her heart, like a wedding bouquet.

"Maman, Jean is lonely in the bedroom," I say.

"I hope he sleeps the whole day," she says, without looking at me.

"Won't ghosts steal him?"

"He'll get used to them. Go get yourself some food, Monique."

"*Oya,* Maman, I don't want to eat."

"Then go and shower."

"Alone? I don't want to shower."

She touches my nightie. "You need to shower."

"Maman, when wizards pee . . ."

"Don't tell me now." She looks at Papa. "She needs a shower."

Hearing this, I raise my nightie to show Maman my swollen thigh, but she slaps it down, saying, "You'll get a new pair of underpants. Your face will be beautiful again."

I return my attention to the pictures. I scratch at Tonton André's face with my nails to erase him from our family. But the glass saves him.

Maman isn't looking at the photos anymore; her eyes are closed, as if in prayer. I pick up a brass letter opener and begin to scratch the glass over my *tonton*'s face. The sound distracts Papa from the window and he gives me a bad look. I stop.

"Why did you come down — come *back*?" he says to Maman, searching my face to see whether I've understood the question.

I haven't.

He turns back to Maman. "Woman, why? Return to where you were last night. Please. Leave."

"Whatever you do," she says, "do not let my daughter know."

"She should!" he says, then recoils from the force in his own voice.

My parents are hiding something from me. Maman is very stubborn about it. Their sentences enter my ears as randomly as a toss of the dice on our Ludo board. Papa looks guilty, like a child who can't keep a secret.

"I can't bear it," he says. "I can't."

"If Monique knew where I was last night," Maman argues, "your family would've forced it out of her and shed blood."

As they talk, invisible people are breathing everywhere — at least twenty ghosts are in the air around us. When Maman speaks, the ghosts let out groans of agreement, but my parents don't seem to hear them.

Papa shakes his head. "I mean, you should never have come back. I could have convinced them . . ."

"We needed to be with the children."

I don't understand why Maman is saying she wants to be with me when she won't even look my way. I see dirty water dripping down the white wall beside me. It is coming from the ceiling. At first, it comes down in two thin lines. Then the lines widen and swell into one. Then two more lines come down, in spurts, like little spiders gliding down on threads from a branch of the mango tree in our yard. I touch the liquid with the tip of my finger. Blood.

"Ghost! Ghost!" I scream, diving toward Papa.

"It's not blood," he says.

"You are lying! It's blood! It's blood!"

Papa tries to get between me and the wall, but I get in front of him and hug him. I cling to his body, climbing up until my hands are around his neck and my legs wrapped around his waist. He tries to muffle my shouts with his hands, but I wriggle and twist until he bows under my weight, and we nearly topple over. He staggers and regains his balance, then he releases his breath, and his stiff body softens. He puts his arms around me and carries me to the sofa. He holds my face to his heart, hiding me from the blood. I stop shouting. Maman is grinding her teeth, and there is a stubborn look on her face — maybe the Wizard has fixed her too.

My body continues to tremble, no matter how hard Papa holds me. I tell him about last night, and he consoles me, telling me not to cry. Tears fill his eyes too, then pour down onto me, warm and fast. I've never seen him cry before. Now he can't stop, like me. He's telling me he will always love me, putting my head on his shoulder, stroking my braided hair. Once again, I'm Papa's Shenge.

"They're good ghosts," he sobs, kissing my forehead. "Good people who died."

"Papa, I tricked the Wizard."

"Don't think of last night."

He gives me a piggyback ride to the bathroom. He takes off my nightie and tosses it into the trash, then turns on the tap to run the bath. In the walls, the pipes whistle and sigh, but today it feels as if I were hearing blood flowing through the strange veins of ghosts. The heat of the bath sends mist through the room, and Papa moves within it, still sobbing and wiping his tears with the sleeve of his shirt.

When he cleans my face, his hands smell like raw eggs. I reach out and switch on the light; his dirty hands seem to shock him. He washes them in the sink. We're sweating in the heat and the steam. But when I try to pull back the window blinds, he stops me. In the mirror, my mouth looks as if I'd been dropped on it. I can't brush my teeth. With warm water and iodine from the closet, he cleanses my lip.

He leaves me to wash myself, tells me that I should not be afraid; he'll be right outside the door. After the bath, he goes with me to my room, and I dress in a pair of jeans and a pink T-shirt.

Back in the parlor, we sit together, away from the blood wall, my head on his shoulder. I'm hungry. He offers to make me food, but I say no, because I can't move my mouth to eat.

"Look, we cannot run away from this," Maman says.

Papa shrugs. "But I cannot do it. How do I do it?"

They're talking about secret things again.

"You can," she says. "Yesterday, you did it to Annette."

"I should never have gone to André's place yesterday. Big mistake."

"We owe André our cooperation. He's a madman now."

Papa goes to the window and looks out. "I think we should run to those UN soldiers by the street corner."

"*Ndabyanze!* No way! If your brother doesn't get what he wants when he returns, he will hurt all of us."

"The soldiers are our only hope."

"They? Hopeless."

"No."

"My husband, whatever you decide, let our children live, OK?"

"Maman, are we going to die?" I ask.

"No, no, my dear," Maman says. "You're not going to die. *Uzabaho*. You will live."

OUTSIDE, THE MIDMORNING SUN is now very bright, and, though the blinds are still drawn, I can see my parents' clothes clearly now. Papa's light-brown jeans are covered with dark stains. Maman is very dirty, her dress covered with dust, as if she'd been wrestling on the ground all night. She smells of sweat. I knew that it was a bad idea for her to go out last night; she never goes out at night. She tells me that there are many bad women who do, because Rwanda is getting poorer and poorer.

"Maman, Maman!" Jean shrieks suddenly. He must be having a nightmare. She shakes her head guiltily but doesn't go to him, as if she'd lost her right to be our mother. I go with Papa into our bedroom, and Jean climbs all over him, but wails for Maman. A muffled sneeze breaks the silence again. A ghost is gasping for air, as if it was being stifled. We hold on to Papa, who has brought holy water into the bedroom with him.

"It's OK, it's OK," Papa says, looking around and sprinkling the holy water, as if he has come to console the ghosts, not us. Together we listen to the ghost's raspy breathing. The breaths come further and further apart. They stop. Papa and the other ghosts start to sigh, as if the ailing one had died a second death.

There are tears in Papa's eyes, and his mouth is moving without words. He is commanding ghosts, like the Wizard, but without a stick.

Someone begins to pound on our front door. Papa quickly hands Jean to me. "Don't open the door!" he hisses to Maman, in the parlor, then turns to me. "And don't take your brother out there!" He stays with us, but his mind is in the parlor, where we can hear Maman pushing aside the table, opening the front door, and whispering to people. We hear chairs and tables being moved. Then there's a grating sound. On the roof, I can hear big birds flapping their wings for takeoff. Then quiet. The people must have left, and Maman is alone again in the parlor.

Somebody wails in a house down the road. Jean begins to cry. I pat him on the back and sing for him in a whisper. He's licking his lips, because he wants food. Papa takes us into the parlor and offers Jean the remains of the oatmeal. He chews the cold chunks hungrily. "Young man, I told you to eat the whole thing in the morning," Papa says. "You children are a burden to us!" He gives me bread slices and milk from the fridge. I soak the slices and swallow them without chewing.

A mob is chanting in the distance; it sounds like it's making its way toward our house. Papa goes to the window. Another voice begins to wail. A third voice, a fourth, a fifth, a child's — it sounds like my friend Hélène. Before I can say anything, Papa says, "Shenge, forget about that Twa girl."

Hélène and I sit next to each other at school. She's the brightest in our class, and during recess we jump rope together in the schoolyard. She's petite and hairy, with a flat forehead like a monkey's. Most of the Twa people are like that. They're few in our country. My parents say that they're peaceful and that when the world talks about our country they're never mentioned.

Hélène is an orphan, because the Wizard fixed her parents last year. Mademoiselle Angeline said that he cursed them with AIDS by throwing his gris-gris over their roof. Now Papa is paying Hélène's school fees. We're also in the same catechism class, and Papa has promised to throw a joint party for our First Holy Communion. Last year, Hélène took first prize in community service in our class—organized by Le Père Mertens. I came in second. We fetched the most buckets of water for old people in the neighborhood. He said if you're Hutu you should fetch for the Tutsis or the Twa. If you're Tutsi, you do it for the Hutus or the Twa. If you're Twa, you serve the other two. Being both Tutsi and Hutu, I fetched for everybody with my small bucket.

"We can't take her in," Papa says, and shrugs. "And how does this crisis concern the Twa?"

Suddenly, Maman yanks the table away from the door again and unlocks it. But she doesn't open the door, just leans on it. More choked cries crack the day like a whip. There are gunshots in the distance. Papa approaches Maman, his hands shaking. He locks the door and takes her back to her seat. He pushes the table back against the door.

Maman stands up suddenly and pulls out the biggest roll of money I've ever seen, from inside her dress. The notes are squeezed and damp, as if she had been holding on to them all night. "This should help for a while," she says, offering the roll to Papa. "I hope the banks will reopen soon." He doesn't touch the money. "For our children, then," she says, placing the money on the table.

I tell Papa, "We must give the money to Tonton André to pay him back."

"*Ego imana y'Urwanda!*" Maman swears, cutting me off. "My daughter, shut up. Do you want to die?"

Her lips quake as if she had malaria. Papa pulls his ID from his back pocket and considers the details with disgust. He gets Maman's card out of his pocket too. Joining the two together, he tears them into large pieces, then into tiny pieces, like confetti. He puts the scraps on the table and goes back to his security post at the window. Then he comes back and gathers them up, but he can't repair the damage. He puts the pieces into his pocket.

EVENING IS FALLING. MAMAN walks stiffly across the room and kneels by the altar. Papa speaks to her, but she doesn't reply. He touches her and she begins to sob.

"By this, your Shenge's crucifix," Maman says, getting up, "promise me you won't betray the people who've run to us for safety."

He nods. "I promise . . . *ndakwijeje.*"

Slowly, Maman removes the gold ring from her finger and holds it out for Papa.

"Sell this and take care of yourself and the children."

Papa backs away, his eyes closed. When he opens them, they're clouded, like a rainy day. Maman comes over to me and places the money in my hands and puts the ring on top of it.

"Don't go away, Maman. Papa loves you."

"I know, Monique, I know."

"Is it because you went out last night?"

"No, no, I did not go out last night!" she says. I leave everything on the altar, kneel in front of Papa, and beg him with all my love to forgive her even though she's lying. He turns away. I go back to the sofa. "Your papa is a good man," Maman says, hugging me.

I push Jean against her, but she avoids his eyes. I think of Le Père Mertens. I plead with Maman to wait for him to return from Belgium to reconcile them. "If you confess to Le Père Mertens," I say, "Jesus shall forgive you."

There's a light knock on the door. Maman sits up, pushing Jean off like a scorpion. Someone is crying softly outside our door. Maman walks past Papa to push aside the table and open the door. It's Hélène. She's sprawled on our doorstep. Maman quickly carries her inside, and Papa locks the door.

Hélène is soaked in blood and has been crawling through the dust. Her right foot is dangling on strings, like a shoe tied to the clothesline by its lace. Papa binds her foot with a towel, but the blood soaks through. I hold her hand, which is cold and sticky.

"You'll be OK, Hélène," I tell her. She faints.

"No, Saint Jude Thadée, no!" Maman exclaims, gathering Hélène's limp body in a hug. "Monique, your friend will be fine."

I can hear a mob coming, but my parents are more interested in Hélène. Papa climbs onto a chair, then onto the table. He opens the hatch of the parlor ceiling and asks Maman to relay Hélène to him.

"Remember, we've too many up there," Maman says. "When I came down, you had five in there . . . and I put two more in just hours ago. The ceiling will collapse."

They take Hélène into my room, and Maman pulls open the hatch. A cloud of fine dust explodes from the ceiling. They shove Hélène's body in.

Now I understand — they are hiding people in our ceiling.

Maman was in the ceiling last night. She tricked me. Nobody is telling me the truth today. Tomorrow I must remind them that lying is a sin.

As the mob closes in on our house, chanting, the ceiling people begin to pray. I recognize their voices as those of our Tutsi neighbors and fellow parishioners. They're silent as Papa opens the front door to the crowd, which is bigger than last night's and pushes into our home like floodwater. These people look tired, yet they sing on like drunks. Their weapons and hands and shoes and clothes are covered with blood, their palms slimy. Our house smells suddenly like an abattoir. I see the man who attacked me; his yellow trousers are now reddish brown. He stares at me; I hold on to Papa, who is hanging his head.

Maman runs into her bedroom. Four men are restraining Tonton André, who still wants to kill us all. I run to Maman and sit with her on the bed. Soon, the mob enters the room too, bringing Papa. They give Papa a big machete. He begins to tremble, his eyes blinking. A man tears me away from Maman and pushes me toward Jean, who's in the corner. Papa is standing before Maman, his fingers on the knife's handle.

"My people," he mumbles, "let another do it. Please."

"No, you do it, traitor!" Tonton André shouts, struggling with those holding him. "You were with us when I killed Annette yesterday. My pregnant wife. You can't keep yours. Where did you disappear to when we came last night? You love your family more than I loved mine? Yes?"

"If we kill your wife for you," the Wizard says, "we must kill you. And your children too." He thuds his stick. "Otherwise, after cleansing our land of Tutsi nuisance, your children will come after us. We must remain one. Nothing shall dilute our blood. Not God. Not marriage."

Tonton André shouts, "Shenge, how many Tutsis has Papa hidden—"

"My husband, be a man," Maman interrupts, looking down.

"Shenge, answer!" someone yells. The crowd of Hutus murmur and become impatient. "*Wowe, subiza.*"

"My husband, you promised me."

Papa lands the machete on Maman's head. Her voice chokes and she falls off the bed and onto her back on the wooden floor. It's like a dream. The knife tumbles out of Papa's hand. His eyes are closed, his face calm, though he's shaking.

Maman straightens out on the floor as if she were yawning. Her feet kick, and her chest rises and locks as if she were holding her breath. There's blood everywhere—on everybody around her. It flows into Maman's eyes. She looks at us through the blood. She sees Papa become a wizard, sees his people telling him bad things. The blood overflows her eyelids, and Maman is weeping red tears. My bladder softens and pee flows down my legs toward the blood. The blood overpowers it, bathing my feet. Papa opens his eyes slowly. His breaths are long and slow. He bends down and closes Maman's eyes with trembling hands.

"If you let any Tutsi live," they tell him, "you're dead." And then they begin to leave, some patting him on the back. Tonton André is calm now, stroking his goatee. He tugs at Papa's sleeve. Papa covers Maman with a white bedspread and then goes off with the mob, without looking at me or Jean. Maman's ring and money disappear with them.

I cry with the ceiling people until my voice cracks and my tongue dries up. No one can ever call me Shenge again. I want to sit with Maman forever, and I want to run away at the same time. Sometimes I think she's sleeping and hugging Hélène under the bedspread and the blood is Hélène's. I don't want to wake them up. My mind is no longer mine; it's doing things on its own. It begins to run backward, and I see the blood flowing back into Maman. I see her rising suddenly, as suddenly as she fell. I see Papa's knife lifting from her hair. She's saying, "Me promised you."

"Yes, Maman," I say. "You promised me!"

Jean is startled by my shout. He stamps around in the blood as if he were playing in mud.

I begin to think of Maman as one of the people in the ceiling. It's not safe for her to come down yet. She's lying up there quietly, holding on to the rafters, just as she must have been last night when the man in the yellow trousers attacked me. She's waiting for the right time to cry with me. I think that Tonton André is hiding Tantine Annette in his ceiling and fooling everyone into believing that he killed her. I see her lying, faceup, on a wooden beam, with her mountain belly, the way I lie on the lowest branch of our mango tree and try to count the fruit. Soon, Tonton André will bring her down gently. She'll give birth, and my uncle will cover her mouth with Belgian kisses.

JEAN YANKS THE CLOTH off Maman and tries to wake her. He straightens her finger, but it bends back slowly, as if she were teasing him. He tries to bring together the two halves of Maman's head, without success. He sticks his fingers into Maman's hair and kneads it, the blood thick, like red shampoo. As the ceiling people weep, he wipes his hands on her clothes and walks outside, giggling.

I wander from room to room, listening for her voice among the ceiling voices. When there's silence, her presence fills my heart.

"Forgive us, Monique," Madame Thérèse says from the parlor ceiling.

"We'll always support you and J-Jean," her husband stammers from above my room. "Your parents are good people, Monique. We'll pay your school fees. You're ours now."

"Get this dead body off me," Grandmaman de Martin groans from above the corridor. "It's dead, it's dead!"

"Just be patient," someone close to her says. "We'll send the dead down carefully before they fall through."

Some praise God for the way my parents' marriage has saved them. Grandmaman de Martin becomes hysterical, forcing everyone else to rearrange themselves in the ceiling in the corridor. I identify each voice, but Maman's voice isn't there. Why hasn't she said something to me? Why doesn't she order me to go and shower?

All the things that Maman used to tell me come at me at once and yet separately—in play, in anger, in fear. There is a command, a lullaby, the sound of her kiss on my cheek. Perhaps she is still trying to protect me from what is to come. She's capable of doing that, I know, just as she stopped Papa from telling me that he was going to smash her head.

"I'm waiting for Maman," I tell the ceiling people.

"She's gone, Monique."

"No, no, I know now. She's up there."

"*Yagiye hehe?* Where?"

"Stop lying! Tell my mother to talk to me."

The parlor ceiling is now creaking and sagging in the middle, and Madame Thérèse starts to laugh like a drunk. "You're right, Monique. We're just kidding. Smart girl, yes, your *maman* is here, but she will come down only if you go outside to get Jean. She's had a long day."

"*Yego, madame,*" I say, "wake her up."

"She's hearing you," Monsieur Pierre Nsabimana says suddenly from above the kitchen. He hasn't said anything all this while. His voice calms me, and I move toward it, my eyes fixed on the ceiling. Someone begins the Catena in a harsh, rapid whisper. It's not Maman. She always takes her time to say her prayers.

"Do you want your *maman* to fall with the ceiling on you?" Monsieur Pierre says.

"No."

"Then, girl, leave the house, and don't come back!"

The ceiling above the altar begins to tear apart from the wall, and people scurry away from that end, like giant lizards. I pick up the broken crucifix and hurry outside.

There are corpses everywhere. Their clothes are dancing in the wind. Where blood has soaked the earth, the grass doesn't move. Vultures are poking the dead with their long beaks; Jean is driving them away, stamping his feet and swirling his arms. His hands are stained, because he's been trying to raise the dead. He's not laughing anymore. His eyes are wide open, and there's a frown on his babyish forehead.

Then he wanders toward the UN soldiers at the corner, their rifles shiny in the twilight. They're walking away from him, as if they were a mirage. The vultures are following Jean. I scream at them, but they continue to taunt him, like stubborn mosquitoes. Jean doesn't hear. He sits on the ground, kicking his legs and crying because the soldiers won't wait for him. I squat before my brother, begging him to climb on my back. He does and keeps quiet.

We limp on into the chilly night, ascending the stony road into the hills. The blood has dried into our clothes like starch. There's a smaller mob coming toward us. Monsieur Henri is among them. He's carrying a huge torch, and the flame is eating the night in large, windy gulps. These are our people on Maman's side, and they're all in military clothes. Like another soccer fan club, they're chanting about how they're going to kill Papa's people. Some of them have guns. If Papa couldn't spare Maman's life, would my mother's relatives spare mine? Or my brother's?

I slip into the bush, with Jean on my back, one hand holding the crucifix, the other shielding my eyes from the tall grass and the branches, my feet cold and bracing for thorns. Jean presses hard against me, his face digging into my back. "Maman says do not be afraid," I tell him. Then we lie down on the crucifix to hide its brightness. We want to live; we don't want to die. I must be strong.

After the mob runs past us, I return to the road and look back. They drag Maman out by the legs and set fire to the house. By the time their fellow Tutsis in the ceiling begin to shout, the fire is unstoppable. They run on. They run after Papa's people. We walk forward.

Everywhere is dark, and the wind spreads black clouds like blankets across the sky. My brother is playing with the glow of the crucifix, babbling Maman's name.

AFTERWORD

Although his parents had played a prominent role in our diocesan events and development for decades, I first came in contact with Father Uwem Akpan in 1988, at his home village of Ikot Akpan Eda. He was one of the 150 parishioners of St. Paul's Parish, Ekparakwa, who were waiting to receive the sacrament of Confirmation that bright Sunday morning. Shortly before Mass, it was realized that the catechist, who had prepared the candidates and led them through the rehearsals for the celebration of the sacrament, had suddenly taken ill and was indisposed. As churchwardens scrambled for a replacement, Uwem stepped forward and volunteered to be the master of ceremonies on that occasion. He was seventeen, rather stern-looking in his dark "French suit," as we say in Nigeria. He had just graduated from secondary school and was bent on joining the Jesuits. He had never been a master of ceremonies before. When I asked how he would lead the other candidates and the congregation through the day, he quickly said he would be coming to the altar to consult the bishop on what to tell the people. Many times during that Mass, Uwem had the church in stitches as he ran the commentary with a straight face, using everyday language to say what the sacrament of Confirmation meant. He was fluent in both English and his native Annang language.

It was when I invited Uwem to live and work with me in the Bishop's House that I really came in contact with his depth, passion, and courage. He always said things straight from the heart. He was impatient with what he called "abstract" theology. He read widely and bombarded me with questions about the Catholic faith. Sometimes, his focus and intensity were made bearable only by his Annang humor and ringing, mirthful laughter. As I followed the progress of his Jesuit priestly formation in Nigeria, the United States, Kenya, Benin, and Tanzania — and in the conversations we had when he visited home, about his struggles to write in the seminary — I began to sense that there was no way this Ikot Akpan Eda man could be a priest without using the common man's language to probe the terrain within which modern Africans are living out their faith. Therefore, I was not very surprised when he started giving African children a voice in fiction.

It is my belief that the publication of *Say You're One of Them* is a bold attempt to enlighten readers about children in Africa, fueled by a passionate desire to create a safer place for children all over the world. Father Uwem, we in your home diocese of Ikot Ekpene are proud of you. May God continue to confirm your faith and bless your talents and courage as priest and poet.

—The Most Reverend Camillus Etokudoh,
Bishop of Ikot Ekpene

ACKNOWLEDGMENTS

This book came together because of the presence of many people in my life.

In the name of the Jumbo Akpan-Ituno and Titus Ekanem extended families, I thank you, my brothers and sisters-in-law — Emem and Joy, Aniekan and Nkoyo, and Mfon and Ekaete — and your children; and you, John Uko and Bishop Camillus Etokudoh. You always said it was possible.

I'm also indebted to you, my friends—among whom are Jesuits—who never tired hearing of my big dreams or reading my drafts: Jude Odiaka, Ubong Attai, Mary Ifezime, Edie Nguyen, Itoro Etokakpan, Ndi Nukuna, Isidore Bonabom, Comfort Udoudo-Ukpong, Emma Ugwejeh, Ehi Omoragbon, Lynette Lashley, Emma Orobator, Caitlin Ukpong, Chuks Afiawari, David Toolan, Bob Hamm, Iniobong Ukpoudom, Vic EttaMessi, James Fitzgerald, Peter Chidolue, Bob Reiser, Larry Searles, Abam Mambo, Bill Scanlon, Rose Ngacha, Gabriel Udolisa, Tyolumun Upaa, Barbara Magoha, Christine Escobar, Wes Harris, Matilda Alisigwe, John Stacer, Aitua Iriogbe, Peter Byrne, Amayo Bassey, Funto Okuboyejo, Gozzy Ukairo, Peter Ho Davies, Nick Delbanco, Laura Kasischke, Nancy Reisman, Dennis Glasgow, Fabian Udoh,

Acknowledgments

Greg Carlson, Mark Obu, Prema Bennett, Bob Egan, Arac de Nyeko, John Ofei, Gina Zoot, James Martin, Madonna Braun, Ray Salomone, Jim Stehr, Wale Solaja, Sam Okwuidegbe, Tom Ebong, Pat Ryan, CC Akpan, Rachel Suhm, Tom Smith, Mike Flecky, Kpanie Addie, Shade Adebayo, Gabriel Massi, Nick Iduwe, Peter Otieno, Dan Mai, Greg Zacharias, Anne Njuguna, Edie Murphy, Alex Irochukwu, Fidelis Divine, Jan Burgess, Jackie Johnson, Chika Eze, Marian Krzyzowski, Eugene Niyonzima, Jeanne Levi-Hinte, Marissa Perry, Celeste Ng, Preeta Samarasan, Peter Mayshle, Anne Stameshkin, Jenni Ferrari-Adler, Phoebe Nobles, Joe Kilduff, Ariel Djanikian, Jasper Caarls, Taemi Lim, Maaza Mengiste, Marjorie Horton, Taiyaba Husain, Rosie and Jerry Matzucek, Ufuoma and Rich Okorigba, Emily and Paul Utulu, Eunice and Dele Ogunmekan, Olive and Thomas Beka, Monica and Cletus Imahe, Mary Ellen and Leslie Guinn, Justina and Raphael Eshiet, the Okuboyejo family, Daniel Herwitz and Mary Price of the University of Michigan's Institute for the Humanities, and the Akwa Ibom priests and religious in Michigan.

I also wish to thank Cressida Leyshon at *The New Yorker;* Pat Strachan, Marie Salter, and Heather Fain, editor, copyeditor, and publicist, respectively, at Little, Brown and Company; Elise Dillsworth at Little, Brown Book Group; and Eileen Pollack, Gerry McIntyre, and Ekaete Ekop, friends and editors at large. Maria Massie, my agent, you are the best out there.

Last, may the Lord bless you, the people of St. Patrick's Church, Ikot Akpan Eda; St. Paul's Parish, Ekparakwa; and the Catholic Diocese of Ikot Ekpene, for your love and generosity to me and my family since my childhood. Through your inspiration, I have stories to tell.

About the Author

Uwem Akpan was born in Ikot Akpan Eda, in southern Nigeria. After studying philosophy and English at Creighton and Gonzaga universities, he studied theology for three years at the Catholic University of Eastern Africa. He was ordained as a Jesuit priest in 2003 and received his MFA in creative writing from the University of Michigan in 2006. *Say You're One of Them* was a finalist for the *Los Angeles Times* Art Seidenbaum Award for First Fiction. The collection was also nominated for the *Guardian* First Book Award, the Caine Prize for African Writing, and the Story Prize. It received the Commonwealth Writers' Prize for Best First Book, African Region.

A Reading Group Guide

Say You're One of Them

Stories by

Uwem Akpan

A conversation with the author of
Say You're One of Them

Uwem Akpan talks with Cressida Leyshon
of *The New Yorker*

Your story "An Ex-mas Feast" is about a family living on the street in Nairobi, Kenya. When did you first start thinking about these characters and the world that they inhabit?

When I went to study theology in Nairobi, in 2000, I was taken by the phenomenon of street kids. I'd never seen anything like it before. . . . I started talking with the bunch of kids around Adams Arcade, which was near my school. These kids were not very wild, because they still went back to their homes in the slums in the evening. There was one kid, Richard, who was their leader. I started calling him Dick. He had some English, and was very respected by the others. If I wanted to give them money, the whole bunch would ask me to give it to Dick, because they knew he would not cheat them. He would talk with me and ask me about Nigeria. I don't know how he managed to be so nice, unlike his friends. After the Christmas holiday of 2000, he disappeared. I started asking questions. Some of his friends told me that maybe he had gone to the city to become a real street kid. I really thought I would run into him someday in the city. But I never did. I kept hoping that he would keep his gentleness even in the very wild gangs of the City Centre.

You're working on a collection of stories about children in various countries in Africa. Can you talk a little about the other stories? Why do you want to write about a number of African countries rather than one or two—for example, Nigeria, where you grew up, or Kenya, where you studied for three years?

I would like to see a book about how children are faring in these endless conflicts in Africa. The world is not looking. I think fiction allows us to sit for a while with people we would rather not meet. I have had the chance to study and to travel a bit. I really hope I can visit these places and do good research, so that the stories can be truly those of the people I am trying to write about. I want their voices heard, their faces seen.

Do you find it easy to move between the two continents, Africa and America, or does it take time to adjust to life in each place again?

The rhythm of life here is different from that of Nigeria. I really liked the efficiency and accessibility of things here, the educational opportunities. And I was touched by the beauty and tolerance it has taken to fashion America. But, for instance, the thing about old people staying in "homes" away from home blew my mind. As did how little Americans know or want to know about life elsewhere.

It is a great thing to be able to move back and forth. I get to see my friends. There's also the challenge of remaining faithful to my roots. Now each time I return to Ikot Akpan Eda, my home, I ask my parents and old people a lot of questions. I am more interested in my Annang culture now than I was before I started coming here. I am always interested in listening to old people in my village. Everybody knows everybody, and people tell tall stories. After Mass on Sunday, people sit together outside the church and share fresh palm wine. One of my mother's cousins used to come around to our home to tell us stories he made up about different people in the village. He seemed to have a license to change any story into whatever he wanted. My granddad, who helped bring Catholicism to my village, became a polygamist at one point and later came back to monogamy. So I have many uncles and aunties. My father and all his brothers live in one big compound. My mother's place is not far off.

Have you set much of your fiction in the United States?

I have not set any of my fiction in the U.S. . . . Not yet. I feel that you guys have tons of writers "discovering" the American experience for you. I feel that the situation of Africa is very urgent and we need more people to help us see the complexity of our lives. Ben Okri has said that rich African literature means rich world literature. Having said that, it would be great to set some of my fiction in this country. A lot of African refugees are coming to America now. So that could be where to begin.

What do you read, mostly?

The stories I find in the Bible keep surprising me. All the crimes are already committed in Genesis, yet God stays with the ones who committed them. I read extensively, though ever since I started writing my reading speed has gone down considerably.

Is your faith important to you when you're writing? What role, if any, do you think it should play in your fiction?

Since it is not something I can put away, my faith is important to me. I hope I am able to reveal the compassion of God in the faces of the people I write about. I think fiction has a way of doing this without being doctrinaire about it.

In "An Ex-mas Feast," two of the main characters, Jigana and his sister Maisha, live in a harsh world. Do you think that they'll survive?

My continent is in distress and has been since the beginning of slavery. Leadership is a big problem. My hope is that things will change in Africa. Europe fought endlessly with itself in past centuries; now they have a European Union, not just in name, like the African Union. I hope that someday all the stupid wars on the African continent will end. I am amazed at the endurance of people, whether in Asia or Latin America or Africa, caught up in harsh situations.

What do you do when you want to forget about everything?

[Laughs.] A priest has no way of forgetting about everything! I like to watch good soccer on TV. Take long, slow drives. Read. Visit with people.

Cressida Leyshon's interview with Uwem Akpan originally appeared at www.newyorker.com in 2005. Reprinted with permission.

Questions and topics
for discussion

1. Each of the stories in *Say You're One of Them* is told from the perspective of a child. Do you think this affected your reaction? If the narrators had been adults, might you have felt differently about the stories? Why do you think Akpan chose to depict these events through children's eyes? How do Akpan's young characters maintain innocence in the face of corruption and pain?

2. In "An Ex-mas Feast," Maisha leaves her family to become a full-time prostitute. Do you think she chose to depart, or did her family's poverty force her to flee? Is it possible to have complete freedom of will in such a situation? Is it reasonable to judge a person for her actions if her choice is not entirely her own?

3. In "Fattening for Gabon" the children's uncle and caretaker, Fofo Kpee, sells them into slavery. How does Fofo's poverty and vanity contribute to his unthinkable actions? Do his pangs of conscience redeem him for you? Why or why not?

4. In "What Language is That?" Hadiya and Selam are kept apart by their parents after the escalation of religious conflict. Have you ever experienced a situation in which friends and family have objected to someone in your life for reasons you didn't understand? What did you do? How did you feel?

5. The bus in "Luxurious Hearses" is a microcosm not only of African hierarchies and religions but also of the continent's

numerous languages and dialects. Discuss how speech is related to class, culture, religion, and heritage. How does dialogue function in the other stories? Do we hold similar attitudes about language in our own culture? What are some examples?

6. This book takes its title from instructions given to a Rwandan girl by her mother in "My Parents' Bedroom." Did the familiar domestic detail in this story—Maman's perfume, little Jean's flannel pajamas, toys like Mickey Mouse in the children's room—intensify for you the horror of what ensued? Is there comparable detail in any of the other stories that helped you to identify with Uwem Akpan's characters?

7. Although the stories in *Say You're One of Them* are fictitious, the situations they depict have a basis in reality. How do the emotions you feel when reading these stories compare to your emotions when reading accounts in the news media of similar atrocities? Has reading *Say You're One of Them* changed the way you think about these issues?

8. Uwem Akpan addressed his other vocation in an interview, saying, "A key Vatican II document makes it very clear that the joys and anguish of the world are the joys and anguish of the Church." While reading these stories, were you ever reminded that this writer is also a Jesuit priest? Does Akpan's subject matter seem to you to be imbued with religious values? In what ways? Do the drama and power of Akpan's fiction call forth any biblical stories for you? If so, which ones?

9. Some of the children in *Say You're One of Them* are not poor. What are the particular obstacles these children face that are not issues in your own country? Are there challenges other than poverty with which you can identify? Do the family dynamics feel familiar to you?

10. The poet and memoirist Mary Karr wrote that Uwem Akpan "has invented a new language — both for horror and for the relentless persistence of light in war-torn countries." Did you find any beauty or goodness in these tragic tales? If so, offer some examples.